Praise for the charming Highlanders series

A HIGHLANDER CHRISTMAS

"Romantic and magical. . . . Chapman dishes up all the passion and tender love she's known for."

—*Romantic Times*

"A humorous plot line, self-deprecating characters, and a decided dose of enchantment make this a warm read for the season."

—*BookPage*

"Filled with poignant realism interwoven with the enchanting magic of the holiday season. . . . Will charm and delight readers. "

—Single Titles

"An extraordinary seasonal story full of laughter, romance, and magic."

—Fresh Fiction

SECRETS OF THE HIGHLANDER

"Liberally spiced with mystery, this story has warmth and genuine love that make it the perfect antidote for stress."

—*Romantic Times*

ONLY WITH A HIGHLANDER

"A mystical, magical book if there ever was one. . . . A perfect 10!"

—Romance Reviews Today

"Chapman's amazing ability to meld rich characterization with passion and romantic adventure is unmatched and unforgettable."

—*Romantic Times*

TEMPTING THE HIGHLANDER

"Chapman breathes such life and warmth into her characters, each story is impossible to put down."

—*Romantic Times*

WEDDING THE HIGHLANDER

"A series that just keeps getting better. . . . This is Chapman's most emotional, touching, and powerful novel to date."

—*Romantic Times*

"Exciting . . . Janet Chapman writes a refreshingly entertaining novel."

—The Best Reviews

And for her latest enthralling contemporary romance . . .

TEMPT ME IF YOU CAN

"Hidden secrets, passion, and a dash of danger all work in perfect harmony to create an outstanding read!"

—*Romantic Times*

"An absolute joy! Books like this are the reason I like to read in the first place."

—Fresh Fiction

"Janet Chapman at her very best. The characters are likeable and believable, and the villain is truly vile. . . . One of the best romance stories—with a hint of mystery—you'll read this year."

—Reader to Reader

These titles are also available as eBooks

Also by Janet Chapman

Dragon Warrior
Tempt Me If You Can
A Highlander Christmas
Moonlight Warrior
The Man Must Marry
Secrets of the Highlander
The Stranger in Her Bed
The Seduction of His Wife
Only with a Highlander
The Dangerous Protector
Tempting the Highlander
The Seductive Impostor
Wedding the Highlander
Loving the Highlander
Charming the Highlander

JANET CHAPMAN

MYSTICAL WARRIOR

POCKET **STAR** BOOKS

New York London Toronto Sydney

Pocket Star Books
A Division of Simon & Schuster, Inc.
1230 Avenue of the Americas
New York, NY 10020

Cover design by Min Choi
Cover art by Craig White

Manufactured in the United States of America

ISBN 978-1-61129-776-8

To Robbie

MYSTICAL WARRIOR

Chapter One

Trace Huntsman would have punched Kenzie Gregor in the face if the bastard hadn't looked too miserable to defend himself. So he hauled the highland warrior several yards down the driveway instead, out of earshot of the two women getting out of the large black SUV.

"Mind telling me what in hell is going on here?" Trace asked through gritted teeth. "And you damn well better start by explaining why the 'lost soul' moving into my house just happens to be your *sister*."

"If I'd told you I wanted the apartment for Fiona, would you have rented it to me?" Kenzie asked, the determination in his eyes warring with his obvious guilt.

Deciding that was a rhetorical question, Trace looked over his shoulder to see Eve Gregor wrap an arm around her sister-in-law and all but drag Fiona toward the outside stairs leading up to the second-floor apartment of his old New England farmhouse. He turned back to Kenzie. "I offered to keep an eye on one of your displaced time travelers; I did *not* agree to babysit the little sister of a powerful drùidh who will turn me into a toad if anything happens to her."

Kenzie shot him a tight grin, although it did little to soften his expression. "It's not as though we pulled your name out of a hat, Huntsman. Matt and I rented your apartment precisely so you can keep an eye on Fiona for us."

"Goddamn it, she's your sister, why can't *you* keep an eye on her? Better yet, why can't your brother? He's a *wizard*, for chrissakes; all he has to do is conjure up a protective bubble to put around her."

"Do ye not think we wouldn't prefer to do just that?" Kenzie asked softly. "But what kind of life can she possibly have if we treat her like a child? Believe me; for as hard as this is on Fiona, it's sheer hell for Matt and me." Kenzie gestured toward the house. "Which leaves us with you. It's our hope that by forcing Fiona to live on her own, she will eventually rediscover the strong, self-reliant woman she was before that bastard raped her and stole her courage."

"Then build a house on your land and let her live under *your* watchful eye."

"Fiona needs to be in town in order to become part of this community. She must learn to trust people—men in particular—and that won't happen unless she realizes society is a blessing instead of a curse."

"But why *me*?"

"Because Matt and I trust you."

"Then you and your brother are idiots. Hell, my own mother doesn't even trust me enough to water her plants and feed her cat when she goes out of town."

Some of the tension eased out of Kenzie's shoulders, and this time his grin actually reached his eyes. "You won't need to water Fiona or feed her. In fact, Matt and I prefer you do nothing for her other than make sure she's safe. Her rent is paid up for the next six months, her cupboards will be stocked with a week's worth of food, and she has five hundred dollars in cash." He shrugged. "When she gets hungry, she will have to walk to the store and buy what she needs, and when her money runs out, she'll have to find a job."

Trace was incredulous. "You expect a woman born in eleventh-century Scotland to just walk into a modern business and get a job?" He snorted. "There's not much call for washing clothes in the creek or spinning wool into yarn these days. No, wait," he said, snapping his fingers. "Fiona was a red-tailed hawk for several centuries; maybe the town could hire her to control the pigeon population."

Kenzie scowled. "Fiona knows how to read and do numbers, and she can be quite resourceful when she's not jumping at shadows. Which is why you mustn't coddle her, either."

"Well, sure. I'll just give you a call, then, when your dead sister's body starts stinking up my apartment."

The towering highlander's grin returned, but quite menacing this time. "Do not underestimate her, my friend, or it's likely *your* body I'll be carting off. Fiona may appear delicate, but I've seen her go after a pack of wolves with only a stick when they tried to snatch one of our spring lambs. She was ten, and the wolves were smart enough never to return."

Trace dropped his head in defeat. "Goddamn it. I didn't sign up for this, Gregor."

Kenzie headed toward his SUV. "Ye may wish to clean up your language around her," he said, his chuckle equally menacing. "When she was eight, Fiona washed Matt's mouth out with soap for taking God's name in vain. But knowing she'd never catch him in a footrace, she waited until he fell asleep that night and then shoved a lathered bar of soap halfway down his throat." He stopped and opened the rear hatch. "So consider yourself warned. Fiona rarely gets mad, but she *will* get even."

Trace grabbed one of the boxes out of the back of the truck and started toward the stairs. Great. Wonderful. Friggin' fantastic. Why should he care if Matt Gregor turned him into a toad? Living under a rock waiting for a fly to land on his nose had to be better than babysitting an eleventh-century woman who had turned her fear of men into openly aggressive hatred.

Which was a shame, really, considering that Fiona Gregor also happened to be stunningly beautiful. Dammit to hell, he'd be beating *two-legged* wolves off with a stick once every bachelor within fifty miles realized a pretty new lamb had just moved into town.

Trace suddenly stopped in mid-step. Wait a minute—did that mean the Gregor brothers thought *he* was a goddamn eunuch?

Well, Christ, they really were idiots if they had never considered they might have just conned the fox into guarding the henhouse.

Fiona squinted against the sunlight shooting through a knothole in the wood and slowly sat up as much as the sharply slanting ceiling allowed, giving a disheartened sigh.

She made no apologies for hating men, but she surely was tired of being afraid of them. And she was quite disgusted with herself for going into a full-blown panic last night when Trace Huntsman had knocked on her door to tell her that electricity didn't grow on trees and that she needed to turn off the lights in her apartment.

Afraid he might decide to push through the rickety old door and turn them off himself, she'd run through the rooms like a madwoman, shutting off lamps and frantically searching for wall switches. She'd turned off every last bulb, even though he'd said she could leave one on just before he'd walked back down the outside stairs.

Thoroughly shaken by the late-night encounter, she had tried resorting to her old habit of sleeping in a closet, only to discover that all three of the apartment closets were simply too small. So she'd dragged her blankets into the large cupboard built under the attic stairway, curled into a tight ball in the dark, and eventually fallen asleep.

Blinking against the bright morning light when she opened the door, she decided to make a latch for the cupboard that she could lock from the inside. And before she started scrubbing every crack and crevice in the kitchen and bathroom, she should probably gather some of the sweetgrass she'd seen growing down by the sea and make a mattress for it as well.

"It won't be my permanent bed," she assured herself as she crawled out and stood up. "But having a hidey-hole is only prudent, and there's no reason it can't be comfortable as well as secure." Maybe she could also disguise the fact that it even existed; some well-placed furniture and a large wall hanging over the door should do the trick.

But her shoulders slumped as she stared down at the gaping cavity. A modern woman wouldn't have spent the night hiding in a cupboard—even if she did live above a big, strong-looking, disgruntled landlord.

"I am well aware that electricity doesn't grow on trees," she muttered, walking to the bathroom. She stopped to look into the mirror over the sink and found gold-colored eyes exactly like her mother's glaring back at her. She began unbraiding her hair. "Just because my brothers tricked you into renting this apartment to me, that's no reason for you to march up here in the middle of the night growling like an angry bear. You could have just called my cell phone and nicely asked me to turn off the lights. Or is acting civilized beyond the ken of *modern* warriors, too?"

Fiona decided it was beyond *her* ken how little men had changed in a thousand years, especially considering that technology had progressed out of this world—literally! People had actually walked on the moon, yet every blasted man she'd ever met—in this century or in her old time— was still a bully.

Including her brothers.

Fiona stripped out of the clothes she'd slept in, then reached past the tattered shower curtain surrounding the bathtub and turned on the water. She felt bad for having spoken so bluntly to Eve yesterday, when her sister-in-law's feigned excitement had turned to horror the moment they'd walked into the apartment. No, she probably shouldn't have said she considered this a rather nice prison compared with her last one, as Eve had grown even more appalled and started to go tell Kenzie the apartment wasn't fit for a dog to live in.

Fiona had immediately stopped her, saying she'd willingly live in a cave if her dear, sweet, loving brothers thought she should, seeing as how they seemed to know far better than she did what was good for her. And besides, with a little work, she could make the place quite cozy. She didn't have anything else to do now that they had each in turn banished her from their homes.

Aye, she'd definitely been too blunt, Fiona decided as she stepped under the hot spray of water. After making up her bed and unpacking some of the boxes they'd spent last week filling with household goods, it had taken her almost two hours to persuade Eve—who obviously felt guilty for siding with Kenzie—that she was actually looking forward to putting her personal touch on her new home.

Not that this old house could ever be as nice as her brothers' homes, especially the veritable castle Matt and Winter were building up in the western mountains of Maine. And even though Kenzie and Eve lived in a century-old farmhouse similar to this one, theirs had just gone through a major renovation that had transformed it into a fortress the devil himself couldn't destroy.

Whereas this place . . . well, Fiona figured the roof was staying attached only by the grace of God, the furnishings and appliances were older than she was, and if the floors creaked any louder, she'd likely be deaf in a month.

On the plus side, however, it did have running water, indoor plumbing, and electricity that she happened to know came from power lines—although she wasn't sure where the power in those lines actually came from.

But just as soon as she worked up the nerve, she planned to visit the building full of books Eve's mother, Mabel, had

Chapter Two

Trace reached into his pickup to start the engine, flipped the defroster on high, and closed the door to scrape off the ice last night's freezing rain had left on his windshield. But as he rounded the front of the truck, he stopped and looked up at the darkened second-floor windows and scowled. If he hadn't heard his ceiling creaking again last night, he might think his new tenant had somehow managed to turn herself back into a hawk and had flown away.

Not actually having seen Fiona since she'd moved in, Trace had feared he really was going to have to tell Kenzie to come get her body. But every night for the last six nights, he'd watched the lights go off the moment he drove into the yard and heard what sounded like a mouse tiptoeing overhead late into the evening. And every morning, he would back out of his driveway and wait on the road, and sure enough, the lights would come on the moment his invisible tenant was certain he was gone.

He felt a tad guilty for having stormed up there the first night to point out that just because electricity was included in the rent, that didn't mean she could keep every damn bulb burning all night. But, still sore at being duped by a couple of eleventh-century highlanders, he hadn't been in a generous mood.

Trace chuckled humorlessly as he scraped the passenger side of the windshield. He'd have liked to have been a fly on the wall in the two Gregor households as Kenzie and Matt discussed Fiona's future with their twenty-first-century wives. He didn't know Winter Gregor very well, having met her only last month when she and Matt had driven Fiona down from the mountains, but he'd gotten the impression the woman had felt a tad guilty herself.

Whereas Matt Gregor had simply looked relieved. Having a long-lost sister suddenly show up while dealing with a new infant and fighting sleep deprivation had obviously been too much for the powerful wizard, and Matt had somehow persuaded his wife—who had also shown signs of needing a good night's sleep—that Kenzie and Eve were in a much better position to help Fiona adjust to her new life.

But seeing his own impending fatherhood and two a.m. feedings fast approaching, Kenzie had, in turn, decided to pawn Fiona off on his good buddy, who just happened to have an empty apartment he desperately needed to rent.

Trace climbed into his truck, directing his scowl at himself. Apparently, working twelve-hour days wasn't as good an excuse as having a baby, whereas his own military background made him a perfect chump to babysit a beautiful woman afraid of her own shadow. "Oh, and while you're at it, Huntsman," Kenzie had said just before leaving, "could ye maybe help us help Fiona get over her fear of men?"

Trace snorted and backed out of the driveway. There was no *us*, as he hadn't seen hide nor hair of the highlander since.

Great. Wonderful. How friggin' fantastic lucky was he to get sucked into the remains of the Gregor clan—that just happened to be a family of magic makers. That's what his other good buddy, William Killkenny, called them, anyway; and William should know, since *he* was a ninth-century Irish warrior. Only instead of traveling through time as a noble little hawk like Fiona Gregor, Killkenny had shown up in Midnight Bay last spring as a goddamn *dragon*.

Trace had thought he'd left his war behind in Afghanistan five months ago, but it seemed he'd only exchanged one nightmare for another. Whereas Matt Gregor was some sort of ancient drùidh, Kenzie Gregor, it turned out, was a soul warrior, who helped time-traveling displaced souls cursed to live as monsters become human again.

Which was what had originally brought William Killkenny here.

But then, Trace's cousin Maddy was why the Irishman had stayed.

And because whoever or *what*ever had cursed the displaced souls didn't care for Kenzie's interference, this desolate section of the coast of Maine had been weathering freak storms every time the evil forces came up against the highlander.

Mainers could deal with good old-fashioned homegrown bogeymen—because any idiot knew you only needed a shotgun to send them scurrying—but dragons, mermaids, demon wolves, and magical tigers . . . well, Afghanistan wasn't looking so ugly anymore. At least he'd understood that fight, even if he hadn't liked his personal role in it, whereas now he couldn't even tell the good guys from the bad guys.

Take the magical tiger, for instance; turned out it was another powerful drùidh by the name of Maximilian Oceanus, from what was supposed to be the *mythical* continent of Atlantis. Mac was the one who had turned Fiona Gregor back into herself, as a thank you to Kenzie for helping his own sister escape some bad-ass fiancé.

Carolina Oceanus had been the area's latest tourist attraction, a mermaid that had quickly displaced Midnight Bay's infamous dragon when Trace, in a moment of outright insanity, had broadcast a Mayday that he had spotted a naked woman swimming ten miles out in the Gulf of Maine.

Noticing that the lights in the upstairs kitchen had come on, Trace blew out a heavy sigh and headed toward the docks. All he'd dreamed about for the last two years was coming home to Maine and living a quiet, peaceful life as a fisherman, where the only battles he waged would be against Mother Nature, and the only demons he had to fight were the ones in his head.

Dammit, magic wasn't *supposed* to be real.

But Matt Gregor and Maximilian Oceanus sure as hell weren't selling snake oil, William Killkenny certainly knew more about the art of war than most modern generals, and Kenzie Gregor . . . well, dammit, he had *seen* Kenzie turn into a panther.

And if that wasn't proof enough, Trace had several new scars on his already battered body as evidence, made by a pack of demonic wolves that had shown up in the last hurricane-force storm that had nearly wiped Midnight Bay off the map.

Yes, he could see his hope of a peaceful life heading to hell in a handbasket.

But that didn't mean he had to let a beautiful woman with vulnerable golden eyes sucker him into going along on the ride. He'd already been there and done that, and he was smart enough to learn from his mistakes.

Especially the ones that nearly killed him.

Fiona stood on the sidewalk at the end of the driveway, snuggled inside an ankle-length wool coat, as the November sun struggled to warm the air above freezing. She smiled down the street in the direction of Dragon Cove, feeling quite proud not only of having survived six whole days living on her own but also of actually *enjoying* herself. She rather liked nobody constantly reminding her how lucky she was or telling her what she should be thinking or doing or planning to do, and this morning, her newfound freedom even had her feeling brave enough to venture into town.

Well, maybe only semibrave, since she wasn't exactly going alone.

Not that Gabriella would be much help if they got into any sort of physical confrontation, but the young girl certainly had plenty of moral support to offer. And truth told, Fiona had every hope that Gabriella's courage, however naïve, might actually prove contagious.

Not seeing any sign of her new friend, Fiona turned toward the house that was slowly starting to feel like home and realized that the sad-looking structure appeared more abandoned than lived in, although attempts had been made to rectify that.

A new coat of yellow paint covered the bottom half of the house, while the top half still had patches of weathered wood showing from years of neglect. Broken shutters—some holding on by a single hinge—hung crookedly beside the upstairs windows, and decades of seagull droppings made the black roof appear almost white. The porch that ran across the front and down the left side of the three-story structure had patches of new lumber holding the rotten wood together, and its roofline sagged so badly that it gave the illusion the house was smiling.

A large maple tree on the front lawn had been felled by a storm—a while ago, judging by the color of the exposed trunk—and the branches were still waiting to be sawed into firewood and stacked inside the long shed that connected an equally run-down barn to the house. And there was enough grass and weeds covering the dirt driveway to feed a small herd of goats, except where a path had been made by her landlord's pickup, which was—thankfully—rarely there.

Such was the life of a lobsterman, Eve had explained in an attempt to reassure Fiona that her landlord would hardly be around. Trace spent not only long hours at sea on his lobster boat but many hours mending and rigging his traps, cutting bait, and repairing the new boat he and his partner had just bought.

It certainly was fine with her that the man left before sunrise and didn't return until after dark. Having the place to herself went a long way toward making her exile bearable.

Well, bearable except for Kenzie's rule that she couldn't ask for help from anyone even remotely related to her. And for some stupid reason, her dear, sweet, loving brother had decided to include Eve's mother, Mabel Bishop, as well as Madeline and William Killkenny, in his imperial dictate.

But then Fiona went back to smiling, this time quite smugly. *Gabriella* Killkenny had not been mentioned by name, likely because Kenzie assumed that William's little sister would be too busy struggling with her own sudden appearance in this century to be helping anyone, much less another displaced time traveler.

Which only showed how little men knew about women. Seventeen-year-old girls, no matter what century they were born in, had the resiliency of oak trees. Beat them, break them, even kill them, and they sprouted right back up— usually even more determined to master their destinies.

Lord, she hoped courage really was contagious.

Because by the time a woman reached twenty-nine years of age, she'd already learned many of life's harsher lessons, not the least of which was that men are by nature brutes and, more often by choice, bastards.

Fiona took a calming breath, willing herself not to go there. She was a human being again, living in a wondrous new century, and she needed to let go of the past if she hoped to have any sort of decent future. Those bastards may have stolen her innocence and ultimately killed her and her son a thousand years ago, but she refused to let them kill her newly resurrected dreams.

She only wished she could have another babe without needing a man to conceive one. Surely in this modern time, there was some miraculous means to make that happen.

Men mostly got in the way of child rearing, anyway, with their endless demands, rules that made sense only to them, and punishments that rarely fit the crime.

"Fiona!"

Fiona turned to see Gabriella running up the sidewalk, her coat unbuttoned and her long auburn hair flapping in the breeze. "What's the matter?" she cried in alarm, rushing forward as her gaze darted behind the girl. "Is someone chasing you?"

Gabriella halted and glanced back down the sidewalk before giving Fiona a quizzical look. "No. What makes you think that?"

"Then why were you running?"

Gabriella shot her a smile, throwing her arms wide. "Because I can." She looped her arm through Fiona's and started walking toward town. "I'm so glad you invited me to go shopping with you. I wish to go to the bookstore and buy something called a magazine that Mabel told me about. It's especially for young women, and Mabel said it will be easier to learn how to read if it's something that interests me."

Fiona started to tell Gabriella that Eve's mother had also taught William to read when he'd been a dragon and that she had sat perched on a branch and learned right along with him, but the girl just kept on talking.

"Mabel said the magazine is filled with pictures as well as with something called articles that explain how I can apply makeup and do my hair. And she said there are even suggestions on how to talk to boys," she continued excitedly. She suddenly laughed. "Only William walked in just then, and he said that I was not to talk to *any* boys. Ever!" She rolled her eyes. "Anyway, Mabel believes that if I stay focused on my lessons all this winter and through next spring, I should be ready to attend school next fall with the other young people my age." Gabriella frowned. "But it appears I'll be in school only one year, and that just when I've made friends with everyone, we're all going off to *different* schools, called universities, in distant towns."

"Did you have much trouble sneaking away?" Fiona asked when Gabriella stopped to take another breath.

The girl laughed again. "Have you met Maddy's daughter, Sarah? She was more than willing to help me sneak off, saying she needed the practice for when *she's* seventeen." Gabriella squeezed Fiona's arm looped through hers. "I believe I'm going to like being an aunt, even if my ten-year-old stepniece is smarter than I am."

"Just temporarily," Fiona assured her. "You'll soon catch up to the women your age in this century." Fiona stopped walking, her bravery suddenly deserting her when she saw all the vehicles and people. "Maybe we should come back later, when the town is less busy."

"But that's when shopping is the most exciting," Gabriella countered, starting them off again. "It's the people that make it interesting." She gave Fiona a curious look. "Was your eleventh-century village very small?"

"We lived high up in the mountains, well away from everyone."

"But you must have gone into a nearby village regularly to barter for goods."

Fiona dropped her gaze to the sidewalk. "My family made a point of keeping to ourselves, as we weren't welcome in society." She stopped and looked Gabriella directly in the eyes. "Unless somebody had need of the magic. Then it was suddenly okay for them to sneak up to our cabin with their trinkets and bribes and ask Mama to cure a sick child or make the rain stop or have her mix them a special potion."

"Your mother was a magic maker? Like Mac?" Gabriella asked in surprise.

"Nay, not like Maximilian Oceanus. The man who gave you your life back and brought you here is a drùidh, whereas my mother was a Guardian. As . . . as I believed I was when I died and came back as a hawk."

"But what's the difference between a drùidh and a Guardian?" Gabriella asked.

"Drùidhs protect the Trees of Life, which are what power the world, whereas Guardians protect people from the drùidhs." Fiona snorted. "Only it seems I wasn't a Guardian after all, since I couldn't even protect myself from Maximilian. He was so certain he was doing my brothers a huge favor by giving me back to them, he didn't seem to care that I didn't *want* to be human again."

"You didn't?" Gabriella asked in surprise. "But why?"

"I was *safe* as a hawk, and I liked helping Kenzie free those poor, displaced souls from the dark magic. But now I'm just a powerless woman again."

Her friend frowned. "Women aren't powerless."

"No? So, you're saying that in the ninth century, *you* could choose who you married or, if you preferred, that you didn't marry at all?"

"Well, of course not. But only because I was too young and inexperienced to make such an important decision."

"So your mother could have made the decision, then?"

"Well . . . no. My father would have chosen for me."

Fiona nodded. "Exactly. And you couldn't hold land in your name, you had no say in political matters, and you even had to ask permission to go visit a friend."

"But this isn't the ninth or eleventh century; it's the twenty-first, and women have lots of power today." Gabriella grinned. "You should be *thanking* Mac for bringing you to this century."

"If that's true, then how come you had to sneak away today instead of simply telling William you were going to town with me? And how come I wasn't even asked if I wanted to live over a man I know absolutely nothing about? I'll tell you why," she rushed on when Gabriella tried to speak. "Because my dear, sweet, loving *brothers* decided it was for my own good."

"But that's not what William—" Gabriella's face suddenly darkened, and she looked away.

"What?" Fiona demanded, nudging her. "What did William say as to why Matt and Kenzie banished me? Come on, Gabriella," she implored more softly. "You're the only friend I have. Please tell me."

"Um . . . I overheard William telling Maddy that your older brother sent you away because you were—" Gabriella finally looked at her. "Because you'd grown possessive of your new niece and that whenever baby Fiona started to cry, you would rush to her before Winter could, as if she were *your* child. And Matt told Kenzie that if he didn't make you leave before *his* son was born, you'd start mothering his new babe, too."

Fiona must have visibly recoiled, because Gabriella took hold of her shoulders. "But then Maddy told William she knows for a fact that your sisters-in-law are the ones who suggested you move into a place of your own," she continued. "They believe that you won't ever become a modern woman if you continue hiding behind your brothers."

"Eve and Winter are the ones who sent me away?"

"No, they set you free!" Gabriella took another deep breath. "I know you died giving birth to your son," she continued softly, "and that he died a couple of weeks later because your papa had gone mad by then and didn't know how to care for a babe. And I know that you were . . . raped just like me." She smiled sadly. "But all that happened over a thousand years ago, Fiona. And Maddy told me that if I don't let go of *my* anger, I will be giving the bastard who raped me even more power. He took my chastity and my life, but that doesn't mean I have to *give* him my spirit."

"But those men took something from us that we can't ever get back," Fiona whispered. "Even if we wanted a husband after what they did, no man would want *us*. We . . . we're used goods, Gabriella, no better than camp followers or whores."

Instead of being shocked, the young girl gave a musical laugh. "Omigod, don't ever let Maddy hear you say that! I said almost the same thing to her last week, and she got so angry I thought she was going to explode." Gabriella started them toward town again. "I think you should invite Maddy over to your new home for tea and ask her to explain how men view women today."

"I'm not allowed to talk to Madeline," Fiona muttered, dragging her feet in an attempt to slow them down.

Gabriella laughed again. "Nobody is the boss of you anymore, Fiona. You are a modern, independent woman now, and *you* are the one who decides who you talk to."

Fiona suddenly stopped walking when she got a strange feeling deep in the pit of her stomach. "You're right," she whispered, the unraveling sensation making her light-headed. "Matt and Kenzie gave up their rights to tell me what to do when they sent me away, and I *am* master of my own destiny." The dizziness blossomed into something akin to euphoria, and Fiona slid her arm through Gabriella's and started striding down the sidewalk. "Come on, my smart friend, let's go see if that bookstore has any magazines for women my age!"

Chapter Three

$\mathscr{F}$iona's renewed bravery lasted less than twenty minutes, however, before that all too familiar knot in her gut returned when the door opened and two men strode into the bookstore, the breadth of their shoulders spanning the aisle and effectively blocking her and Gabriella's escape.

The store owner, who had introduced herself as Ruthie, looked up from the magazine she was showing Gabriella. "Oh, hello, Johnnie," the older woman said, her smile immediate. "And Jason. How's your dad doing?"

"We're just heading over to Ellsworth to bust him out of the hospital," the bearded man said, although his sharp dark eyes were focused on Fiona.

Feeling like she couldn't breathe, Fiona pretended to be interested in a magazine farther down the aisle. But when she tried pulling Gabriella with her, the girl gave her a frown and tugged free, apparently not the least bit alarmed that they were trapped.

"That was quick," Ruthie said in surprise. "Clive's only been in the hospital for what, five days? He broke his leg in *three* places, and they're already letting him come home?"

The sharp-eyed bearded man, who was the older of the two and about Fiona's age, gave a chuckle. "It's more like they're kicking him out—or, rather, kicking *Mom* out. Ever since Dad fell off the roof, she's practically been living at the hospital, complaining that the nurses are doing everything wrong and that he'd heal faster if she could bring him home and get some *real* food into him."

Ruthie snorted. "Sonja's just as opinionated at Grange meetings. Still, I'm glad Clive is—Jason, why is your jacket squirming?"

Fiona tried leading Gabriella out of grabbing distance of the men, but the young girl tugged free again and actually stepped toward them. "What have you got in there?" she asked. "It sounds like an animal whimpering."

The man named Jason, who appeared three or four years older than Gabriella, slid down the zipper on his jacket as he walked closer, and a dark pink nose and yellow fluid eyes popped out in a tangle of frenzied legs and dust-colored fur.

"Oh, a puppy!" Gabriella cried, reaching for it.

The squirming pup gave an excited yelp as it vigorously strained to get to her. Nearly dropping it in the process, Jason lunged forward just as the puppy leapt into her arms. "Careful," he said with a chuckle. "Or he'll wash all those pretty freckles off your face if you let him."

Fiona stood frozen, so overwhelmed by feeling trapped that she couldn't even rescue her friend when the young man's large hand shot out to turn the pup's eager tongue away from Gabriella's face, as the girl had also gone perfectly still, her huge blue eyes locked on Jason as a blush crept into her freckled cheeks.

Jason suddenly groaned, his own face darkening, and tried to take the puppy away from her. "Aw, hell, I think he just peed on your coat."

Gabriella hugged the puppy to her chest. "That's okay, I don't mind. My niece has a puppy that piddles on me all the time." She finally looked down at the squirming bundle in her arms, and the puppy immediately started lapping her face, making Gabriella giggle as she fought to control it. "What's his name?" she asked between licks as she looked up at Jason again.

"He hasn't got one, so we've just been calling him Pest," Jason said. "Because you're a great big pest, aren't you, boy?" he added, rubbing the puppy's head even though his gaze remained locked on Gabriella. "You want him? Mom said we have to find someone to take him before we bring Dad home from the hospital, because she's afraid Pest will trip him up when he's trying to walk with his crutches."

"And if we can't find a home for him," the older man said, "then we have to take him to the animal shelter in Ellsworth. Ruthie, didn't I hear you were looking for a dog?"

"I was," Ruthie said, her expression growing distressed as she reached out and let the puppy lick her fingers. "But I adopted a couple of kittens instead, so I won't have to rush home every night right after I close the store. Oh, Johnnie, you can't just drop him off at the shelter! All those barking dogs will traumatize the poor thing, and he might catch one of those kennel diseases. Thelma Goodie got her dog there, and after paying a fortune in vet bills, she still ended up putting the poor thing to sleep."

"This one's the only pup we haven't been able to place," Jason interjected. He shot Gabriella a smile. "He sure seems to like you. He's got an impressive pedigree. His daddy is a three-time grand champion field hunter, and we drove all the way to Nova Scotia to get his mom five years ago, and she's the best ocean duck dog in the area." He nodded toward his brother. "Johnnie trained Maggie himself. We got nine hundred bucks each for his six litter mates, which is a steal for a Chesapeake Bay retriever with great bloodlines, but we could sell you this little guy for seven hundred."

"Oh, I would love to have him," Gabriella said, lifting the pup to rub its fur on her cheek. "But where I'm living right now is bursting with people. I couldn't possibly get a dog of my own until my brother's house is finished being built and we move into it." She suddenly thrust the pup into Fiona's arms. "But you could take him. You have that whole apartment to yourself, and your landlord doesn't have a dog."

"I . . . but . . ." Fiona couldn't say anything because every time she opened her mouth, the puppy kept licking her. She was finally able to wrestle the quivering mass of muscle under control, and after darting a frantic glance at the two men, she grabbed Gabriella's sleeve and dragged her farther down the aisle.

"I can't just bring home a dog without asking my landlord's permission," she quietly hissed. "What if he doesn't like dogs and says no? Then what am I supposed to do with this little guy?"

"But you said he's never there," Gabriella countered. "Heck, it would probably be months before he even realized you had a dog. Oh, Fiona, think of how much company he would be for you. And you'll be able to take him for walks around town, and he'll grow big and strong and protective. A dog is just what you need."

"Who's your landlord?" Johnnie asked, making Fiona jump when she realized the two men had followed them down the aisle.

"It's Mr. Huntsman," Gabriella answered for her. "Do you know him? Fiona is renting his upstairs apartment. His is the large yellow and sort of white house down by the ocean on the edge of the village, just a short walk from here."

"You live over Huntsman?" Johnnie asked in surprise, looking at Fiona. "Hell, I went to school with Trace, and I know for a fact that he likes dogs. I tell you what," he said, reaching out and rubbing the puppy's ear. "You take this little guy off our hands right now, and you can have him for six hundred."

Fiona couldn't even speak, much less think; she could only picture the seven months she'd spent in hell the last time she hadn't done something a man had asked her to do.

"But you said you're taking him to the shelter," Gabriella interjected when Fiona didn't respond. "So you should *give* him to my friend, and that way, you would know he's going to a good home."

Johnnie Dempster continued looking directly at Fiona. "Five hundred," he said quietly.

"I'll buy him from you!" she blurted out when Gabriella started to protest again. She immediately shifted the puppy to one arm, reached into her pocket and pulled out the small money purse Eve had given her, and thrust it toward him.

But Gabriella snatched it out of her hand. "Three hundred," the girl said.

Fiona shot Gabriella a threatening glare and spoke to her

in Gaelic. "You will not barter with this man," she hissed. "I am naming the puppy Misneach, and to pay any less would demean my new pet."

"Misneach?" Gabriella repeated, slaughtering the word with her ancient Irish brogue. She suddenly smiled. "You're naming the pup *courage*?" she asked in Gaelic.

Speaking in her native tongue seemed to have a calming effect on Fiona—that is, until Johnnie Dempster said, "I have no idea what language that is, but we really have to get going." He shot Gabriella a frown and then looked at Fiona again, his direct stare somewhat menacing. "I heard that Barry Simpson at the Shop 'n Save across the street might be looking for a new duck dog, and that's our next stop after we leave here. So I'm actually doing you a favor by offering him to you for five hundred, considering Barry would probably pay seven."

Fiona clutched Misneach to her chest. "I beg you, Gabriella," she pleaded, once again in Gaelic, "give the man his five hundred dollars, and please let's get out of here." *So I can run home and crawl into my cupboard and never, ever come into town again,* she silently added.

Gabriella lifted the flap on the wallet and pulled out the money inside. The girl painstakingly counted the paper bills out loud, until she reached five hundred dollars exactly—all the money Fiona had to her name.

But if that was the price of getting out of the store without angering the men, so be it. She nudged Gabriella. "Pay him for the puppy," she said, this time in English.

Just as soon as Gabriella handed him the money, Fiona grabbed her friend's arm, dragged her past the man named Jason, and headed for the door.

Only Johnnie Dempster started following them. "How about if I bring his papers over to you this evening?" he asked, reaching around Fiona to open the door.

She took a relieved breath when she stepped onto the sidewalk and saw all the people milling about. "What do you mean by papers?" she asked, feeling slightly more in control now that she was no longer trapped.

"His kennel club papers," Johnnie said, giving her a frown. "If you ever want to stud him out, you're going to have to register him."

"That won't be necessary," she said, again pulling Gabriella closer when Jason came up beside her. For hadn't she seen firsthand how men would separate their prey under the guise of being nice, just before they turned into brutes?

"We'll follow you ladies to the Shop 'n Save," Jason said, "and show you what food the puppy should eat. You can also buy a collar and leash there."

Fiona didn't want either of these men following them anywhere. "Misneach will eat what I do," she said, wondering why they thought she would buy special food for a dog. She started walking in the direction of home. "And I saw a soft rope hanging in the barn, so I don't need a collar or leash."

"Gabriella, you forgot your magazine!" Ruthie called out, waving it in the air as she stood on the sidewalk.

Gabriella pulled Fiona to a stop. "Oh, I really want to buy that magazine," she said. "Wait right here; I'll only be a minute."

"You're just going to tie a rope around his neck?" Johnnie Dempster asked, his expression incredulous.

"And you can't feed him people food," Jason added, equally appalled. "It'll make him puke."

"Not to mention turn him into a beggar," Johnnie growled.

Fiona bumped into a lamppost, as she'd slowly been inching away from them. "I've had several dogs before, and I've never fed them special food." She glanced back toward the bookstore, wishing Gabriella would hurry.

"Come on," Johnnie said, making her bump into the post even harder when he suddenly plucked Misneach out of her arms. He shoved the dog at his brother. "You stay here and wait for Gabriella, and I'll take—" He smiled at her. "Fiona, isn't it? I'll take Fiona across the street and help her pick up what she needs."

As desperately as she wanted to wait for Gabriella, Fiona didn't dare resist when Johnnie took hold of her elbow and led her off the sidewalk, stopping only to look for traffic before guiding her across the street to the Shop 'n Save. But surely Gabriella was safe with Ruthie, and they *were* in the middle of town, after all, whereas she had been all alone in the woods, far from anyone who might hear her scream, when that bastard had stolen her a thousand years ago. Not wanting to cause a scene, she let Johnnie Dempster lead her across the street. But she did feel it was important to point out that she had no money left, so he wouldn't think she expected *him* to pay.

"I have no money to buy food and a leash and collar," she said, clutching her coat closed at her throat and wishing she was still a hawk so she could fly away. "All I had was the five hundred dollars I gave you," she told him, glancing over her shoulder for signs of her friend.

He didn't even slow down when the grocery store door suddenly opened all by itself. "Don't worry; it'll be my treat. Mismatch needs a collar and proper dog food."

"Mis*neach*," Fiona said, even as she wondered where she got the courage to correct him. "And I can't possibly accept such a gift from you."

As if she hadn't even spoken, Johnnie led her down one of the many aisles in the large store and stopped in front of a display of goods that had pictures of cats and dogs on them. "What in hell kind of name is Misnutch?" he asked. He looked at her, his expression disgruntled. "He's a *hunting* dog; you have to give him a noble name like Winchester or Magnum or Decoy. Or at least give him a masculine name like Bruce or Henry or Rex or something."

"*Misneach* is Gaelic for 'noble one,'" she blatantly lied.

Apparently mollified, he turned to the display. "I haven't seen you around town before," he said, fingering several ropes with clasps on the ends. "Did you just move to Midnight Bay? And was that Gaelic you and your friend were speaking back there at the bookstore?"

"Yes," she said, finally able to breathe normally now that he'd let her go.

He glanced over his shoulder and lifted one brow. "Isn't Gaelic some old Irish language or something?"

"I'm Scots."

His beard bristled around his grin. "And you have a lovely accent, Fiona . . . ? What's your last name?"

"Gregor."

His grin disappeared. "You related to Kenzie Gregor?"

Fiona took the opportunity to step away when a woman pushed a cart full of food past them, although she didn't quite have the nerve actually to bolt. Johnnie Dempster was a big, long-legged man, and she probably wouldn't even reach the door before he caught her. "He's my brother."

"Then how come you're living at Huntsman's?"

"Because I wish to be independent."

Simply stating it out loud—to a complete stranger and a man, no less—made her feel somewhat braver, despite the fact that she was still effectively trapped.

No, she never should have come to town today.

"What's your favorite color, Fiona?"

"Excuse me?"

"How about gold, to match your beautiful eyes?" he said, his own eyes smiling. "Or maybe red, like your hair—although I suppose it's more of a strawberry blond. I don't believe I've ever seen such a long, thick braid of hair on a woman."

Recognizing that his interest in her had become more than just a means to get rid of his dog, Fiona felt the knot in her belly rise into her throat, leaving her unable to speak.

Johnnie blew out a sigh and returned to fingering the ropes on display. "You're a bit gun-shy, aren't you?" he murmured, pulling a bright orange rope off the hook. "Some guy must have burned you really bad. Here, forget about matching anything," he said, thrusting the rope toward her. "No self-respecting Chesapeake would be caught dead wearing any color other than blaze orange." He picked up one of the shorter orange belts from the display and snapped it closed to visually gauge its size. "This collar should fit Mismatch, but you're going to have to buy him a bigger one in a few months."

Not daring to correct him again, Fiona thrust the leash toward him. "It's very generous of you, but I can't let you buy these for me. You have my word of honor; I will come back another time and buy them myself."

Instead of taking the rope, he snapped the collar onto the end of it, leaving it dangling from her hand, and then turned and began searching the colorful bags with pictures of dogs on them.

Fiona eyed the display of leashes and collars, calculating her chances of hanging hers on the hook and running out of the store before he could catch her.

But then what? She couldn't just abandon Gabriella.

"Come on," Johnnie said, hefting a large bag onto his shoulder and heading back up the aisle. "Jason and I will give you and your friend a ride home."

"But I thought you had to go get your father," she said, rushing after him like an obedient child. But she was *not* getting into his vehicle. "We can walk home; it's just a short distance."

He tossed the bag onto the counter, took the leash and collar out of her hand and tossed them down, then pulled the money out of his pocket that Gabriella had given him. "There's no way you can carry a forty-pound bag of dog food all the way to Huntsman's house," he said, pulling one of the fifty-dollar bills free and handing it to the woman behind the counter. "We'll drop you ladies off on the way, and then I'll return tonight and bring you Misnutch's papers," he said, this time at least trying to pronounce the name correctly.

"How's your daddy doing, Johnnie?" the woman behind the counter asked as she ran first the collar and then the leash in front of a machine that gave a soft beep each time. She took a small device and pointed it at the bottom of the bag, causing the machine to beep again. "I heard he fell off the roof."

"He busted his leg in three places, but Jason and I are bringing him home this afternoon." He smiled crookedly. "I guess that'll teach me to do stuff when Mom asks. I told her I'd stop in and clean that chimney first chance I got, but could my old man wait? Oh, nooo, he had to climb up there and do it himself, thinking he's still thirty goddamn years old."

The woman scrunched up her nose. "When I went home last Saturday, I caught my father standing on a ladder washing the second-story windows." She snorted. "Not that he'd know they were dirty, since his cataracts are so thick his eyes look white." The woman smiled at Fiona. "Who's your friend, Johnnie?"

"This is Fiona Gregor. She's new in town."

The woman's eyes widened. "You related to Kenzie Gregor?"

"He's my brother," Fiona told her.

Instead of handing Johnnie his change, the woman used the money to fan her face as she sighed. "They sure as hell don't make men like that anymore," she said. Her eyes took on a sparkle. "But if they did, I guarantee I'd be the first one in line."

Johnnie plucked the money out of her hand. "I believe your *husband* might have something to say to that," he muttered. He shoved the money into his pocket, handed Fiona the leash and collar, hefted the dog food over his shoulder again, and, after a nod at the woman, headed for the door. "It's a good thing I'm driving my mother's car," he said, stepping through the automatic door. "We'd have been a bit crowded in my pickup. There's Jason and your friend. Come on."

Again like an obedient child—or even worse, an ador-ing *puppy*—Fiona rushed after him, silently vowing that if she and Gabriella somehow managed to get home in one piece, she would never again put her friend in such danger.

Chapter Four

Trace pulled into the Shop 'n Save parking lot and realized his horrible day was about to get even worse when he spotted Fiona Gregor and Gabriella Killkenny—two obviously very lost souls—standing next to Johnnie and Jason Dempster. Jason was holding a large bag of dog food and talking to Gabriella, who was looking up at him with what could only be described as rapt attention. Johnnie was down on one knee, fitting a collar around a puppy's neck, and Fiona, holding the leash attached to the collar, was looking as if she wanted to be anywhere but where she was.

Trace shut off his truck with a muttered curse.

And so it had begun. Little miss scared of her own shadow had finally worked up the nerve to come into town, and judging by the paleness of her complexion, hell would have to freeze over before she ever left the house again. As for Gabriella . . . well, from what his fishing partner, Rick—who also happened to be Trace's cousin and William

Killkenny's new brother-in-law—had told him, the medieval teenager was too excited to be living in this century to be frightened of anything.

Trace got out of his truck and headed toward them, already having figured out what was taking place. Word down at the docks was that Dempster had unsuccessfully been trying to sell the runt of his litter for the last three weeks, and it was obvious the logger had decided that marketing the perfect companion to a single woman had proven easier than trying to convince anyone the dog would ever make a decent hunter. And although he couldn't exactly say why, Trace felt himself walking a little taller when he noticed that Fiona actually looked relieved to see him.

Or at least she did until the puppy made a lunge for him. Her face turning quite pale again, Fiona immediately pulled the puppy back and then actually attempted to hide it behind her long coat. "Misneach, no!" she softly hissed when it continued all the way around her, nearly toppling her when the leash wrapped around her legs.

Trace dropped to one knee to catch the pup when it leapt at him again. "Hey there, squirt," he said, taking hold of its head to keep its slobbering tongue away from his face. "Aren't you a bright-eyed and bushy-tailed monster."

Fiona tried pulling it off him again, and Trace realized that the pup might be a runt, but it was a damn strong little beast, when, instead of being dragged away, it pulled Fiona off balance again.

She would have fallen if Johnnie hadn't caught hold of her shoulders. "Let go of the leash!" Johnnie growled, pulling her upright.

Fiona let the leash go as if it had burned her.

Trace grabbed hold of it and slowly stood up, then just as slowly handed it back to her. "Here, why don't you start heading home with him?"

But it was Gabriella who finally got her to move. The young girl looped her arm through Fiona's with a laugh. "Come on, it's probably going to take us forever, as Misneach will to have to stop and smell every tree on the way." She shot Trace a smile as they walked past him. "Could you bring his dog food home with you?"

Trace nodded.

"And I'll bring his papers over this evening," Johnnie called after them.

Trace stepped to block Johnnie's view of the women and folded his arms over his chest. "The lady is off limits, Dempster."

"Funny, I didn't see your name on her."

"Then I suggest you get glasses—though if you do come sniffing around her, you might have to trade them in for a white cane."

Though it was subtle, Trace saw his old school buddy tense. "What are you gonna do, beat me up like you did that guy in Afghanistan? You think I can't hold my own against a soldier who got sent home with his tail tucked between his legs?"

"I *think* you wouldn't even hear me coming." Trace took a deep breath and blew it out slowly. "Look, I've got no quarrel with you, Johnnie; I'm just trying to give you a friendly warning. The lady is Kenzie Gregor's sister. And trust me, he's not somebody you want to piss off." He looked over at Jason. "And I suggest that if you're interested in Gabriella, you speak to William Killkenny first." He gave the boy a tight grin. "Though when you do, you might want to bring a change of underwear."

He took the bag of dog food from Jason and headed toward his truck, but then he stopped and looked back. "And for the record, my discharge was honorable," Trace told them. "It's the other bastard who'll be missing Christmas with his family for the next five years. And Johnnie, you bring those papers to me at the docks tomorrow, along with whatever money Fiona gave you over a hundred bucks."

"Five hundred dollars was a bargain."

Trace tried not to show his shock. She'd given him all her money?

Because she had wanted the dog that badly?

Or because she hadn't dared say no to Dempster?

Taking an educated guess, he gave a negligent shrug. "It's your funeral when Gregor finds out you bullied his sister into buying that dog."

"Bullied?" Johnnie glared at him for several seconds, then suddenly snorted and reached into his pocket. "What in hell is up with that woman, anyway?" he muttered as he walked over and handed Trace a wad of fifty-dollar bills. "Just tell her I changed my mind and she can have the dog. All the money she gave me is there, minus what I spent on the collar and dog food." He shook his head. "I swear she thought I was going to drown the little runt if she didn't buy it, and a couple of times she acted as if she thought I might drown *her*. Was she married to some bastard who abused her over there in Scotland?"

Trace shoved the money into his pocket. "Your guess is as good as mine. All I know is that she likes to keep to herself."

Johnnie arched a brow. "Maybe she prefers women."

Even though he was tempted to solve his future problems by letting Dempster spread that particular rumor around town, Trace shook his head. "Naw, she's just leery of men. That, and she's trying to get used to living in a new . . . country."

Johnnie extended his hand. "No hard feelings, okay?" he said, his beard curving into a smile. "I'm sorry for that crack about Afghanistan." His smile broadened. "Although I still say I could take you. I've packed on some muscle since that time you punched me in the first grade."

Trace shifted the dog food to his other shoulder and shook Johnnie's hand. "Yeah, I suppose it takes plenty of muscle to run the toggles on your skidder and tree harvester. You come out fishing with me some day, Dempster, and I'll show you what real work is."

Johnnie gave a laugh and headed to a small blue car. "I'll bring my skidder down to the dock, and we'll hitch it to the stern of your boat and go chain-to-chain."

"Last I knew, skidders can't swim, and neither can you."

Johnnie climbed into the car and rolled down his window. "I appreciate the heads-up on Fiona." He snorted again. "I really need to stop being a sucker for a pretty face. I just spent all last month pulling one woman's claws out of my flesh; I should probably let the wounds heal before I let another one maim me again."

"Been there and done that myself," Trace drawled, "and personally, I don't ever intend to let another woman get that close again." He gestured toward Jason. "And if your brother's half as smart as he is pretty, maybe he'll learn from your mistakes."

Johnnie started the car and put it in gear but looked at

Trace. "I'll call you, and we'll go over to that new bar in Oak Harbor and toast our bachelorhood," he said, pulling onto Main Street and heading toward Ellsworth.

Trace set the dog food in the back of his truck, then leaned his arms on the fender to watch Fiona and Gabriella walking down the sidewalk toward home. The puppy apparently had never worn a collar before, much less had to deal with a leash restricting its movements. One minute it was lunging ahead to go after something, and the next it was fighting Fiona's efforts to pull it along.

Trace glanced over his shoulder at the sound of a powerful small engine and saw William Killkenny veer his motorcycle into the parking lot, missing a car by inches before coming to an abrupt stop beside him.

"It's a little cold to be riding a bike, isn't it?" Trace asked when William shut off the engine.

"Real men don't get cold, Huntsman," the Irishman said with a chuckle. But then he turned serious. "Ye haven't seen Gabby, have you? She and Sarah were supposed to be tidying up the woods around my building site, but when I went to check on them not twenty minutes later, my sister had disappeared."

"You mean that sister?" Trace asked, pointing down the sidewalk.

"Goddamn it," William growled. "I should have known something was up when the girls *volunteered* to go pile brush along the driveway." He shook his head even as he grinned. "Sarah made up some outrageous story that Gabby had gone to my cabin to make them both some hot chocolate." He sighed. "My sister's been here less than a month, and she's already corrupted that sweet child."

Trace gave a laugh. "You want to blame anyone for corrupting Sarah, blame your wife. When Maddy was Sarah's age, she could have given snipers lessons on sneaking around."

William sighed again. "Gabriella's not supposed to associate with Fiona."

"Why in hell not?"

"Because Kenzie believes Fiona will never find her backbone again if any of us help her."

"That's bullshit, and you know it. Gabriella understands Fiona's fears better than anyone. They both were brutalized by men, and they both got thrust into this century by your crazy drùidh buddy, Mac the Menace. Have you or Kenzie considered that maybe the two women can help each other?" He shook his head. "Because dumping Fiona on my doorstep and telling her to figure it out on her own sure as hell isn't working." He pointed at the bag of dog food in the back of his truck. "She bought a puppy today because she was afraid to say no to the man selling it."

William gazed down the sidewalk, watching the two women and the puppy disappear around a curve. "Maybe you're right about them helping each other. For the most part, Gabby acts like any normal teenager, but some nights she wakes up screaming bloody murder. Maddy has tried talking with her, but the girl refuses to discuss anything about that day, saying she's decided to pretend it never happened." He looked back at Trace, his eyes filled with pain. "I don't know how to help her," he said thickly. "Maybe I *should* ask Fiona to befriend her."

"Or maybe you should just leave them both alone," Trace suggested. He nodded down the sidewalk. "Neither of them needed any prompting to get together today, and they both managed to survive their little adventure."

William looked appalled. "Ye expect me to ignore the fact that Gabriella snuck off? The brat left her cell phone with Sarah, along with instructions to say she was indisposed if I happened to call. I've spent the last four hours going out of my mind looking for her."

"Now you know to try Fiona's cell phone the next time Gabriella goes missing," Trace countered, chuckling at William's thunderous scowl. "Or simply tell the girl she doesn't have to sneak off in the first place, because you happened to notice she's all grown up now and quite capable of making her own decisions."

"Do *you* have a sister?" William growled.

"Quite happily, no. But I did spend many nights riding every back road in the county with my uncle Marvin, which taught me that it's a lot easier if they *tell* you where they're going than it is to find them if they don't want to be found. Marvin finally gave up and suggested that if I ever have daughters just to hand them the car keys. He said they'll live up to my expectations if they know I trust them, instead of putting all their energy into outfoxing me."

William visibly shuddered. "I don't know if Mac thought he was doing me a favor or trying to kill me when he brought Gabby here. If I do survive her antics long enough to get her safely wed, I'm just going to have to suffer through it again with Sarah." He suddenly grinned. "But Maddy is giving me a son, according to Mac, and at least I won't have to worry about *him*."

Trace gave a bark of laughter and started backing toward the store. "You hold on to that fantasy, Killkenny. Raising boys today is a damn lot harder than it was in the ninth century, and by the time your son reaches manhood, you're going to think Gabriella and Sarah were saints."

Trace turned away from the Irishman's scowl with another laugh and headed into the Shop 'n Save to the sound of the powerful motorcycle roaring out of the parking lot. But he quickly sobered, remembering Fiona's relief to see him and how good it had made him feel. Dammit to hell, she'd better not think he was going to come to her rescue every time she got into trouble, because he *wasn't*. He'd left his hero uniform in Afghanistan, and he sure as hell wasn't ever putting it on again.

Not even for a pair of vulnerable golden eyes.

And that clueless puppy had better not come scratching at his door with its nose full of porcupine quills, either, because he was just as immune to soulful *canine* eyes.

Goddamn it, didn't the woman know she was supposed to ask her landlord if she could have a pet before she brought one home?

Chapter Five

$\diamondsuit$

Watching Gabriella disappear up the road on the back of William's motorcycle, Fiona stood at the bottom of the stairs leading up to her apartment, torn between wanting to run inside and staying to face her landlord like a confident, modern woman. She started walking Misneach around the yard, trying to persuade herself that she wasn't afraid of Mr. Huntsman and that there wasn't any reason they couldn't have a calm, civilized discussion about her owning a pet. But half an hour later, worried he might not be in the mood to hear how having a dog would benefit the both of them, Fiona found herself waiting for him *halfway* up the stairs.

Just as soon as she'd sat down, Misneach had flopped down with a doggy sigh and immediately fallen asleep on the step above her, apparently exhausted from all that had happened to him today. The poor little bugger; he must be so confused and frightened and feeling so powerless that falling asleep was his only defense. For didn't she herself know the horrors of waking up one morning belonging to one master, only to be bartered off before nightfall to another one for a few measly coins?

"Don't worry, my little friend," she whispered, stroking his wavy coat of dust-colored fur. "If Mr. Huntsman says you can't stay, you have my word of honor that I will not hand you off to another master. I learned all about surviving the elements when I was a hawk, and we'll just go live in the woods if he won't let me keep you. You'll give me courage, and I will give you my loyalty, and together we will make a formidable team." She kissed the top of his head. "And if by some miracle Mr. Huntsman does agree to let you stay, then you must also become a perfect tenant and do your business in the tall grass and not jump on him with muddy paws. Oh, and no barking when he's home, as he works very long hours and needs his sleep," she added in a stern whisper.

Fiona sat upright when she heard the distinct rumble of her landlord's pickup turning into the driveway, and that persistent knot in her gut rose into her chest, squeezing her suddenly pounding heart. She stood up, hoping it would help her breathe normally, only to realize that she might appear to be looking down her nose at him. So she sat back down and folded her hands on her lap, again wishing she'd never gone to town.

But when Misneach gave a soft little puppy snore, Fiona realized that if she hadn't, there was a good chance he would be in that terrible shelter right now, praying that he could go to sleep and *never* wake up.

The old green pickup came to a halt just out of her line of vision, and she heard the engine shut off and the vehicle's door open and close.

And then nothing.

She leaned forward and frowned down at the porch. He had to have seen her sitting on the stairs when he'd driven in. Why wasn't he coming to discuss her new pet?

Gathering her courage, because she knew that postponing the confrontation would only add to her angst, Fiona started down the steps. But she plopped back down with a gasp when her landlord silently rounded the corner of the house carrying her bag of dog food. He set it on the bottom step, then pulled some money out of his pocket and held it up for her to see.

"Johnnie Dempster asked me to give this to you. He told me once he thought about it, he decided he wanted you to have the dog when he realized it was going to a good home," he said, tucking the money under the bag of food.

Fiona stood up in alarm. "Oh no, you must give it back to him! I do not wish to feel beholden to Mr. Dempster."

"Hey, I tried to get him to keep at least a hundred, but he insisted on giving it all back minus what he spent on the food and leash. Don't worry; Johnnie's not looking for a new girlfriend. He just got rid of the last one with his skin barely intact." He stared up at her for several seconds and then suddenly blew out a sigh. "Dempster's a good man, Fiona, and he has a passion for dogs. But your new little friend there," he said, gesturing toward Misneach, "was the runt of the litter, and Johnnie knows he'll make a better companion than a hunter, so *he's* beholden to *you* for taking it off his hands."

Fiona plopped back down on the stairs, trying to decide if she believed him or not. "And you . . . you will let me keep Misneach?" she whispered, looking at his broad chest because she wasn't quite able to meet his gaze.

She saw him shrug. "I've wanted to get a dog myself but didn't think it was fair, considering the long hours I'm gone from the house. Truth is, I like the idea of having a dog around to keep the raccoons and skunks out of the barn." Although it didn't quite reach his eyes, he smiled up at her. "Just teach him to do his business in the woods, and keep him out of the trash."

Fiona jumped to her feet again, unable to contain her excitement. "I *promise,* you won't even know he's here!"

Misneach came awake with a startled yelp and tumbled down several steps before he slammed into Fiona's legs, knocking her off balance. She tried to grab the railing with one hand and Misneach's leash with the other, only she missed both when the leash tangled in her legs. But just as she felt herself falling, she was suddenly swept off her feet and gently set on the stairs.

"Th-thank you," she whispered in horror.

But she was talking to Trace Huntsman's back. And if she hadn't still been shivering from the feel of his warm, powerful arms around her, she might have thought nothing had happened as she watched her landlord disappear around the corner of the house—with Misneach, leash flapping behind him, yapping excitedly at his heels.

Fiona shivered again. She couldn't believe a man could move that fast or so silently; yet he must have, or she would have been lying in a heap on the ground right now.

Hearing a sudden yelp followed by strangled cries of distress, Fiona rushed down the remaining steps to find Misneach hanging off the side of the porch, frantically pawing the air. But before she could even reach him, Mr. Huntsman was there, unsnapping the leash from his collar before lowering him to the ground.

Fiona swept the whimpering puppy into her arms and whispered soothing words into his trembling fur. But when she lifted her gaze to thank her landlord, the man had once again disappeared as silently as a ghost.

She frowned down at the leash. The handle had wedged in a crack between two rotten boards, apparently bringing Misneach to an abrupt halt before flinging him off the porch. She kissed the top of his head and set him down, then pulled the leash free. But before she could snap it onto his collar, the pup was off again, racing after his savior.

"Misneach, no!" Fiona cried, chasing after him. "Come he—"

The rest of her command got muffled in Trace Huntsman's chest. She bounced off him and would have fallen back if he hadn't caught her by the shoulders.

"Just out of curiosity," he muttered, setting her on her feet and turning away, "how many trees did you crash into when you were a hawk?"

Fiona gaped at his retreating back. Was he implying that she was *clumsy*?

"None!" she snapped, marching after him. "I'll have you know I could pluck a dove right out of the air, even in a strong gale. Misneach, come here!" she demanded when the pup started nipping at his heels again.

He reached into the bed of his pickup and pulled out a large roll of plastic and a bundle of thin wooden sticks. Then he stepped over her pet and walked past her without breaking stride as he headed toward the front of the house.

"Misneach, come!" she shouted, rushing after them again.

Her landlord dropped everything at the foot of her stairs, then walked past her again back in the direction of his truck. This time, Fiona managed to capture the pup, who immediately started struggling when she tried to snap the leash onto his collar. "You will behave yourself," she quietly hissed, "before Mr. Huntsman changes his mind about letting you live here."

But the moment she got the leash on him, the little contortionist slipped out of his collar and ran off again. "Misneach!" Fiona cried, growing truly frantic when he disappeared into the barn.

She barged in after him, but her eyes didn't adjust to the darkness quickly enough, and she would have smacked into a post if a large hand hadn't caught hold of her sleeve and pulled her around it at the last minute.

"Leave the pup be," he said, striding out of the barn carrying a leather pouch with a hammer hanging on it and a small pail filled with nails. "He's following me because he's used to being around men," he continued, stopping to fasten the belt around his waist. "And there's really no reason for you to restrain him here in the yard."

"But he might run out to the road and get hit by a vehicle."

He took the leash and collar out of her hand before she even realized what he was doing, and replaced it with a pair of leather gloves that he pulled from his hind pocket. "He'll stick close to us," he said, picking up the pail and heading back around the front of the house.

Fiona looked at the gloves in her hand, wondering what

she was supposed to do with them. She ran to catch up with him and Misneach, but when she reached the foot of her stairs, neither of them was there. The roll of plastic and bundle of wood were gone, and the pail was sitting in their place.

"Bring the nails," he called from somewhere behind the house.

The stiff breeze blowing in off the bay caught the hem of her long coat just as she rounded the corner, and Misneach lunged toward the material with a playful yelp. Only the pup bumped into the pail instead, knocking it out of her hand. She let out a cry of dismay, and despite her attempts to catch it, all of the nails flew out of the pail and disappeared into the tall grass.

It took every ounce of courage Fiona possessed not to turn tail and run, even though she knew Mr. Huntsman would catch her before she reached her stairs. And it definitely was beyond her ability to look at him, knowing the anger she'd see in his eyes.

But several pounding heartbeats later, when he still hadn't said anything, she finally worked up the nerve to look up.

Only he was gone.

And so was Misneach.

Fiona bent at the waist, the memory piercing her like a sword of that long-ago day when her pet goose had caused her to spill an entire pot of stew. She had been forced to make a new one with the young goose—and then she'd been forced to eat it.

She dropped to her knees, grabbed the pail, and started picking up whatever nails she could find, praying to God that Trace Huntsman wouldn't take out his anger at her on a poor, innocent puppy.

"I'm picking them up!" she screamed as she frantically searched the ground. "I'll find every last one, I promise! Please, just give me time to find them!"

"Here, this will help," he said quietly, setting a rectangular piece of metal the size of a shoe on the ground and then walking away.

Misneach bounded up and started licking her face, and Fiona blindly pulled the puppy under her as she leaned over him. She swiped at her eyes with the back of one hand as she held her pet protectively beneath her, and picked up the heavy piece of metal—only to discover several nails stuck to the underside of it.

"It's a magnet," her landlord said from several feet away as he started unrolling the plastic. "Just run it over the ground, and it will attract the nails. Then brush them off into the pail and run it over the ground again."

With a whispered plea for Misneach to behave himself, Fiona began working as quickly as her shaking allowed, her silent tears of relief dripping onto her hands. She could actually hear the nails clinking against the mysterious metal as she pushed the tall grass aside to slide it over the ground.

The magnet held such power that she had a difficult time prying off the nails. But every time she lifted it up, several dozen more nails were clinging to it, and in less than five minutes, she had the pail nearly full.

But even more magical than the magnet was that Trace Huntsman hadn't flown into a rage. In fact, she saw him giving Misneach playful little shoves as he unrolled the plastic along the back side of the house. But as fewer and fewer nails clung to the magnet each time she lifted it, and her shaking subsided and her tears dried up, Fiona's terror slowly turned to shame.

She had utterly humiliated herself in front of this man, and probably lost any chance she might have had of getting him to respect her as a modern woman.

Maybe she *should* go live in the woods.

"You've found most of them," he said, pulling a knife out of a large pocket on his work belt and cutting the plastic. Then he cut the cord binding the bundle of wood. "Here, take these laths down to the other end of the house," he said, holding out several of the flat sticks when she stood up. Only he didn't immediately hand them over. "But first, you might want to put on the gloves I gave you."

Fiona patted the pockets of her coat, then spun around so he wouldn't see her further humiliation as she tried to remember what she'd done with the gloves.

Her cheeks burned like hot coals when she heard him sigh. "You're not getting those gloves back," he said, giving a chuckle, "unless you have a spare set of hawk wings under your coat."

Fiona turned to see him looking toward the ocean, and she spotted Misneach racing along the bottom of the bluff the house sat on, her leather gloves in his mouth. The pup splashed into one of the shallow tidal pools without even slowing down, tossed the gloves into the air, and then pounced on each one as it started to sink.

"Misneach!" she shouted, looking for a place to descend the steep bank.

But she came to an abrupt halt when Huntsman thrust the sticks toward her again. "Forget the gloves," he said, walking away as soon as she took them. "We have only about an hour of daylight left to get this side of the house banked."

"Banked?" she repeated, although she was once again talking to his back and had to chase after him.

"What did you do in the eleventh century to keep the snow from blowing through the cracks in your house?" he asked, lifting one edge of the plastic. He held it against the clapboards, about a foot above the granite foundation. "Here, hold one of those laths over the plastic while I nail it in place."

Fiona dropped the flat sticks onto the ground, picked one up, and then held it in place. He pulled his hammer and a couple of nails out of his belt and started nailing through the wood and plastic directly into the siding on the house.

Holding her end of the lath by the very tip the moment he got one side of it nailed, Fiona leaned away when he nailed her end.

Not because she was afraid of him but because he smelled strongly of fish!

And for some reason, the thought of this big, powerful man doing what might be considered woman's work, stuffing little bags with bait fish he had to cut up himself, made her feel somewhat giddy.

Then again, it could be the fish fumes causing her light-headedness.

Either way, that knot in her belly slowly started unraveling.

"We cut fir and pine boughs and tucked them around the bottom of our house," she told him, grabbing another lath and placing it over the plastic he held up.

"We'll do that tomorrow afternoon," he said around a nail he'd stuck in his mouth as he pounded in another one. "The boughs will keep the plastic from billowing up and hold the snow against it for added insulation."

We? He expected her to help him again tomorrow?

"I assume *Misneach* is Gaelic. What does it mean?" he asked, waiting for her to set another lath in place.

Fiona didn't answer him right away. If she said it meant "noble one" as she'd told Johnnie Dempster, Mr. Huntsman might discover she had lied to him if Kenzie or William told him otherwise. But neither did she want to further humiliate herself by revealing her weakness.

"I named him 'Courage,'" she finally admitted. "Because of how brave he was today when he lost the only home he's ever known," she added in a rush.

He glanced over at her, and then with a snort drove a nail through the lath in one powerful stroke. "That pup's not courageous; it's clueless." He walked to the pail and filled his work belt with another fistful of nails. "Mother Nature designed all babies that way, so they'll attach themselves to anyone who pays attention to them. Hell, they'll even remain loyal to someone who kicks them around for sport."

Hearing the slight edge in his voice, she didn't respond.

They continued working their way down the house in companionable silence, and the unraveling sensation inside her made Fiona realize how wonderful it felt to be working. She held another lath in place and stared at her hands, trying to remember the last time she'd done anything truly constructive. She'd helped Kenzie with his displaced souls when she'd been a hawk, but when was the last time she'd helped another human being without being forced to?

It really was quite empowering.

And she didn't even mind that it was a *man* she was helping.

Nor was she bothered when he inevitably brushed up against her, not even when his large, callused hand suddenly shot out to cup her face protectively when her feet got tangled up in the blowing plastic and she nearly fell against the house.

"Thank you," she murmured, tucking several strands of hair back into her braid.

"The wind's picking up, and the temperature's dropping with the sun," he said, turning to the ocean. He gave a sharp whistle, causing Misneach to stop right in the middle of a tidal pool and look up. When he gave another whistle, the pup started running toward them. "Why don't you and Misneach head inside? I can finish this."

"But it will go faster if I continue to help."

He took the lath out of her hand and used it to gesture at Misneach, struggling up over the bluff. "A full-grown Chesapeake can splash around in cold water all day, but he hasn't got much meat on his bones yet. You'd better get him warmed up before he catches a chill. There's dry firewood in the shed, and the stove in your front room works if you want to build a fire. In fact, I prefer you burn wood once it gets really cold, to save on heating oil. I assume you know how to run a woodstove?"

She picked up Misneach and started around the house. "I know how it works."

"Fiona."

She stopped at the corner and turned toward him.

"Thank you." He gestured toward the plastic. "I appreciate your help."

Before she even realized what she was doing, Fiona shot him a beaming smile. "You're welcome, Mr. Huntsman."

"It's Trace," he said when she turned away. "My old man was Mr. Huntsman."

Wondering at the edge in his voice again, she shot him another smile, although this one was a bit forced. "You're welcome, Trace."

Chapter Six

"Goddamn it, Gregor, I am *serious*. You have one week to find Fiona a new place to live," Trace growled into his cell phone as he stood in the middle of his neatly organized, cobweb-free barn. "Because if you don't, I swear the next time she goes into town, I will torch my own damn house to get her out of here."

"What's the matter, Huntsman, do ye not like having fresh eggs for breakfast?"

"Eggs? You think this is about the chickens? Or the goat? Or the goddamned horse the size of an elephant? It's about your sister cleaning and rearranging every square inch of my barn. She organized my *tools,* Gregor. And she found an old scythe and leveled every damned last weed all the way to the street!"

"Aye," Kenzie said on a sigh. "Women do have a tendency to nest."

"Nest?" Trace repeated through gritted teeth. He walked

over to look out the side window, only to scowl again when he saw Fiona—wearing his tool belt around the waist of her long coat—nailing a board she'd obviously found during her cleaning spree to one of the rotten paddock posts. "Dammit, Gregor, if she keeps fixing up this place, they're going to raise my taxes."

The horse and goat were in the paddock, the horse nuzzling Fiona's shoulder and the goat, its neck stretched through the fence, trying to reach the leather pouch on her tool belt. Misneach was standing in a small water trough that Trace had never seen before, and the pup kept driving his head under the water, only to surface with a rock in his mouth, which he would then drop into the water again.

Trace's mood darkened even more when he caught himself noticing how the low-hanging November sun made Fiona's hair look like spun gold—especially the tendrils framing her flawless face—and how gracefully and efficiently she moved. And he sure as hell didn't like that he *liked* coming home to a house that wasn't empty, with the smell of wood smoke and the aroma of fresh-baked bread assaulting him the moment he stepped out of his truck.

Thank God he kept his door locked; if she ever saw his living quarters, she'd probably have a field day, or more likely a month of field days, cleaning the kitchen and organizing his sock drawer.

"Don't ye see," Kenzie said, turning serious. "Fiona's nesting must mean she's grown comfortable with you. That's amazing progress in only two weeks, considering Killkenny got nothing but grief from her."

"When he was a *dragon* and she was a *hawk*," Trace growled. "But whenever William or any other man stops by, she still vanishes and doesn't reappear until they're gone. And," he continued when Kenzie tried to say something, "she can't be comfortable with me, as we haven't spoken two entire sentences to each other since I agreed to let her keep that puppy. Which," he continued hotly, glaring at the chickens scattered through the yard, "has turned into twelve hens, a goat, and a horse. And when I stopped in just now to pick up some tools, I found two *skunks* curled up in some rags in a box on my workbench."

"They're orphans," Kenzie said, the amusement back in his voice. "Fiona called this morning and asked me to go over there and check them out, and they told me they hadn't seen their mama for many, many days."

"They told you they're orphans," Trace repeated, deadpan, remembering that this was the man he had seen transform into a panther.

"Aye," Kenzie said. "And they gave me their word they won't spray anyone not directly threatening them."

Trace closed his eyes on a silent groan. Great. Wonderful. How friggin' fantastic nice of them.

"Ye needn't worry; they'll be taking their winter sleep soon, and Fiona offered to let them stay in the barn only until spring."

Trace snapped his eyes open. "Can *she* talk to animals?"

Kenzie chuckled at his alarm. "Nay, but she does have a certain . . . empathy for creatures. Ye might remember she was a red-tailed hawk for several centuries."

What he remembered was that he was dealing with a clan of *magic makers*.

One of whom could turn him into a toad.

Trace scowled out the window again when he saw Fiona

wrestling another board into place, two nails held between her pursed lips and a fine sheen of perspiration making her hair cling to her flushed cheeks. "One week," he snapped, not caring if Matt turned him into a goddamned slug. "You get your sister and her zoo off my property by next Tuesday, or I swear, this place is going up like a rocket on the Fourth of July."

A loud sigh came over the phone. "Can ye not give this arrangement more of a chance? It means a lot to me, Trace," Kenzie said, his voice growing thick. "When I brought the mare to her, I saw a hint of the woman Fiona was becoming before that bastard assaulted her. Just give me enough time to explain to her that she can't take over your home, and I'll persuade her to turn her energies toward pleasing *herself* instead of you."

Trace suddenly stiffened, not knowing which shocked him more, that Fiona was working her pretty little ass off making sure *he* liked her or that he hadn't realized what she was doing. The eggs and fresh-baked bread he kept finding on his doorstep, the boughs she had tucked along the house before he could do it himself, the barn swept clean of every damn last cobweb, his tools organized, her living in virtual darkness every evening—she'd been building brownie points against his ever getting angry at her.

How in hell had he missed that?

For chrissakes, he was *trained* to read people.

Which was why, when he had seen it was taking every ounce of courage she possessed just to ask him if she could keep Misneach, he'd folded like a house of cards. And going against his own better judgment, he'd conned her into helping him bank the house, hoping she would see that he wasn't anyone to be afraid of.

Only he'd nearly blown it when she'd dropped that pail of nails.

Christ, he'd wanted ten minutes alone with the bastard who had caused the terror he'd heard in her screams.

And when he'd continued having her help him as if nothing had happened, she'd become no better than her clueless puppy, eagerly pitching in and even appearing disappointed when he'd sent her inside. And then she'd worked nonstop for the next six days, turning his house into a goddamned *home*.

"Your sister's demons are not my problem, Gregor. And if *you* can't deal with them, then move her in with some little old lady who needs mothering." Remembering the flood of inquiries he'd gotten down at the docks about his pretty new tenant, Trace snorted. "Just make sure you find one who owns a shotgun, because some of the idiots around here have the finesse of a bull moose when it comes to courting women."

"This is why it's important that Fiona live over you."

"Dammit, Gregor, I am the *last* person you want around her."

Trace immediately realized his mistake, and the prolonged silence on the other end of the phone told him that Kenzie hadn't missed it, either.

"You're attracted to her," the highlander said quietly.

"Goddamn it!" Trace growled, kicking the wooden barrel he was standing beside as hard as he could. "I am—"

Trace snapped his mouth shut when the air compressor sitting on top of the barrel rolled off and slammed down onto his workbench.

Or more important, it slammed into the box holding the

skunks, the startled screams of its occupants mixing with his own panicked shout. Trace dropped the phone to catch the box, at the same time trying to turn the opening away from himself.

He'd have succeeded, too, if the heavy compressor hadn't continued its descent and slammed into his knee. Trace fell with a shouted curse, shoving at the box as he tried to scramble away. And that's when the damned compressor struck his head, just as the skunks tumbled onto the floor beside him.

Apparently believing that this was well within the bounds of being directly threatened, both skunks let loose everything they had, hitting him point-blank.

Trace's roar ended on a choked gag when a cloud of putrid musk enveloped him. He blindly rolled in the direction of the door, his eyes burning as if they'd been dosed with acid, his mouth and throat on fire as he held his breath while fighting the urge to vomit. But finding that he couldn't crawl on his right knee, he ended up dragging himself from the barn even as he scrambled out of his jacket and ripped off his shirt. He tried getting to his feet then, only his knee gave out, and he fell to the ground.

He threw up and lay there gagging, gasping for breath.

"I've got you," he barely heard over the roaring in his head.

"No, get away," he choked out on a series of convulsing heaves. He blindly swatted at her, but she still managed to manacle his wrist in a surprisingly strong grip and then wedge her shoulder under his armpit as she straightened to lift him.

They stumbled toward the house. "Water. Outside fau-cet," he rasped, fumbling with his belt buckle with his free hand.

Christ, he couldn't breathe!

He slammed against the granite foundation as he felt for the faucet and gave a shout of relief when the deluge of water gushed over his head. He lay on his side, not caring if he drowned in the icy water, because it sure as hell was better than drowning in skunk piss and vomit.

Trace felt something tugging at his feet and realized that Fiona was taking off his boots. He unfastened his jeans and gritted his teeth against the pain in his knee when she pulled them off. He dragged himself back under the spigot again and let the water continue to flush his eyes and pum-mel his body.

Misneach, who'd been barking incessantly the whole time, jumped at him but gave a strangled yelp and ran away in a fit of sneezes.

Trace didn't know how long he lay there and didn't even care that he was naked; he only knew that whenever he moved from under the water, he started gagging again.

The water suddenly shut off, and his protest got lost inside the heavy material that enveloped him. "Go away!" he shouted, blindly feeling for the spigot as he tossed the material away and turned the water back on.

"Oh, thank God you stopped by!" Trace heard Fiona cry as she was moving away. "You have to help me get him into the house. He hurt his knee and can't walk."

The water shut off again, and the material returned, this time wrapping around him like a straitjacket just before he was hauled to his feet.

"Christ, Huntsman, did ye kiss their asses?" Kenzie growled. "Fiona, grab that jug of vinegar I brought."

When Trace's knee gave out on him again, the highlander hefted him over his shoulder with a muttered curse and started off.

"Not the house!"

"Nay, I'm taking you down to the salt marsh. Fiona, go get a blanket and bring it and the vinegar down to us."

Great. Wonderful. Friggin' fantastic. A swim in the freezing ocean was exactly what he needed. Trace vomited again, which started his nose and throat burning all over again. "Forget the week," he ground out, wiping his face on the back of Kenzie's jacket. "I'm torching the house *today*."

Kenzie chuckled. "You'll likely want to burn the barn, at least, along with your clothes and my sister's coat."

After wiping the tears pouring from his eyes, Trace held his head to keep it from bobbing with Kenzie's strides. "My face is numb," he muttered. "I swear, skunk piss is worse than pepper spray. The military should bomb the bastards out of those Afghan tunnels with this shit."

"Aye, I've seen the little buggers send warriors scattering right in the middle of battle. Here we go," Kenzie said with a grunt, shrugging Trace off his shoulder and dropping him next to a tidal pool. "Hell, Huntsman, couldn't ye have left your shorts on, at least?"

Trace leaned over to splash some seawater on his face and gave a snort. "Apparently, your sister isn't so shy that she wasn't afraid to strip me naked in a matter of seconds." He looked toward the house and saw the blurry figure of Fiona racing down the path along the paddock fence, a blanket in one hand and a jug in the other. He glared up at Kenzie. "She goes home with you *today*."

The highlander bent over and gave the coat Trace was sitting on a sharp tug, rolling him into the pool—his roar of outrage turning to curses when he landed in freezing water up to his chest.

Kenzie turned to block Fiona's view as she approached them. "Just leave the blanket and vinegar," he told her. "And go put Trace's clothes in a pile in the middle of the driveway, along with your coat," he instructed, handing it to her, "and light them on fire. Then go change your own clothes," he continued, moving slightly when she tried to see past him. "And after ye do, go in his home, fill his bathtub with hot water, and put a kettle on to boil."

"No!" Trace shouted, making the highlander turn to look at him. His vision might be blurry, but he could see the amusement on the bastard's face. "I can run my own bath. And besides, the door is locked." He splashed more seawater on his face and screwed his fists into his eyes, trying to clear them. But when he leaned around Kenzie to look at Fiona and saw that her own eyes were puffy with skunk fumes and filled with concern, he blew out a deep sigh. "Just don't burn my clothes without taking my wallet out of my pants first, okay?" he asked calmly.

She nodded. Holding her coat away from herself, she turned and started back toward the barn at a run.

"His house key is likely on the key ring in his truck," Kenzie called after her. "Ye run a bath and put the kettle on."

"Dammit, Gregor, I don't want her in my house."

"Why? Are ye keeping a naked woman tied to your bed?"

Kenzie drawled, unscrewing the cap on the vinegar. "Close your eyes; this may sting."

Trace snorted, which ended on a sputter when the vinegar cascaded down over his head and into his mouth. He gargled, then spit it out and ran his hands over his face and through his hair. "How did you get here so fast?" he asked, shuddering against the cold as he rubbed the steady stream of vinegar over his chest and arms.

"I was in town, at Eve's store. Lucky for you, she uses vinegar to wash the windows," Kenzie said, directing the stream over his back. "Mind telling me what possessed you to disturb those skunks?"

Trace stopped washing to glare up at him. "I didn't; my air compressor did. Apparently, your sister thought it belonged on top of a barrel beside my workbench, and when I kicked the barrel, the compressor fell on the box of skunks. Then it hit my knee just before it smashed into my head." He touched the stinging lump on his forehead. Finding his fingers covered in blood, he glared up at Kenzie again. "That compressor must weigh as much as she does, so not only *why* did she think it belonged up on the barrel, *how* did she get it up there?"

Kenzie shrugged and poured the last of the vinegar over him. "That will have to do for now," he said, picking up the blanket. "We better get you into a hot bath before the cold takes your strength." He laid the blanket out on the grass and reached out to Trace. "If ye have Scotch, I'll dose your tea with it for you to sip while ye soak."

"Not that I'll taste it," he said, giving a grunt when Kenzie hauled him out of the tidal pool and dropped him onto the blanket. "I'll be lucky if I ever get the smell of skunk piss out of my nose hairs, let alone taste anything again." He pulled the blanket around himself and dropped his throbbing head into his hands with a groan.

Kenzie squatted down in front of him. "I'm asking as a friend, Trace, that ye please let Fiona stay," he said quietly.

Trace lifted his head to look the highlander in the eyes. "I came within one blow of killing a man the last time I got between a woman and her demons, and now she's dead, the guy who killed her is serving five years for manslaughter, and I got kicked out of the military." He dropped his head back into his hands. "As much as I'd like to help you, I've got my own demons to fight."

"What stopped you from killing him?"

He looked up again. "Only the knowledge that I was as much to blame for her death as he was."

"It's been my experience that intelligent men learn from their mistakes, my friend, and I have every reason to believe you won't make that particular mistake again."

"Oh, I won't. I have no intention of ever getting involved with another woman."

Kenzie chuckled at that and lifted Trace with him as he stood up. "No offense, Huntsman," he said, hefting him over his shoulder. "But with your stones—even shriveled as they are from the cold—I can't quite see you becoming a monk."

"Lovely, Gregor," Trace muttered, gritting his teeth at being carried like a stinking sack of grain. "How friggin' *nice* of you to notice."

Chapter Seven

"Go ahead, Peeps," Trace drawled, shifting the ice pack on his knee. "You keep right on talking about me as if I'm not here, and I'll continue telling your husband all about your more colorful teenage antics."

Maddy turned away from Fiona and Gabriella to glare at him, her nose wrinkled against the eau de skunk still oozing from every pore on his body. "Don't you believe one of his stories, William. I was a saint compared to Midnight Bay's infamous hell-raising Huntsman." She moved her gaze around the room. "Jeesh, Trace, would it kill you to pick up a dust rag once in a while? Everything in this place looks like it was here when you bought the house, including the dirt."

"That's because it was."

Maddy looked around again in surprise. "All this stuff is old man Peterson's junk?" Her eyes turned sad. "Do you own anything?" she whispered.

"I own my boat, my truck, and a falling-down house that sits on twelve acres of oceanfront property. But if you don't slap a bandage on my knee so I can go fishing tomorrow, I won't be able to pay the taxes on any of them."

"Sorry, big man, you're laid up for at least a week. If you push that knee, you might end up needing surgery, and that'll put you out of commission for over a month."

Trace closed his eyes on a stifled groan.

He'd lost the battle with Kenzie. Not only was Fiona still there but she was in his living room, receiving instructions from his cousin—who was a *geriatric* nurse—on how to take care of him for the next few days. It was the least Fiona could do, Kenzie had said right after he'd called Maddy, for not immediately putting the skunks in a dark corner of the barn as he'd instructed.

God only knew where the little pissants were now; probably hiding under the porch recharging their stink guns for another shot at him.

He still couldn't feel his face, his constantly weeping eyes were so bloodshot that everything appeared red, and half a bottle of Scotch hadn't done a damn thing to kill the foul taste in his mouth except make him just drunk enough not to care that he smelled like a skunk.

"If ye want, I can go out fishing with Rick tomorrow," William offered.

"And I'll come back in the morning," Gabriella interjected, "and help Fiona . . . um . . . straighten things up here."

Wonderful. Then he'd have *two* women messing with his stuff.

Trace gave the young girl a drunken smile. "That's very kind of you, Gabriella, but I rather like my things just as they are." He looked at William. "And no offense, Killkenny, but I still haven't recovered from the last time I took you out fishing."

William gave him a pained look but then suddenly grinned. "Not a problem; Rick can run the winch this time, and I will drive the boat."

"No!" Maddy yelped, drowning out Trace's muttered curse, both of them horrified at the thought of William getting behind the wheel of his boat, considering the Irishman couldn't keep his *truck* off the shoulder of the road. That's why William was still riding his motorcycle long after everyone else had put theirs away for the season, as he claimed straddling a bike was just like riding a horse. And drivers and pedestrians—and mailboxes—everywhere thanked God that Killkenny didn't mind the cold.

"I mean, really, William," Maddy said more softly, smiling at her husband. "Rick is more than capable of pulling Trace's weight for the next few days."

Feeling his burning eyelids growing heavy, Trace sighed in defeat. Maybe he'd just stay drunk for the next few days. That way, he wouldn't care if they all climbed onto his boat and sailed away—just as long as he wasn't on it with them.

He finally found relief from the fumes by falling asleep to the rhythmic chatter of everyone planning his week without him, likely right down to which one of them got to organize his sock drawer.

When Trace woke up to sunlight hitting his face and found himself in his bed, although he had no recollection of how he'd gotten there, he snapped his eyes shut again with an agonized groan.

Christ, he stank.

His head felt like someone was striking it with a sledge-hammer, and he hoped like hell that was a bandage on his knee and not fluid making it so swollen he couldn't even bend it. His eyes were still running and apparently had been all night, judging by the crust around them, and when he opened them again, everything was still blurry.

He was tempted to just roll over and go back to sleep, but somewhere in the foggy regions of his throbbing mind, he remembered hearing Maddy say something to Fiona about rubbing his knee with horse liniment.

He sat up with another groan. No way was he letting that walking disaster anywhere near him; if she wasn't tripping over her own two feet, she was setting booby traps for *him* to trip over.

How in hell had she gotten that heavy compressor up on that barrel? And for chrissakes, why? The damn thing had wheels on it, so why hadn't she simply wheeled it under the workbench? What, was he going to find his microwave on top of the fridge when he hobbled into the kitchen this morning? And the TV sitting on a footstool next to the fireplace—would he find it on top of the china cabinet he was using to hold his rifles?

Trace threw off the blankets to take a look at his knee and saw that he was wearing pajamas.

Only he was pretty sure he didn't own pajamas.

And he sure as hell wouldn't own any with Big Bird and Elmo on them.

He pulled the shirt away from his body and found a cardboard note tied to one of the buttons. He rubbed his blurry eyes, trying to focus on the words. *You're getting your Christmas present early, cousin,* he read, *so you won't give Fiona nightmares.*

He tore the card off with a snort. Just as soon as he could walk again, he was shaving Maddy bald.

Where in hell had she found adult-sized *Sesame Street* pajamas?

Trace suddenly stilled at the sound of his porch door squeaking open. He lay back with a muttered curse when he heard Misneach race into the kitchen, and pulled the blankets up over his head. But when that only imprisoned him in fumes, he tucked the blankets under his chin and pretended to be asleep.

He heard his bedroom door squeak open and cracked his eyes just enough to see Fiona's head appear, her own eyes huge with a bit of curiosity and a whole lot of caution and her nose wrinkled against the smell. Trace gave a soft snore, but instead of that getting her to leave as he hoped, she crept up to the foot of his bed.

Misneach was far less shy. The pup ran past her and jumped up onto the bed with an excited yelp, making Trace bolt upright when the dog nearly unmanned him.

God save him from women and puppies.

"Misneach, no!" Fiona cried, scrambling after her pet.

Seeing the train wreck heading his way, Trace shoved the sneezing pup off the bed in order to catch Fiona when she tripped on some of his clothes on the floor, and deftly guided her past his groin by spinning her around and laying her down beside him.

The woman gave a startled gasp that ended when she went perfectly still, and Trace realized she was holding her breath—and probably not because he stank.

He tossed back the covers and swung his pajama-clad legs over the side of the bed, stifling a groan when his right knee protested the movement. "Here's an idea; why don't you go into the kitchen and . . . cook something while I get dressed? And then while I'm eating, you can hunt through the closets for a pair of crutches I'm pretty sure old man Peterson owned. Then I'll go to work, and you can . . ." He waved at the air, keeping his back to her. "Oh, I don't know, maybe you could ride your elephant into town and buy yourself a new coat or something."

"Madeline said you can't go to work for a week," she whispered, still lying on the bed, still holding herself perfectly still.

Trace gave a snort. "The last time I listened to Peeps, I spent two nights in the county jail." He started unbuttoning his pajama top, figuring that stripping it off might get her to leave. "You could try looking in the closet in the mudroom for those crutches. I remember seeing them, I'm just not sure where." He shrugged the shirt off and let it fall onto the bed behind him. "Or they could be hanging in the shed," he added, just as the bed dipped and he heard her gasp.

Oh, Christ. He'd forgotten. This time, *he* went perfectly still at the feel of her fingers moving over the maze of scars that ran from his shoulders down to his waist.

"What happened?" she whispered.

He stood up to get away from her feathery touch, pulling on the pajama top as he gritted his teeth and limped to the door. "Yeah, I'm pretty sure I saw those crutches in the shed," he said, hobbling down the hall to the bathroom.

He shut the door softly behind him, then lowered himself onto the hamper and stared at the floor. Goddamn it, if Gregor thought he was bluffing about torching his own house, the highlander obviously didn't know shit about fighting real demons.

Fiona was so mad at herself she could just spit. How could she have been so insensitive as to ask him about his scars, much less be so rude as to touch them, too? It was obvious that Trace was self-conscious about them, even if he had tried to appear otherwise. She didn't know what sort of weapon made such terrible scars, but she did wonder how any man could survive that kind of horrible injury.

She should apologize to him for being so insensitive.

Or maybe she should start by apologizing for his getting sprayed by the skunks.

And for his knee injury, and for her being responsible for his not being able to earn the money it was apparent he desperately needed.

Fiona stopped scrubbing the counter and threw the dishrag into the now spotless sink filled with hot, soapy water. No, she should probably start by apologizing for cleaning his barn and cutting the weeds out of his driveway and *then* move on to her other transgressions.

Kenzie had explained to her yesterday, while Trace had been soaking in the tub, that even though he knew she had meant well, men did not care to have a woman point out their shortcomings by doing their chores for them. Men— and, apparently, Trace Huntsman in particular, Kenzie had explained—didn't like feeling indebted to anyone, especially a woman.

Her brother had then gone on to point out that a man's possessions were always off-limits. She'd had no business rearranging Trace's tools, much less borrowing them without asking his permission first. And if she'd been work-ing so hard because she wanted Trace to like her, Kenzie had said, she was going about it all wrong. Sharing her eggs was neighborly, but taking over his home was a wife's privi-lege, not a tenant's.

Fiona looked around the dirty, disorderly, completely dysfunctional kitchen and gave a disheartened sigh at the realization that she was doing it again.

But she simply couldn't stand to see anyone living like this.

And really, she didn't care if Trace liked her; she was only protecting herself. As it was now, she wouldn't be able to stop picturing him lying in his bed, his clothes smelling of fish and thrown onto the floor, gobs of cobwebs hanging from his ceilings, and dust an inch thick covering his furniture.

She'd noticed that the rifles in the china cabinet didn't have any dust on them. And even though his truck wasn't pretty to look at, its engine sounded like a purring kitten.

So what made a man particular about some things but not about others?

And really, did she even care?

Well . . . maybe she cared a little bit, because she'd no-ticed that Trace seemed to be working equally hard to make sure that *she* liked *him*.

She just didn't know why.

Unless it was because of his friendship with her brother.

When Kenzie had told Fiona he was moving her to her own apartment, he'd also told her that if she ever got scared or felt threatened, she just had to go downstairs, and Trace would protect her. At the time, she'd been horrified that he expected her to approach a complete stranger for help, but she certainly had been relieved to see her landlord arrive at the grocery store and rescue her from Johnnie Dempster.

And he had let her keep Misneach, and he hadn't once said anything about her leaving the skunks on his work-bench. Nor had he confronted her about rearranging his tools, or the goat, the horse, and the hens he hadn't given her permission to have.

No, he'd obviously taken his grievances to Kenzie instead.

"Did you find the crutches?" he asked, limping into the kitchen, the fine sheen of sweat on his forehead telling her he was in pain. He pulled a chair out and plopped down with a relieved sigh, absently rubbing his knee. "Were they in the shed?"

Fiona went over to the stove and pulled out the plate of eggs and toast she had warming in the oven. "I looked, but I . . . I'm not sure what crutches are," she admitted, setting the plate on the table in front of him.

When he only stared at her, saying nothing, Fiona spun away and headed to the fridge, from which she took out a jug of milk. She grabbed one of the glasses she'd washed earlier, filled it with milk, and set it beside the plate of eggs.

"Crutches," he said, lifting his hand to the height of his shoulder. "Two tall . . . canes that I can stick under my arms, to take the weight off my bad knee when I walk."

"Oh! Yes, I saw something like that!" she said, escaping down the hall and not stopping until she reached the cold shed. She took a steadying breath. How in heaven's name was she going to spend the next several days taking care of a man who didn't want her around?

But even worse, how was she going to stop herself from cleaning his house?

Chapter Eight

"Have you seen my boots?" Trace asked when Fiona came back into the kitchen carrying a pair of dusty old crutches.

She stopped by the door, and he saw her eyes widen as she glanced out the window, then back at him. "Your boots?" she repeated, looking out the window again.

Trace stuffed the last of the eggs into his mouth—eggs he couldn't taste—and drained the last of the milk just before he used the table to push himself to his feet. "My work boots, the ones I was wearing yesterday," he said, frowning when she glanced out the window again, her face turning as pale as new snow.

"I . . . um . . . I burned them with your clothes," she whispered.

"You what?" he yelped, limping to the door to look out the window. Only he stopped in mid-limp when she flinched and raised the crutches protectively.

He smiled, and slowly reached for the crutches as he blew out an exaggerated sigh. "I suppose that was the only thing to do," he said, tucking the crutches under his arms and hobbling the rest of the way to the door. "I probably wouldn't ever have gotten the smell of skunk out of that leather," he added, masking his consternation when he saw the pile of ash in his driveway.

All that remained of his brand-new work boots were the steel toes.

He looked down at the floor and saw that the space under the coat pegs was empty. "Have you seen my sneakers, then?" he asked. "Or my rubber mud boots?"

"Madeline took all of your shoes and boots with her last night," she whispered. But after several heartbeats of silence, she took a small step toward him. "And I think you should know that she raised the hood on your truck, pulled something out of the engine, and took whatever it was with her, too."

Trace couldn't decide if he wanted to roar that Maddy had left him stranded or hug Fiona for tattling on her. He snorted instead. "Peeps believes that just because she's married to Killkenny now, I can't threaten to cut her hair when she pisses me off. But you know what I think?"

Fiona pushed her own thick braid of hair back over her shoulder, presumably out of his reach. "No, what?"

"I think our little stink-bomb buddies would like to spend the winter sleeping under Maddy's cabin down at Dragon Cove."

Fiona's eyes widened. "You want to put the skunks— But that's William's cabin, as well. And Gabriella and Sarah also go there during the day."

"You're right," he said, shaking his head. "I wouldn't mind playing a dirty trick on Killkenny for costing me three lobster traps and all their rigging, but I've got no quarrel with Gabriella and Sarah." He grinned. "I know; we'll put the little stinkers in the back of Maddy's SUV."

"We? But I don't have a quarrel with Madeline. She didn't steal *my* shoes."

"No, but she did leave you here to take the fall for her." Trace hobbled toward the living room, the crutches a blessed relief to his knee. "I'm going to watch the morning news while I figure out how to catch those skunks, and then I'll have to figure out how to get them over to the nursing home where Maddy works, since my truck obviously isn't running." He stopped in the doorway and looked at her. "I appreciate your cooking me breakfast. I couldn't taste any of it, but my belly certainly thanks you."

"Trace," she said when he started off again, making him turn to her. "Would you mind if I just . . . picked up a bit? Just in the kitchen," she quickly added, her gaze darting to the counter and her body language all but begging to start cleaning.

It must be a woman thing, he decided, this compelling need to clean. He waved a crutch at the room. "Sure, have yourself a field day."

"Wait," she said when he turned away again. "I saw a washing machine in the mudroom. If you'd like, I can wash some of your clothes while you're figuring out how we can catch the skunks and get them to the nursing home."

He arched a brow. "So you're going to help me get revenge on my cousin?"

One corner of her mouth lifted, and her eyes actually

took on a bit of a sparkle. "Well, Madeline did leave it to me to tell you about your shoes."

He couldn't believe she thought he was serious about putting those skunks in Maddy's truck. Hell, he couldn't really do that to the little pissers, despite the fact that his face was still numb and he couldn't smell a damn thing.

The latter being a blessing, he supposed.

He shrugged. "Sure, you can do a load of laundry. And could you also hunt around for something for me to put on my feet? Old man Peterson was the size of a gnome, but maybe some of his sons' boots are still kicking around. What did you do with my wallet?"

She walked to the counter, picked up his wallet, and, holding it away from herself, carried it over to him.

"Thank you," he said, ignoring her gasp when he shoved it into his hind pocket. "You didn't happen to see my cell phone, did you, when you were burning my clothes? I think I dropped it in the barn, and I need to call Rick."

"I'll go look for it." She reached into her pocket and pulled out her own cell phone, and handed it to him. "You're welcome to use mine until I find yours."

He slid it into his shirt pocket. "Thanks," he said, turning away again.

"Trace? How come Mr. Peterson didn't take all his belongings when he left?"

He kept hobbling toward the living room. "Probably because there wasn't enough room in his casket."

"Please tell me you're not still mad at me," Gabriella said from the kitchen table, where she was working on matching up Trace's clean socks.

Fiona stopped using the metal spatula to scrape a glob of something off the floor and looked up at her friend in surprise. "What are you talking about? What makes you think I'm mad at you?"

"Because you haven't called me since the day I persuaded you to buy Misneach. Was Mr. Huntsman angry that you brought home a puppy without asking his permission?"

Fiona scrambled to her feet and rushed over to her friend. "Oh, Gabriella, I didn't call you because I was too ashamed for putting you in danger."

"What are you talking about? How was I in danger?"

"I let Johnnie Dempster take me across the street, which left you all alone with his brother." She touched Gabriella's shoulder. "And friends do not abandon friends in a dangerous situation."

"Neither one of you ladies was in danger," Trace said, hobbling into the kitchen. "Midnight Bay in broad daylight is about as safe as it gets."

Feeling her cheeks flush at the realization that he'd overheard them, Fiona wondered how the man could possibly move so silently on crutches.

"Did you happen to find any food that doesn't have mold growing on it when you cleaned the fridge?" he asked, going to the refrigerator. "Well, hel—heck," he muttered, leaning back on his crutches. "I didn't know this thing was white; I honestly thought it was almond." He pivoted, his gaze moving around the kitchen and his eyes widening with shock. "Holy . . . heck, the counters are blue. And it looks like I won't have to replace the floor after all; it just needed a good cleaning. You ladies have done quite a job. The place looks really nice."

"It's all Fiona's doing," Gabriella said. "I've been here only a short while."

"And I see she put you to work organizing my socks," he drawled. He looked at Fiona, his expression hopeful. "Is there anything for lunch? I won't really taste it, but the rumbling in my belly must mean I'm hungry. Anything will do—stale bread, leftover pizza, *skunk* stew." He visibly shuddered. "Only not goat's milk; just the thought of drinking anything from an animal that eats baling twine and tin cans makes me queasy."

When Fiona noticed that his smile wasn't quite reaching his eyes, she decided Trace was putting on a show, appearing overjoyed to have two women in his house.

She beamed him a brilliant smile—hers was sincere—and walked to the fridge. "I'll make you a sandwich," she said, taking out the package of meat and the container of cheese she'd brought down from her apartment. Then she grabbed the jug of milk and set everything on the counter. "I'll bring it to you in the living room. Go on," she said, shooing him away. "Maddy said you're supposed to keep your knee elevated, and that means it has to be higher than your heart. Would you like me to find some other place to set the television, so you can use the footstool?" she asked, stifling another smile when she saw him suspiciously eyeing the jug of milk. "Pillows would make the stool high enough that you could sit in your chair instead of having to lie on the couch."

"I already moved the TV," he said, a slight edge in his voice as he hobbled back to the living room. "And the chair's a recliner, which means it has a footstool built in."

Gabriella walked to the counter. "Fiona, this is too pale

to be cow's milk," the girl whispered, picking up the jug. "And Mr. Huntsman said he doesn't like goat's milk."

"He drank it this morning." Fiona took the jug and filled a tall glass with the milk. "And it certainly hasn't stopped him from wolfing down the bread I make with it or the cheese spread I put on his eggs this morning. And since I haven't gotten around to getting a cow yet, he's just going to have to settle for this." She slathered a thick slice of bread with some of the delicious goat cheese Eve made and sold in her store and then piled on several slices of meat. "Besides, my nanny does not eat twine or tin cans or any other nasty thing."

Gabriella looked around the half-cleaned and still cluttered kitchen. "How does anyone live like this?" she whispered, glancing toward the living room. She gave a soft snort. "My mama told me men don't even see dirt, and that's why they need wives. She said having someone to wash their clothes and cook their meals is the only reason they get married." She looked back at Fiona and grinned. "That, and for sex." But then she frowned. "Only when I asked her why any woman would get married if cooking and cleaning and having sex were all men wanted from us, you know what she said?"

Fiona stopped making the sandwich. "No, what?"

"She said that women are born with a powerful yearning to have children, and for that we need husbands. She claimed women are stronger than men in every way except physical strength, and so we need them to provide us with a safe home. She said that putting up with all their posturing is well worth the security we get in return."

Gabriella walked back to the table and sat down, and

started hunting for stray socks again. "I remember her showing me a drawing of lions in Africa once, and she explained that they were a perfect example of how marriages work. Apparently, the female lions do all the hunting and raise the cubs while the male lions just lie around all day, basking in the sun. But when the pride—that's what a family of lions is called—is threatened, it's the males that do the fighting."

The young girl suddenly stilled, and her eyes grew distant as she stared down at the sock in her hand. "Just like Papa and all the men did when our keep was attacked." Gabriella looked up, her face awash with pain. "I guess I still have that powerful yearning my mother spoke of," she continued shakily, "but now, whenever I think about having babes, I remember my father standing in front of Mama and me, trying to protect us. Papa's roar of outrage still wakes me up sometimes at night, and the smells and horrible sounds of battle fill the room as if it's happening all over again. I keep seeing those men slashing at him with their swords, and then I see him lying in his own blood, his eyes filled with a terrible pain as he helplessly watched them dragging Mama and me away."

Fiona rushed over and hugged Gabriella to her. "Shh, it's okay," she crooned. "He's no longer in pain, Gabriella. It's over."

"I know that. I've been with my parents all these centuries, and we were at peace." She leaned away just enough to look Fiona in the eyes, her own eyes welling with tears. "But I'm alive again, and I still yearn to have babes someday. Only . . . only now I'm afraid."

"What is it you're afraid of?" Fiona smoothed down her

hair. "Of being with a man? But it won't be anything like what happened to you, Gabriella. If you find a man you care for, and he cares for you, making a child is not a violent act."

"I am aware of that. Unlike in most arranged marriages, my parents actually loved each other, and they would often disappear up to their room for hours, and Mama was always smiling when she came down later. Being with a man doesn't scare me nearly as much as having children. The look on my mother's face when those men were killing my father and the expression in Papa's eyes as he lay there dying, watching us being brutalized, that's what really frightens me," she whispered. "Loving a husband and children is supposed to be the most wonderful thing in the world, but now I'm afraid to love that much. What if something just as bad were to happen to my husband or child?" she quietly sobbed, her eyes brimming with pain. "I . . . I don't think I could go through that again."

"William survived losing all of you, didn't he?" Fiona offered softly. "And he was able to find peace and happiness with Madeline."

"But it took him centuries to get past his anger at not being there to save us," Gabriella said. "And I don't have centuries. Mac said I was only returning to live out the remainder of my natural life. But what kind of life will it be, if I'm too scared to love anyone?" The girl swiped at her eyes. "I don't think I have what it takes to be a nun, Fiona, because I still have that powerful yearning to get married and have babes."

Fiona brushed her distraught friend's hair off her face, smiling encouragingly. "I believe your mama also said that women are stronger than men, didn't she? Of course, it took William centuries to get over what happened, because he didn't even know he had a heart to *risk*. It took a strong woman like Madeline to bring him to his senses." She shook her head. "Although I have no idea why she wanted to."

That got a tentative smile from Gabriella. "You only pretend to dislike William."

Fiona arched a brow. "Are you sure about that?"

"William told me that when you were a hawk and he was a dragon, the two of you spent a lot of time together."

"Only so I could rub his misery in his face."

The girl snorted. "So you really didn't mean to tell William how he could find Kenzie Gregor and lift the old hag's curse? And when he broke his dragon wing and couldn't hunt, are you saying you *accidentally* dropped all those doves and rabbits on the ground near him every day for several weeks?"

"I was bored, and your brother was entertaining."

Fiona started to leave, but Gabriella held on to her, the girl turning serious again. "Do *you* have yearnings?" she whispered.

"I would give anything to have another babe," Fiona told her honestly. "But I have no yearning to be with a man in order to get one."

"Did you . . . before?"

"Yes," she softly admitted. "I spent my entire childhood wanting a husband and children, as well as to live in a village, to go to festivals, and to have women friends I could talk to about all sorts of things."

"But you can have all that now. We've both been given second chances."

Fiona pulled away before Gabriella could stop her again and walked back to the counter. "Oh, I definitely intend to find a way to have another child, only I will be the one to give it a home and protect it. Madeline raised Sarah for six years without a husband, and I've seen where plenty of women today are single parents."

"Or you could make things a whole lot easier by simply falling in love and living happily ever after," Gabriella said, walking to the counter. She bumped Fiona's hip with her own. "Mr. Huntsman might be a bit . . . rugged-looking, but he does have a home, and according to William, he's a formidable warrior, so he would certainly be able to protect you and your babe."

Fiona started gagging on the bite of meat she'd popped into her mouth. She spit it out in her hand and gaped at Gabriella, utterly speechless.

The girl sauntered back to the table, picked up an armful of folded clothes, and headed toward the bedroom. "And the poor man does appear to be in desperate need of a wife," the girl said, her laughter trailing behind her.

Chapter Nine

She was actually going to do it. The little witch intended to serve him goat's milk again, even though he'd told her he hated the stuff. She must have figured out that he'd been messing with her about putting the skunks in Maddy's truck, which meant that Kenzie hadn't been jesting when he'd said Fiona rarely got mad but that she did like to get even.

He couldn't let her get away with it, of course, or the next thing he knew, she'd be *buying* his socks. What in hell was it with women, anyway, that they refused to leave a man alone in his misery? Single women were the worst kind of snipers, waiting to ambush the first available chump to step into their crosshairs. And apparently, the more miserable a guy was, the more attractive a target he made.

Yeah, well, he was quite capable of taking care of himself, thank you very much. Any soldier who managed to survive boot camp knew how to make a bed, put a crease in a pair of pants sharp enough to cut paper, and shine a toilet with only a toothbrush.

Except he wasn't in the military anymore, and if he wanted to sleep on dirty sheets, dress in marginally clean clothes, and wash dishes only once a week, it was his God-given right to do so, dammit. And what was so god-awful wrong with a little dust, anyway? Any idiot knew that sterile environments made a person's immune system so weak that even a common cold could prove deadly.

It wasn't like he was going to become one of those crazy old hermits who walked around town muttering obscenities at everyone; he was physically and mentally strong. Hell, old Rusty Peterson had looked after himself for nearly a quarter-century, and the feisty ninety-four-year-old probably would have lived to be a hundred if he hadn't walked in front of that delivery truck on his way to the mailbox last winter.

Seeing Fiona approaching with a tray of food, a large tumbler of milk prominently on display, Trace swept his arm across the table beside his recliner. "Here, let me make a place for you to set that," he said over the sound of books and magazines, a couple of empty beer bottles, and other small items clattering to the floor.

"Thank you," she said sweetly, though maybe a tad aggressively. She set the tray on the table, then dropped a spotless hand towel onto his lap, presumably for him to use as a napkin. "Is there anything else you'd like me to get you before Gabriella and I go try and catch our two little stink-bomb buddies?" she asked, her smile warm enough to melt butter.

Trace rubbed his hands over his face, tempted to ask her

to get him one of his guns so he could shoot himself. "No, I'm fine. Thank you," he said, keeping his face covered as he listened to her quietly walk away.

Dammit to hell, he didn't like being waited on by a woman trying to atone for her supposed sins against him. And he sure as hell didn't like how he noticed the intrinsic grace of her movements, or the way her eyes sparkled like sunshine, or how his heart seemed to speed up and all his blood rushed south whenever he caught sight of her.

Okay; either it had been way too long since he'd had sex, or he really was fatally attracted to walking disasters.

Because he sure as hell was attracted to her.

Trace spread his fingers to make sure she was gone and then lowered his hands to glare at the tray sitting beside him. It was obvious that Fiona Gregor was familiar with at least some of men's baser appetites, because she'd made him a sandwich big enough to choke a horse. He grabbed the glass of milk and downed half of it in one swallow, then sat staring toward the kitchen, listening to her explaining to Misneach that if he didn't want to smell like their landlord, he'd better stay away from the skunks.

Trace wondered when his ego had gotten so big that he thought he had to be everyone's hero. Although he certainly had a knack for pulling off impossible military missions, when had he decided that his personal mission in life was to save the world one person at a time?

And why in hell did that person always seem to be a woman?

He gave a derisive snort and downed the rest of the milk. As near as he could tell, he'd started acting the hero at age seven, when he'd punched Johnnie Dempster—his best buddy at the time—in the nose for saying something to Paula Pringle that had made the first-grader cry. Having remembered how good it had made him feel, that punch had been the first of many schoolyard and then gravel-pit fights, which had eventually led to one massive explosion at age seventeen.

That's when he'd gone into the military in order to escape going to jail.

After spending the night cruising the roads with his uncle Marvin in search of the man's missing daughters, Trace had walked into his kitchen at two in the morning to find his mother cowering in the corner beneath his drunken father, cradling her ribs and holding her other arm protectively over her head.

The towering brute had even had the balls to kick her in front of Trace, when she'd tried getting to her feet so she could pretend—again—that nothing was wrong. Trace had stood staring at his mother's battered face for several raging heartbeats, only to realize that he was finally strong enough, and sure as hell angry enough, to rescue a woman who had needed a hero for her entire miserable marriage.

All of his life, Trace had watched his father repeatedly make his mother pay for getting pregnant at sixteen and listened to the bastard blame her for trapping him in a dead-end job in order to support a wife and a child he'd never wanted.

That was the day the unwanted child had liberated his father by beating him to a bloody pulp and kicking his drunken ass out the door and all the way down to the docks. Trace had then thrown the bastard into the ocean with a final warning that if he ever came near either one of them again, he would kill him.

After taking her to a hospital to have her cheek sutured and her ribs wrapped, Trace had driven his mother to a divorce lawyer in Ellsworth. He'd changed the locks on the doors when they'd gotten home, tossed his father's belongings into the old man's truck and driven it to the cannery, and walked away without once looking back.

Their peace had lasted exactly one week, before the sheriff had shown up with a restraining order against him and his mother in one hand and a warrant for Trace's arrest for assault in the other.

Waving a list of juvenile altercations under his nose and pointing out that Grange Huntsman would probably walk with a limp the rest of his life, the DA—who just happened to be female—had given Trace a choice between fighting for his country or prosecution, pointing out that he couldn't very well support his mother from a jail cell.

Three months later, on his eighteenth birthday, Trace had left for boot camp.

His mother had moved in with her sister, Maddy's mom, and started building a new life for herself. She'd gone back to school to become a paralegal, eventually growing independent enough that she'd started depositing the checks Trace sent home into an account in his name. And six years ago, she'd married a man who thought she alone was responsible for making the sun shine.

Grange Huntsman had left Midnight Bay not long after Trace had, to pursue the life he claimed they'd stolen from him, only to die a couple of months later in some alley in Boston from alcohol poisoning. Uncle Marvin was the only one to attend the bastard's funeral, and then likely only so he could spit on his brother's grave.

Blowing out a sigh that did nothing to quell his frustration, Trace picked up the sandwich and peeled back one of the slices of bread. And yup, that sure as hell looked like Eve Gregor's award-winning goat cheese to him, slathered over all that meat.

What a terrible thing to do to perfectly good chicken.

He took a large bite and chewed without tasting, wondering how a person went about getting revenge on a walking disaster without overstepping the bounds of fair play. He didn't want to actually scare the woman, much less crush her blossoming spirit; he just wanted to pay her back for organizing his tools and turning his home into a zoo, and for the skunks, for his being laid up, and for the goat's milk.

But mostly, he wanted to make her stop making him want her.

Threatening to cut off all of Maddy's hair had certainly served him well when his then-thirteen-year-old cousin had caught him screwing Leslie Simpson in the woods behind his house. But he'd dared to make such a threat only because he'd known that not only would Maddy have survived the injustice but the little Peeping Tom would have risen to the challenge. And then the brat would have one-upped him, just like she had last night by stealing his shoes, disabling his truck, and dressing him in *Sesame Street* pajamas.

Hell, maybe he *would* put the skunks in her SUV.

As for Fiona . . . well, old lady Peterson had been a schoolteacher, and Trace was pretty sure he'd seen one of those handheld antique school bells kicking around here somewhere—the ones teachers would ring to call kids in from recess that could be heard nearly all over town.

It could definitely be heard as far as his upstairs apartment.

And seeing how it was his tenant's fault that he was out of commission for a week, he should probably find that bell and ring it whenever he needed something.

Hell, maybe he'd been going about this attraction thing all wrong. Instead of going out of his way to make sure Fiona wasn't afraid of him, he should be making sure she absolutely, positively, without question disliked him.

Because really, what man could possibly be attracted to a hostile woman?

It certainly had worked on Mac when the fool had tried to steal Maddy from William. But after spending a single afternoon with Peeps, the drùidh had decided he sure as hell didn't want to spend a lifetime with a woman who called him pond scum to his face.

Trace took another large bite of his sandwich and felt some of the cheese plop onto his chest. He frowned down at the clean shirt he'd spent twenty minutes hunting for this morning and tried wiping it off, only to end up *smearing* it into the material.

Well, Christ, he'd been out of the military only five months, and he'd already turned into a slob. Come to think of it, he hadn't gotten his hair cut since he'd come home, and he bothered to shave only once a week, and then only because he went to his mom's for Sunday supper—usually wearing clothes still damp from the dryer because he'd forget to throw in a load of wash the night before.

Giving up on the shirt, Trace stuffed the last of his sandwich into his mouth and used the towel to wipe the cheese off his face. He stopped in mid-wipe to crush the soft material into his nose and frowned. Apparently not all of his olfactory cells were dead, because he'd swear he could smell roses—just as he had the afternoon Fiona helped him bank the house.

Great. Wonderful. How friggin' *nice* of her to spread her scent over all his stuff.

The porch door slammed open, and Trace dropped the towel when he heard footsteps running through the kitchen. "There's a storm coming," Fiona said, barging into the living room. She kicked the footrest closed on the recliner and tried to haul him out of the chair. "Come on, I have to get you to the basement where you'll be safe."

He refused to budge. "What do you mean, a storm's coming? As in a plain old nor'easter or a storm involving one of Kenzie's displaced souls?"

She hauled Trace to his feet—but only because he let her. "All I know is that it's an unnatural storm," she said, thrusting the crutches under his arms. "Gabriella's bridling Buttercup so I can take her home." She started shoving at him. "I promise I'll be gone only twenty minutes, and then I'll gallop right back here to protect you," she said, giving him a harder shove when he didn't move.

Was she serious? She intended to come back and *protect* him?

Trace let the crutches fall to the floor, grabbed her arms to stop her shoving, and held her facing him. "Calm down," he said evenly, "and tell me how you know it's not just a plain old snowstorm."

"I just know!" she snapped, struggling to get free. But when he wouldn't let her go, she went perfectly still. "Don't make me hurt you," she softly threatened.

Was she *serious*?

Christ, he was tempted to let her try.

His shirt pocket suddenly started ringing and vibrating at the same time Fiona's jacket also started ringing. Gabriella came rushing into the kitchen just then and ran into the living room to the sound of *her* phone blaring out a jaunty tune.

Fiona jerked free and reached into her pocket even as she reached toward his chest with her other hand. "This one's yours," she said, handing Trace his cell phone as she plucked hers out of his shirt pocket.

All three of them said hello at the same time.

"We have company coming, Huntsman," William growled into Trace's ear. "And I need ye to keep Gabriella there with you until it's over."

"But I want to help!" Trace heard Fiona cry into her phone.

"What's coming in?" he asked William. "And what do you need me to do?"

"There's not enough time for ye to get the women to Kenzie's," William said. "So we're counting on you to keep them safe. Can ye manage okay with your knee?"

"I'll manage. Do you have any idea what we're facing?"

"Nay, except it appears to be an unusually powerful energy. Kenzie believes whoever is chasing the soul seeking sanctuary is hell-bent not to let him reach us, so this may run well into the night. Maddy is talking to Gabriella right now, but I need ye to . . . my sister might . . ." The Irishman blew out a heavy sigh. "Hell, there's a good chance the girl may get hysterical."

"I will keep her and Fiona safe," Trace promised, closing his phone when the line went dead. He turned to find Fiona still arguing with her brother. He plucked her phone out of her hand and snapped it shut.

"Hey!" she cried, trying to grab it back.

He shoved it into his pants pocket. "You want to help," he said quietly, nodding toward Gabriella, who was staring sightlessly ahead at nothing, "then help your friend get through this." Trace picked up his crutches and hobbled into the kitchen. "Where's Misneach?" he asked, stopping at the door to slip into a jacket.

"He's still outside," Fiona said, her arm around Gabriella as she followed him.

"Go to the mudroom," he instructed. "You'll find a door hidden inside the back wall of the closet. It opens onto a set of stairs that leads down to a corridor. Take a left at the bottom, and you'll eventually come to another door made of steel. Open it, and you'll find a flashlight on a shelf on the right. Take Gabriella into the room and then bolt the door closed behind you. And Fiona?"

"Yes?"

"You don't unlock that door for any reason, unless you hear me knock on it three times, and then not until I've done it twice. Got that? Two sets of three knocks, and that way, you'll know it's me."

"But—"

"There's enough food and water to last you several days," he cut in. "But you wait at least two days before you come out if I don't show up before then."

"But you must come with us. You can't even walk!"

Trace shot her a slow grin. "Don't worry. I promise I'll hurry back to protect you."

The look she gave him was fierce enough to turn away the coming storm. He opened the outside door and found Misneach standing on the porch, the pup's hackles raised as he growled menacingly toward the ocean.

Hell, there seemed to be an epidemic of heroes going around.

Trace scooped up the pup, limped over to Gabriella, and placed him in her arms as he nodded at Fiona. "Let her be responsible for Misneach so she'll have something to do. Go on, head down to the room." He had to physically turn her around and then nudge her. "And don't forget, two sets of three knocks, or two days."

He was surprised that she didn't argue, even though it was obvious that she wanted to. But then, eleventh-century women were taught from birth not to contradict men, weren't they? Which was nice in a crisis, he supposed, but likely boring the rest of the time.

Trace followed as Fiona led Gabriella into the mudroom, and he waited as she opened the closet door and pushed against the back wall. "There's a hidden latch on the left, and it opens inward, so watch that first step. It's going to be pitch-black, and you won't find a flashlight until you reach the room, so you'll have to feel your way."

Fiona scowled at him standing there watching her. "Did they kick you out of your war because it took you all day just to get to the battle?"

Apparently, being obedient didn't mean she had to be silent.

God help him, he wanted to kiss that scowl off her face.

He handed Fiona her cell phone. "It won't work in the room, because the walls are thick and lined with steel, so shut it off to save the battery for when you come out. Oh, and Fiona? Don't touch any of the equipment I've got down there." He shot her a grin. "Or you just might find a *real* mess to clean up when you come out."

"Please come down with us," she whispered, her eyes filled with concern.

"I will, just as soon as I see exactly what we're up against."

Gabriella gave a soft scream when something slammed onto the porch roof before it smacked against the railing on its way to the ground.

Trace figured that was one less shutter he'd have to take down.

He touched the young girl's chin to make her look at him. "You're safe, Gabriella. Nothing and no one can breach that room. But it's going to be your job to keep Misneach calm, okay?"

"M-madeline told me she and Sarah were on their way to Kenzie's house," Gabriella whispered, "because Eve has a powerful weapon to fight off the dark magic. Did Kenzie give you a magical pen, too?"

Trace smiled. "I have something just as magical and even more powerful."

"What is it?"

He brushed the girl's hair over her shoulder and gave Misneach a quick scratch on the ear. "It's called modern technology. So if you hear a loud boom and the room shakes around you, you'll know that I'm making my own kind of magic," he said, giving Fiona a nod and softly closing the closet door.

Just as soon as he heard them start down the stairs, Trace looked around the mudroom. He grabbed one of the folded sheets he spotted on the dryer. He limped into the kitchen, sat down, pulled his multitool out of its sheath, and cut the sheet into strips. He wrapped a couple of the strips tightly around his right knee and stood up to test his leg.

Leaving the crutches by the back door, Trace limped onto the porch and then shouldered his way through the blinding snow and gale-force wind blowing in off the bay. Seeing the fidgeting horse tied to a post when he entered the barn, he slipped off its bridle and pushed it into the storm, figuring that it stood a better chance of surviving outside. He shooed the goat out behind the horse, then went to the chicken coop and opened the door to let them choose to stay or leave.

He walked to the back of the barn and looked out the window, but the blizzard conditions wouldn't let him see more than a couple of feet. The old barn gave a loud snap when a strong gust shifted the structure, and over the howl of the wind, he heard a large branch snap off a tree out front and crash to the ground.

A cold chill that had nothing to do with the plummeting temperature raced up his spine when Trace heard the eerie and now familiar sound of screaming demons.

Christ, they sounded close.

A dark . . . something . . . momentarily cast the window in shadow, causing him to step back in surprise. Why in hell weren't they chasing the soul to An Téarmann—which was a good six miles away—instead of coming here? It was supposed to be known throughout all of time that Kenzie's home was a sanctuary the black magic couldn't breach.

Trace headed into the attached shed at a limping run, scattering several of the hens, and squeezed behind the rows of stacked firewood. Dammit, he wasn't prepared to face an army of demons; about the only thing he *was* prepared for was to ride out whatever sort of hell they brought with them.

He folded back a heavy canvas tarp, grabbed his backpack, and slid it over his shoulders, then strapped his sidearm around his waist and lashed it to his thigh. He had hoped he'd have more time to be fully operational, but even though he'd been working like a madman for two months, he'd only been able to build the safe room, secure the immediate perimeter, and install less than half the electronics he needed.

He'd had no idea the tunnels even existed when he'd bought the house, and he probably never would have known if he hadn't stumbled upon them when he'd been searching the cellar, looking for a structurally sound place to build a safe room.

Apparently old man Rusty Peterson's grandfather had done a bit of smuggling in the late eighteen hundreds and early twentieth century, and based on some of the old newspapers and crates Trace had found in them, Gavin Peterson, Rusty's father, had continued the family tradition and actually expanded the tunnels during prohibition.

If Rusty's sons had been aware of their family history, they hadn't told Trace what a gem he was getting when they'd sold him the house.

Then again, there was a good chance the secret had died with Rusty Peterson. He hoped it had, as the fewer people who knew about a hidey-hole, the better.

Except that now Fiona and Gabriella knew about the room, but considering their own laundry list of secrets, Trace figured he could trust them with his.

When he heard what sounded like a window blowing

out in the barn, he sidestepped his way farther down the back side of the woodpile. Since he wouldn't be much help to William and Kenzie with a bum knee, and because he didn't know shit about fighting *physical* demons without Kenzie's magic, the only sensible thing to do was retreat.

Sliding a few heavy boxes out of the way, relieved that Fiona hadn't gotten this far in her cleaning, he stuck his finger in a knothole in the floor and lifted a hidden doorway. Taking one last look around, Trace stepped down into the darkness—even as he wondered if the women had noticed how spotless he kept his hidey-hole.

Chapter Ten

$\mathcal{S}$eeing that Gabriella had actually managed to fall asleep and that Misneach was softly snoring cuddled in her arms, Fiona leaned forward on the narrow bed she was sitting on to see better the television screen Trace had been watching almost constantly since he'd arrived. He pushed a button on a small electronic box beneath it, making the screen change to four separate pictures—one of the front dooryard, one looking from the house toward the ocean, another of the tunnel outside the room, and the last one of his half-cleaned kitchen. She had asked him how they could see into the pitch-black corridor without a light, and Trace had told her that the camera taking the picture used something called night-vision technology. So only the kitchen and tunnel pictures were clear, the other two screens showing mostly blowing snow.

"What is this room?" she asked. "And why do you have it?"

He glanced over his shoulder at her and arched a brow. "Are you telling me you've never had a hidey-hole to escape to for when things got a little scary?"

Fiona felt her cheeks heat up. "You don't think it's cowardly to hide in a closet or . . . a cupboard?" she whispered.

He looked back at the screen and gave a soft snort. "Hell, near as I can tell, the only reason I'm alive today is because I spent the first sixteen years of my life hiding."

Fiona noticed that Trace's cheeks also darkened, his scowl as he went back to studying the screen indicating that he probably hadn't intended to disclose that bit of information—at least, not to her.

But then, didn't she know how men hated to admit any weakness?

Nevertheless, his comment piqued her curiosity. "I can't imagine anything sending you into hiding," she said lightly. She beamed him a warm smile when he glanced at her sharply. "I thought the only thing young boys were afraid of was girls."

He snorted again and looked back at the screen. "I *wish* I'd been afraid of girls. It would have saved me a lot of rides in the backseat of the sheriff's car."

"So, what did you hide from?" she asked, even as she wondered where she got the courage to pursue her questioning. But then, hadn't she already figured out that Trace was more bark than bite, at least when it came to women?

"From a drunken old man whose idea of discipline involved a thick leather belt," he growled, hitting another button that changed the screen yet again.

Fiona straightened in surprise. "The sheriff beat you?"

He looked at her. "Not the sheriff; my father."

She gestured dismissively with her hand. "Whose father *didn't* beat them?" she said, giving him a crooked smile when he scowled at her again. "Heck, I can remember Papa chasing Kenzie and Matt halfway down the mountain to give them a good whooping at least once a week. And if you think a belt hurts, you've obviously never been on the wrong end of a willow stick." She broadened her smile at his incredulous look. "Didn't you know that hiding would only worsen the punishment when you eventually showed up?"

He turned on his stool to face her. "Did your father beat you? With a *stick*?"

"Just once, when I was ten, just so I'd appreciate his restraint because I was female, he told me." She smiled again. "I remember that his being lenient on me certainly didn't sit well with Kenzie and Matt, when we were all guilty of the same crimes."

"What sort of crimes warranted a beating?"

Apparently, she had managed to pique *his* interest. "Neglecting our chores often got us a good smack, but sneaking down to the village, which was strictly forbidden, almost always meant a trip to the barn for Kenzie and Matt. So, what sort of crimes do modern boys commit that will send them running from their fathers?"

He turned back to the screen. "Sometimes all a kid has to do is be born." He gestured at the room, not looking at her. "Did you happen to notice how clean my hidey-hole is?"

Guessing he wanted to change the subject, Fiona stifled a frown. His father had beaten him simply because he'd been born? "I did notice," she said, making sure she sounded impressed. They'd been sitting down here for nearly two hours, and the storm outside—from what she could see on the television—didn't show any sign of letting up. "Only I'm afraid you made it too impenetrable, as even fresh air can't get in." She wrinkled her nose when he looked at her. "No offense, but you stink."

He stood up with a pained groan, keeping his weight on his left leg, and slowly stretched his arms over his head. "I guess that's the price you have to pay for leaving skunks on my workbench." He stopped stretching and frowned at her. "How in hell did you get that heavy compressor up on that barrel? And for gosh sakes, why?"

Fiona leaned back on the bed against the wall and gazed down at what she guessed was a weapon strapped to his bandaged thigh. "I was trying to make it easier for you to find all your tools." She raised her gaze to his and shrugged. "And I'm stronger than I look. Are you divorced?"

As she'd hoped, her question caught him completely off guard, and he actually took a step back. "What?"

"You have to be in your early thirties, and even though I realize men and women get married later in life today, I was wondering if you were married and are divorced. And if so, why?" She arched a brow, just to confound him further. "Did she divorce you, or did you leave her?"

"I've never been married," he growled. Only when he spun around to pace away and drew up short against a wall of the tiny room, he spun back toward her. "And for your information, I don't intend to *ever* get married."

"Do you prefer men, then?"

"No!" He blew out a harsh breath and glared at her. "What is it with you women, anyway, that you can't stand seeing a guy happily single?"

"God designed everything in pairs."

He snorted. "He sure as hell didn't think that one through, did He?" He pointed at her. "If you women would spend less time trying to figure out how to drive us men insane and more time—"

Knock-knock-knock; knock-knock-knock.

Trace stiffened, his gaze whipping to the door.

Fiona sat forward and also stared at the door. "That's the secret knock," she said, frowning when he didn't move. "Aren't you going to let them in?"

Knock-knock-knock; knock-knock-knock, this time a bit harder.

"Here's the thing," he said quietly, going to the television screen. "There is no secret knock, because I just made that up for you this morning." He hit several buttons, then straightened and looked at the door again. "And you, Gabriella, Misneach, and I are the only ones who know this room even exists."

Knock-knock-knock; knock-knock-knock, this time a whole lot harder.

Fiona jumped to her feet when something slammed into the ceiling over their heads, shaking the walls of the room. She looked at Gabriella, but the girl remained sleeping. Misneach, however, was curiously staring at the door, his ears perked forward and his tail gently thumping against Gabriella's coat.

Trace bent down to look at the screen more closely, then straightened with a muttered curse. "I can't tell what that is," he said, pointing at the television. "Can you? It looks like it's . . . half man and half some sort of . . . animal."

Fiona squinted at the screen. "Whatever it is, it appears

to be covered in snow." She looked at Trace. "But how can it know the secret knock?"

"It can't, because there *isn't* one." He slipped into the backpack he'd been wearing when he arrived, then pulled what she recognized as a handgun out of the sheath on his hip, did something to it, and slid it back into the sheath. "Okay, time for plan B," he said, turning to push a shelf full of supplies away from one of the walls.

He turned back to her and pointed at the door. "You don't open that door for anything, you understand? No matter what you hear or what you might see on the monitor, you stay put. The batteries in the surveillance system will last only about another six hours, so after that, you . . . well, just don't open the door."

He reached on top of the cabinet he'd moved, took down a leather pouch, and unzipped it. He pulled out another handgun and held it for her to see. "This is a weapon that shoots projectiles when you pull this trigger," he said, showing her a small lever inside a metal ring on the underside. He took her hand and wrapped her fingers around the handle, holding the shaft of the weapon away from them. "It's a revolver, and it's loaded, so you point it at whatever you want to kill and just pull the trigger. It's going to make a deafening noise and jerk violently, so don't be surprised. You have six bullets, and after that, you hold it by the barrel and use it like a club. Got that?"

"I've got it."

"Good. Only you be careful what you shoot at. If the bullet hits a wall or the steel door, it's going to ricochet and possibly come back and hit you or Gabriella. So, pull the trigger only when you're sure of your target."

He took the gun from her and set it on the table beside the television, then cupped her face between his large, callused hands. "I don't think I've ever seen anyone quite as calm as you are," he murmured, his sharp gray eyes looking directly into hers. "Why aren't you hysterical?"

"Because I already know that dying is nothing to fear," she whispered. "And getting hysterical serves no purpose."

"You must be aware that some fates are worse than death," he returned softly.

"Aye. But I also know that I can survive most of them."

He started to lower his head but then hesitated. "Aw, hell," he muttered as he tilted her face up and covered her mouth with his own.

The gentleness of his kiss surprised her. He didn't take possession of her mouth but *gave* her his. And when he slid one arm around her shoulders and pulled her up against him, Fiona was even more surprised to feel herself melting into him.

Knock-knock-knock; knock-knock-knock, this time hard enough to rattle the heavy door.

"Don't read anything into what just happened," Trace growled as he straightened, although he continued holding her. "That kiss was only in case I don't make it back."

"You needn't worry; I know how men's minds work."

"What in hell is that supposed to mean?"

She smiled. "Are you sure they didn't kick you out of your war for being tardy, or are you waiting for this particular battle to come in here to us?"

He still didn't let her go; if anything, his arm around her tightened, and his hand cupping her head twitched slightly. "I'm changing the signal to one knock, then three, then two.

If you hear anything else, you wait two days before you come out."

Knock; knock-knock-knock; knock-knock.

Trace jumped back and spun toward the door, his expression incredulous. "Goddamn it, what in hell is going on!"

Gabriella sat up with a gasp at his shout, and Misneach jumped down and ran to the door, his tail wagging excitedly, and started whining.

"For the love of Zeus, Huntsman, let me in before these demon bastards can finish me off!" came a muted shout from the other side of the door.

"That's Mr. Oceanus!" Gabriella cried, rushing to the door.

Trace pulled her back when the girl reached for one of the latches. "We can't know that for sure," he said, nudging her toward Fiona. "It could be a trick."

"Or it really could be Mac," Fiona said, wrapping an arm around Gabriella. "Kenzie told me the energy coming in with the storm is very powerful, and Mac is one of the most powerful drùidhs ever to exist." She turned Gabriella and pointed at the screen. "Do you recognize either the man or the animal?" she asked.

The girl bent down to see better, but whatever was out there was leaning with its back against the door, and Fiona could only see what appeared to be a pitchfork in its . . . was that a flipper?

"What was Mac the last time you saw him?" she asked Gabriella.

"He came to me as a little boy," the girl said. "So I wouldn't be afraid, he told me. The picture isn't very good, and it's black-and-white. But that appears to be some sort of sea creature." She looked at Fiona. "You know, like one of those . . . walruses, I think they're called, that live far to the north on the ice." She pointed at the screen. "See, doesn't that look like the end of a tusk? Oh! I do recognize the trident! That's the drùidh's staff Mr. Oceanus used to bring me here," she said excitedly, turning to Trace.

But he had disappeared.

Fiona walked over to look behind the cabinet but found only solid wall.

"Where'd he go?" Gabriella whispered, also looking behind the cabinet.

Fiona took hold of the girl's trembling hand and moved back to watch the screen. "He mentioned something about a plan B," she said. "I guess that means he's gone out to see for himself what's knocking at our door."

"But how did he leave? Is *he* a magic maker, too?"

Fiona shot her friend a reassuring smile. "I believe Trace prefers technology over magic. And he strikes me as the sort of man who wouldn't build a hidey-hole with only one way in and no second way out. There must be a secret door in the wall."

"H-how can you be so calm?" Gabriella asked, looking back at the screen.

"We have a drùidh and a powerful warrior on our side, Gabriella. They won't let any harm come to us."

"But Mr. Oceanus is wounded," the girl quietly cried, pointing at the screen. "See, he's slumped against the door. And Mr. Huntsman is also wounded."

"Not badly enough to slow him down, apparently. And Mac—" Fiona snapped her mouth shut when she saw what looked like the shadowed figure of a man appear on the screen at the far end of the darkened corridor.

"That's Mr. Huntsman," Gabriella said with a gasp. "But what's he holding?"

"It's a handgun." Fiona picked up the revolver Trace had left her and tucked it into the waist of her pants, being careful not to touch the trigger. "It shoots bullets out of the barrel, and that way, you don't have to be close to something to kill it."

They both turned silent then as they watched Trace slowly make his way along the edge of the corridor. Whatever was leaning against their door tried to get up, and Fiona saw it lift what now looked like a human hand, the three-pronged trident pointed at the ceiling over Trace's shoulder.

A thunderous boom suddenly shook the air as a blinding flash filled the television screen. Gabriella screamed and grabbed Fiona, and Misneach gave a frightened yelp and scurried under the bed.

The deafening boom continued rumbling overhead like rolling thunder, making the walls and floor shudder violently and the air throb with energy. The shelf of supplies toppled over, and Gabriella screamed again as they both scrambled out of the way.

Seeing that the television screen had gone blank, Fiona ran over and pressed her ear to the door. She heard rocks and beams falling and what sounded like a faint shout that ended abruptly when something heavy slammed into the metal she was leaning against.

And then everything went eerily silent except for Gabriella's weeping.

"Be quiet," Fiona whispered, waving at Gabriella as she

pressed her ear back to the door. She heard a weak groan and felt the metal shudder as she heard more rocks shifting and another groan.

She straightened and slid open the first of the four latches.

"What are you doing?" Gabriella cried, rushing over and pulling her hand away. "Mr. Huntsman said we aren't to open the door for any reason."

Fiona shrugged free and slid open the second latch. "Do you see Trace here to tell me I can't?"

"But what if the demons got him and Mr. Oceanus, and they're on the other side of the door? Let's find the secret way out that Mr. Huntsman used."

"He doesn't like to be called Mr. Huntsman," Fiona informed her, now knowing why. She slid open the third bolt. "And exactly where do you intend to go? There's a storm of demons still raging outside." She placed her hand on the last bolt. "And if we don't get Trace and Mac in here where they'll be safe, we may all die."

She tried sliding the fourth bolt, but when it didn't budge because something on the other side was holding pressure against it, Fiona leaned her shoulder into the door and tried pushing on it as she tugged on the bolt.

Gabriella stopped her again. "Wh-when did you become so brave?"

Fiona stared directly into her friend's huge eyes. "Sometime last week after our trip to town, when a clueless little puppy reminded me that courage doesn't require having control over what happens to us but having control over how we *react* to what happens to us. No matter what happened to him, Misneach simply went about the business of living."

Gabriella's eyes widened. "Are you saying your pet really did give you courage?"

"Even better, he gave me hope. Mac gave me back my life, Kenzie and Matt gave me my freedom, Trace unwittingly gave me a purpose—however misguided or temporary it may have been," she said with a laugh. "And I gave myself permission to get on with the business of my own life."

Gabriella suddenly smiled. "So, does that mean you're not afraid to fall in love now, and get married and have babes and live happily ever after?"

Fiona pushed against the door again. "I'll settle for two out of four. Having another child is all I need to be happy. So, come on, help me get Trace and Mac in here so we can *all* live happily ever after."

With Gabriella's weight added to hers, Fiona was able to slowly slide the last bolt free. The door suddenly shot open, sending them both scurrying out of the way when rocks and dirt cascaded into the room—along with the bloody and battered body of an unconscious man Fiona didn't recognize.

"You see if he's still alive," she told Gabriella as she grabbed the flashlight and stepped past him. She crawled up over the debris littering the corridor, having to shove broken beams and a couple of heavy rocks out of her way, stopping every so often to listen as she aimed the light around the tunnel.

"Trace!" she shouted. "Make a noise so I can find you."

"What part of 'don't open that door for anything' didn't you understand?" he growled from about ten paces away.

"I think it was the 'for anything' part," she said, crawling toward him. "Or maybe the 'don't' part." She stopped when she spotted his bloody face but quickly aimed her flashlight at where his body should be; he gave a curse and blinked furiously against the light in his eyes. Only instead of his body, all she saw were rocks.

She shone the beam farther down the tunnel and saw that debris had filled it nearly up to the ceiling. A screaming howl pierced the air just then, and several large rocks tumbled down, one of them knocking the flashlight out of her hand.

"Get the hell out of here!" Trace shouted. "Go back to the room and lock the door! Now!"

She crawled over to him, the beam of the fallen light allowing her to see his scowl. "Yeah, about closing that door," she said, carefully removing the rocks from around his shoulders. "That might take a while, as a portion of the cave fell into the room—along with a man I really hope is Mac."

"I thought eleventh-century women actually did what they were told," he muttered, wiggling his shoulders in an attempt to help her free him.

She stopped digging. "Whatever gave you that idea?"

He blinked at her—or maybe he was only trying to see past the blood seeping into his eyes. "Kenzie believes you're too afraid of men to even talk to them."

She started moving rocks again. "I'm not afraid of men; I merely don't like them. Can you feel your legs?"

"I hope you're not all that attached to your hair," he said tightly, "because a good two feet of it is coming off just as soon as I get out of here."

She flipped her braid over her shoulder and started shoving rocks away from his chest and stomach. "I would love to have short hair like some of the women I've seen on television." She shot him a quick smile. "You would cut it for me? Truly?"

The glare he gave her was hot enough to *burn* off all her hair.

His hands now free, he started tossing rocks off his legs.

"Fiona! Did you find Mr.—Trace?" Gabriella called from the doorway.

"I found him, and he's definitely alive. How's Mac?"

"He's alive, too, but I can't get him to wake up. And one of his arms is still a flipper. What should I do?"

"Drag him into the room and move the rocks away from the door so we can close it," Trace called to her. He glared at Fiona. "The bastard actually shot at me."

She shook her head. "I don't think he was shooting *at* you, more like over your shoulder." She picked up the flashlight and shone it toward the entrance of the corridor. "Can you see that?" she said. "Doesn't that look like some sort of webbed foot sticking up past those beams?"

The air shook with another thunderous boom, and Fiona leaned over Trace, wrapping her arms around his head and shoulders. A blood-curdling scream came from behind the wall of debris, and rocks began moving at the far end of the tunnel.

Fiona suddenly went flying toward the room. "Crawl!" Trace shouted at her.

"Not without you."

"I'm right behind you."

When she glanced over her shoulder because she didn't believe him, he placed his hand on her backside and gave her a shove. "Keep moving!"

She ended up falling into the room but quickly sprang to

her feet, grabbed Trace when he faltered, and dragged him all the way inside. "Help me close the door, Gabriella!" she cried, stepping over Trace to reach the door.

But when she saw the screaming dark shadow rushing toward them, Fiona pulled the revolver from her waist, aimed down the corridor, and pulled the trigger.

The gun exploded in her hands, jerking upward so violently that she nearly dropped it. She brought it back down and immediately pulled the trigger again, but knowing what to expect this time, she held it steady and fired four more times.

Her ears ringing with the sharp peal of gunfire echoing through the room, mixing with the god-awful screams of several more charging demons, Fiona barely heard Trace shouting at her to close the goddamned door.

But just as she tucked the gun back in at her waist, another deafening round of gunfire filled the room, this time several shots in rapid succession.

She and Gabriella shoved as hard as they could, both of them using their backs to push the door through the dirt, which allowed Fiona to see Trace lying on the floor, his own gun held straight out in both hands as he fired into the tunnel.

Only he wasn't pulling the trigger each time but merely holding it back, and small pieces of metal were flying out the side of the gun.

And he had a heck of a lot more than six bullets.

He stopped firing. "You've almost got it!" he shouted, dragging himself to the door and reaching for the bottom latch. "Harder! Push!"

Her ears ringing so loudly that his shouts sounded like

whispers, Fiona felt rather than heard the bolt slide into place. She immediately turned and seated the top bolt and finally the other two.

She spun around, grabbed Gabriella, and hugged her. "We did it!" she cried, although she barely heard her own words. She leaned away to grin at her friend. "You were so strong and courageous; we couldn't have done it without you!" She cupped the girl's trembling face between her hands. "Don't you ever again tell me you're afraid of *any-thing*." She hugged Gabriella to her. "You will have your babes, and you will be a fearsome mother. You just wait until I see William. I am *so* going to rub your courage in his ugly face the next time he tries to tell me women are the weaker sex."

"Do you suppose we can hold off patting ourselves on the back until *after* we take stock of our injuries and come up with plan C?" Trace muttered, rolling to sit up and lean against the door. His eyes suddenly widened. "Holy shit, get that gun out of your pants! Revolvers don't have safeties, and if you fall, you could blow off your leg!"

"You might have mentioned that earlier," she muttered, pulling it out and handing it to him when he held out his hand. "Not that it matters now, as I believe it's empty."

He grinned. "Remind me never to piss you off when you're holding a gun."

"Can I buy one of those at the Shop 'n Save?" she asked, nodding at his hand.

His grin disappeared. "No!" He blew out a breath, looked over at the man lying beside him, and used the barrel of the gun to give him a poke.

When he didn't move, Trace poked him harder.

The man grunted and opened his eyes, blinking several times as he grabbed his head and finally focused his glare on Trace. "Sweet mother of Neptune, Huntsman, you poke me again and I swear you'll smell like a skunk's ass the rest of your life."

"Why are you bleeding all over my floor instead of Kenzie Gregor's?" Trace ground out. "And shooting at me instead of at him?"

"I was shooting at the demon behind you," Mac returned. He lifted his head enough to glance toward Fiona, then back at Trace. "And I wasn't sure how welcomed I'd be at An Téarmann." He rolled onto his side. "What's she doing here?" he asked softly, although Fiona still heard him. "I would have thought she'd be at de Gairn's."

"Matt pawned her off on Kenzie," Trace said, not at all bothering to whisper. "And Kenzie pawned her off on me."

Mac lowered his head to the floor with a groan.

Trace chuckled. "Don't you just love it when a good deed comes back and bites you on the ass? Hey, your sister's not with you, is she?"

Mac snorted. "I wouldn't be surprised if Carolina was *leading* the demons."

"Can you make them go away, Mr. Oceanus?" Gabriella asked.

She bent down to pick up the trident, but Mac snapped open his eyes and moved it out of her reach. "Gabriella," he said cordially—or at least as cordially as he could, Fiona guessed, considering that he appeared to be half dead. "You're looking well." He smiled weakly. "Other than today's little . . . event, how's life been treating you?"

Gabriella straightened and actually curtsied to him. "It's

been treating me very well, Mr. Oceanus. I love everything about this century."

"Please, I've asked you to call me Mac." He moved his gaze to Fiona. "And Ms. Gregor, life seems to have . . . I believe you've changed a bit since I last saw you."

"Not really. I'm still being pawned off from one man to another, apparently."

"O-kay," Trace injected. "Now that all the niceties are over, can we get back to figuring out plan C?"

"I vote for we resume your original plan," Mac said, closing his eyes on a sigh, "and not open the door for anything and wait two days before we emerge. Surely Kenzie and William will have turned the storm away by then."

"How in hell did you know what the knock was?" Trace asked.

"Mr.—Mac is a powerful drùidh," Gabriella said before he could answer. "And drùidhs know everything."

"Apparently, not everything," Mac muttered. "I don't have a clue who is after me, much less why."

"Some woman's enraged father, most likely," Fiona said. Ignoring Mac's glare, she crouched in front of Trace and started to take off the sheath strapped to his leg so she could check his knee.

He stopped her by grabbing hold of her hand. "No, I need to leave it on. If you want to help, see if you can find the medicine kit that was on the shelf so I can stop this bleeding," he said, wiping his face. But when she started to stand up, he held her in place. "You did good today."

"Does that mean you won't cut off my hair for opening the door?"

He grinned, and for the first time since she'd met him, it actually reached his eyes. "I haven't decided yet."

Mac snorted. "Are you still using that silly threat, Huntsman?"

Trace arched a brow at him. "You got a better one, Oceanus? No, wait, I forgot; you can't even get *close* enough to a woman to threaten her. How'd your little trip to the mountains pan out, anyway? Did you find any single MacKeage women in Pine Creek willing to date you?"

When Fiona saw Mac's hand twitch—the one holding his trident—she pulled free and stood up. "Gabriella, have you seen Misneach?"

"Oh!" Gabriella gasped, looking around. "He was right here before . . . before . . ." She looked toward the door, her eyes wide with worry as she looked back at Fiona. "Could he have followed you into the tunnel?" she whispered. "Oh, Fiona, I lost him!"

"Take it easy," Trace said, rolling onto his stomach toward the bed and pushing some of the fallen supplies out of his way. "The pup's smarter than that. Misneach, come here, boy. Come on, come to Papa."

Fiona heard Mac chuckle. "Siring dogs now, are you, Huntsman?"

Trace pulled Misneach from under the bed and sat up to hold the trembling pup in his arms, and glared at Mac. "At least he doesn't call me pond scum to my face."

Fiona rolled her eyes and started searching the debris for the medicine kit, wondering if the upcoming week wouldn't prove to be one of those fates worse than death, if she was expected to nurse *two* men back to health now.

Chapter Eleven

Not caring that he was getting dirt and blood all over his recliner, Trace clenched his jaw and shifted the ice pack on his knee—the one Fiona had negligently tossed at him on her way by—as he tried to stay focused on what Kenzie and William were saying. He might be keeping his mouth shut, but that didn't mean he had to like that Fiona was kneeling beside the couch to suture what appeared to be nothing more than a scratch on Mac's shoulder. It was bad enough that William and Kenzie had carried the drùidh upstairs—while Trace had *dragged* himself upstairs—but the two warriors hadn't even bothered to thank him for keeping their sisters safe from the demons.

Which Mac the Menace had brought here, he might point out.

And he sure as hell didn't like how Gabriella kept fawning over the jerk, dabbing Mac's brow and constantly asking if he was in pain. Christ, he was tempted to cram a pillow down over the bastard's face the next time he moaned.

"We still don't know why they're after Mac," Kenzie said, "or who they are. But what really worries me is they don't seem to be afraid of him. Nor do they seem even to care if they incur his father's wrath. Titus Oceanus isn't exactly known for his leniency when it comes to dealing with anyone who threatens his family."

Trace took another sip of Scotch—which he'd had to find and pour himself—and glared toward the couch. Dammit, Fiona should be tending *his* injuries.

"There seemed to be more than one entity controlling the demons," William said, "as there were at least three separate waves of attacks."

Didn't either of them see that Gabriella had contracted a horrible case of hero worship? And Mac sure as hell didn't seem inclined to quell it; in fact, he appeared to be encouraging her, holding the girl's hand and sucking in a shuddering breath each time the needle pierced his ugly flesh.

Why in hell wasn't Fiona putting a stop to Gabriella's foolishness? *She* certainly was bright enough to know that Maximilian Oceanus was a pompous ass.

The bastard had better not suddenly decide he could fall in love with the new and improved Fiona Gregor. She was *his* tenant, dammit; he was the one bringing her out of her shell, and he wasn't about to let some love-starved pond scum of a drùidh reap the benefits of his hard work.

Trace absently rubbed Misneach, sleeping on his lap, pleased that at least the pup knew where to place his loyalty. Probably irrevocably gun-shy now, if not also deaf, the little Chesapeake had been the only one to notice that Trace was injured and had even tried licking the blood off his face back in the safe room. And when he'd set Misneach down when they'd finally heard Kenzie and William shouting for them overhead, the loyal little pup had lifted his leg and whizzed on Mac's one remaining . . . flipper.

Only to everyone's surprise, the flipper had magically turned back into a human hand just as soon as the warm urine had hit it.

Hell, if Trace had known that was all it would take, *he* would have volunteered.

Seeing that Fiona was finally done, Trace started unbuttoning his shirt so she could rub horse liniment on the bruises on his ribs. A soak in a hot bath was out of the question until the electricity came back on, and he'd have to ask Gabriella to hunt around for some kerosene lamps, so they could conserve the battery in the lantern.

Only Trace suddenly stilled in the middle of trying to pull his shirttail out of his jeans without disturbing Misneach. He blinked at Kenzie and William. "Come again? Did you just say you think the *tooth fairy* was leading the demons?"

Kenzie didn't even try to hide his amusement. "I would offer to bring Mac to An Téarmann to recuperate, but it appears he's already made himself comfortable on your couch." He leaned forward on the footstool he was sitting on next to the woodstove. "I'd hide that trident if I were you, though, the moment he falls asleep. When he gets his strength back, there's no telling what sort of havoc he might wreak."

William snorted. "Aye, there's a good chance he's still a wee bit miffed at ye for rejecting his sister's marriage proposal."

"Is he miffed at you for rejecting Carolina *and* for marrying Maddy?"

"Nay," William said with a chuckle. "Mac likes me."

"Lucky you," Trace muttered.

Kenzie stood up with a tired groan when he saw Fiona heading to the kitchen. "If you're done here, sister, go upstairs and pack a few of your things, and I will take you to An Téarmann."

She spun toward him in surprise. "Excuse me?"

"We'll return in a few days to get the rest of your belongings."

"But I'm not moving back to An Téarmann. This is my home now. I mean, that's my home now," she said, pointing at the ceiling.

Kenzie gave her a gentle smile. "I've decided this may not be the best arrangement for you after all, so you can live with us until I'm able to find a better one."

"Yeah, well, *I've* decided that you aren't the boss of me anymore. And neither is Matt. I will live where I want, and say and do and *think* what I want, from now on, just like any other twenty-first-century woman."

Trace very nearly jumped out of his chair, he was so pleased.

Not because he wanted her to stay or anything but because she was very politely telling her brother to go to hell.

Kenzie pointed at the ceiling rather . . . pointedly. "You will do as you're told and go get your things, and we will discuss this at home."

Fiona folded her arms under her breasts and arched a brow. "Exactly which part of 'you're not the boss of me anymore' didn't you understand?" she asked ever so softly, obviously trying to rein in her anger. "Because I have to tell you, I'm damn tired of sitting through your one-sided *discussions*. You and Matt can discuss my arrangement until hell freezes over for all I care, but it's not going to change the fact that neither one of you *men* knows shit about what's good for me."

Wow. When the woman decided to break out of her shell, she came out swinging! Christ, he wanted to kiss her again.

"Your language is unbecoming!" Kenzie snapped, his anger growing in direct proportion to his realization that he'd lost control of her.

She actually laughed. "Are you sure it's my language you find unbecoming, or is it my unwillingness to jump at your command like a clueless eleventh-century lass?"

Hell, she was even starting to *sound* like a Mainer.

Kenzie was so taken aback that he seemed to have been rendered speechless.

"Gabriella, get your coat," William growled as he stood up and used his bloodied sword to point toward the kitchen.

"Nay." The girl thrust her chin out defiantly. "I believe I'll spend the week here with Fiona and help her take care of Mac and Trace." She walked over and looped her arm through Fiona's. "Friends do not abandon friends."

Instead of also being rendered speechless, William turned a thunderous glare on Trace, pointing his sword at *him*. "This is your fault, Huntsman. We leave these two perfectly obedient women in your care for one day, and suddenly, the only word they seem able to utter is *no*."

Trace grinned at the confounded warrior. "Kind of dents

the ego, doesn't it, when a woman tells you no? I would think you'd be used to it by now, seeing as how you've been married to Maddy for over a month and a half." He turned his grin on Kenzie. "And how's your campaign coming along to get Eve to have her baby in a hospital? Has she agreed with you yet that just because the MacKeage women all had their children at home, that doesn't mean she should?"

"Are ye saying you *won't* burn down your house to make Fiona leave?" the vengeful highlander ground out.

Trace looked directly at Fiona when he heard her gasp. "I've changed my mind. I've decided I like having a tenant I can count on when things get scary." He continued to answer Kenzie even as he continued staring into Fiona's no longer vulnerable but definitely wounded eyes. "Especially when that tenant handles a gun better than you do, Gregor, and knows that retreating is not an act of cowardice but one of intelligence."

Giving her a wink, he looked at Kenzie and William. "I realize you might have a hard time wrapping your ancient minds around the concept, but today wasn't the first time a female has pulled my neck out of the wringer. I've fought side-by-side with women in Iraq and Afghanistan, and for the record, I don't have a problem facing screaming demons with either one of your sisters. In fact, Killkenny," he said, giving the wide-eyed Gabriella a wink as he slid his gaze to William, "neither do I have a problem with Gabriella also becoming my tenant, should she decide to move in with Fiona."

William's hand on his sword flexed. "Ye overstep your bounds, Huntsman!"

"Not by twenty-first-century rules, I don't. When we

were waiting for you to finally come to our rescue, Gabriella just happened to mention that her birthday is next week. And in this century, eighteen is the age of independence."

"Are ye deliberately trying to anger us?" Kenzie asked tightly. He lifted a brow. "Or maybe you've decided ye like having a clean house and home-cooked meals."

"Personally," Mac said from the couch, "I think he's looking to get himself some milk without having to buy the cow." He snorted. "Or should I say *goat*?"

"Enough!" Fiona snapped. "You will all shut the fuck up, or I swear, I'll find my gun and shoot every damned last one of you."

"Sister!" Kenzie shouted, taking a step back. "You will mind your tongue! Where did you even learn such a word?"

Equally shocked but utterly enthralled, Trace could only gape at Fiona as she shot her brother a scathing glare. "You'd be surprised at what a camp whore learns," she hissed, "other than just how to pleasure a man."

Kenzie took another step back, his knees obviously gone weak as he staggered into the wall. "What are ye saying?" he whispered.

Her brother's shock apparently doing nothing to quell her anger, Trace saw Fiona's hands ball into fists. "I'm not the innocent little girl you remember, Kenzie. I grew up the day you walked away from Mama and Papa and me, and I grew wise the day that bastard caught me alone in the woods and turned me into a whore."

When Kenzie slid down the wall to squat on his heels, his face as pale as snow, Fiona took a hesitant step toward him. "I honestly tried to be the baby sister you and Matt remembered," she said huskily. "And for a while, I actually became her—to the point that I even began fearing men again. But even worse than losing her virginity, when a woman's *innocence* is stolen from her, she can't ever go back to pretending she is something more or anything less than she is."

She took another step forward and held her hand out, and Trace was proud to see that it wasn't trembling even a little. "Where you and Matt left to find your destinies, mine was thrust upon me." She snorted. "Several destinies, actually, and always at the hand of some man. Well, brother, I'm done. My future is in *my* hands now, and if I screw up, then I have no one to blame but myself." Her mouth curved upward. "And if all of my dreams do come true, they will be all the sweeter for being mine alone. I will have children again, and I'll raise them to know that the only thing they need to fear is their mama's wrath, if I ever catch them being afraid of anything."

That said, she started toward the kitchen but then stopped and faced Kenzie again, her shoulders thrown back and her head held high. "Please tell Eve and Winter for me that I thank them for speaking their minds. I realize now that as long as I continued living with you or Matt, I would have continued trying to be your baby sister."

Fiona walked over to Trace and lifted Misneach off his lap. "There are enough like-minded males in this room already," she muttered, heading to the kitchen again. "I don't need any of you corrupting my pet. Come on, Gabriella," she said as she walked past her gaping friend. "We'll go upstairs and build a fire and make ourselves a cup of tea. But first, grab that unopened bottle of Scotch in the cupboard next to the sink and bring it with you."

The porch door closed a moment later, and the ensuing silence lasted several more moments until it was broken by the sound of the ceiling creaking over their heads.

"Holy Christ," Kenzie whispered. He raised pain-filled eyes first to William and then to Trace. "I thought she'd only been raped. One time. I thought some man had caught her alone in the woods and that . . . that she had . . ." He dropped his gaze to the floor and shook his head. "She called herself a whore."

Mac sat up on the couch, cradling his arm against his side. "You didn't know Fiona had gone missing for nearly seven months?" he asked softly.

"Nay," Kenzie said, not looking up. He ran his hands through his hair and then held his head as he stared at the floor. "What kind of hell was she forced to endure for seven months?" He looked up, his haunted gaze focused inward. "I thought I killed the bastard who'd raped her, but . . . hell, it appears he was only the first of many."

Trace quietly closed the footrest on his recliner and stood up, then limped over and pulled the highlander to his feet. "I'm sorry," he said softly. "But you need to realize that what didn't kill your sister only made her stronger."

"And now she's fighting to remain strong," Mac said as he limped over to them. "And if you truly love her, you'll not only let Fiona go forward on her own terms, you will help her. But only when she *asks*, Kenzie, and then only what she asks for, instead of what you believe she needs."

Although he hated like hell to admit it, Trace found himself agreeing with the drùidh. "Your sister is a lot stronger and smarter and more capable than most *men* I know," he added. He grinned, trying to lighten the mood. "And a hell of a lot prettier."

"Aye," William said, even as he glared at Trace. "Fiona proved her mettle today."

"She called herself a whore," Kenzie whispered, apparently unable to get past that. He looked at Trace. "You're attracted to her, Huntsman, and she seems to trust you. Ye must help us show Fiona that she isn't a whore."

"You're not getting it, Gregor," Mac growled. "It's you who needs help, because you obviously can't let go of your guilt for leaving home to go find your destiny."

"I didn't leave to find anything but freedom," Kenzie hotly countered. "And I abandoned my family even though I suspected our father was starting to lose his mind." He waved angrily toward the ceiling. "Fiona was twelve! You heard her; she grew up the day I walked away and left them without protection. I was the worst kind of coward, running from my responsibilities." He spun away from them, his hands clenched at his sides. "I sold my soul for the dream of becoming a warrior, wanting to be some village's hero."

Trace snorted. "Welcome to the club."

"You were fifteen," Mac said. "What did you know, other than your dreams?"

Kenzie threw his head back and stared at the ceiling. "I must go apologize to her," he said. "And ask her forgiveness and beg her to let me make this right."

When he started toward the kitchen, all three of them moved to block his path. "The only thing you're going to do," Trace said, nudging him down onto the stool beside the woodstove, "is call your wife and tell her you're going to be late getting home from work tonight." He limped over and grabbed the bottle of Scotch off the table beside his chair. "And like those two smart women upstairs, the four of us are going to toast our good fortune that we all survived to fight another day."

"Here's the thing," Fiona said, smiling when Gabriella took another sip of tea and started gasping for breath again. "I'm worried that having freedom and knowing what to do with it are two very different things."

"Wh-what do you mean?" the girl choked out with a violent shudder. "Freedom means we can do anything we wish now," she said before lifting her cup and taking a noisy slurp.

Waiting for her friend to catch her breath again, Fiona sipped her own tea, relishing the warmth spreading through her slowly relaxing muscles. "But what is it we want?" She shot Gabriella a grin. "Other than to have children, that is."

"I told Maddy that I might like to be a nurse, like she is," Gabriella said. "Only Maddy said there wasn't any reason I couldn't be a doctor." She snorted and then immediately covered her face when tea shot out of her nose. "Omigod, that burns," she muttered, wiping her nose on the back of her sleeve. "Only William walked in just as I asked Maddy how I could go to school to be a doctor and raise children at the same time, and he said that it wouldn't be a problem because I wasn't allowed to talk to boys."

"You're going to have to talk to at least one if you want to conceive a child." Fiona drained what tea was left in her cup. They were each on their third cup of the Scotch-laced tea—and they'd each taken a good swallow directly from the bottle while they waited for the woodstove to get hot enough to boil the water. That one swig had gone a long way toward calming Fiona's nerves, but hadn't done much to lessen her embarrassment.

She couldn't believe she had spoken so crudely downstairs, much less that she'd actually told Kenzie some of what she'd gone through a thousand years ago.

What must he think of her? What must they *all* think of her, knowing she'd spent months serving every need a man had? She wondered if modern wars had women who traveled from battle to battle, cooking and washing and tending the wounds of the warriors by day and warming their beds by night.

And if so, had Trace had ever sought them out?

Fiona reached for the simmering kettle on the stove. If he truly had changed his mind about her continuing to live here, he certainly must have changed it back again now that he knew why his kiss hadn't shocked her.

"What do you want to be?" Gabriella asked.

"Be?" Fiona repeated, at a complete loss as to what they'd been talking about.

The candle cast enough light for her to see the girl's frown as she held her cup out for a refill. "Other than to have another child, what do you want to do with your life?" Gabriella asked. "You have to earn a living if you don't intend to get married."

Fiona picked up the Scotch and added some to each of their cups. "I have no idea." She set the bottle back on the table and suddenly grinned. "But I like children; maybe I can take care of other women's children while they go out and earn *their* livings. Surely there's a need for such a service. In fact, there's an interesting television show every weekday in the afternoon that I've been following, and on it, a woman is trying to find someone to watch her two-year-old child so she can go to work."

But then Fiona frowned again. "Only the child's father— she isn't married to the man and he just found out he *is* the father—is trying to take the little girl away from her, claiming she's an unfit mother. It seems the person she had been leaving the child with drank too much, and the little girl wandered off and got lost for an entire day."

Wide-eyed and utterly intrigued, Gabriella leaned forward in her chair, not even noticing that she spilled tea on her bosom. "There's a television show that follows people around, letting us see what's going on in their lives?"

"I started watching it when I lived with Matt and Winter, and Winter explained that it's only pretend. You know, like a play. Didn't you have minstrels come to your village and act out stories of great battles or what was happening at court?" Fiona leaned back in her chair with a smile. "I saw one once, when Matt and Kenzie and I snuck down to a nearby village. That was the only time Papa ever took a switch to me, but it was worth it. I don't think I'd ever laughed that hard in my life."

"Then you should write to that woman and tell her that *you* will take care of her child," Gabriella said, waving her cup and spilling the tea on her lap this time. "And that way, the father won't take the little girl away from her."

"I can't write to her; it's only pretend." Fiona leaned forward again, warming up to her idea even as she formed a plan. "But I could put a notice in Eve's store that says I'm willing to take in children who live here in Midnight Bay.

Why, there's no reason I couldn't watch three or four babes. Damn," she said, plopping back into her chair again. "I would need to ask Trace first, wouldn't I? He might tolerate having animals around, but men feel differently about children."

Gabriella waved her concern away. "He won't even be here during the day when they are. Hey!" she cried, standing up and spilling her tea all over the floor. "If I move in with you like he suggested, together we could probably watch *ten* children. And we could even make enough money to buy a vehicle of our own."

Fiona shook her head. "I'm certain we need to ask Trace first."

Noticing that all of her tea was gone, Gabriella grabbed the bottle of Scotch and poured some into her cup, then sat down. "We can still live together, though, can't we, and take care of each other's children while we become working women?"

"I doubt a modern husband would let an unwed mother live with you, Gabriella."

Gabriella grinned. "Just as soon as you figure out how to have a babe without a man, you can tell me, and I'll do the same." She lifted her chin. "I don't need a husband to live happily ever after any more than you do."

"Oh, Gabriella," Fiona said on a soft sigh. "There's more to marriage than just cooking and cleaning and having sex. Remember that powerful yearning your mama spoke of? Well, it's all tied up with love. You'll always feel like something's missing if you have no one to be . . . intimate with. Unlike lions in Africa, women need someone to hold us in the middle of the night when we're frightened and to share our joys and sorrows." She leaned forward. "Can I tell you a secret?"

Gabriella nodded vigorously.

"I came close once. I stayed with one particular warrior for almost a month, and we grew quite comfortable together. I even talked myself into believing he would take me home with him," she said softly.

"And did he?"

"Nay; he was killed in battle." She pulled in a shuddering breath. "And I moved to another man's tent that very night."

"What was it like being a wh—a camp follower?" Gabriella whispered, her cheeks turning pink. "I remember when William escorted Mama and me to her sister's wedding when I was eleven. I snuck out of our tent one night to see what all the noise was down in the woods, as William had pitched our tent well away from his warriors. The camp appeared quite festive, with the women laughing and the men teasing them." She frowned. "But I remember thinking, where are the children? If those women were having sex every night, how come they didn't get pregnant?"

"They did," Fiona told her. "But once a woman became too heavy with child to keep up with the demands of constantly moving, she was abandoned and left to find her own way home—if she dared go home at all."

"But that would mean the men abandoned their children, too."

Fiona snorted. "There was little way to know who had fathered the babes."

"But why didn't they let the women stay? As soon as they gave birth, they would have been able to keep up again."

"Children were strictly forbidden in camp, as young ones are unpredictable and might get in the way. And sound carries on clear, windless nights; a crying infant could give away a battalion's position to the enemy."

"And when you became heavy with your babe, you were abandoned?"

Fiona nodded. "It took me three weeks to make my way back home, but I managed to get back just in time to have Kyle." She dropped her gaze to her empty cup. "Only I had no strength left to get out of bed, and I wouldn't stop bleeding," she whispered. She looked at Gabriella. "I tried to explain to Papa how to take care of my son, but he had become so mad by then that he couldn't remember from one feeding to the next that he had to give Kyle only goat's milk." She shrugged. "And then one night I went to sleep and Mama came to me in my dreams, and I simply didn't wake up. And two weeks later Kyle died, and I held him in my arms again before he returned to earth as someone else's child—because, he told me, he still had earthly lessons to teach."

"And that's when you became a hawk?"

Fiona poured more Scotch into her cup without bothering to add any tea. "Aye, within days of Kyle leaving me." She smiled sadly. "I went in search of Matt and found him lying on a battlefield, bleeding to death. All the people in the village where he had been living had been slaughtered."

"And you saved his life," Gabriella pronounced. "And then you came to this century as a hawk with him, and Kenzie came here as a panther."

Fiona shook her head. "Nay, I didn't travel to this time with them, because I didn't approve of why Matt was coming here. He was seeking out Winter MacKeage—another powerful drùidh, although she didn't know it at the time—to help him keep his promise to make Kenzie human again." She waved her cup in the air. "I didn't come to this century until William did, and then only to show him how to get here." Fiona stood up when Gabriella gave a loud yawn. "Come on, my new roommate, it's been a long day, and it's time we got some sleep."

Gabriella drained the last of the Scotch in her cup and stood up, only to giggle when she staggered and bumped into a table. "Oh, these old floors are really slanted. We'll need to have Trace fix them before we bring children here."

Fiona wrapped an arm around her unsteady friend and guided her to the couch. "I'm sure he'll put that right at the top of his list of things he must do." She turned Gabriella around and let her fall back onto the couch. "Just after he repairs his hidey-hole, digs his tunnel out again, gets his truck running, shovels the snow out of the driveway, and catches the skunks and puts them in the back of Madeline's truck."

Gabriella grabbed a throw cushion and hugged it to her face, then plopped sideways with a sigh. "If we ask him nicely, maybe Mr.—I mean, maybe Mac can use his magic to remove all the snow from the dooryard," she murmured. She smiled up at Fiona. "Don't you think he's handsome? I know you don't like men," she rushed to say, "but if you did, wouldn't it be exciting to fall in love with a drùidh?"

Fiona snorted. "About as exciting as childbirth."

"You know who else is handsome?" Gabriella asked.

Fiona took the blanket off the back of the couch and tucked it around her. "No, who else is handsome?"

"Maddy's brother, Rick. Have you met him?" Gabriella grabbed Fiona's hand to keep her from straightening away. "He's Trace's fishing partner, you know, and he lives with all of us at Maddy's mother's house. I slept in Sarah's room at first, but when I started having bad dreams and would wake up screaming . . . well, Rick suggested I take his room over their garage." She smiled crookedly. "Wasn't that nice of him? And sometimes, when I've had a bad dream and can't get back to sleep, he brings me downstairs and makes me hot cocoa."

She pulled Fiona closer. "And a couple of times, he's even given me a bottle of something he calls beer, saying it will relax me." She fell back against her pillow with another sigh. "It tasted similar to the mead I used to sneak out of my papa's cup when he wasn't looking, only I think the Scotch we put in our tea works better. I feel as if even my bones have melted, I'm so relaxed."

Fiona patted her shoulder, deciding that the Scotch had certainly relaxed the girl's tongue. "Your dreams will all be pleasant tonight, I promise," she whispered. "And in the morning, we shall put our minds together and come up with a plan we can present to Trace *before* we implement it."

"Mama told me that when she wanted Papa to let her do something, the less she told him, the better," Gabriella said without bothering to open her eyes. She sighed again, snuggling into her pillow. "And that she always made him think it was *his* idea."

"I believe I like your mama," Fiona said, walking out of the room.

She went to her cupboard under the attic stairs, pulled out the mattress of sea grass she'd made, and dragged it to the front room next to the woodstove. Fiona finally lay down with a tired groan and stared up at the ceiling. She touched her fingers to her lips as she remembered Trace's kiss down in the safe room.

And how very much alive and very womanly it had made her feel.

Or, rather, how womanly *he* had made her feel.

She slowly rubbed her finger back and forth over her lower lip and smiled at the realization that Trace Huntsman desired her. And to her surprise, Fiona found herself wondering if that wonderful, exciting sensation she'd felt in the pit of her stomach when he'd kissed her—which had spread through her like warm, soothing Scotch—might in fact have been her own desire for him.

Lord, she hoped so. Because if what she felt toward Trace really was desire, her prospects of becoming a truly modern woman, one who could *choose* to be intimate with a man, meant that her new life had just gone from a curse to a blessing.

And this time, by God, she intended to have some say in the matter.

Chapter Twelve

Trace couldn't imagine what sort of crime he might have committed—at least not recently—that would have compelled the universe to send his life to hell in such a crowded handbasket. Honest to God, he was thinking about burning his house down again, only this time to get Mac the Menace to leave. How in hell could anyone sit sprawled on a couch watching television for three friggin' days and not go insane?

Unless Mac's real intention was to drive everyone insane with him.

It was no wonder Fiona and Misneach kept disappearing. The woman might claim that she was spending time in the barn to help her animals get over the trauma of the storm, but Trace suspected she was secretly sneaking down to clean his safe room, as well as to escape the woe-is-me antics of their uninvited . . . guest.

Only Gabriella seemed blissfully unaware of the building tension.

Trace decided he was going to have to take the girl aside and point out that her little hero-worship thing was starting to border on the ridiculous. Nobody needed their pillows fluffed every ten minutes, and the next time she lugged another tray of food in to Mac, Trace was tempted to trip her.

Three endless days of waiting for his knee to mend was taking its toll. He'd swear his muscles were atrophying from not being used, his butt had gone numb from sitting in his lumpy old recliner, and his teeth ached from grinding them every time Mac rang the little bell Gabriella had given him to call her whenever he needed something.

About the only bright spot Trace could find was that his taste buds had recovered enough for him to discover that Fiona was one hell of a cook. Well, and that the goat had stopped giving milk.

And he did have to admit that being laid up had afforded him the time to catch up on his paperwork, which in turn only added more fuel to his growing frustration. Even with Rick pulling double duty, they'd be lucky to break even this year, and Trace couldn't for the life of him figure out where they would find the money to get their second boat up and running and in the water.

"Could you please keep your sighing to a minimum, Huntsman?" Mac asked from somewhere inside his throne of fluffy pillows. "The batteries in the television remote are wearing down because I have to keep adjusting the volume."

Trace was tempted to tell him exactly what he could do with that remote, but he merely let out a sigh loud enough to override the blaring . . . oh, for chrissakes, the man was watching *Sesame Street*!

Mac hit the mute button and pivoted on the couch to look at him. "What is it that has you so depressed, anyway?"

Before he realized what he was doing, Trace held up his checkbook. "I'm trying to figure out where Rick and I are going to get the money to put our new boat in the water." He sighed again. "Because according to our bank balance, we might as well sink the damn thing and use it as a mooring."

Mac arched an imperial brow. "You and Madeline's brother are broke?"

Trace snorted. "We're not just broke; we're in debt up to our eyeballs. And if we don't start catching more lobsters, we won't be able to finish repairing the second boat we bought." He pointed his checkbook at the window. "Every time another army of demons chases one of Kenzie's displaced souls here, the storm not only stops us from going to sea but it also messes up our fishing grounds. We're lucky if we find one lobster in our traps when we haul them now, whereas we used to find several."

Mac arched his other brow. "So, merely catching more lobsters is all it would take to get rid of your foul mood?"

Trace eyed him suspiciously. "It would help."

Mac raised one of his hands in the air, waved his index finger in a circle, and shot Trace a smug smile. "Consider it done," he said, turning back to the television and hitting the volume button.

"Wait. Consider what done?" Trace asked over the sound of Big Bird talking to some scruffy-looking puppet in a trash can. "What in hell does this mean?" he growled, waving his own finger in a circle when Mac turned to him. "What did you just do?"

Up went that imperial brow again. "I simply told all of the older lobsters to seek out your and Rick's traps and go inside them."

"You told them," Trace repeated evenly. He moved his fingers to imitate running. "And they just scurried into our traps like good little lobsters."

"Not the little ones, Huntsman, the *older* lobsters. Do you not prefer to catch the larger ones? I was under the impression that your commerce system paid by the pound."

Realizing that he was gaping, Trace snapped his mouth shut with a muttered curse. Did the man honestly think he was that gullible? Of all the outrageous— "Wait, do the lobsters know they're going to end up in a pot of boiling water? Aren't you afraid of bad karma or something, for telling them to commit . . . lobster suicide?"

Mac shrugged. "They've had a good twenty-year run already, and every creature understands its place in the food chain. I merely asked them to fulfill their destinies."

Holy hell, twenty-year-old lobsters weighed at least five pounds!

Man, he wanted to believe him.

But Mac was a drùidh; Trace knew that much about him because he'd actually seen him *do* stuff. Hell, the guy even had a fancy robe and a pointy hat and everything, just like a real wizard. "So what other tricks can you do?" he asked, this time over the sound of Elmo belting out a song at the top of his little puppet lungs.

Mac hit the mute button again. "Tricks?" he repeated softly. "You mean, like turning annoying people into toads?"

As threats went, Trace supposed that one was as good as any. "Actually, I was thinking more along the lines of you fixing my bum knee, and getting my truck running again, and making a new pair of work boots magically appear. Because if you could do all that, I would get the hell out of here and stop interrupting your . . . quality television time," he offered, nodding towards the TV.

"Consider it done!" Mac snapped, turning back to the television.

"Wait. You didn't wave your finger in the air this time."

Mac hit the mute button again, and Trace actually braced himself when the man shot him a glare fierce enough to turn him into a . . . well, something not pleasant.

"So, it's true, then, what Gabriella told me?" Mac drawled. "They kicked you out of your war because you had a hard time to get . . . moving?"

"I was kicked out for beating a man nearly to death when he pissed me off. If you're going to perform fancy tricks, the least you could do is say abracadabra or make a puff of smoke or something."

Mac's glare turned downright ominous. "I'm not one of your modern charlatans, and my *performances* are not de-signed to entertain. Rearranging time and space and matter is serious business." He suddenly smiled. "But if you insist."

Trace gave a strangled shout when a bolt of electricity suddenly shot through his chair. He lurched to his feet without even closing the footrest and spun around just in time to see the recliner burst into flames.

"For chrissakes, put it out! You're going to burn down my house!"

"I'm sorry; I thought that was your intention," Mac said with a chuckle.

Trace had to jump back when a deluge of water

suddenly came out of nowhere and landed on the burning recliner, sending up a cloud of sizzling steam. "What, you read minds, too?" he muttered, bending down to pluck his checkbook out of the puddle of water on the floor.

This time it was Mac who sighed. "I wish. No, I can't read minds. But like you, I do have a knack for reading a person's intentions." He grinned. "After hearing Kenzie say you had threatened to burn down your house to get Fiona to leave, I assumed you were considering doing the same to get rid of me."

"Only unlike with Fiona," Trace said, "I'm not worried about hurting your feelings. I don't have a problem *telling* you to get lost to your face."

Up went that damned brow again. "Then why haven't you?"

"I figured since I was laid up, having you around might prove entertaining." Trace gave a shrug. "But it turns out you're only irritating." He used his soggy checkbook to point toward the kitchen. "So, you can leave anytime, Oceanus. Just don't let the door hit you in the ass on your way out."

Mac turned to face the muted television. "If I leave now, the demons will get me." He looked back, and Trace went perfectly still at the utter seriousness in the drùidh's eyes. "And if they somehow manage to kill me, half the earth's population could be wiped out in the ensuing war my father will wage to extract retribution."

"Who in hell did you piss off?" Trace whispered.

Mac looked back at the television. "I honestly have no idea. I only know that they seem unconcerned about annihilating anything or anyone that gets in their way."

"And so you led them *here*? But if your father is such a bad-ass . . . whatever," Trace growled, angrily waving at nothing, "then why in hell didn't you go running home to him instead of to us?"

Mac finally stood up and faced Trace directly. "My father and I haven't exactly been on speaking terms for several years."

"But six weeks ago, you came here to get Carolina for him," Trace countered.

"No, actually, I came after Carolina for her sake, not my father's. I did not wish to see the brat on the wrong side of his anger."

"Exactly who is Titus Oceanus that everyone—including even Kenzie's brother, apparently—gets all quiet and serious at the mere mention of his name?"

"You've heard of Atlantis?" Mac asked.

"Sure, everyone's heard of the *mythological* continent."

Mac's grin was somewhat provoking. "Well, Titus Oceanus is what you would call the patriarch of Atlantis. He created the entire . . . okay, let's use *myth* for lack of a better word." His grin turned indulgent. "I can see I had best give you the short version, as well as endeavor to use terms you can relate to. So, where was I? Oh yes, I believe I was at the beginning of modern time, when dear old Daddy built Atlantis as a hidey-hole in which to protect and cultivate his Trees of Life."

"Wait. Who's he protecting these Trees of Life *from*?"

"From the gods."

"As in Zeus and Poseidon and all the other *mythical* gods?" Trace drawled, folding his arms over his chest.

Mac's grin disappeared. "Believe what you wish, Huntsman,

but the fact is, the gods were so busy trying to wrestle control of the world away from one another that they were all but destroying it. So, my father," he continued sharply when Trace tried to ask another question, "stepped forward to champion humanity. He created Atlantis, planted groves of his Trees, and educated several hand-picked humans to become drùidhs. But when the gods discovered what he was doing, they actually worked together for once and tried to destroy him." Mac's grin returned. "And the myth of a wondrous lost continent began when Titus sank Atlantis and all of its inhabitants into the sea."

"Into the sea *where*, exactly?"

Mac gestured dismissively. "It matters not. All that matters is that Atlantis truly exists and that as long as it does, humanity shall remain safe. But only if the Trees of Life, which are now growing all over the world, continue to thrive."

"Let me get this straight. I'm supposed to believe there's a bunch of trees that . . . what? What makes them so special?"

"In layman's terms, they're what power the world. They hold all knowledge, like a library of sorts, and keep the energies balanced. In actuality, they are humanity's conscience. If you consider how trees are designed, you'll see why my father chose them to hold everything together; they reach toward the heavens while their roots anchor civilization to the earth."

"So, if these trees are scattered all over the world now instead of safely growing in Atlantis, who or what is protecting them from . . . the gods?" Trace couldn't help but ask, despite knowing that he was hearing the mother of all tall tales.

"Each drùidh is charged with protecting his or her Tree. In fact, Cùram de Gairn, whom you know as Matt Gregor, and his wife, Winter, are protecting a new species right here in Maine, which grows on the mountain where they're building their new home."

"So where's *your* tree?"

Mac smiled. "I'm not a drùidh, actually. I've just let everyone continue to believe I'm one because it's less intimidating."

Trace went perfectly still again. "Then what are you—*actually*?"

"Titus Oceanus's son."

When Trace just glared at him, Mac gave an impatient sigh. "The drùidhs protect the Trees of Life, and my father and I protect the drùidhs."

"Lucky you," Trace muttered. He rubbed his forehead, trying to dispel the uneasy feeling rising inside him. Christ, he hoped the bastard was lying, because if Mac was telling the truth, that he was even more powerful than the drùidhs, a quick trip to hell in a handbasket was starting to sound appealing.

"Look, I've enjoyed the history lesson," Trace said, "but that still doesn't explain what is going on *here*. I've seen you do stuff I can't even come close to understanding, so tell me why you don't just magically heal yourself and then zap on home to Daddy and tell him you're sorry for whatever caused the rift between you, and would he please kill whoever is trying to kill you? Because I gotta tell you, if you just made up that elaborate tale so I'll let you sit on my couch and watch television, you picked the wrong *hidey-hole* to hide in. I don't know shit about any of this; I'm just a highly trained weapon the military would point at a target they wanted destroyed. Kenzie and William are the demon-fighting experts, and An Téarmann is impenetrable because it's under Matt Gregor's protection. So tell me, why are you endangering Fiona and Gabriella after you went through all the trouble of giving them back their lives?"

Mac stared at him for several heartbeats, then turned and quietly sat down on the couch. "I can't go to An Téarmann because I can't get past de Gairn's magic any more than the demons can. And I can't heal myself." He looked at Trace. "Haven't you heard the saying that a physician who operates on himself has a fool for a patient? Hell, I could turn *myself* into a toad."

"Your sister didn't seem to have any trouble staying with Kenzie."

"Carolina is not Titus Oceanus's heir; I am. But my father had the foresight to implement a fail-safe system that, in effect, makes me . . . allergic to the energy a drùidh emits." Mac grinned derisively. "Which he did on the off chance that his heir turned out to be a no-good rotten bastard." He looked back at the television, his hands balled into fists on his thighs. "And to answer your questions as to why I can't seek my father's protection . . . well, I can't return to Atlantis unless I happen to bring along a wife, preferably one who's already pregnant with my child." He looked back at Trace. "The rift between my father and me is over my failure—or, according to him, my stubborn refusal—to give him a grandson."

Trace stepped toward the couch, his own hands balling into fists. "Are you saying that all you wanted Maddy for was as a broodmare?" he asked ever so softly.

Mac stiffened in surprise. "No! I truly was enamored with Madeline, and I sincerely felt I could grow to love her . . . in time." He relaxed back against the pillows. "I certainly knew there would never be a danger that I would grow tired of her; Madeline's light comes from within, and when she gets riled, that light outshines the sun." He looked down at his lap. "And as much as I envy Killkenny's good luck to have won her heart, I probably envy his courage to love her even more." Mac waved dismissively without looking up. "Go away, Huntsman. Your knee is healed, and your truck is running again, so go pull your traps full of lobsters."

It was only then that Trace realized he had been standing on two good legs for the last ten minutes, and when he looked down, he saw a pair of shiny new boots on his feet. Holy hell, the bastard really had healed him!

The porch door opened, and Trace heard Misneach race into the kitchen. "Oh, we're just in time," he heard Gabriella say. "The show is starting in ten minutes. But maybe we should watch it upstairs," she continued in a whisper. "Mac might be having a nap, and we shouldn't disturb him. The poor man needs to rebuild his strength."

"You will put a stop to this, Oceanus," Trace growled softly. "How in hell can you live with yourself, letting the girl idolize you like that?"

Mac dropped his chin to his chest. "Because I am a needy bastard, apparently." He looked at Trace and nodded. "I will have a talk with her. But for the record, I felt I was helping Gabriella by letting her see that not all men are brutes."

Trace scooped Misneach up in his arms. "No, some of us are just—"

"Good Lord, what happened?" Fiona cried, staring at the recliner.

"He did it," Trace said, pointing at Mac. "He set my chair on fire—while I was in it, I might point out—and then doused it with water. So you make him clean it up."

Gabriella shot Trace an accusing glare as she rushed over to Mac. "You don't worry about cleaning up anything," she said, fluffing several of the pillows and then pushing Mac back against them. "I'll have that ratty old chair out of here in two shakes of a lamb's tail. Are you hungry? I could fix you a snack before our show starts."

Trace cleared his throat rather loudly, giving Mac a pointed look.

Blowing out a huge sigh, Mac captured Gabriella's hand and pulled her down beside him. "I'm fine, Gabby. And I made the mess, so I will clean it up." He handed her the remote. "You find which channel our show is on, and I'll go get us a snack."

"Oh no!" Gabriella said, jumping up. "You need to conserve your strength."

Mac gave a laugh and pulled her down beside him again, then stood up and handed the remote back to her. "I knew our show was coming on, and I tried to find the correct channel but couldn't. I'm afraid you're going to have to do it for me. Besides, your tender care has already worked its magic, and if you truly wish to help me finish healing, you must start encouraging me to stretch my muscles."

Rolling his eyes, Trace set Misneach down and headed for the kitchen, but stopped when he saw Fiona's surprise.

"You're not limping," she said.

"Nope, my boo-boo's all better." Trace pointed down at his feet. "And look, Mac gave me a new pair of work boots, and he claims my truck is running again."

"A minor miracle to grant," Mac said, coming to stand with them, "if it gets him out of the house."

Fiona frowned. "If you could heal him with magic, why didn't you do it sooner?"

"And miss out on all our male bonding?" Mac drawled. He looked over Fiona's shoulder toward the kitchen. "Do you have any corn I can pop?"

She quickly stepped to block the doorway, her frown turning to a threatening glare. "I just spent three days cleaning that kitchen, and I'm not about to let either one of you anywhere near it." But then her cheeks suddenly darkened as she glanced toward Trace and quickly looked away. "I mean . . . I . . . ." She stepped past them and marched toward the couch, waving over her shoulder. "Oh, go on. Have yourselves a friggin' field day," she muttered, flopping down on the couch beside Gabriella.

Mac shook his head. "You're a bad influence on that woman, Huntsman, as she's even starting to sound like you."

"That's because imitation is the best form of flattery," Trace said, walking into the kitchen—only to stop dead in his tracks.

"Sweet Neptune," Mac whispered, coming up behind him. "I'm not the only one making magic around here."

Trace stood speechless, trying to take it all in. Not only didn't he recognize his own kitchen but he didn't dare touch anything in it.

"Forget about the free milk," Mac continued in a reverent murmur, "and claim Fiona now, before some fool shows up here wanting to *buy* an entire cow."

"I'm not looking for a wife," Trace snapped, striding to the door.

"And you dare accuse me of using Gabriella," Mac muttered, following him.

Trace slipped into his jacket but stopped with his hand on the doorknob. "I can't help it if Fiona's got something against dust bunnies." He nodded toward the living room. "When you replace my recliner, make sure the new one is soft Italian leather." He grinned in the face of Mac's glare. "We'll consider it one of those thank-you gifts smart guests bring along when they show up *unannounced* for an *extended* visit."

"Mac!" Gabriella called out. "Hurry up, our show is starting!"

"Good fishing," Mac said, giving a wave over his shoulder as he walked away. "Try not to let the door hit you in the ass on your way out, Huntsman."

Trace walked onto the porch, frowning at the uneasy feeling in his gut, which only worsened when he saw that a good portion of the snow had been shoveled out of the dooryard. He walked to his truck—which had also been brushed off—opened the door, and reached in to turn the key.

It started right up and quickly fell into a purring idle.

But instead of climbing in and heading to the docks to see if Rick was offloading today's catch, Trace stood staring at the house, trying to figure out what was bugging him. And then he suddenly stiffened.

Goddamn it, *Mac* was the one looking for a wife!

Trace reached in and shut off the truck. "You're not getting rid of me that easily, you conniving bastard," he muttered, trudging down the path Fiona had shoveled to the barn. "The only fox in this henhouse is *me*."

Chapter Thirteen

$\mathscr{D}$id he have Fiona's number or what? As he'd suspected, when he'd walked into his safe room not an hour ago, it had been to find it just as spotless as his kitchen. She had put all of the supplies back in the cabinet, shoveled out the debris, washed the blood off everything, remade the cots, and swept every damn last particle of dirt off the floor.

But had the woman stopped there? Oh no, she had gone on to completely reorganize everything. She apparently thought the cots should be at a ninety-degree angle to each other in the back corner, the cabinet obviously had no business blocking his secret exit, and the heavy folding canvas stools belonged on *top* of the cabinet. As near as he could tell, the only thing she hadn't moved was the monitor, and then probably only because she hadn't dared to mess with the wires.

Fiona Gregor didn't merely have something against dust bunnies; she had an obsessive-compulsive disorder. And like most OCD neat freaks, she had a sense of order with a theme only she could see, hers seeming to be that she liked to put stuff on top of other stuff. Stools belonged on the floor so they could be sat in, not stacked on top of the cabinet; which was why *he* had kept them lined up against one of the walls. And he kept his rifles hanging on the wall rack organized by caliber, but Fiona obviously felt they should be stacked according to length, with the longer ones on top, making an upside-down pyramid. She had rearranged all of the boxes of ammunition, too, and it had taken Trace a good twenty minutes to unstack them in the cabinet so he could grab the correct box in a hurry without having to read every damned label.

And she must have filched his revolver, because he couldn't find it anywhere—or the bag he kept it in, or the box of bullets he kept in the bag.

But that discovery had actually made him smile; that is, until he'd remembered that the revolver had been shoved inside her pants the whole time she'd crawled through the tunnel and dug him free. He was going to have to take her to the gravel pit the first chance he got and teach the little thief how to handle a gun before she shot a hole in her floor—which was his ceiling—and killed him right there in his brand-new leather recliner.

Trace stopped trying to push the heavy beam back into place at the far end of the tunnel and stretched the kinks out of his back. Maybe he'd get her a nice little compact automatic instead, and that way she could keep the clip loaded without having a bullet in the chamber. He pushed several small rocks out of the way with the toe of his new work boot, and then threw his shoulder into the beam as he kicked the bottom up against the dirt wall. The only problem was, Fiona needed a permit to carry a handgun, and he didn't know how to go about getting her one if she didn't have any documentation proving she actually existed.

He stepped away and eyed the beam, then gave it a couple of whacks with his fist to seat the top into place. Maybe good old Mac the Magician could rearrange time and space and matter for him again and simply conjure up a birth certificate.

Hell, why stop there? Why not give Fiona a bachelor's degree in . . .

Trace snorted as he hunted around for a scrap of wood to trig the beam in place. The only thing Fiona knew anything about was cooking and cleaning.

Well, that and the fine art of driving a man crazy.

Especially if that man had sworn off women.

No, wait. He was pretty sure he'd only sworn off *vulnerable* women.

Yeah. He hadn't even considered that he might find himself attracted to a demon-shooting, Scotch-drinking, potty-mouthed neat freak—who also happened to have the body of an athlete, hair he just itched to unbraid and get lost in, and eyes so golden they made the sun look like a mere dot in the sky.

Well, great. Wonderful. How friggin' fantastic *smart* of him to be lusting after a woman who unapologetically admitted that she didn't like men.

Trace stilled at the sound of footsteps on the stairs that entered the tunnels from the shed. He reached up and unscrewed the lightbulb over his head and pressed back against the wall beside the beam, then silently watched Fiona step into the corridor and go into the safe room.

He took a steadying breath, willing himself to imagine her checking for dust bunnies under the cots instead of how inviting she'd look lying naked on one of them. But it didn't work, as now all he could picture was walking into that room and seeing her lush little bottom in the air. He ran a hand over his face, hoping to wipe away the image, only to realize he was sweating. He had been moving heavy rocks and beams, but that didn't explain why his heart had just kicked into overdrive.

Trace eyed the stairs leading up to the mudroom and then looked at the open door to the safe room again. His head was telling him to go upstairs, but his lower brain was screaming at him to walk down the tunnel, close the door, and lock it—and make damn sure he was *inside* the room when he did.

Christ, he wished she'd never told him she wasn't afraid of men.

Or maybe if she'd slapped his face when he'd kissed her the day the demons had been trying to kill them . . . maybe that's all it would take to make him walk away.

But she hadn't slapped him, or appeared even a little bit afraid of him, or been outraged or disgusted or even confused. No, all he could remember was how she'd relaxed into him and how soft and sweet and promising her lips had tasted.

Trace stilled again at the sound of weeping, his heart pounding even harder at the realization that he was standing just outside the room—only he couldn't recall moving.

He heard another wrenching sob, followed by what

sounded like an angry curse. So help him God, if Mac had made a pass at her, he was going to— "What's the matter?" he asked, rushing inside. "What happened?"

She stopped unbraiding her hair with a startled scream and spun toward him.

"Hey!" he yelped, rearing back from her clenched fist and then jackknifing away from the knee heading toward his groin. He grabbed hold of her swinging arm and spun her against him, wrapping her up in a tight embrace. "Calm down, it's just me," he growled into the mess of her curls fanning across his face.

She went limp in his arms. "You startled me."

"Why are you crying?" He brushed her hair out of the way as he continued holding her against him. "What did Mac do to you?"

She turned her head in surprise. "Mac? What makes you . . ." Her eyes widened. "You think Mac made an advance toward me? A *sexual* advance?" She laughed, turning to face forward again—but not pulling away, he happened to notice. In fact, she relaxed back against him. "He knows better than to even try," she said huskily.

Trace turned her in his arms and brushed his thumb over her damp cheek. "If not Mac, then what's upset you?"

She dropped her forehead to his chest with a heavy sigh. "I can't believe they let that bastard take that poor little child away from her mother. It was heart-wrenching."

Trace smoothed down her hair, only to get his fingers tangled up in her curls. He didn't have a clue what she was talking about. He leaned away and tilted her chin up. "Who's the bastard, and what poor little child are you talking about?"

"That evil man, Rory. He didn't even know little Sophia existed until Charlotte's vengeful sister told him a month ago. And Charlotte is a *good* mother." Fiona gathered Trace's shirt in her fists. "What sort of laws do you have in this time that allow a man to rip a two-year-old child away from her mother? Rory made up all sorts of lies about Charlotte, and he got several of his friends to lie for him, as well, and that stupid judge *believed* everything the lying bastard said."

Trace stared into her tear-filled, angry eyes, wracking his brain trying to figure out who all those people were. "Is Charlotte a woman you befriended when you lived with Matt and Winter?"

Her brows knitted into a frown. "What? No! She's on the television show."

He pulled her to his chest with a strangled laugh. "Sweetheart, you're upset over something that happened on a *soap opera*. Charlotte's not real, and neither is Rory, or Sophie, or any of his lying friends."

She wrapped her arms around his waist and relaxed into him with another heavy sigh. "I know the show is only pretend, but the feelings I get watching it are real. And the little girl's name is Sophia, not Sophie." She craned her head back and smiled up at him. "Mac and Gabriella got angry, too. And when the judge gave Rory custody of Sophia, Mac jumped up, pointed at the screen, and said something I didn't understand, and . . . well, you now own a really large, very flat television."

When she moved to rest her head back on his chest, Trace captured a lock of hair trailing down her back and lowered his mouth to hers, stopping just short of actually kissing her. "Slap my face or kiss me, Fiona," he whispered. "Either way, just put me out of my misery."

She stretched upward inside his embrace, hesitated less than a heartbeat, and then he felt her soft, delicious lips touch his. Trace ran his fingers up through her silky hair and cupped her head, being careful not to overwhelm her despite every one of his muscles protesting against his restraint. Only he nearly lost it when she pressed her strong, delicate hands to the sides of his face to angle his head and parted her lips.

She had no business not being afraid of him, and she sure as hell shouldn't feel like warm, pliable butter melting into him. Nor should she be making those sweet little sounds as her tongue darted out to let him taste her or be pressing her hips forward into his groin.

The fact that she felt so right in his arms should have set warning bells off in his head, but every brain cell he processed had already headed south, and the best Trace could do was aim them toward the closest horizontal surface without breaking their kiss. Turning slightly and opening one eye to gauge the distance to one of the cots, he pivoted and gently dropped onto his back, bringing Fiona with him.

Expecting that maybe now she'd slap his face—since asking for a kiss was one thing and finding herself lying on a bed with him was another—Trace nearly came unglued when she started unbuttoning his shirt.

Still not hearing any warning bells, he threaded his fingers through the waterfall of curls cascading down over her arms and onto his chest, only he got lost somewhere inside the intimate curtain of silky sunshine and greedily pulled her mouth down to his.

Apparently quite good at multitasking, she kept undoing

his buttons even as her tongue sparred with his, and Trace felt his shirttail being pulled from his jeans just as he remembered that he'd forgotten to lock the door.

He broke the kiss with a groan, certain that he'd blown his chance. "The door's not locked."

Her hands stilled on their way to his belt buckle, her moist, swollen lips parting in surprise. She was suddenly gone, and Trace sighed when he saw her running away, and closed his eyes on a muttered curse.

The door slammed shut with enough force to rattle the walls.

He snapped open his eyes when he heard one of the bolts slide into place and sat up when he saw her unbuttoning her blouse as she walked to the table and turned out the light, plunging them into absolute darkness.

"You're sure?" he asked quietly, even as he twisted to reach into his back pocket and pull out his wallet. He opened it and felt around for the condom. "Because if you're not one hundred percent okay with this, then you're on the wrong side of that door."

"Does . . . does it bother you that I've been with other men?"

Trace stopped trying to tear open the packet. "Not if it doesn't bother you that I'm not exactly a virgin, either," he said thickly, realizing that this really was going to happen when he heard a sigh, then clothes rustling, and then what sounded like her hopping around on one foot.

Trace wanted to kick himself for asking but asked anyway. "I need to know why you're doing this, Fiona."

He heard one of her boots fall and roll up against something. "Because I can."

Deciding that was as good an answer as he could hope for, he ripped open the packet and slid it under the pillow behind him. He really wished she'd left the light on, though, because he really needed to see her eyes in order to figure out how okay she really was with this.

But he wasn't exactly twisting her arm, now, was he?

And *he* hadn't locked the door.

If he'd found himself in this position a week ago, he would have slapped himself in the face for even considering making love to her. But fighting an army of demons with a person was a hell of a way to get to know them, and not only had the real Fiona Gregor emerged four days ago, she hadn't gone quietly back into the safe little bubble her brothers had tried to put around her.

He heard what sounded like her bumping into the table, which was followed by a truly impressive curse. "Would you like me to take down one of the stools from the *top* of the cabinet and put it on the *floor* so you can sit on it to take off your boots?"

Something heavy hit the wall beside him.

Trace started to lie down with a chuckle to unbuckle his belt and slide off his pants but was suddenly pushed backward by a pair of strong, delicate hands, followed by a pair of wonderfully naked legs straddling his hips. "No, thank you. I'm managing," she said thickly, her hands pinning down his arms. He heard her sigh. "You really need to work on your lack of urgency, Trace. You're still dressed. What have you been doing for the last two minutes?"

"I've been imagining what you look like naked. A man likes to see what he's touching, you know."

"I am aware of what a man likes," she whispered, her

mouth mere inches from his and her wonderfully naked breasts brushing his sensitive chest hairs.

Trace tried to reach up to cup her breasts, but she continued to hold him down. He lifted his hips to let her know that he wasn't lacking urgency in some matters.

She made a little noise that sounded sort of surprised, and then she didn't move for the longest time.

He suspected that she was trying to figure out how to get him out of his clothes without letting go of his arms, and although he had a few suggestions, he decided to wait and see what she came up with—seeing as how she was an expert on what a man liked and everything. And while he waited, he tried to recall the last time he'd had a naked woman sitting on top of him and if he'd taken this long to get straight down to business.

Maybe he *was* a little too laid-back.

"What's the matter, sweetheart?" he drawled. "Did you just remember you prefer the heavy stuff on top? Here, let me help you," he said, gently bucking her off and twisting to spin her beneath him, chuckling at her startled gasp. "There, see? The next time you need something heavy moved, just ask, and *I'll* move it."

"I . . . but you're . . . that's not—"

He covered her sputtering mouth with his own, deciding that he urgently wanted to see her hot and wet and frenzied while he was still young enough to enjoy it. She settled down fairly quickly, but instead of kissing him back, she went kind of passive on him all of a sudden. Trace lifted his head to see what was wrong, only to realize that he couldn't see a damn thing in the absolute darkness.

So he asked, "What's the matter?"

"I—I'm not sure what you want me to do," she whispered. "You're not . . . I don't . . . I can't pleasure you if you're holding me down."

"Excuse me?"

"Do you prefer that I lie perfectly still and not touch you?" she asked, a frantic edge creeping into her voice. "Or we can get up, and I'll hold on to the desk, and you can take me from behind if you want," she rushed on anxiously. "Just tell me how you like it, and that's what I'll do."

Trace was off her and standing in the middle of the room in half a pounding heartbeat. "I think you better get dressed," he said quietly.

He heard her scramble off the bed. "But why? What's wrong?"

He silently stepped away from her groping hands trying to find him in the dark.

"T-Trace, please," she whispered. "I don't know what I did wrong, but I'm sorry." He heard her bump into the table. "Do you prefer having the light on? I don't mind if you do. Really. I just thought you might be—"

"Leave it off," he growled. Sensing her going perfectly still, he stepped toward the back wall. "You didn't do anything wrong, Fiona, I did," he said as calmly as he was able to, considering that there was an axe buried in his chest.

"But I don't know what I did wrong!" she cried, the panic back in her voice. "I told you I'd do whatever you wish. I can give you pleasure if you would just let me."

The axe jerked sharply, making it impossible to breathe. Christ, what a mess. He reached back and silently tripped the hidden latch on his secret exit.

"Trace. Please!"

He slipped into the side tunnel, every cell in his body shaking with rage, some of it aimed at himself and some at her, but a good deal of it aimed at the bastards who had stolen the very thing that made her a woman.

Fiona stood pressed up against the metal door, as still as a statue but for her trembling long after she realized Trace had left. She couldn't stop replaying like a television show what had just happened, watching it over and over in hopes of understanding what she'd done wrong. She couldn't even move to dress when her trembling turned to shivers, but merely pull her hair around her like a curtain of shame.

She was so confused; one minute Trace was asking her to kiss him, and even teasing her about cleaning his room, and the next thing she knew he was angry.

And then he'd simply left.

Fiona groped through the darkness to find the bed, and pulled the blanket free and wrapped it around herself as she sat down, then buried her face in her hands.

Trace had said *he* had done something wrong, but she knew better. It had been obvious for days that he desired her, and apparently so angry at what had happened on television that she hadn't seen his truck in the yard, she had come down to his secret room to revisit the notion that she had an equal desire for him.

Or see if what she really desired was simply to be like other modern women.

So when Trace had startled her by walking in, looking strong and powerful, with his handsome gray eyes darkened with lust, and he'd taken her in his arms and asked her to kiss him . . . well, she had boldly offered him her body without asking for or even expecting any sort of commitment in return.

Because that was how things were done today. She knew women were free to sleep with men they had no intention of marrying without being considered whores and that what had once been only a man's privilege was now a woman's as well. And she had desperately wanted Trace to see how bold and confident she'd become . . . and maybe to show him that she was just as capable of giving him sexual pleasure as any of the modern women he knew.

Which only showed that pride really did go before a fall.

She'd been so determined to prove to Trace how quickly she'd adapted to this century and all of its freedoms, she hadn't once stopped to consider *his* feelings. Nay, she hadn't thought past giving the man the best sex he'd ever had, so *she* could feel like a twenty-first-century woman.

She had to fix this. She had to go after Trace and apologize, and she had to promise that she would never, ever throw herself at him again.

And then she had to get the hell out of his life.

Fiona pulled in a shuddering breath and stood up, not liking that last part but realizing there was no way she could continue living here. She walked to the table and turned on the light. She didn't think she could rent a new apartment with only the three hundred dollars she had left, though, so until she found a job and saved up more money, she would simply have to avoid Trace.

She quickly dressed and started braiding her hair. It shouldn't be too hard, now that his knee was healed. He'd be going back to work, and she would simply stay in her apartment when he was home. And no more leaving eggs and bread on his doorstep, or cleaning, or new animals, or touching his tools or any of his belongings.

And she would bring back his revolver and never come down to his room again.

Fiona squared her shoulders as she looked around and took another shuddering breath. She would begin by putting Trace's hidey-hole back the way he'd had it. Then she would go upstairs and send Gabriella home, tell Mac to cook his own dinner, and take Misneach for a long walk down by the ocean and explain to him that he could no longer pester their landlord.

And tonight she would sleep in her cupboard, because . . .

Because today she'd learned it was only in there that she should dream of soaring strong and free and proud.

Chapter Fourteen

Trace set his drink on the table and gave the man sliding into the booth across from him a warning glare. "Go away, Oceanus, preferably far, far away."

"I'll have whatever the gentleman is having, please, and bring him another one at the same time," Mac added as the waitress walked off. "Believe me, Huntsman, I would if I could. But I need to stay as close to An Téarmann and de Gairn's magic as I possibly can without it killing me. If I leave Midnight Bay, I'm unprotected."

"Then you're as good as dead, because this is Oak Harbor."

"And so when you bring my cold, dead body back to my father, maybe then you'll explain to him why you forced me to come looking for you."

Trace downed the last bit of ice-diluted Scotch in his glass. "What's the matter, did the women run out of pillows to fluff or food to cook you? Or did you end up burning down my house after all?"

"I've been on my own for the last two days. Fiona came in about an hour after you finally drove off the other day, and sent Gabriella home and then disappeared upstairs. I haven't seen either one of them since, except when Fiona went to the barn to feed her animals and yesterday morning, when she walked out the driveway and headed toward town."

Trace stared down at his empty glass, saying nothing.

"You need to come home and fix this, Trace. The energy surrounding your house is so muddled that even the seagulls refuse to land on your roof."

"Go away, Oceanus."

"You haven't answered your phone for two days," Mac continued. "And your excited fishing *partner* finally had to come over last night to tell you he had to hire a man to help him at sea and that the winch broke twice because the traps were so laden with lobsters." Mac took a sip of the drink the waitress set in front of him and made an appreciative sound. "Are you not pleased that the fishing is going well?"

"Ecstatic."

"But you don't feel guilty for leaving a nineteen-year-old boy to fend for himself?"

"The *man* is more than capable of carrying both our loads and obviously smart enough to hire help if he needs it."

Mac slid Trace's new drink toward him. "If you have anything running through your veins besides Scotch and cold, stark fear, you will come home and fix this before she does something . . . foolish."

Trace disguised his flinch by lifting his glass and taking a long swig, letting the Scotch sit in his mouth awhile and then swallowing.

"Brooding doesn't become you, my friend," Mac continued quietly.

"I'm not brooding; I'm sitting here wondering where I'm going to hide your body when I finally lose my patience and kill you. I can't stuff you in a lobster trap, because I don't know where in hell Atlantis is. And the way my luck's been running lately, I'd probably sink you right on top of your father's goddamned house."

Mac stopped with his drink halfway to his mouth and gave Trace a small salute with his glass. "I can see you're finally starting to believe."

"What I *believe* is that you're a . . . what in hell are you, anyway, if you're not a drùidh? I'd like to know what to call you other than a pain in the ass."

Mac eyed him for several heartbeats. "I suppose 'Your Highness' is out."

Trace snorted. "We'll go with *royal* pain in the ass, then."

"The accurate term is *theurgist*," Mac growled. "Which I obviously must explain means 'supernatural agent of human affairs,'" he said when Trace shot him a glare. But then he sighed. "Okay; then let's just go with *wizard*."

Trace took a sip of his Scotch before leveling his gaze on Mac again. "So if you're some big, bad-ass wizard, you ought to be able to fix Fiona's problem all by your supernatural self," he said, waving his finger in a circle. "So why in hell don't you?"

"Because the thing about being a theu—a wizard is that I'm not supposed to actually meddle in human affairs."

"Then what do you *do,* actually?"

Mac grinned. "I protect everyone's right of free will, so all you people can mess up your lives and then fix your own damn problems."

"You don't think bringing Fiona and Gabriella here was meddling?"

"I merely granted them something they were already wishing for."

"Fiona sure as hell wasn't wishing to be herself again," Trace countered. "She made no bones about the fact that she preferred being a hawk."

Mac made a dismissive gesture. "She only thought she did, but hidden inside her so deeply that even she couldn't see—likely because she didn't dare look—Fiona dreamed of coming back." He leaned forward on the table. "More than anything else, she desires to be a mother and to be able to live long enough to raise her child. If she hadn't wanted a second chance, of her own free will, not even my powerful magic could have made it happen."

Trace stared down at his glass, running his thumb over the condensation on the side. "Can you bring anyone back?" he asked quietly. He looked up when Mac didn't answer, and sucked in his breath at what he saw in the wizard's eyes.

"I'm sorry," Mac said softly. "But Elena's deepest wish was to move on."

"You can't know that."

"I'm afraid I do, and if you take a moment and look deep inside *yourself*, you will find not only the knowledge that I'm right but also a sense of relief." Mac leaned forward on the table again. "You can't save them all, Trace, because sometimes an individual's journey is more about dealing with their own demons than helping you fight yours."

"You could at least try to bring her back."

"Unlike Fiona, who remained herself even as a hawk because she wasn't ready to move on, Elena is already walking the earth again as someone else." Mac grinned tightly. "And with any luck, maybe the woman will have learned from her mistakes and get it right this time."

Trace scowled down at his drink, trying to decide if he believed him or not, suspecting that the man might be too caught up in his own problems to be interested in helping anyone else. He'd brought Fiona back as a gift to Matt and Kenzie to trade her for his own sister, but bringing Elena back wouldn't gain him anything, now, would it?

Trace narrowed his eyes. "What did you mean when you said I'm relieved? You think I'm *happy* Elena's dead?"

"No," Mac said evenly. "I think deep down you know that if she'd lived, you would have found yourself tied to a woman you couldn't save. And I also think you innately know that death is not a punishment, and that life is not some sort of reward." He leaned forward again. "They're two sides of the same coin, Trace, and the difference between them is really quite insignificant."

"Then what in hell *is* significant?"

"How you choose to spend that coin."

Trace took a swig of his drink, again letting it sit in his mouth before swallowing.

"You saved your mother," Mac said quietly.

"Sure," he said with a snort. "And it only took me seventeen friggin' years." He set his glass down and leaned on the table. "Since you seem to know so much about everyone else's problems but your own, then tell me why my mother—or any woman, for that matter—would stay with a bastard who kicked her around for sport."

"Because women are hardwired to stay." Mac blew out a heavy sigh when Trace just glared at him. "Since the beginning of humanity," he continued, "if a woman didn't stay with her mate, she and her children faced certain poverty and even death. So, she stayed and endured, and because she had no other choice, she went to sleep every night praying the bastard would miraculously wake up a changed man."

"My mother had choices. There were agencies she could have gone to for help. And she had two sisters and a bunch of cousins who would have helped if she'd *asked*. Yet she spent seventeen years hiding the fact from everyone that she was married to a drunken bully."

"You think a survival instinct can vanish in only a few generations?" Mac said quietly. "As recently as the nineteen-hundreds, what did women with children have to rely on except the kindness of their families? And if they had no family to take them in, then they were on the street or living in a poorhouse. That's why even today, even with all of the help available to them, women continue to stay: because in the backs of their minds, they ask themselves a hundred *what ifs. What will I do to support myself if I leave him? What if I'm unable to make it on my own? I can't live with my sister forever. What if the drunken bully causes trouble for my family? What if no other man will want me? What if the bastard is right, maybe I did trap him into marriage because I was too afraid to leave Midnight Bay to go to college?* She was sixteen, Trace, and scared to death. And she had you to think about, which only added to her list of *what ifs.*"

"You mean, like what if the bastard ended up killing his son in a drunken rage?"

"No, I believe it was more like *What if he blames me for*

his father hating him? And then there was her greatest fear of all: *What if my son hates me when he becomes old enough to realize I can't even put food on the table or a roof over his head because I truly am a weak, husband-trapping woman nobody wants?"*

"How in hell do you know all about my mother? And Elena?"

"The Trees of Life truly are humanity's conscience, Trace, and all that has happened and all that will happen is stored in them."

"Which you can't get near, because you can't get past the drùidhs."

"Ah, but I don't need to get past them," Mac countered. "I believe you would like my father, Huntsman, as the two of you have a lot in common. He didn't trust anyone, either." Mac shrugged. "Probably because he understood human nature only too well. Dad knew better than to cut himself—or his heir—completely off from the Trees, so he fashioned a secret entrance through which we could access the knowledge they hold." Up went Mac's brow again. "And knowing I'd be forced to rely on your *generous* nature to take me in, I did a little research before I came here."

Trace ran his thumb along the side of his empty glass. "Then you know what happened two days ago down in my safe room."

"No, actually, I don't. Rearranging time and space and matter is simple enough, but it takes a good deal of energy to access and then sift through all the knowledge in the Trees. And right now, I need to conserve my strength in order to be prepared for another attack." He shrugged. "Besides, my problem is more important to me than your little lovers' spat with Fiona. *Except*," Mac growled, leaning forward again, "when it forces me to hunt you down to some seedy bar three towns away from An Téarmann." His glare turned threatening. "So, are you coming home, or am I *taking* you home?"

Trace leaned back in the booth and dropped his chin to his chest. "I can't fix the problem," he quietly muttered, "because I don't know how." He looked up. "Exactly how thoroughly did you research Fiona before you decided to give her a second chance?"

Mac folded his arms over his chest. "I am aware of all that she endured."

"Then do you have any suggestions how one goes about giving a woman back her . . . femininity? Those bastards turned her into a pleasure machine."

Mac sighed. "I don't think I'm the man you should be asking." He canted his head. "That is, if you should be asking a *man* at all. Maybe this is a question for Madeline." He grinned tightly. "Although I would take her advice with a grain of caution if I were you. She sent me on a wild-goose chase after those MacKeage women."

Trace waved that away. "Peeps has a thing for getting even with people who piss her off." He remembered the *Sesame Street* pajamas, her stealing his shoes, and how she'd sabotaged his truck, and he smiled. "Although I have to admit, she's taken one-upmanship to a whole new level." He nodded to himself, thinking maybe he would ask her. But then he started shaking his head. "Nope. If I ask Maddy what to do about Fiona, she'll hound me to hell and back for a play-by-play of the proceedings and then start planning my wedding."

"What about Eve Gregor?" Mac suggested.

Trace gaped at him and then snorted. "Don't you know *anything* about women? You even hint to one of them that you're interested in someone, and women turn into matchmaking tyrants. And they *always* tell their best friend, and Maddy and Eve are so tight you can't slip a piece of paper between them."

"You have to ask someone, Huntsman, because you have to fix this."

Trace looked Mac directly in the eyes. "No, I don't have to fix a damned thing, because none of this is any of my business. I didn't create the problem, so why in hell should I be the one to fix it? You said yourself I can't save them all, so why are you expecting me to save Fiona?"

Up went Mac's brow yet again. "If not you, then who? Johnnie Dempster? Or the first man who asks her out on a date? I'm sure there are plenty of single men in town who would love to give Fiona her wish."

"You think it's her wish to let some man use her again?"

Mac frowned. "Her wish is for a *child*. I told you that deep down, Fiona wanted a second chance because she wants another baby."

"But she openly admitted to me that she doesn't like men, so I don't exactly see her dating every guy in town, much less marrying the first one who asks her."

"You don't think Fiona's going to figure out that she doesn't need a husband to get her wish? Hell, half the women on that show she's been watching have had children out of wedlock."

Trace stiffened. "Are you saying the only reason she . . . that she only wanted to . . . you think she was hoping I'd get her pregnant?"

"Isn't that what the two of you fought about?"

"Goddamn it! She was *using* me."

Mac looked around and then leaned forward. "And I suppose your intentions were completely honorable?" he whispered tightly.

"I sure as hell didn't have a hidden agenda. I asked her flat-out if she was okay with it." Trace threw himself back with a snort, waving angrily at the air. "Of course she was okay with it, because she thought she'd found herself a sperm donor."

"And your fight was over your using a condom?"

"We didn't get that far. Wait. How do you know there even was a condom?"

"I found the empty packet on the cot in your safe room this morning."

"But I never took it out from under the pillow. And the packet shouldn't have been empty, because I opened it and put it under the pillow but then never touched it." He snorted again. "Fiona must have found it when she was tidying up."

"So, if you didn't know this had anything to do with a child, what exactly did you think I was asking you to come home and fix?"

"Her inability to . . . her attitude toward . . ." Trace dropped his head in his hands. "I knew I had sworn off women for a reason." He glared across the table at Mac. "I got the impression Fiona thought her only role in love-making was giving pleasure, and it appeared to me she didn't have a clue how to *receive* it."

Mac nodded. "That is what she spent seven months learning."

"And now she intends to use her ill-gotten skills to get pregnant." Trace stood up. "Only that sure as hell isn't going to happen on my watch!"

But he had to grab the edge of the table when the room started spinning. "Shit. I guess that last drink gave me a bit of a buzz." He pulled out his wallet and tossed it to Mac. "Pay the waitress and give her a nice tip, and then meet me out front. I'm going to see if I can find someone headed to Midnight Bay to give us a ride."

Mac scrambled out of the booth with a laugh. "You're not buzzed, my friend, you're stinking drunk." He pulled out all of Trace's money and tossed it onto the table, then tucked the wallet into his own pocket before hauling Trace's arm over his shoulder. "And I'll drive," he said, heading for the door.

Trace pulled them to a stumbling halt. "You know how?"

"I fixed the truck, remember? Driving it can't be all that hard."

Trace shuddered as Mac headed them toward the door again. "Maybe you should go for a ride with Killkenny sometime." He sucked in a deep breath when they hit the frigid night air, then bent over to brace his hands on his knees as he craned his neck to look around. "Damn, I can't remember where I parked." He waved his finger in a circle next to his spinning head. "Conjure up my truck, magic man, and have it come pick us up." He set both hands back on his knees. "And make it snappy, because I gotta go save some unsuspecting chump before Fiona fixes her own damn problem."

Mac hauled Trace's arm over his shoulder again and started them down the sidewalk. "Mind telling me exactly how you intend to save her?"

"Not her, the unsuspecting chump!" Trace grinned, feeling quite smug that he knew exactly what to do and that he hadn't had to ask anyone. "I'm going to use Fiona's own tactics against her, only instead of her *stuff,* I'm going to rearrange the lady's *thinking.*"

Chapter Fifteen

Misneach was a perfect example of why children weren't allowed to be anywhere near an army when it was camped close to the enemy. The moment he heard Trace shouting Fiona's name at the top of his lungs out in the yard, the pup started whining and scratching at the cupboard door. And when Trace stomped up the outside stairs and started banging on her door hard enough to rattle the windows, Misneach became so frantic to get to him that he piddled all over the floor.

Fiona unlocked the cupboard door and scrambled out as her pet ran off in such a rush that she heard him slip on the floor, tumble into one of the kitchen chairs, and knock it over. She pulled on her bathrobe, tossed back her braid and squared her shoulders, and calmly walked to the woodstove in the front room as she remembered the last time Trace had banged on her door. It had been her first night here, and she'd been so frightened she'd spent the night shaking like a leaf.

"Fiona! Get out of bed and open this door!" he shouted, banging on it again so hard she was surprised the window didn't break.

She took her time setting another log in the woodstove, contemplating how she'd spent the last two days trying to figure out what she'd done wrong. But this afternoon, she'd finally concluded that the only mistake she'd made was to forget that Trace Huntsman was about as *male* as a man could be. And in her experience, either men got angry and lashed out, or they stormed off in a huff when something didn't go the way they were expecting, especially when that something involved their precious manhood.

"Fiona! I want to talk to you!"

She just bet he did. But if he thought *she* wanted to talk to *him* after he'd run off and spent two days . . . slaking his lust on some other woman, most likely, he was either out of his mind or drunk—or both.

"Misneach," she heard him say, his voice suddenly encouraging. "Hey there, squirt. Yeah, I missed you, too. Go on, go get Fiona and tell her to come open the door so I can play with you. Go on, go get her, boy."

She heard Misneach whine and then return to scratching frantically at the door.

But then she heard another man's voice, to which Trace responded heatedly. Something bumped into her door; she heard a strangled yelp, and then muttering from the other man.

Mac, most likely.

She'd wondered how long it would take the drùidh to get sick of his own company—as well as his own cooking— and finally go hunt Trace down. Not that she cared. And she certainly didn't care if that beautiful kitchen downstairs now looked worse than it had before she'd cleaned it. She was even getting used to the smell of burnt toast that wafted upstairs every morning, as well as the pungent and equally burnt smell, along with the smoke, every afternoon.

She figured they must not have modern appliances in Atlantis.

"Open the goddamned door!" Trace shouted.

Apparently ignoring him wasn't going to work. Fiona tightened the belt on her robe, walked to the kitchen and pushed Misneach out of the way with her leg, and unlocked and opened the door.

Trace gave the pup a quick pat, then straightened and thrust his hand toward her, palm up. "I want my condom back."

She certainly hadn't been expecting that. "Your what?"

He lifted his outstretched hand just under her nose, apparently assuming she couldn't see it. "You know, the thin rubber thingy that's about this long when you unroll it," he said, raising his other hand and holding them a short distance apart, "that's shaped exactly like a man's cock." He thrust his open hand at her again, arching one brow. "Ring any bells, Fiona? It's what every red-blooded, twenty-first-century male hoping to get lucky carries in his wallet, just in case some woman walks up and starts undressing him. I believe you found one under the pillow in my safe room. Well, it's mine, and I want it back." He shot her a rather nasty grin. "In case I find some other woman who wants to get me naked."

"For the love of Zeus, Huntsman," Mac growled, grabbing Trace's sleeve and trying to tug him around. "*This* is your solution, to make her jealous?"

Trace pulled free and shoved his hands in his pockets as he hunched his shoulders against the cold—although Fiona couldn't see why he should be cold, as the glare he was giving her was hot enough to boil a kettle of water.

"People with hidden agendas don't get jealous," he growled as he continued glaring at her. "They just move on to their next target when the first one doesn't cooperate."

She was at a complete loss as to what he was angry at, other than her taking his condom. But she hadn't known what it was, only that it hadn't been under the pillow when she'd cleaned the room the previous day. So, after taking it out of the packet and unrolling it, suspecting what it was for but not quite sure, she'd brought it upstairs with the intention of asking Madeline if it truly was something men wore during sex.

But beyond her taking his property, she didn't know what else he was mad at.

"What are you talking about? What hidden agenda are you implying I have?"

"If you want another baby, lady, you're going to have to put up with a husband to get it. I even catch a hint of you undressing in front of anyone else, and I swear, I'll . . . I'll . . ." He pulled a hand out of his pocket to point his finger at her. "You just stay away from Johnnie Dempster, you hear me? And any other chump unlucky enough to bump into you in town. Your brothers might not be the boss of you anymore, but a landlord sure as hell has some say over his tenant dragging home innocent men at all hours of the day and night."

"Excuse me?"

"Besides," he growled, "you won't have time even to

smile at another man, because you'll be too busy working for me." He took his pointer finger and pointed down the stairs. "You be standing on my porch at four a.m. tomorrow, and make sure you're dressed warm, because it gets friggin' cold at sea this time of year."

"*That's* your plan?" Mac barked, appearing even more shocked than she was. "You're going to take her to work with you?"

"Rick and I need help, and she needs a job," Trace said, turning back to Fiona. "Because your rent just went up a hundred bucks a month. Landlords always charge extra for animals, and my deal with Kenzie didn't include a zoo." He pointed his finger at her again, only this time Fiona noticed it was shaking quite badly. "And your brother's not paying the difference, *you are,* which means you need to get off your duff and earn some honest money."

"That's telling her," Mac muttered, grabbing Trace's sleeve again. "Can we please go inside to have this discussion?" He gave him a shove. "It's freezing out."

Trace pushed back against Mac as he tried to elbow the drùidh in the ribs but missed. "Are you nuts? You don't ever go inside a woman's apartment, day or night, even if she was civil enough to invite you in." He turned his glare on her again. "And you *especially* don't go in if she's looking for a sperm donor."

Even though she couldn't stifle her gasp of surprise, Fiona glared right back at him. "I'm not inviting you in because you're drunk."

"Here's a suggestion," Mac said, blowing into his clenched fists. "Let's all go downstairs to have our little . . . chat. I will even do the honors of making us hot cocoa."

"If a little chill in the air bothers you, then go sit in the truck." Trace snorted. "No, wait. You can't, because the truck is sitting in a snowbank a mile down the road." He turned back to Fiona and pointed his finger right at her nose. "Five a.m. sharp and not a minute later, or I'll dock your pay an hour."

She very generously refrained from pointing out that he'd originally wanted her standing on his porch at four, not five. But still at a loss as to why Trace was so angry at her—other than that he didn't seem to want her smiling at men—Fiona gave him a warm smile. "Thank you for offering me a job, but I already have one."

He swayed back on his feet. "You what?" he yelped as Mac caught him.

"And it starts at the civil hour of eight," she continued. "And goes until six."

He narrowed his bloodshot eyes at her. "Doing what?"

"Watching a gentleman's two young children."

He leaned toward her. "At his house or here?" he asked ever so softly.

"Um . . . here," she said, leaning away.

"Why aren't you watching them for the gentleman's *wife*?"

Fiona inched away from his escalating anger. "His wife died two years ago, so he's been raising his two children all by himself. And when he came here tonight to—"

"When he *what*?" Trace shouted, stumbling toward her.

"Enough!" Mac snapped, shoving him the rest of the way inside and closing the door behind them. "This is getting interesting, actually, but I'm starting to miss parts of the conversation because my teeth are chattering too loudly."

He dragged Trace into Fiona's front room, then shoved him down onto the couch and turned to hold his hands over the woodstove. "Would you happen to have any . . . coffee, I believe, is what they think sobers them up." He smiled at her. "If not, tea or anything hot will do."

They both turned at the sound of snoring coming from the couch.

Mac sighed. "It would have helped if the truck heater had hit him that hard and knocked him out." He looked at her, shaking his head. "You would think being a warrior would have hardened his nerves, but when he wasn't gripping the dash on our ride back from Oak Harbor tonight, he was grabbing the steering wheel and shouting at me to keep to one side of the road." He shrugged. "Which made no sense if there wasn't another vehicle coming toward us. I slowed down and veered to the edge whenever I saw headlights coming at us."

"Mac, do you know why he's so angry at me?" she asked, gesturing at Trace, who was flopped over sideways on her couch in an awkward position.

God help her, it was all she could do not to go over there and straighten him out.

"He's angry that you tried to seduce him with the intention of making a child."

"What?" she gasped, taking a step back. "But I wasn't . . . I didn't . . ." Fiona felt her cheeks fill with heat. "He *told* what happened down in the safe room?" she squeaked, deciding she'd rather go over and kick Trace instead.

Mac tucked his hands behind him as he backed toward the stove. "Not the details, just the generalities of what led up to your little misunderstanding." He arched a brow. "Are you saying that at the time you never once thought of the possibility that you could make a child?"

"No!" She pointed at the couch. "And you better tell him that the moment he wakes up." She dropped her hand, fighting tears. "I can't believe he thought I would deceive him about something as important as fathering a child."

"You'd have to know about his childhood to understand why he jumped to that conclusion," Mac said gently. "Trace's father blamed his mother for getting pregnant when she was sixteen and trapping him in a marriage he didn't want."

"Th-that's why his father beat him?" she whispered, seeing one more piece of the puzzle fall into place. "Just because he'd been born?"

The drùidh nodded. "I'm afraid Trace is quite sensitive about fathering children, which is why you mustn't take his anger tonight personally. It's not about you, Fiona, it's about him." He folded his arms over his chest. "And so I would ask, if you weren't looking to get with child, what *were* you doing down in that room?"

Fiona spun away and ran to the kitchen. "We forgot Misneach outside."

But when she couldn't get the door to open, even after she checked to make sure it wasn't locked, she turned to find Mac standing in the front-room doorway.

"I'm only asking because I'd like to know if you are attracted to Trace or not," he continued, apparently unconcerned that her pet was freezing to death.

"You locked the door."

"It will open just as soon as you answer my question."

"But what does my liking or not liking him matter to you?"

"It shouldn't, really." He smiled sheepishly. "But it appears I have a romantic side I wasn't aware of until just recently." He shrugged. "Probably because I'm finding it's easier to stick my nose in other people's affairs than it is to get my own affairs in order. So, are you attracted to that drunken lout on your couch or not?"

She turned back and rattled the doorknob again as she looked down through the window to see Misneach sitting on the porch, his whole body shivering as he stared up at her. She spun back to Mac. "Okay, here's the thing. I'm sure you know how much I don't like men, but I don't . . . dislike Trace." She pointed her finger at the drùidh. "And if you tell him that, I swear I'll poison your dinner."

Up went that brow again, and his eyes took on an amused twinkle. "So, you were merely *not disliking* him two days ago when you took off all your clothes?"

"I was trying to be modern!" she snapped. "Women today can sleep with a man simply *because we can.*"

"And Trace just happened to be available and willing and . . . what? Safe? You felt comfortable with him because he's a friend of Kenzie's?"

"Well, yeah," she said, deciding that was as good a reason as any for why she'd made a complete fool of herself.

"Then can I ask how you're planning to go about getting a child, if you don't want anything to do with men and hadn't been trying to have one with Trace?"

Fiona immediately brightened. "Oh, but it truly is possible now! I was watching a show on television yesterday, and there was a woman getting something called artificial insem . . . insem . . . I wrote it down," she said, rushing to the counter. "Artificial insemination," she read from the piece of paper she picked up. She looked at Mac. "A doctor places a man's seed inside the woman, and she gets pregnant without having to have sex. Isn't that wonderful?" She waved the paper at him. "I knew there would be a miraculous way to have children without involving a man in this modern time."

Up when Mac's brow again. "I believe a man's got to be involved somehow, if you want his seed."

"Oh, but the show said there are *banks* of it, just like the banks that hold people's money. I can get the seed from one of them."

"Without knowing whom it belongs to?" he asked. "What if the gentleman who put his seed in the bank is . . . oh, I don't know," he said with a shrug. "What if he's stupid or a ne'er-do-well, or he's sickly or old?" He smiled. "Or so ugly that no woman will sleep with him? Is it not important to you what sort of lineage your baby will have? And do you not question why a man would give his seed to a woman he doesn't even know, to create a child he will never see?"

Fiona dropped her hand holding the paper, her shoulders slumping as she looked down at the floor. "I—I hadn't thought about any of that," she whispered.

Mac walked over and lifted her chin. "You will have your babes, Fiona," he said gently. "But maybe not today or tomorrow or even next week, okay? Why don't you focus on just being alive for the moment and let good old-fashioned Mother Nature take care of the details of when and how and with whom?"

"But I'm thirty years old, Mac. If Mama and Papa hadn't kept us isolated from society, I would have had several children by now."

"Your parents were trying to protect you, Fiona. They

knew that the very society you yearned to be part of had a tendency to fear and ultimately annihilate anyone who was different. Did you not learn that lesson the hard way, when that man caught you alone in the woods and asked you to come home and heal his dying father?"

"But I'm not a healer. My mother was the Guardian, only she was dead."

"And when he realized you didn't have your mother's magic and couldn't help him, that's when he turned on you, isn't it?" Mac took hold of her shoulders. "I'm sorry, Fiona, for all that you went through, and if I could, I would undo it. But it's important for you to understand that what you endured served to make you the strong, resilient, and determined woman you are now. No man will ever take advantage of you again, because you won't let him." He brushed a finger down her cheek. "Especially not that drunken lout snoring on your couch."

Mac stepped away just as the door popped open on its own, and Misneach ran straight to the front room without even looking at them. And when Fiona followed Mac into the room, it was to find the pup sitting on Trace's chest, licking his snoring face.

"Your pet's really not all that discerning, is he?" Mac said with a chuckle, lifting Misneach off and handing him to Fiona. He then grabbed Trace's wrists and hauled him into a sitting position, then pulled him to his feet and flung him over his shoulders in one smooth movement. He straightened and turned to Fiona, and grinned. "Will you be okay alone here, if I decide to go to sea with Trace and Rick?"

"But isn't it dangerous for you out there? Won't the demons get you?"

He started toward the door with Trace hefted over his shoulders. "Ah, but I'll have a secret weapon with me this time," he said, stopping on the top landing to turn to her—and bumping Trace's head on the doorjamb.

The drunken lout didn't even flinch.

"What secret weapon?"

He shrugged his shoulder, which caused Trace's head to bump the doorjamb again. "Huntsman told me he was a weapon the military would aim at anything they wanted destroyed, so I figure to aim him at the demons if they happen upon us."

"Mac," she said when he started to turn away. "You'll tell Trace that I wasn't trying to make a baby with him?"

"I don't think he's going to believe me. Or even you, if you tell him yourself." He nodded. "But I will give him your message. The gentleman you're working for—how did you find out he needed someone to watch his children?"

Fiona tucked Misneach up under her chin to keep the pup from straining toward Trace. "Eve Gregor allowed me to put a notice in her store that said I would take in children during the day. Mr. Getze stops in regularly to buy bread and eggs from her, and he saw my notice the very same afternoon I put it up. He called me yesterday and asked if he could come over and meet with me tonight and see my apartment."

"Did you check to see if Eve knew anything about him before you let Mr. Getze come here?"

"I did. And she assured me that he's a nice man and that she knew him because he went to her school, only he was a year ahead of her. She said he married a woman he met in college and works as a lawyer in Ellsworth. But his wife died of something called cancer two years ago, and Mr. Getze told me that he's been taking the children to a day-care center near his work. But he'd prefer to have someone here in town watch them now, as it's time for the older child, a little boy named Daniel, to start preschool. He wants Daniel to be with the same children he'll be going to regular school with. He brought them with him last night," she told Mac, smiling at the memory of those two precious children. "Daniel is four, and Kate will be three in May. They're both so adorable I nearly offered to watch them for free."

Mac arched his brow, and Fiona smiled again. "Don't worry; he's paying me very well. When I asked Eve what I should charge, she called a friend and found out the going rate in the area is a hundred and forty dollars a week for each child. But Mr. Getze said that if I supply their lunches, he'll pay me three hundred dollars a week to watch them Monday through Friday." Her smile turned sad. "I wish you could have seen those children, Mac. Kate's hair looked like her brother had braided it instead of Mr. Getze, and Daniel was missing a button on his shirt, and his pants were too small." She shook her head. "The poor man is obviously doing the best he can, but he doesn't seem to know much about children. Any time he told them not to do something and they did it anyway, he just sighed." She smiled. "I'm hoping that with a little encouragement, he can learn how to make them behave before they grow to be brats."

Mac shifted Trace's limp body on his shoulders. "Would you mind a friendly word of advice?" he asked. He gestured toward his shoulder when she nodded. "Try to avoid talking about Mr. Getze to Trace. Just so he doesn't get the idea that you're attracted to your employer," he explained when she frowned. "Trust me; it'll make life easier for all of us."

Mac turned down the stairs, but stopped and looked back, causing Trace's head to barely miss the rail. "Oh, and you be careful you don't get too attached to the children, okay? You can love them, but not like a mother loves her child. Mr. Getze is a young man and will likely remarry, and it will be his new wife's place to instill herself in their hearts."

"I understand," she whispered, stepping back inside the kitchen. She closed the door and rubbed Misneach's fur with her chin as she watched Mac walk down the stairs. Trace's head kept bumping the railing occasionally, only Mac didn't seem to notice—or maybe he just didn't care.

She set Misneach down when they disappeared around the front of the house and went into her front room and sat on the couch and stared at the woodstove. She absently picked up one of the pillows and hugged it, drawing in the scent of fish mingled with a good deal of Scotch, and wondered why she was so relieved that Trace had spent the last three days in some seedy bar instead of with a woman.

Chapter Sixteen

Scowling at the Norman Rockwell scene playing out in his driveway, Trace tried swallowing the burnt toast lodged in his throat by taking a sip of tea, only to jerk away when he scorched his tongue. He wiped the spilled tea off his *Sesame Street* pajama top, then tried lifting the glob of jam—which hadn't done a damned thing to help the taste of the toast—off Big Bird's beak without smearing it in.

He sucked the jam off his finger and looked back out the window at Gabriella pulling two laughing children through the snow on a small plastic sled. A totally ecstatic Misneach was chasing after them as Fiona gently lobbed snowballs at the pup, making sure she missed by a mile as she called to Gabriella to save the children from the mitten-stealing monster.

And John Getze, apparently in no hurry to get to work, was standing beside his car in his three-piece suit and overcoat, smiling at the women playing with his children.

Trace decided that smile looked more feral than amused.

"I wonder when the last time was that Fiona looked that happy," Mac asked—rhetorically, Trace hoped—as he stood beside Trace at the window.

"If she's the youngest in her family," Trace said, "and she didn't have any women friends or ever go down to the village, then what makes her think she knows anything about babysitting kids?"

"She was born to be a mother." Mac looked over at him. "And she raised enough lambs and young orphaned wildlife to know that, animal or human, all any baby wants is to be nurtured and protected and loved."

"Why in hell isn't Getze going to work?" Trace muttered, lifting his mug to his mouth, this time remembering to blow on the tea before he took a sip.

"I believe he's making sure his children are in good hands, as any concerned father would do. Wouldn't you be doing the same in his position?"

"I guess we'll never know, will we, because I'm never having kids." Trace turned and strode to the counter. He'd make his own goddamned toast, and just as soon as he found out where Fiona had hidden the coffeemaker, he was replacing the bog water in his mug with something strong enough to get rid of the foul taste in his mouth.

"You would punish your mother for giving you life by robbing her of the joy of having grandchildren?" Mac asked, still standing by the window.

Trace spun toward him. "I'm not punishing anyone. I'm saving some unborn kid from having the likes of me for a father."

"So Grange Huntsman succeeded, then, in his desire to break his son's spirit?"

"No!" Trace ran his fingers through his hair and turned to brace his hands on the counter. "The bastard never broke me," he said quietly. "Though God knows he tried." He looked at Mac. "But he sure as hell didn't set much of an example for me when it comes to being a father."

"You had many fine role models, Trace, if you would only look back. You were close to your uncle Marvin, as well as Maddy and Rick's father. They were the dads you wished for, and you merely have to treat your own children the way those good men treated you." Mac walked over and leaned against the counter, crossing his feet at his ankles and folding his arms over his chest. "And if I remember correctly, you were the go-to man in Afghanistan for a good number of street urchins, because instead of simply handing them money and trinkets, you gave them the gift of your time. And those you couldn't help you buried with dignity."

"Which begs the question as to why I would want to bring a kid into this screwed-up world in the first place," Trace whispered, staring down at the counter.

"Because children are the epitome of hope. They are the nutrients that feed the Trees of Life, Trace. And every time someone like you refuses to hope, a branch will die and fall off, becoming dust scattered on the winds of despair."

"And yet you continue to stubbornly refuse to give your father a grandson."

"Not for lack of trying. Do you have any idea how many women through all of time that I've proposed to, only to have them run from me in terror?"

Trace arched a brow, trying to look imperial. "Why? Were you dressed in your fancy robe and pointy hat when you asked them?"

Mac walked to the window. "No," he said quietly, shoving his hands in his pockets as he stared out the window. "I only thought it honorable to be . . . myself when I asked. And trust me," he growled, glancing over his shoulder before looking out the window again, "I'm not exactly a woman's idea of a dream husband, much less someone she would want fathering her children."

Trace stilled at the edge in the wizard's voice. "Why? What are you, really?"

Mac turned to face him, and Trace stumbled against the counter in shock. "For chrissakes, change back!" he shouted. "Now!"

"Do you see my problem, Huntsman?" Mac asked. Or, rather, whatever the hell he'd turned into asked.

"I believe the word you're looking for is monster," Mac said softly. "Or bogeyman. Or creature. Or beast. Your quaint little story of *Beauty and the Beast,* which parents read to their children to teach them not to judge a person on looks alone . . . well, it's not a fairy tale, my friend. It's my life."

"Change the hell back," Trace ground out, darting a quick glance at the door. He wiped a trembling hand over his face, only to have it come away wet with sweat, but when he looked up again, Mac had changed back to himself.

Or, rather, the wizard was once again the *image* he wished to portray.

Trace took a steadying breath. "Maybe you'd have better luck if you didn't do that until after they said yes," he said, gesturing weakly. "Or better yet, after the honeymoon."

Mac shoved his hands in his pockets again. "I may lack

honor in some things, but I draw the line at deceiving women into sleeping with me."

"You're a virgin?" Trace asked in surprise.

"No! Let me rephrase that; I draw the line at deceiving women into *marrying* me." A hint of a grin lifted one side of his mouth. "But bedding a beauty for our mutual pleasure doesn't even come close to that line."

"Then maybe that's your problem. Have you thought about asking an ugly woman to marry you? Because I've heard," he rushed on when Mac glared at him, "that they can be quite grateful." Trace turned away and started opening cupboard doors to disguise his shudder as he attempted to shake off the image of Mac the Beast. "How many women have you actually asked to marry you, anyway?"

Mac walked over and sat down at the table. "After several . . . um, refusals, I stopped even trying. But I actually came close once again, in England in the fourteenth century." He smiled somewhat sadly. "I honestly thought Lady Cordelia Penhope might be the one."

"So what happened? Did she also run screaming in fright when you changed?"

The wizard's face darkened. "I never got the chance. Just when I had finally worked up the nerve to ask for her hand in marriage, Delia suddenly sent me away." He scowled. "She claimed I was starting to bore her."

Trace snorted. "She sounds a tad high-maintenance to me. Maybe you should consider yourself lucky Lady Penhope took off *her* mask before you took off yours."

Mac sighed. "I have spent a good deal of my adult life traveling through time to all four corners of the world searching for a woman I could be content with, but I'm quickly running out of centuries to search in."

Trace found the coffeemaker and went hunting for the filters. "Have you ever considered that maybe you're just too damned picky, Oceanus?"

"Would *you* not be picky if you knew you had to live with a woman for thousands of years? And besides being pleasant, there's also the fact that she'll be married to a theurgist, which isn't exactly something for the faint of heart."

"What do your parents look like?" Trace found the filters in a drawer, then started looking for the coffee, but stopped when he realized Mac wasn't answering him.

The wizard was smiling again, though. "You've met my sister, Carolina."

"I've met her," Trace said, remembering how he'd barely dodged that high-maintenance bullet.

"Carolina is the mirror image of our mother."

"I saw a beautiful young woman, but Kenzie and William saw a heavily whiskered harbor seal," Trace said with a chuckle. "So, how do I know that if I *had* agreed to marry your sister, she wouldn't have turned into . . ." He waved at the window and shuddered again. "Into the mirror image of you on our wedding night?"

"You saw the true Carolina, despite the fact that she had disguised her looks. That's why she was so sure you were the man she was destined to spend the rest of her life with. I don't know if you realize your gift, Huntsman, but you have a knack for seeing past the masks people try hiding behind."

Trace continued hunting for the coffee, hoping it was in

the fridge. "So if you take after your father, then why don't you just ask him how *he* got your mother to say yes?"

"Titus is legendary for his good looks."

Trace straightened from searching the fridge. "Then what in hell happened to you? Was your mother doing drugs or something?"

Mac went back to glaring at him. "I wasn't born this way. I was a perfectly normal, beautiful child—right up to puberty."

Trace bent to look in the fridge again, mostly to hide his grin. "So you're saying that instead of your voice cracking, your face did?"

The interior of the fridge suddenly exploded, and Trace instinctively lunged to the side and rolled away from the shower of food that shot halfway across the kitchen. He continued rolling and sprang to his feet, and spun to face Mac. "Don't you *ever* make something explode near me again," he ground out, taking a threatening step toward him. "Or finding a wife will be the least of your worries, you ass."

Mac merely arched a brow in response, saying nothing.

Trace pointed at the floor. "And you made the mess, so you're cleaning it up. Where in hell did she put the coffee?" he said when Mac still didn't respond. He started opening cupboards again. "I know I bought some a couple of weeks ago, because I distinctly remember putting it in a stainless-steel canister." He gave up and headed toward the door. "Dammit, I'll just ask her."

Mac scrambled to his feet and cut him off. "I don't be-lieve that would be wise."

"Why in hell not? If she couldn't be bothered to draw a

map of where she put all my stuff, then she'll just have to tell me where everything is."

"I'm fairly certain she doesn't wish to speak with you at the moment. Or anytime soon, I would imagine."

Trace waved that away. "I was drunk. And besides, you would have jumped to the same conclusion if you had been in my boots." He turned away and went back to opening cupboard doors. "And you might want to believe she was just looking to get laid like any other modern woman, but the jury's still out for me."

"I think you might find your coffee in Mrs. Peterson's old Christmas cactus."

Trace pivoted toward him. "Why would Fiona put my coffee in a plant?"

"Probably because when she opened the canister to see what it was, she assumed it was potting soil. At least, that's what I suspected when I saw her sprinkling the contents of a small container into the planter."

Trace grabbed the filter and a spoon, and strode to the living room. He didn't care if he ended up brewing dirt; he needed something stronger than sissified tea if he had any hope of feeling human again.

Along with women, he decided he was swearing off Scotch.

Trace hadn't believed Mac when the wizard had told him this morning that he'd actually asked Fiona for his condom back, and he was pretty sure he still didn't believe him. He'd said and done enough stupid things in his life to realize that he might have made an ass of himself last night; but really, asking a woman to return a condom? *Really?*

Had he thought she was running around with it in her pocket?

Hell, did she even know what a condom was?

Trace spooned what he hoped was coffee out of the planter and into the filter. But on his way back to the kitchen, he stopped dead in his tracks at the sight of what had to be the biggest television he'd ever seen. And not only was it taking up an entire wall, the wall it was hanging on had been completely remodeled to house a state-of-the-art multimedia center that Mac must have also . . . conjured up.

Trace glanced around and saw a pair of dark brown leather recliners on either side of a granite-topped table, and on that table sat a remote control that could probably run a nuclear submarine.

"Would you consider this an appropriate thank you from an unannounced guest?" Mac asked from the doorway.

"Is it cable or satellite?"

"That would depend on which you prefer."

Trace shrugged. "It doesn't matter, because either one comes with a monthly bill I can't afford to pay."

"I believe I already solved your little money problem, Huntsman, to the point where you may have to buy a third boat."

Trace looked at him. "Yeah, about that; I've been thinking that it might not go over all that well with the other fishermen when Rick and I suddenly start hauling in boatloads of giant lobsters while the rest of them are going broke. It's just not . . . honorable." He took a painful breath and blew it out slowly. "So you can tell all those big, fat, juicy lobsters that they can go back to whatever they were doing before you told them to fulfill their destinies."

"Or I could just tell them to go into everyone's traps," Mac said quietly.

Trace stared at him for several heartbeats. "Works for me," he said, heading into the kitchen with his filter full of . . . something.

"So it's honorable to let magic earn your living for you?" Mac asked, following.

"It seems to be earning *you* a good living." Trace shoved the filter into the coffeemaker and filled the tank with water. "And besides, it's not like we're sitting on our duffs and the traps are hauling themselves." He hit the on button and turned to see Mac picking up the contents of the fridge off the floor. "Tell me, if you can make anything you want happen, how come you don't make the magic do everything for you?" Trace pointed at a bottle of mustard that had rolled under the table. "Like clean up the messes you make, cook toast without burning it, and have my truck drive itself home."

Mac straightened with his arms full of food. "Because when I find myself standing in front of the pearly gates, I don't want to be explaining why I spent ten thousand years sitting around on my duff doing nothing. Life is not a spectator sport, Huntsman, and all of it, the good, the bad, and the *ugly*," he said with a pained grin, "must be embraced." His grin turned sheepish. "Although I will admit to taking an occasional shortcut."

"Ten thousand years? How the hell old are you?"

"I'm not sure, exactly," Mac said, staring off at nothing. "Three and a half, maybe four thousand years old."

"Wait, you said the pearly gates. They really exist?"

Mac started putting everything back into the fridge. "All myths are based in some form of reality," he explained. "But the gates aren't really made from pearls, you know; it's the energy they emit that makes them appear iridescent."

"Then what are—" Trace snapped his mouth shut when he saw Mac suddenly stiffen and look out the window.

"Do you hear that?" Mac whispered.

Trace strained to listen but heard nothing.

The wizard ran for the kitchen door, flung it open and ran onto the porch, and then sprinted toward the barn. Not even bothering to slip into his boots, Trace was only two steps behind him.

"Take the children upstairs," Mac told Fiona on their way by.

Instead of going to the barn, Mac didn't stop until he reached the end of the paddock fence, his gaze trained on the ocean. Trace stopped beside him, looked back to see Fiona and Gabriella carrying the children around the front of the house, then looked out at the ocean, trying to discover what Mac was looking at.

"There," Mac said, pointing to their left. "No more than a mile out. Do you see the dark shadow beneath that swelling wave?"

Trace caught only the slightest movement but then saw what looked like the mother of all whales shoot straight up out of the water over half the length of its body. It twisted and fell on its side, creating a splash that sent spray a good twenty feet into the air, its tail slapping the water so forcefully they heard the sound not a couple of seconds after the whale slipped out of sight.

"How in hell could you have heard that from inside?"

"Listen. He's telling us something," Mac said, gesturing for him to be quiet.

The whale was *talking* to them?

Trace saw the water swelling again, only this time instead of breaching, the whale twisted on its side, waving a flipper that had to be as long as a school bus. And then Trace heard a series of deep, guttural moans of varying pitch and length, the haunting song sending chills down his spine.

He turned when he heard vehicles driving into the dooryard and saw Kenzie's SUV followed by his own truck—which the two men must have recognized and pulled out of the snowbank—with Killkenny behind the wheel. They spotted Trace and Mac and walked over, William's gaze moving up and down Trace's body.

"Cute, Huntsman," the Irishman said, his eyes filled with amusement. "Does your mama know ye snuck out of the house in your pajamas?"

Kenzie, however, was stone-cold sober, his attention directed at where Mac was looking. "What's going on?" the highlander asked softly. "What are ye watching?"

Trace also turned to look out to sea, but the whale had slipped below the surface again. "Mac is talking to a friend of his," he drawled.

The four of them stood silently and watched, and Trace curled his toes against the cold seeping through the heavy wool socks he'd barely managed to slip on this morning when he'd stumbled out of bed, his head pounding so hard he hadn't even been able to get dressed.

"Can you contact Rick at sea, Huntsman?" Mac asked, still watching the ocean.

"I have a marine radio in my truck."

"Then I suggest you call and tell him to come back to

port. And also radio all of the other fishermen out on the bay, and have them come in as well."

"What's going on?" Kenzie asked.

The whale suddenly breached again, letting out a long, chattering whistle as it fell back into the water with a spectacular splash. Mac turned to them. "It appears Midnight Bay is about to find itself at the center of a fierce battle, gentlemen, and according to my father's messenger," he said, waving toward the ocean, "we have less than a day to prepare."

"Does that mean your father is coming here?" Kenzie asked.

Mac merely nodded, rather curtly.

"Thank God," William said. "He'll dispatch those bastard demons to hell."

"I wouldn't be too quick to claim victory if I were you," Mac said evenly, "because whoever has angered Titus Oceanus enough to bring him here is obviously someone very powerful, as my father hasn't left Atlantis in more than nine thousand years."

"Who in hell did you piss off?" Trace whispered. "You must have some sort of idea. And if you don't know, then *guess*. Who would have the balls to come after you, if it means going up against your father?"

"I honestly wish I knew," Mac said, his hands balling into fists at his sides. He turned to the ocean again. "I'm sorry; I never should have come here and involved all of you in my personal problem." He took a deep breath and blew it out slowly. "And in the end, it matters not if we know the names of our enemies or the reason they want us dead, only that we face them with courage and dignity." He nodded toward the truck. "Go make your broadcast to your fellow fishermen, and tell them they need to come in."

"Any suggestions as to what I should say?" Trace asked, gesturing toward the ocean. "Considering the seas are as calm as a swimming pool."

"Tell them Midnight Bay is about to come face-to-face with an unknown enemy and that they need to lock themselves in their cellars with their women and children." He looked directly into Trace's eyes. "With the storms your town has weathered recently and with the September eleventh attacks still fresh in your countrymen's minds, they won't take a chance that it might be a hoax."

"Is the battle taking place here in town or at sea?" William asked. "We need to know what to prepare for."

"I will do my damnedest to keep it offshore," Mac said tightly, turning away and heading for the house. "And you only need to prepare to defend yourselves, on the off chance I don't succeed."

Trace followed a little more than a step behind him. "Oceanus."

When Mac turned to see what he wanted, Trace drew back and gave him a hard uppercut to the jaw, sending the wizard flying backward without so much as a grunt of surprise, knocking him out cold before he even hit the snow.

"For the love of Christ, are ye insane?" William said, his shocked gaze lifting from Mac to Trace. "What in hell are ye doing?"

"Or more importantly," Kenzie said, "what are you intending to do when he wakes up?" A slight grin tugged at the corner of the highlander's mouth. "Or are you thinking ye might enjoy living under a rock with the other toads?"

"I had to do something before the idiot went out there alone and got himself killed." Trace bent down to grab Mac by the wrists and pulled him into a sitting position. "So if you gentlemen don't want to join me under that rock, then help me get him down to the tunnels before he wakes up."

Chapter Seventeen

◆

$\mathcal{U}$sually considered the curse of living in a small town, the speed at which the latest news spread throughout Midnight Bay was actually a blessing. Within six hours of Trace's broadcast that the mother of all storms was brewing out in the Gulf of Maine, all of the fishermen were back in port, their boats lashed to storm moorings and their heavy morning's catch of giant lobsters tucked safely in tanks at the co-op.

Just as Mac had surmised, no one was taking any chances that this might be a hoax, since a series of unusually fierce and unpredicted storms had hit this section of the coast beginning last spring. Word had even spread to the surrounding communities, and after lashing down anything that might blow away, everyone was safely tucked in their homes, waiting to see what Mother Nature had in store for them this time.

Well, everyone except John Getze. He was in Trace's

dooryard, having what appeared to be a sometimes coaxing, sometimes heated discussion with Fiona as he strapped his kids into their car seats.

Trace was actually proud of himself for continuing to prepare for the storm, when he really wanted to go out there and tell the three-piece suit to get the hell off his property. But then, he was just as curious to find out how long it would take Fiona to see through the man's carefully crafted disguise.

Trace suspected that Mrs. Getze would have found herself divorced in another couple of years if she hadn't died first, considering that John had changed girlfriends in high school nearly as often as people changed their underwear. Trace was surprised his old high school nemesis had gone into law, though, because he wouldn't trust the guy to write a simple will without naming himself as one of the heirs.

Hell, even Misneach didn't like the jerk, he noticed as he glanced out the window for the tenth time in as many minutes. The pup was actually tugging on Fiona's coat, trying to get her to come inside. Trace went to place some cans of food in the box he was packing, only to step back to the window when he saw Getze trying to coax Fiona into the passenger's seat of his car, all while kicking Misneach away, as the pup was now tugging on *his* overcoat.

Trace dropped the cans and was out the door and at the car in a heartbeat. "Fiona," he said cordially, giving John a cursory nod as he pulled her away. "Could you come help me find some blankets for us to use down in the cellar?"

Only when he started to lead her away, Getze grabbed hold of her other sleeve, actually placing her in a tug-of-war between them. "I was just suggesting that Miss Gregor come with me and the children," John said, smiling tightly. "I have a condo up at Sugarloaf, and it would be safer for *your tenant* up in the mountains."

Trace nearly lost his grip on her when he noticed Fiona's eyes sparkling with amusement. "I believe Miss Gregor prefers to stay *home*."

Christ, he was tempted to kiss that smirk off her face right in front of Getze.

She quickly turned her smile on her employer. "Yes, thank you for the offer, John," she said sweetly, pulling out of his grip. "But despite looking like a good wind could blow it over, I believe this old house is a safe haven." She pulled away from Trace next, then opened the back door of the car and leaned inside. "You two have fun at Sugarloaf, okay?" she said to the children, adjusting the little girl's hat. "And when I see you in a couple of days, we'll make cookies together for you to take home."

"With frosting?" the boy asked.

"And colored sprinkles," Fiona promised. She kissed her finger and then touched each child's cheek. "You be good for your papa, okay?"

"You're sure you won't come with us?" John asked when she straightened.

"She's sure," Trace said before she could answer, grabbing Fiona's hand and leading her toward the house. "No need to hurry back, Getze; I'm sure this storm's going to last several days," he said, giving a wave over his shoulder. "You can wipe that smirk off your face now," he softly growled the moment they were out of earshot. "I can't believe he thought you'd run off to his condo after meeting him only two days ago." He snorted. "The bastard still thinks he's God's gift to women."

She actually laughed. "I haven't seen that much posturing since a couple of male peacocks showed up in our camp one day when we were laying siege to a castle."

He stopped and turned to her. "I hope you know your safety was the last thing on his mind, because the only thing Getze has ever been concerned about is nailing anything with boobs."

"By nailing, I assume you mean having sex?" She actually had the nerve to arch her brow. "Maybe you should have asked John if *he* had any condoms he could give you, so you can be prepared when another woman undresses you."

Trace leaned down until his nose was nearly touching hers. "I already replaced the one you stole," he said ever so softly, his heart kicking into overdrive when instead of leaning away, she simply smiled again. "In fact, I put three in my wallet."

"I can see you and John have a lot in common. Maybe one evening I can watch his children and the two of you can go to your bar in Oak Harbor and *both* get lucky."

Unable to believe she'd just called his bluff, Trace pivoted away with a growl, still refusing to let go of her hand when she tried veering toward her apartment stairs. "I need you to come show me where you hid all my stuff."

"I'd rather not."

"I'd rather you did."

He hauled her up onto his porch, but the moment he dragged her inside, she gasped as she glanced around, her glare finally coming to rest on him. "How can two people make such a mess in less than three days?" She jerked free, but instead of bolting for the door, she walked over and started closing cupboards, only to gasp again when she slipped and nearly fell on an exploded potato.

"Mac made the mess. Or at least most of it," he said, picking up the cans he'd dropped by the window. He straightened and pointed over her shoulder. "And the cupboards are open because I was trying to find stuff to take down to the safe room. Will you please tell me why you stacked all of the canned goods in the mudroom?"

"Because it's cooler in there."

"And the microwave—does it need to stay cool, too?"

"No," she said, her cheeks turning pink. "I simply didn't see why that confounding machine should be cluttering your counter," she whispered, her gaze dropping to his chest. "It's unnatural to cook without heat, and when I tried using it to fix your eggs the other day, they blew up." She thrust her chin out. "I attempted to use a microwave when I lived with Matt and Winter, but the potato I was trying to cook also exploded, even though I had pushed the potato button."

When Trace only stood there staring at her, watching her cheeks slowly turn a deep red, she spun away and started stacking things back in the cupboards.

And still he continued to stare, utterly speechless.

Christ, he was an ass. He didn't even deserve to breathe the same air as this woman. And he sure as hell didn't have any business being angry at her for messing with his stuff, driving him crazy with lust, and for not knowing that lovemaking was supposed to be something two people did *together*.

Even after all she'd been through, from being treated no better than a piece of property a thousand years ago to being thrust into a new and confounding world, she never stopped *trying*. Who in hell was he to judge her, when he doubted he'd be half as courageous in her shoes?

Not only didn't Fiona Gregor need anyone to save her, she had been, in her own upside-down way, trying to save him from his own miserable self.

Trace quietly walked over and turned her around, and, ignoring her stiffening in defense, he pulled her into his arms and cupped her head to his chest with a heavy sigh. "I'm sorry for being a jerk," he whispered against her hair. "I should be shot with my own gun for running away from you the other day, and as soon as I find where you put that revolver, I'm going to show you how to load it so you can use it on me. Just promise me you'll shoot Mac next, for messing up my kitchen that you worked so hard to make beautiful."

Still holding her against him, afraid that if he lifted her chin to see her face, he might lose it altogether, he used his thumb to caress her cheek gently. "And I'm pretty sure I forgot to thank you for cleaning the barn and organizing my tools, cooking me the best meals I've eaten in ten years, and for chasing every damned last dust bunny out of my house."

He felt her stiffen again and realized that pointing out her little cleaning compulsion probably wasn't a good idea. So he finally lifted her chin so she could see the truth in his eyes. "But mostly," he continued, "I want to thank you for having the courage to leave that safe room to dig me out of the tunnel and save my life. Can you forgive me, Fiona, and maybe find it in your heart to give me a second chance?"

She dropped her gaze, held herself perfectly still, and said nothing.

He let her chin go and wrapped his arms around her with another sigh. "I understand I'm asking for more than I deserve, but I . . . well, I'm sorry."

He let her go when she pulled away and returned to packing his box as she mutely walked to the counter and started putting things back in the cupboards again.

"There's still time to change your mind and go ride out the storm at An Téarmann with Eve and Maddy and Gabriella," he said into the deepening silence.

"I believe I made it clear to you and Kenzie that I prefer to stay here," she said, keeping her back to him.

"Can I ask why?"

She bent down to put a pot in one of the bottom cupboards. "Because I can."

He wanted to tell her the real reason she was still here was because he'd nearly gotten into a fistfight with her brother earlier when the highlander had threatened to drag her to An Téarmann kicking and screaming if he had to, but Trace decided it was better that she believe Kenzie respected her enough to let her make her own decisions. He tucked his box of supplies under his arm, walked over and took hold of her hand, and led her to the mudroom.

"We don't need to go below yet," she said, trying to wiggle free. "The wind isn't even blowing, and the sun's shining; there's still plenty of time. And I still have things to do upstairs," she whispered when he opened the closet door with his foot.

"There's something I want you to see while there's still time for you to change your mind," he said, nudging her ahead of him into the closet.

She glanced back over her shoulder, her golden eyes a mixture of curiosity and suspicion. "What?"

Trace tripped the latch on the back wall. "You'll see."

"You've added light," she said as she walked down the

stairs. "Only it's not coming from bulbs. It seems to be everywhere."

"Go to the right instead of left," he said, standing on the step above her when she reached the corridor. "The tunnel opens into a small chamber just around the corner."

After only a quick glance over her shoulder, she headed down the tunnel, and Trace decided that she might not be ready to forgive him, but at least she still trusted him.

He hoped she would feel the same way a minute from now.

The light emanating from the very walls of the tunnel grew more intense the closer they got to the chamber, until it was nearly blinding. She stopped, and Trace bumped into her. "It's okay, keep going. The chamber's lit with only a lantern."

"But what's making the walls glow like that?"

"Your brother's magic," he said, giving her a gentle push.

"Matt?" She stepped into the small chamber and turned to look at him, blinking against the change in lighting. "Matt's come here to help us?"

"No. It's his magic, but I got it from that fancy pen he gave Kenzie."

She beamed him a smile. "That was very wise of you. Now we'll be just as protected here as at An Téarmann."

"Yeah, I guess that's one advantage," he said, setting down the supplies. He took hold of her shoulders and slowly turned her around. "But more than just keeping the demons out, your brother's magic is keeping Mac in."

"Oh, my God, what have you done?"

Trace held her back when she tried to step forward. "I can't let you near him, Fiona. I don't know how . . . sedated he is or what he's still capable of doing."

"But what's wrong with him? He looks sick."

"Mac isn't really a drùidh, I'm afraid. He's more or less in charge of them, like some sort of prince of the drùidhs. Only thing is, he's allergic to their magic." He waved toward Mac. "And as near as I can tell, when he gets too close, it puts him in a stupor, and hopefully keeps him too weak to do anything . . . magical."

"But why?" she asked, craning to look at Trace. "If you know my brother's magic makes him sick, then why expose him to it?"

He finished turning her around to face him. "Titus Oceanus is coming here after whoever's trying to kill his son, and I'm just making sure he still *has* a son when this is over."

"But if Mac is even more powerful than the drùidhs, then . . . wait. How do you know he's allergic to their magic?"

Trace grinned. "He told me." He shook his head. "Rule number one: Never tell anyone your weakness, because first chance they get, they'll use it against you."

"He thought you were his friend," she snapped, spinning away to go to Mac.

Trace caught her by the shoulders and hauled her backward against him. "I am his friend. And right now, I'm all that's stopping him from committing suicide in the name of *courage* and *dignity*. The idiot intended to go out there and meet those demons head-on, all by himself." He flexed his fingers on her arms. "So choose, Fiona; stay and help me keep him safe, or go to Kenzie's where I know *you'll* be safe."

He felt her go perfectly still. "I'm staying."

"Goddamn it, *why*?"

"Becau—"

He gave her a small shake. "Don't you dare say *because you can.*"

"I was going to say," she said quietly, "because it's obvious someone needs to stay here and keep you from committing suicide." She turned to face him when his hands slackened in surprise. "*Because,*" she continued a tad more forcefully, "there's no way I will ever be able to stuff all your precious belongings into your casket!"

She bolted then and was halfway up the mudroom stairs before Trace could even shake her again. He heard chuckling coming from the other side of the chamber and saw Mac, half propped up against the dirt wall, grinning like a sailor on shore leave.

"You think that's funny, you drunken idiot?" Trace took a step toward him. "If you care for her at all, you'll help me talk her into going to An Téarmann."

Mac tried to gesture but only managed to slap himself in the thigh. "You can't handle a mere slip of a woman long enough to carry her to Kenzie's if you have to?" He shot Trace an unfocused glare. "You didn't seem to have any trouble blindsiding me."

Trace folded his arms over his chest and relaxed back on his hips. "She's had her fill of men either telling her what to do or *forcing* her to do something."

Up went that brow—sort of.

"Whereas you," Trace continued, "have obviously needed a good punch in the face since you were twenty."

Mac heaved himself forward with a grunt and quickly rested his elbows on his knees in order to hold his head in his hands. "For the love of Zeus, Huntsman, you're killing me. At least move de Gairn's magic farther down the tunnel."

"Not a chance. If you're strong enough to laugh at me, I think you'll live."

"Why are you doing this?"

"Because I can."

Mac looked up. "This is my fight, not yours. I don't need your and Fiona's deaths on my soul."

"Sorry, but I guess that's what you get for protecting people's free will."

Mac dropped his head back in his hands with a groan.

Trace started to leave but hesitated. "While you're sitting here with nothing to do but figure out ways to get even with me, why don't you try being useful and think back to all Fiona went through in the eleventh century and come up with something to persuade her to give me a second chance?"

"I don't have to think back; I already know," Mac said as Trace started to turn away. The wizard looked up again, his bloodshot eyes heavy with . . . Christ, the man actually looked smug. "And you dare call me an idiot, when the answer is as plain as the nose on your face. What is the most important thing that was stolen from Fiona in the eleventh century?"

"I sure as hell can't give her back her virginity." He stiffened. "Or another child."

Mac dropped his head to his hands again. "Those bastards stole her value as a woman, Huntsman." He looked up. "Fiona is determined to do everything completely on her own now, from supporting herself to having children. And you know why? Because she feels she will never have value to anyone other than herself."

"For chrissakes, that's crazy!"

"It isn't if you're an eleventh-century woman," Mac said quietly. "You want Fiona to give you a second chance, you only need ask her to do you the honor of becoming your wife. And then don't bed her until *after* the wedding."

Trace stumbled back, groping for a wall to support him. "Are you serious?" He straightened, his hands balling into fists. "No, you're out of your friggin' mind!"

"I may be half dead, but I assure you, I still have enough of my faculties to know that you can't keep toying with her. If you truly care for Fiona, then either walk away and let her get on with her life, or find the courage to make her an equal and cherished partner in your life."

"She doesn't want anything to do with men, so how in hell would asking her to marry me be anything but an insult?"

"You of all people should know that Fiona's not liking men is merely a defense. Do you think she offered you her body the other day because she's *not* attracted to you?"

"She was just . . . experimenting."

"Yes; likely to prove to herself that *she* has the power to initiate sex rather than it being forced on her. And she honestly believes that men do desire her, only as a means to slake their lust but never as their wife. In Fiona's eleventh-century mind, a woman's value is in being cherished by her *husband*."

"Goddamn it, I don't ever intend to get married."

Mac leaned against the wall and closed his eyes. "Then walk away, Huntsman. Go crawl back into that dark, miserable place you've been hiding in most of your life, and stop trying to pull Fiona down there with you. Because I assure you, she intends to live the rest of her life in the light—be it with you or despite you."

Chapter Eighteen

Fiona sat on the top rail of the paddock fence, watching the dark, churning clouds building along the horizon out over the bay, and wondered if she was ever going to get the hang of living in this century. It seemed like everything about this time was so much more complicated, from all the different foods being sold in huge stores and all the technology that was supposed to help do chores but only created more work to a society that had as many rules as it did people.

Even the men were more complicated. A thousand years ago, all they had required was a full belly, occasional sex, and a good war to take out their aggressions on. But today, men apparently still wanted their basic needs met, only now they also wanted to stick their noses into women's affairs.

It was obvious Trace didn't know the first thing about preparing a decent meal, much less how to organize a kitchen, yet he got all prickly over a few moved items—and then apologized for being upset with her for moving them. And one minute he was pulling her into his arms and kissing her, making her believe he desired her, and the next he was turning all prickly again and running off. But then he shows up on her doorstep falling down drunk, and accuses her of trying to trick him into making a baby.

And then he apologizes yet again, and asks her not only to forgive him for being an ass but to give him a second chance.

She was getting friggin' tired of all his pulling and pushing.

How could she ever have thought she might be attracted to him? The man didn't even shave regularly, and she was fairly sure his hair hadn't seen scissors in almost a year. And he obviously didn't understand the difference between a dishwasher and a clothes washer, because, honest to God, she had found a pair of socks lying in the top rack next to the dirty cups and bowls. There was also the fact that he drank quite a bit of Scotch, which meant that he didn't even know a drunken warrior could easily be a dead one if his enemy caught him in such a state. And really, what could she possibly find attractive about someone who smelled of fish much of the time?

Just because he spent twelve grueling hours a day on a boat and didn't have anyone to wash his clothes for him didn't mean he had to be a walking bait bucket. And even when he was cleaned up and dressed in nice clothes, he was a little too tall and broad-shouldered and strong-looking, and a bit too handsome for her liking.

Because, really, what woman wanted anything to do with a handsome man who walked around with condoms in his wallet, hoping he'd get lucky?

No, she was better off having nothing to do with Trace Huntsman, even if she did find herself drawn to him. And now that she had a paying job, just as soon as this storm was over, she had to move to a new apartment before she not only forgave him but undressed for him again.

Fiona sighed. She'd just have to find a much less attractive man, she supposed, to see a condom actually being used.

Misneach suddenly stopped running through the tall marsh grass below and looked up, only Fiona realized the pup was actually watching Trace when she saw him come from behind the barn, looking as if he was searching for them.

She sighed again. It had been so much easier when he was working twelve-hour days, as it seemed she couldn't get away from him now.

He spotted Misneach first, and after scanning the marsh, he turned and finally saw her sitting on the fence. He walked over and hopped up onto the rail beside her. "It looks like the storm could reach us sometime after midnight," he said, staring out at the horizon. "Unless Mac's father manages to keep the battle out on the bay."

"I've seen at least two dozen whales in the half hour I've been sitting here." She pointed to their right. "There's another one. They seem to be swimming back and forth just offshore, like sentries."

"They probably are, sent by Titus to protect his son."

Fiona looked around the barnyard. "I miss the animals. I'm glad they're safe at An Téarmann, but without them here, the place feels rather empty."

"Yeah, I've gotten used to having them around, too." He

looked over at her. "I guess we never know how much we'll miss something until it's gone."

"I think I'll go fix something for Mac to eat," she said, setting her hands on the rail to jump down. "Maybe a full belly will make him feel less sick."

Trace stopped her by grabbing her arm. "Wait. I'd like to talk to you first."

He let her go when she settled back on the rail. "About Mac?"

"No," he said, looking out at the ocean. "About us."

"There is no us, Trace," she said, folding her hands on her lap so he wouldn't see them trembling. "You need to leave me alone."

He gave a humorless chuckle. "So I've been told."

"By who?" she asked in surprise.

"By Mac," he said, still staring out at the ocean. "But the more I try to stay away from you, the more I find I can't."

Fiona felt her heart start to pound—in dread, she decided, because she really didn't want it to be pounding in hope. "But why?"

The faintest grin tugged at the edge of his mouth when he looked over at her. "Because I happen to like women." His grin broadened, actually reaching his eyes. "And you in particular."

"But *why*?"

"I think partly because you're smarter than I am."

She leaned away. "I am not."

"Sure you are," he said, looking back out at the ocean. "Not only do you seem to know what you want but you go after it with hell-bent determination and courage. Whereas I've spent my entire life focused on avoiding what I *don't* want. I've only recently realized that I've always been afraid to have dreams, probably because I've always figured why get all excited about something just to have it taken away from me."

He shifted on the rail toward her and took her hand in his. "But then you showed up, and I watched you change from a frightened, confused, almost childlike mouse into a woman every damned last red-blooded twenty-first-century man would give his right arm just to date. I swear you grew more and more beautiful with each passing day."

Fiona's heart started pounding so hard she was afraid he would hear it.

He looked down at her hand clasped in his. "And I remember thinking," he continued quietly, "that if I could just get close enough to you, then maybe some of your courage would rub off on me." His hand tightened around hers. "Only every time I caught myself believing it might actually work, I'd get scared and turn into an ass." He looked her directly in the eyes. "Because I kept feeling things for you that I had no business feeling."

He dropped his gaze again and ran his thumb over the back of her hand. "I swear, you have more courage in your little finger than I have in my entire body. How do you do it?" he asked, looking up. "How do you go after what you want so courageously? Tell me," he said, squeezing her hand again when she didn't immediately answer.

"I'm not brave," she softly admitted. "I'm really afraid that if I ever stop dreaming, I won't even get out of bed." She leaned toward him. "You want to know a secret? I discovered that a person can't will herself to go to sleep and never wake up. I tried for nearly two whole months, but

I couldn't make it happen. And then I realized I was with child, and I started praying to God to please let me wake up every morning."

"But why?" he whispered. "If you and your son had lived, weren't you afraid the two of you would have known nothing but hardship?"

"No, Kyle was my salvation. Each new generation is another chance to get it right, Trace, and that's why we always have to keep trying. Just because my dreams weren't coming true exactly the way I'd imagined they would, it didn't mean my son's dreams wouldn't. I intended to give Kyle the best chance at a good life that I could, and in doing so, I would have been living my own dream." She gave him a lopsided smile. "I died, remember? And that's when I discovered that life isn't about reaching our goals; it's about having them to begin with and then going after them every day. And now Mac has given me another chance to make some of my dreams come true."

"Just some of them?"

She looked down at their clasped hands. "I'm willing to settle for the ones most important to me. In fact, I've already achieved several of them. I'm living in a village now and have women friends, and I've found a way to earn a living by doing something I love. And someday I will have children of my own."

"But not a husband?" he quietly asked. "Was getting married ever one of your childhood dreams?"

She looked up, smiling crookedly again. "It was until I was old enough to realize that husbands are more trouble than they're worth."

He didn't return her smile, but he did pull his hand

away. "So are you saying that if some man here in the twenty-first century—say, some guy you might actually be able to *like*—were to ask you to marry him, you'd say no?"

"Yes, I would probably say no."

"A flat-out no without even thinking about it? You wouldn't even take a couple of days or weeks to even *consider* his proposal?"

Wondering at the edge creeping into his voice, Fiona gave him a tight smile. "I believe that's the best thing about this century. I can have a child without it being ostracized for being born out of wedlock, which means I won't have to put up with a husband bossing me around in order to achieve my dreams."

"Husbands and wives are equal partners today, so nobody's bossing anybody around," he growled. "Marriage is about *teamwork*."

She snorted. "Tell that to Winter and Eve. When I lived with them, those poor women spent half their time trying to avoid an argument and the other half figuring out ways to make their husbands believe everything was *their* idea."

"They're married to eleventh-century men!" he snapped. He took a deep breath, apparently to calm himself, although she didn't know why he was getting so riled up to begin with. "Look," he continued quietly. "My mother remarried, and she's the happiest woman on the planet right now. She *loves* being married."

"Is her husband a warrior?"

"What? No. What's that got to do with anything?" he asked, the edge creeping back into his voice.

"I don't care what century it is; warriors give orders and expect to be obeyed, and they don't leave that habit on the battlefield." She beamed him a smile, hoping to soothe whatever had gotten him so riled. "I'm really glad your mother found someone who obviously cherishes her the way your stepfather must. But few marriages are love matches, even today. Oh, they start out lovely," she said, waving at nothing, "but a majority of them turn nasty, and the men and women stay together for the sake of the children while having affairs with other people, and before you know it, everyone ends up either drinking too much or taking medicine to dull their heartache."

He blinked at her, and then his face suddenly darkened. "For chrissakes, those are soap operas! They're not *real*."

She gripped the fence rail to keep from falling when she leaned away and kicked her smile up another notch. "I am aware the stories are exaggerated to make them interesting." She sighed. "Why are we having this conversation, Trace? What does it matter that I don't want to get married?" She tried smiling at him again, feeling more like Eve and Winter than she cared to admit. "You have my word of honor; I will not drag home innocent men all hours of the day and night."

He suddenly jumped down off the fence, grasped her waist, and lifted her down, then started leading her toward his truck.

"I'm not going to An Téarmann," she hissed, clawing at his hand.

He pulled her off-balance with a muttered curse, forcing her to grasp his sleeve to keep from falling. "I'm not taking you anywhere. I'm giving you a shooting lesson."

"Is there a reason you can't *ask* me to go with you instead of dragging me around like a recalcitrant child?"

He finally let go of her to open his truck door. "Is that an eleventh-century word?" he asked, reaching in to his seat. "Because in this century, we just call them brats. Here," he said, shoving a belted pouch at her. "Put this on. And you keep it on until I tell you to take it off."

She nearly dropped it, she was so surprised by its weight. But then he grabbed it away from her when she merely looked at it, too late realizing that it was just like the gun sheath he was wearing on his own thigh.

She immediately snatched it back. "No, I want it," she said, unbuttoning her coat one-handed as she held the gun out of his reach. She contorted out of the coat and let it fall to the ground, so excited that she started undoing the sheath's buckle before her arm was even out of her sleeve.

"You've got it upside down," he said, taking it from her again. "Wait. Are you right- or left-handed, so I know which leg to strap the holster to?"

She held up her right hand.

"Okay. Good," he said, crouching to sit on his heels. He reached around her to put the belt around her waist, and she heard the buckle close with a soft snap. But then she had to grab the belt when it started sliding down her hips from the weight of the gun. "Hold it up while I adjust it," he said, placing it at her waistline.

"Make it tight, so it doesn't pull down my pants," she told him as she bent over and lifted the holster. "This gun looks smaller than the one you're wearing. Why can't I have one just like yours?"

He pulled the holster out of her hand and let it fall back to her thigh. "Trust me, it's big enough to knock you on your bottom. It's a semiautomatic pistol, with nine bullets.

Spread your legs," he said, sliding his hand between her knees.

Fiona did as he instructed but then went perfectly still, looking toward the house so he wouldn't see the heat climbing into her cheeks. She felt him wrap a strap around her thigh just above her knee and then felt his hand slowly move up her leg.

"Open wider," he said thickly.

"Let me do it," she said as she bent over and shoved his hand away. "I need to know how to put it on for when I go to the . . . bathroom," she ended on a whisper.

She spun away to hide her blush as she fumbled with the straps—which didn't seem to have a buckle—only her hip smacked into Trace, sending him backward to land sprawled in the snow.

"Will you calm down!"

"There aren't any buckles on this strap," she muttered just as the two ends suddenly stuck to each other. "Oh, nice," she said, lifting the flap on the holster. She pulled out the gun and straightened. "Do I just pull the trigger on this one, too, or do I have to push one of these buttons?"

"For chrissakes!" he yelped, jumping up and grabbing her arm to spin her toward the woods. "You need to treat every gun as if it's loaded."

"But I didn't have my finger on the trigger, see?" she said, lifting her hand to show him, even though he was still gripping her arm. "Can I shoot it? I want to see the bullet hit something," she said, looking around. "Does it explode whatever it hits?"

She heard him take another deep breath. "You're really scary, you know that?"

"There," she said, pointing at the fallen maple tree on the front lawn. "That stump looks just like one of those bastard demons," she said, pointing the gun at it.

"Will you hold on," Trace growled, wrapping his arms around her from behind and grabbing her wrists. "It's not loaded."

She frowned up at him. "Then what did you get all excited about?"

"Because you always need to *treat* a gun as if it's loaded. Now, pay attention while I show you how it works. First, you have to slide a bullet into the chamber."

He wrapped his fingers over her hand holding the gun and used his other hand to push a button on the side. Fiona gasped when something fell out of the bottom of the handle, and she tried to catch it.

Only Trace beat her to it. "This is the magazine, or clip, and it holds nine bullets. That means you can have a total of ten shots if you keep one in the chamber, which is right here," he said, touching the top of the gun.

"Then why isn't there one in it?"

"Because even though the gun has a safety," he said, pointing to another button on the side, "it's actually safer to keep only the clip loaded. That way, if a kid gets hold of the gun, he can't just pull the trigger and fire it."

"That's wise," she said, looking over her shoulder to smile at him.

"Turn around and watch what I'm doing," he said, nudging her again. "You slide the clip up in the handle like this. Listen," he said, pushing on it firmly. "Hear that click? That means it's fully seated." He readjusted her grip, then took hold of the top of the gun and pulled it back toward her, although by the way the handle dug into her hand, she could see that he had to use a lot of pressure.

"I think I prefer the revolver," she said, frowning, "because I don't want to have to do that every time. No, wait. You just pulled the trigger on yours the other day."

"That's what makes this a semiautomatic," he said. "Once you've loaded the chamber, every time you pull the trigger, it fires, until the clip is empty. And you'll know it's empty because the slide will stay cocked back."

"But I watched you firing at the demons the other day, and you just pulled the trigger once and held it back."

"Yeah, I modified mine to do that."

"I want mine to do that, too. It will be quicker."

He nudged her to face forward again. "No, for you, it would be really, really dangerous," he drawled. "And there's also the fact that fully automatic guns are illegal."

"Why?"

"Because they're really, really dangerous," he growled. He pulled the gun out of her hand and stepped away. "I'm going to shoot a couple of rounds at the stump first, and I want you to watch the gun, not the tree, okay? Plug your ears."

"Wait. I saw parts of the bullets shoot out the side of your gun the other day."

"Those are the empty shells that hold the powder. Trust me, the bullets went out the barrel. Plug your ears."

"Wait. Won't we scare the townspeople? It was quite deafening in the room."

He looked over at her and sighed. "Nobody around here's going to get worried about a couple of gunshots. Any more questions?" he growled.

She mutely shook her head, stifling her smile.

"Okay, plug your ears and watch," he said, holding the gun out in both hands.

She saw his thumb flip the little button on the side and realized she'd have to remember to push the correct button so she didn't end up popping the clip out instead. She stuck her fingers in her ears but still jumped when the gun went off, then flinched again when he shot a second time almost immediately.

He suddenly popped the clip out while still pointing at the tree, pulled the trigger a third time—just as she dropped her hands because she thought he was done—and made her jump again in surprise as her ears rang painfully.

"Okay, now, watch this," he said, still pointing toward the tree. "See how the slide stays back because the gun's empty? There are two more full clips on your holster, so when you've fired all your rounds, you just pop out the empty clip and slide in a new one. But remember to make it click," he reminded her as he pushed the clip back in the handle. "And here, you push down on this button with your thumb, and you're back in business."

The slide slammed forward rather violently, and she saw Trace push the safety back on. She reached out for the gun, but he pulled it back.

"No, I want you to load it yourself," he said, dropping the clip out and then pulling the slide so that the bullet popped out of the chamber. He pushed the bullet down into the top of the clip, handed it to her, and *then* handed her the empty gun.

"I still believe I prefer the revolver," she said, staring at the two items in her hands. She looked up at him. "Because honestly? If the demons are chasing me, I don't think I'll have time to remember which buttons to push in what order."

He stared at her for what seemed like forever, and she could tell by how his eyes darkened that he was probably picturing the demons chasing her.

So she smiled. "Then again," she said, shoving the clip into the handle, making sure she heard it click, "nine shots are better than six, and I prefer not to blow my leg off in the meantime." She had to stiffen her right arm and point the gun toward the ground in order to pull the contrary slide back, but when she let it go, she was fairly certain there was a bullet in the chamber. She held the gun out in both hands, making sure the skin between her thumb and finger wasn't in the way, and slipped off the safety and aimed at the tree.

"You need to line the notch in the rear sights up with the white bead on the front of the barrel," he said, bending down behind her. He reached around and held her arms to lift the gun, tucking his head against her ear. "See where my bullet hit the tree? Line the sights up so it's right behind that front bead, and then slowly pull the trigger."

"I won't have time to line them up if I'm being chased," she said, finding it difficult to line up the white dot, probably because his being so close was distracting her.

And he certainly didn't smell like fish today.

"You have to aim only if your target's at a distance. Within ten paces, just point and shoot. But if your target doesn't know you're there, you can take the time to aim for a vital spot." He stepped away and plugged his ears. "Okay. Fire two shots, then put the safety back on before you lower the gun. Just remember, it's going to pack a hell of a wallop, so be prepared. No, wait!" he said.

Fiona clicked the safety back on, still holding the gun aimed at the tree, and turned to see him sit down in the snow and pat his legs as he looked toward the barn. "Come on, Misneach," he called excitedly, slapping his legs again. "Come, boy!"

"No, don't bring him here. The noise will scare him."

"Naw. He must have come up from the marsh when he heard my shots, so he can't be gun-shy. I was afraid all that gunfire the other day had ruined him for life. I'll cover his ears so it won't be too loud. Hey, Misneach, you're not afraid of a little noise, are you, you big demon fighter?" he said when the pup barreled into him. Trace turned Misneach around and tucked him up against his chest, and covered the pup's ears with his hands and smiled up at Fiona. "Okay, you can kill your demon tree now, and then go give Mac some lunch while I have one last look around."

She turned and lined up the front bead on the gun with the hole Trace had made and pulled the trigger—but nothing happened.

"Safety's on," he said with a chuckle.

Fiona slid it off with her thumb, aimed, pulled the trigger, and stumbled backward several steps when the gun discharged, giving a yelp of surprise when her right hand felt like she'd just been stung by a swarm of bees.

"Again," Trace said with a laugh. "Then, while still aiming, drop the clip out and shoot it a third time."

She braced herself and fired, dropped the clip and fired again, and with her ears ringing and her entire arm numb but for the thousand needles sticking into it, she lowered the gun and turned to him, smiling broadly. "Can I buy this pistol from you after the battle? And the holster and the extra clips?"

"Absolutely, unequivocally, *no*," he said as he scrambled to his feet—though he was laughing. He took the gun from her and closed the slide, then picked the clip up off the ground. "But maybe after a month of lessons, I'll consider giving it to you as a gift."

Fiona felt heat creeping into her cheeks again. "I believe I prefer to buy it from you," she whispered, spinning away when she saw the laughter leave his eyes. She walked to the tree stump, wanting to kick herself when she realized she'd just hurt his feelings. "Not that I don't appreciate your offer," she said without looking back. "But really, teaching me how to shoot it is gift enough. Oh no!" she cried when she reached the tree. "I didn't hit it even once."

"That's because you closed your eyes each time you pulled the trigger," he said, coming up behind her. She saw him reach into his pocket, pull out some bullets, and push them one at a time into the clip. "You need to keep *both* eyes open. Here, put this in your holster, and sleep with that gun on your hip until this is over."

"I'm sorry," she whispered, sliding the gun into her holster. "I . . . you . . . I don't want to be—"

"Forget it," he said, spinning away. "You'd better go check on Mac."

Fiona stared at his back as he walked away, wondering if *she* wasn't an ass. The man might be pushing at her one minute and pulling her the next, but he'd confessed that it was because he was scared.

She walked over and picked up her coat, and started

toward the house. The only thing was, she didn't know what Trace Huntsman was scared of, exactly.

Not her, surely. Although he'd admitted to having feelings for her, he'd also admitted that he didn't particularly *like* that he had them. And it certainly couldn't be that she was a woman, because he'd also admitted that he liked women in general.

He was so different from any other man she'd ever met, including her brothers. Trace was a warrior, but any warrior she'd ever known simply saw something he wanted and took it, usually by brute strength, whereas Trace seemed to prefer to . . . coax whatever he desired to come to him.

Like the first time he'd kissed her; she'd expected him to overwhelm her, but after initiating the kiss, he had simply waited for her reaction. And the second time, he'd asked her either to kiss him or slap his face, as if he hoped *she* would make up his mind for him. She blew out a sigh as she walked onto the porch. Trace wasn't just the most interesting man she'd ever met; he was also the most confounding.

She stopped with her hand on the doorknob when she heard Misneach barking frantically, sounding as if he was running down the path to the marsh. She spun around and ran to the end of the paddock, stopping when a gust of moist, frigid wind nearly knocked her over. Grabbing the fence post for support, she saw Trace running down the bluff behind the house through the snow, trying to intercept the dog.

She could see the waves crashing against the shore, sending spray high into the air. And on the swelling waves, for as far as she could see, were dozens of huge whales swimming back and forth, with hundreds of what looked like dolphins weaving in and out among them, their incessant chattering carried inland on the wind.

She started down the path, Misneach's footprints in the snow making it easier for her than Trace, as he was having to wade through drifts that came up to his thighs.

"Misneach!" she heard him shouting. "Come on, boy! Come back!"

The daylight was fading, but Fiona couldn't tell if it was from the storm clouds moving closer to shore or merely dusk descending.

Trace broke onto the path several paces in front of her, still calling to Misneach, and Fiona realized he didn't know she was there. The young dog didn't even slow down when he reached the rocky beach and barreled right into the crashing surf.

"Misneach!" she cried, coming to an abrupt halt when Trace spun around in surprise and caught her.

"No, you can't go in after him," he growled.

"But what's he after?"

"There!" Trace said, pointing at the waves a short distance away. He let go of her and pulled his gun out of his holster but grabbed her arm to stop her when she started to pull out her own gun. "No, I need you to keep your hands free," he said as he pulled her along the beach to follow Misneach. "There," he said, pointing with his gun. "He seems to be going after something that's floating in on the waves."

She clutched his arm as she strained to see. "Is it a body?" she asked, having to speak loudly against the raging wind.

"No, it looks like a fancy stick or . . . shit, it looks like some sort of wizard's staff. Misneach!" he shouted. "Get back here!"

When the young dog just kept swimming, Trace fired two shots in the air—to get the pup's attention, she assumed.

"Goddamn it, get back here!" he shouted, walking farther down the rocky beach, pulling Fiona out of the way when a wave splashed over a rock beside them.

"He's got it!" she cried. "He's bringing it in."

Trace held her back when she started down the beach to intercept Misneach. "Don't touch it, okay?" he said. "It might be a trick."

A large whale came unbelievably close to shore, swimming very fast, causing a wave to swell behind Misneach, who was struggling to keep his head above water because of the weight of the stick.

"The whale's helping him," she said when the wave pushed the pup in to shore.

Misneach waded onto the beach sideways, dragging the long stick right up to them. He dropped it, gagged, and spit up with hacking coughs, then shook all over to shed his coat of seawater. He stood with his legs splayed, staring up at them, his tongue hanging out of his mouth and his chest heaving with his ragged pants.

"Can I at least pick Misneach up?" she asked over the wind and the loud chattering of the whales and dolphins.

"He'll catch his breath easier if you don't. What do you think it is?"

"I believe you're right; it looks like a drùidh's staff to me. Papa drew me a picture of a sword once, claiming he had one hidden in a cave that had belonged to his father, and it had jewels on it just like this does. I believe Matt has it now, only he turned it into a pen so it wouldn't be conspicuous in this century." She shrugged. "Drùidhs turn their staffs into all sorts of different things. Father Daar, the priest who lives with Kenzie and Eve, used to have a crooked old cherry-wood cane."

Still keeping his gun pointing in the general direction of the staff, Trace looked out at the bay and then back down at it. He bent and picked up a rock the size of his fist and tossed it, striking the jeweled stick. When nothing happened, he stepped closer, motioning for Fiona to stay back, and touched it with his foot.

And still nothing happened.

"Do you suppose Mac's father sent it?" she asked. "Maybe it's to help us protect him or for us to give to him so he can protect himself."

"Or whoever's trying to kill Mac sent it, and the moment he touches it, he's dead."

When they both just stared down at it, Misneach clawed the stick with his paw. He stopped and looked at them, then used his nose to push it toward Trace's foot.

"He seems to think we should pick it up," Fiona said. "But I wonder how he knew it was floating in the sea to begin with?"

Trace looked out at the ocean and shrugged. "Maybe he speaks whale."

"Then I wish he spoke English, too, so he could tell us what they told him," she said, smiling when Trace looked at her. "Let me pick it up and see what happens."

"No," he said, glaring at her. "I'll pick it up."

She grabbed his arm when he started to bend over. "And if something happens to you?" she asked when he straightened. "Then who's going to protect Mac?"

His glare instantly disappeared, and he touched his finger to her chest just below her neck. "You are, Miss Calamity Jane."

She grabbed his finger. "And just who is Calamity Jane?" she growled.

He laughed, snatching his hand away. "A feisty cowgirl who had a thing for guns. I'll rent you the movie one of these days, and we'll watch it on my big new television." He turned, bent down, and picked up the staff before she could stop him, stepping away as he straightened. "It's really quite heavy," he said, hefting it in his hand as he studied it. "I can't believe it was floating."

Misneach started whining, rising on his hind feet and pawing at Trace's thigh.

"He's shivering," Fiona said, trying to pick him up.

The pup scooted behind Trace, and when she reached around to get him, he ran a couple of feet away. Then, when she straightened, he ran back to Trace and started pawing at him again and whining.

Trace slid his gun into his holster and scooped Misneach up in his arm.

"I can carry the staff," she said, holding out her hand. "Are we going to give it to Mac?" she asked when he hesitated.

He turned the staff over, studying it again, and then looked at her. "I don't know. Maybe I'll leave it outside, and we can describe it to him and see what he thinks."

He tried handing Misneach to her, but the pup struggled to stay with him.

Fiona unbuttoned her coat, grabbed the dog, and immediately shoved him inside and buttoned him in.

"I can see Getze's kids aren't going to give you any grief," Trace said, nodding approval. "Let's get going. It's getting dark and starting to snow again."

They hadn't made it halfway down the beach when Trace suddenly tripped and fell. He sat up with a muttered curse, glaring at the jeweled stick lying in the snow. "I swear the damned thing tripped me," he said, getting to his feet. He picked up the staff again and started walking toward the path they had made getting down here.

Misneach had finally settled down, and Fiona felt him shivering only occasionally, although now *she* was starting to shiver as he was soaking her chest and belly. Still, she couldn't help but smile, her arms wrapped securely around him over her coat.

"What are you smiling at?" Trace helped her up over the incline where the beach stopped and the tall grass started. "You think it's funny that I fell?"

"No," she said, rubbing a hand down over the lump sticking out in front of her. "I was just remembering how it felt to be carrying Kyle inside me." She laughed outright. "I waddled like a duck the entire way home the last three weeks that I carried him."

He started to smile but then sobered. "You can laugh at the hardships you faced?" he asked quietly, wrapping an arm around her as they trudged through the snow. "Lean into me to keep your balance."

She laughed again. "I certainly could have used you a thousand years ago. I swear, I walked halfway across Scotland."

"How in hell can you laugh about it?"

"Because for those few weeks, I was as free as the hawk I eventually became. I was so looking forward to having my child, wondering if it was a boy or a girl, and anxious to get home to Papa." She smiled up at him again. "It was hard, Trace, but I think it was the most alive I'd ever been."

He stopped in mid-step, looked down at her protruding coat, and then lifted his gaze to hers, his eyes dark with some emotion she couldn't quite read.

"I would have carried you across Scotland if I'd been there," he said quietly, "and then called your son my own."

"You'd have been a wonderful father to him," she whispered.

He wrapped his other arm around her and leaned over Misneach, and Fiona couldn't stop herself from stretching up to meet him. But before his lips actually touched hers, a powerful vibration shot up the length of her back just as a loud hum filled the air.

Trace tried rearing away, but the staff seemed to be stuck to her, just the way those nails had clung to the magnet he'd given her to use.

"Let it go!" she cried, shoving at him. "Get away!"

"I can't pull it off!" he snapped, tightening his arms around her. "Hang on to me!"

Misneach yelped, popping his head out of her coat just as a blinding light suddenly engulfed them. Fiona balled her hands into Trace's jacket, trying to hold on to him as his arms tightened around her. The humming became deafening, sounding like it was coming from the whales behind her.

"Fiona! Where are you? Where in hell did you go?"

What was he saying? She was right here. He was holding her, squeezing her so tight she could hardly breathe.

"Goddamn it! Fiona! Where'd you go?"

It wasn't until she could see him standing below her in the tall grass, his gun held straight out in his hands as he spun around looking for her, that Fiona realized what she'd thought were his arms around her was really the contorted staff dragging her out over the ocean.

Couldn't he see her? She was right here, dammit, being carried away!

She twisted and squirmed, trying to break free, but the more she struggled the tighter the staff squeezed her. She screamed Trace's name but couldn't even hear her own voice, only Misneach's soft whimpers as he licked her chin.

"Fiona! Come back! Fiona, where the hell are you?"

His shouts faded to nothing as she continued moving farther out to sea, a halo of brilliant light protecting her from the storm. And then Fiona screamed again when she suddenly plunged into the ocean, and everything went dark and eerily silent.

Chapter Nineteen

Trace gave Mac's feet a kick. "Get up, Oceanus." He kicked him again when Mac only groaned. "Come on, wake the hell up." He started to reach down and haul him up, but quickly stepped back when Mac finally rolled over and he saw the wizard had changed into the beast—only sort of a pasty green.

"Leave me to die in peace, Huntsman," Mac rasped, trying to roll away.

Trace hauled him into a sitting position. "You can die after you help me get Fiona back."

"I can't do anything in this condition," Mac groaned, holding his ugly head in his hands. He looked up, his bloodshot eyes blinking against the light coming from the tunnel. "Kenzie has every right to take Fiona to An Téarmann, whereas you have *no* rights over her."

Trace hauled Mac to his feet, then shoved him against the wall to keep him standing. "Kenzie didn't take her; your enemies did."

"What?" Mac straightened in surprise. "The battle's moved over land?"

"No, a fancy stick washed ashore. When I picked it up nothing happened, but the moment it touched Fiona, it stuck to her like a magnet, and I couldn't pull it off. And then she suddenly vanished into thin air, along with Misneach." Trace grabbed his sleeve. "Come on. We need to go get her. Now."

Mac pulled away, stumbling farther down the wall. "Go where, exactly? You said she vanished into thin air."

"All the action's taking place out on the bay, so we start looking there."

"How?"

"In my boat."

Mac straightened, swaying drunkenly. "Then get rid of de Gairn's magic, or I won't be any help to you."

"So you can vanish on me, too?"

"I love Fiona as much as you do. Like a *sister*," Mac snapped when Trace glared at him. He waved toward the tunnel. "Get rid of the magic."

"Yeah, about that; I don't exactly know how," Trace muttered, frowning at the intense light. "Kenzie zapped the walls with some sort of fancy pen, and they started glowing like that. But then he took the pen home with him."

"Sweet Neptune, you're an ass," Mac hissed, leaning over to brace his hands on his knees. "Wait," he said, looking up to scan the chamber. "You always have a second way out."

"*I do,* but not you. I had Kenzie wrap the entire room in light."

Mac dropped his head to stare at the floor. "I take back my suggestion that you ask Fiona to marry you; she deserves better."

"She sure as hell didn't deserve to be kidnapped. Come on, we're wasting time," Trace said, grabbing Mac's arm.

Mac flung himself free and lurched away again. "I won't be any help if I cross that light, because I'll be dead." He braced his hands on his knees again. "Tell me what the stick you found looked like."

"It was as long as I am tall, with a bunch of cut stones surrounding a ball carved in it about a quarter of the way down. It was heavy but floated on the waves. Misneach swam out and got it, only one of the whales had to help him get back to shore."

Mac's head snapped up. "The whale? He's still here?"

"I don't know if it's the same one or not. There've been dozens of whales swimming back and forth out front all afternoon, as well as hundreds of dolphins." He shrugged. "I thought your father had sent them to protect you, but after that stick made Fiona vanish, I figure they were sent by whoever's trying to kill you."

"But you said the staff did nothing until it touched her." Mac shook his head. "There's no reason for my father to take Fiona." He looked directly at Trace. "Unless he's planning to use her to force you to let me go."

"Then he's about to get his wish," Trace said, driving his shoulder into Mac's gut.

He straightened with Mac flung over his back and, ignoring the wizard's shout of protest, ran into the blinding light of the tunnel. Mac let out a painful roar, but Trace turned and ran up the stairs without even breaking stride, and heaved him into the mudroom as he fell to his knees.

He got up and dragged Mac into the kitchen, then ran back and shut the wall of the closet, then the closet door, and then the door separating the mudroom from the house. Mac lay motionless, curled up in a fetal position, moaning. Trace walked over to the sink, filled the coffee carafe with water, and threw it on him.

"I hope you rot in hell," Mac snarled, rolling away to curl back into a ball.

"We'll keep each other company, then," he said, filling the carafe again. But when he turned to throw it, Mac was up on his hands and knees.

"Give me a minute to get my bearings!"

"We don't have a minute." He set the carafe on the counter, hauled Mac to his feet and hooked the wizard's arm over his shoulder, then dragged him out the door.

"How in hell do you think to find her?" Mac asked, lurching upright when the blowing snow hit his face. "It's a big ocean, and right now it's the site of a fierce battle."

"I figure if your father took her to trade, one of your buddies will swim out and tell him where you are," Trace said, heading toward his truck. "And if your enemies took her, they'll find us quick enough."

Mac pulled them to a halt. "The ocean's that way," he said, waving at the bay.

"But my boat is moored in the harbor."

Mac blinked at him, and Trace leaned away. Christ, the guy was scary ugly.

"It will be quicker if my friend takes us to my father."

Trace scrambled away. "Your *friend*? You think I'm going to . . . that we're . . . for chrissakes, I'm not riding on a whale!"

"Not *on* it, Huntsman, *in* it." Mac lifted what barely passed as a brow on his ugly face. "Surely you've heard the story of Jonah and the whale." He swayed on his feet as he held his arms apart. "They have really big bellies, which are quite warm and cozy."

Trace caught one of Mac's outstretched arms and dragged him to his truck. "We go in my boat or I'm tossing you back in that tunnel and leaving you there." He shoved him in the passenger's side and ran around and climbed in behind the wheel. The truck was already running, since he'd started it and turned on the heater when he'd brought out his back-pack and a couple more weapons before he'd gone after Mac. "Here," he said, shoving a jacket at him before pulling the gearshift into reverse. "Put that on. I don't want you dying of pneumonia before I hand you over."

"Maybe you should try *asking* people to do something instead of dragging them around and snapping orders at them," Mac muttered, leaning forward to put on the coat.

"So I've been told." Trace backed out to the road and sped toward town, his gut clenching at the thought of Fiona out there alone, probably scared out of her mind.

Until he remembered she was wearing a gun. He turned onto the harbor road without even slowing down, slam-ming Mac up against the door. "Christ, I wouldn't put it past her to shoot your father. And if she's with your en-emies . . ." He shuddered, unable to complete the thought.

"She's *armed*?" Mac yelped, looking over at him. "With a gun?"

"You mean, as opposed to a frying pan?" Trace drove directly onto the pier and stopped next to the ramp leading down to the floating docks. Only instead of getting out, he stared at his boat riding on swells being pushed into the harbor by huge waves rolling in from the point. "It looks like we're in for one hell of a ride," he said quietly, glancing over at Mac. "Hey, you're starting to look . . . less ugly." He eyed him suspiciously. "You getting your strength back?"

"Not quickly enough to save our asses if you insist on doing this your way."

"As opposed to yours?" He snorted. "I realize there might actually be something to this magic thing, but I draw the line at becoming some whale's dinner."

Mac glared at him. "At least my way you won't die of hypothermia within twenty minutes of our capsizing."

"You mean *we* won't die."

"Atlanteans can't drown; we have ocean water in our veins." Up went that brow again. "So now which one of us seems determined to commit suicide?"

Trace opened his door, grabbed his backpack and slipped it over his shoulders, and, tucking his head against the blowing snow, he headed down the ramp.

"Have you ever trusted anyone, Trace?" Mac asked when they reached the dock.

He untied his dinghy and shoved it into the water. "I trusted the bastard I asked to keep an eye on Elena when I went out on a mission." He held the small boat while Mac got in the front then climbed in after him, sat down with his back to Mac, and picked up the oars. "And we both know how that turned out, don't we?"

"Are you certain it was your friend who betrayed you, and not Elena?"

Trace strained into the oars to row toward his boat, having to fight the gale-force wind as well as the swells. "Jon made promises to her that he had no intention of keeping."

"And when Elena found herself in a . . . lovers' triangle,

you don't suppose she realized she could lose *both* chances to go to America when you returned and found out she'd seduced your friend?" Trace felt Mac lean closer. "And did you never consider that she may have confronted Jon and threatened to claim that he'd raped her if he didn't help her get to America?"

"That's the story he spewed the whole time I was beating the hell out of him," Trace said, elbowing Mac on the pretense of rowing harder. "I guess we'll never hear Elena's version, will we?"

"Do you care to hear my version, Huntsman?"

"No."

"Elena told Jon she was going to tell your commanding officer that both of you had seduced her with promises of taking her to America. She also intended to claim that she was pregnant and that she didn't know which one of you was the father."

Trace stopped rowing and spun on his seat. "Was she?"

"No," Mac said, shaking his head. "But your friend believed her, and when he confronted Elena, she ran into the night." Mac leaned toward him again. "Jon didn't drive her toward that minefield deliberately, Trace, as you believe; he was trying to stop her when he realized the danger." Mac straightened. "The only thing Jonathan Payne is guilty of is having bad judgment when it comes to women."

"Then, according to your version, I'm guilty of the same thing."

Mac merely lifted a brow, saying nothing.

Trace turned and started rowing again, trying to decide if Mac wasn't just pushing his buttons to get even for his using Matt's magic against him. Then again, Jon *could* be innocent, and Elena *could* have duped them both. Trace snorted. It wouldn't have been the first time a woman had used her body to get him to do something.

"If what you're saying is true, Jon's serving time for a crime he didn't commit."

"Would your military court believe an eyewitness?"

"The base police questioned everyone who might have seen or heard anything. And by the time Jon got out of the hospital and could tell his side of what happened, public sentiment was already against him—a good deal of it fueled by Elena's family."

"And by you," Mac said evenly.

"And me."

"If we don't die today, Huntsman, I'll produce a witness to exonerate your friend."

They bumped into Trace's boat, and he grabbed the gunwale and held the dinghy steady as both vessels rose and fell with the swells. He turned on his seat to look at Mac. "You can do that?"

"If we survive the day." He smiled tightly. "If we don't, I'm afraid Jon's plight is on your soul, not mine."

Mac was nearly back to his old self again, although Trace wasn't quite sure if he looked exactly the same. He'd met the man on three different occasions, and the wizard had appeared different each of those times.

Except for his eyes, which were always a sharp, vivid green.

"Climb in," Trace said, nodding at the boat. He climbed aboard right behind him, letting the dinghy drift off, and immediately started the engine.

"You forgot your extra guns in the truck," Mac said,

dropping onto a coil of rope with a groan to lean against the wheelhouse.

"I decided I don't need them. How are you feeling?"

"A bit better, thank you. Why?"

Trace waved his index finger in a circle. "Can you unhook us from the mooring so I don't have to go up front and do it?"

"You really don't trust me, do you? You think I'm faking."

"I'll trust you just as soon as I get Fiona back."

Mac waved his finger in the air. "Let's go."

Trace set his hand on the throttle, hesitating just long enough to make sure they were drifting away from the mooring, but when he looked at Mac he could see that the little magic trick had cost the wizard. He slowly eased the throttle forward and guided them through the maze of moored boats, all the time eyeing the rough seas ahead.

Oh, yeah, they were in for one hell of a ride.

"You know, Huntsman," Mac said, stretching his legs out as he settled back against the wheelhouse. "I believe if you are truthful with yourself, you'll admit that your gut was telling you something wasn't quite right with Elena. Why else would you have asked Jon to keep an eye on her while you were gone?"

"Because I didn't know if my mission was going to take a week or a month." He felt heat creep up his neck. "And she told me her brother had pledged her to some warlord, and I didn't want to come back and find he'd married her off."

Christ, he really was a gullible chump, wasn't he?

"So is that why you panicked when I suggested that you ask Fiona to marry you, because you're incapable of trusting a woman? Even one you admire for her strength and independence?"

Trace glared at him. "For your information, I *did* ask her, and she said no."

"You asked Fiona to do you the honor of being your wife?"

"Well . . . not exactly. I asked if some guy here in the twenty-first century were to ask her to marry him, if she would. And she gave me a flat-out no." He snorted. "Because, she said, husbands are more trouble than they're worth."

Mac just gaped at him. "You are such an ass."

"Have you even once considered that maybe Fiona really doesn't want to get married?" Trace asked, spreading his stance when the boat rolled with the growing swells as they neared the point.

"All women want to get married," Mac snapped as he was thrown off the rope.

"Apparently not badly enough to marry you. Hang on!" Trace shouted, shoving the throttle forward. The boat lurched into the open bay, sending spray crashing over the wheelhouse as the bow slammed into waves he estimated were ten to twelve feet high—which was way bigger than any he'd ever been out in before.

"For the love of Zeus!" Mac roared, springing to his feet and pulling Trace out of the way to grab the wheel. "I've met farmers who were better seamen!"

Trace took hold of the console to brace himself, turning to hide his smile.

He'd wondered how long it would take the wizard to get in the game.

Only he quickly sobered when he heard his boat's foghorn go off. "What in hell are you doing?" he shouted.

"Shut up and look for them!"

Them? As in tails and flippers and big, warm bellies *them*?

Mac started blowing the horn again in a series of long and short bursts.

"Goddamn it, Oceanus!" Trace scrambled to grab the wheel. "I am not—"

Something slammed into the boat, knocking him down and sending him sliding all the way back to the stern. He caught hold of the gunwale and started to stand, but the boat was slammed from the other side, nearly tossing him over the side before he finally got to his feet on the rolling deck just as he heard the engine die.

"Take a deep breath, Huntsman!" Mac shouted, charging toward him.

Trace shot to the side, but the wizard read his intention and veered toward him, snagging him in his arms, his momentum sending them both flying over the stern.

Chapter Twenty

$\mathcal{T}$race unzipped his jacket, pulled his shirttail out of his sopping-wet jeans, and wiped his face. "Fess up, Oceanus; you were dropped on your head as a kid, weren't you?" He cleared his eyes enough to glare at Mac, only to find the bastard smiling.

"Are we not here, Huntsman?"

Yeah, they were definitely here; only problem was, Trace wasn't sure exactly where *here* was. They appeared to be on some sort of ship. Or rather *in* a ship, as he suspected they were several hundred feet underwater. "This boat got a bathroom," he asked, "or do Atlanteans just whiz in the ocean?"

That made Mac's smile disappear. "Now? You need to go *now*?"

"Well, yeah." He gestured at Mac and then at himself. "And I'd rather not meet His Holy Highness, King of the World, looking like this." He smoothed down the front of his sopping jacket. "I can't very well negotiate Fiona's release looking like this."

"Negoti—you have nothing to trade, you idiot, because you just *hand-delivered me to him.*" Mac stepped closer. "And I would caution you to show only respect toward my father, or you might discover a whale's belly is preferable to this ship's brig."

Mac angrily twirled his finger in a circle, and Trace nearly came out of his skin at the feel of a thousand ants crawling inside his clothes. But when he looked down, he saw that he was still dressed, only his jeans, shirt, jacket, and even his boots were so clean they looked brand-new.

He rolled his shoulders to make sure he was still wearing his backpack and beamed Mac a smile. "I could use you on Sunday afternoons when I'm getting ready to drive up to Bangor for supper at my mom's." He shifted uncomfortably. "But I still need a bathroom. And I prefer to do it *myself,*" he quickly tacked on when the wizard raised his hand again.

Mac spun on his heel and headed toward a closed hatchway. Trace followed, trying not to gawk like a tourist. The massive room had to be three stories high, and he figured it was on the lowest level of the vessel, judging by the huge pool of seawater in the center through which they'd entered the ship.

Mac led him into an airlock, sealed the door behind them, and exited through another hatch into a long hallway. "And my father prefers to be addressed as sir, especially in front of the crew."

Trace was about to say something but took a misstep when he saw several men dressed in what had to be the gaudiest uniforms on the planet. They all stopped what they were doing to snap to attention, only instead of saluting, every damned last one of them bowed as Mac strode past without even acknowledging them.

Holy hell, the guy really was royalty.

Trace lengthened his stride to catch up, and tried to keep track of every twist and turn they made down countless hallways. "About that bathroom," he said when they started up a set of stairs. "I really need to *go*."

Mac turned and continued down the hall a short distance, then slapped open a door. "One minute. My father knows we're here, and he doesn't like to be kept waiting."

"For chrissakes, can you see yourself? The closer we get to your old man, the more uptight you become," he said, walking past him into the bathroom.

"I haven't seen or spoken to him in nearly a *century*," Mac growled. "And our parting wasn't exactly pleasant." He gestured stiffly. "We had a fight that sent most of Atlantis's population scurrying to the other side of the island, nearly capsizing it."

"Atlantis *floats*?" Trace narrowed his eyes. "Why haven't our satellites seen it?"

"Because it's a *myth*!"

Trace softly closed the door on Mac's angry face and stepped back into the hallway three minutes later. He walked over to Mac, who was sitting on the bottom step, his arms resting on his knees as he stared down at his hands. "Come on," Trace said, gently lifting him to his feet. "Let's get Fiona and get the hell out of here."

"Only the two of you will be getting the hell out of here," Mac muttered, taking a left at the top of the stairs. "I can't very well run off and leave my father to fight my battles for me."

"I'm pretty sure you don't need him to fight them *with* you, either."

Mac stopped and turned. "You don't understand; I'm his only heir, and if anything happens to me, the Trees of Life will start dying, and so will all of humanity."

"He's got Carolina."

Mac shook his head and started up another set of stairs. "He refuses to leave the fate of mankind in the hands of a woman."

Trace snorted. "We'd have fewer wars if women ruled the world."

When Mac started up yet another set of stairs, Trace slowed enough to glance down the hallway, getting an uneasy feeling that he might have underestimated the size of the ship. As near as he could tell, it was some sort of underwater craft, like a submarine—only it appeared to be as big as a goddamned aircraft carrier.

Then again, its massive size might actually work in his favor.

"So I take it your father is the one who passed down your ethics about not using magic to do every little thing for him," Trace said, figuring they must be getting close, because if Mac's spine got any stiffer the man was going to snap in half. He snorted. "Only he's not above using magic to steal my girlfriend to get you."

Mac stopped just outside a set of huge wooden doors that had a large multibranched tree carved into them. "Girlfriend?" He arched a brow. "Does Fiona know she's been elevated from your tenant to your girlfriend?"

Trace blew out a sigh. "No, I haven't told her yet." He grinned. "But don't you think she'll like the idea? It's got a very twenty-first-century ring to it."

Mac turned to the door. "The only ring she needs is one she can wear."

Trace pulled his friend's arm away. "He puts his pants on one leg at a time, Mac, just like all of us," he said quietly. "And really, what's the worst he can do?"

Trace saw the first hint today of an honest smile on the wizard's face. "When I was a kid he would take away my magic as punishment, and I'd be forced to go to Carolina when I got myself in a jam." He shook his head. "And she would make me play dolls with her as payment." He sobered, and Trace saw his spine stiffen again. "Your word, Huntsman, that you will not antagonize him. We will humbly ask that he give you Fiona and then safe passage back to Midnight Bay for the two of you."

"How about we humbly ask him to give the *three* of us safe passage back?"

"Why do you insist that I go with you?" Mac gestured at nothing. "It's past time I face my responsibilities, even if that means agreeing to let my father choose my bride. At least then maybe I can find some peace."

"So you're saying everyone has free will but you?"

"Yes!" the wizard snapped, opening the door before Trace could stop him. "Father," he said, giving a slight bow as he entered the room. "I'm sorry for not getting here sooner, but I was . . . detained."

For Mac to have claimed that his father was legendary for his looks was one hell of an understatement, Trace decided. Titus Oceanus had to be nearly seven feet tall, with shoulders a linebacker would sell his sister for and a ruggedly handsome face that women would turn somersaults just to have smile at them.

Which made Trace wonder what Mac *really* looked like when he wasn't trying to look like someone else. He and his father had the same vivid green eyes, though, a similar set to the jaw, and that same damned imperial brow—which the old goat raised as he gave Trace the once-over.

"Mr. Huntsman," Titus said. "I'm glad to finally meet you, as I've been wondering whether you've been trying to save my son's life or kill him."

"Yeah, me, too," Trace returned evenly, stepping forward. "I'll see Fiona now. If you please," he tacked on when he heard Mac growl behind him.

"In good time." The elder wizard's gaze slid to Mac, and his eyes hardened, but not before Trace saw the hunger of unconditional love flash briefly. "Maximilian, do you have any idea what sort of unholy war you've started?"

Trace stepped between them. "That's just it. Your boy here doesn't know who in hell's out to get him, much less why. And since I seem to be caught smack in the middle of this unholy little war, I'd really like to know, too." He took a step toward the giant. *"Right after I see Fiona."*

Trace saw a hint of amusement creep into those vivid green eyes as Titus raised a finger and silently waved it in a circle. A door at the back of the room suddenly opened, and Misneach came barreling through it, his claws scraping for purchase as he raced toward Trace with an excited yelp. Keeping his eye on the door, Trace crouched down to catch the pup while slipping a hand inside his jacket pocket when he saw Fiona appear. Only he quickly pulled his hand back out when he noticed the child walking beside her, the young boy's brilliant green eyes huge with uncertainty, his hand clutching Fiona's in a death grip.

Trace stood and shoved Misneach at Mac, then strode over and pulled Fiona into his arms and buried his face in her hair. He wanted to say something but for the life of him couldn't, so he settled for squeezing her until he heard her squeak. Only then did he open his eyes, and looking down over her shoulder, he saw the kid all but twisting her arm off trying to hide behind her.

Trace straightened and cupped Fiona's face in his hands. "We're moving on to plan B," he quietly told her. "So stay sharp, okay?"

Her beautiful, safe, and very much alive eyes sparkled like sunshine up at him. "What does plan B involve?" she whispered.

"I'm not sure yet. Where's your gun?"

"Mr. Oceanus took it. He said any man who gives a woman that kind of weapon should be shot with it."

Trace felt her arm being tugged on and grinned. "How old is he?"

"Six. His name is Henry."

"I'm going to go over and stand beside Mac to stop him from falling flat on his face when his father tells him, okay? You just follow my lead when you hear the signal."

"What's the signal?"

He gave her beautiful mouth a quick kiss. "You'll know when you—"

"It's quite nice that Mr. Huntsman is so concerned for Miss Gregor's welfare," Titus said with all the authority of a king nearing the end of his patience. "And I realize that twenty-first-century men have little regard for tradition, but have you lost all sense of propriety, too, Maximilian?"

"Excuse me?" Mac said, his spine stiffening to the point that Trace decided he'd better get over there now.

He gave Fiona a wink and strode over to Mac. "Brace yourself, my friend," he whispered out the side of his mouth. "We're moving on to plan B."

Mac shot Trace a threatening glare just before he smiled tightly at his father. "By propriety, I assume you mean his display of affection?" Trace nearly kicked Mac when the ass bowed to the old man again. "I assure you, sir, it's perfectly acceptable for a man to kiss his girlfriend in front of others."

Up went that brow, only it was far more imperial than his son's. "You're saying it's acceptable for one man to kiss another man's betrothed right in front of him?"

Trace counted four, maybe five heartbeats before Mac caught on, only he didn't catch his friend when he staggered, because he felt like he'd just taken a punch to the gut himself. What in hell was he talking about? Fiona wasn't *anyone's* betrothed.

"In front of . . . what in hell are you saying?" Mac shouted. He pointed at Fiona. "She's not my betrothed." He swung his outstretched arm toward Trace, smacking him in the chest. "Fiona belongs to *him*."

"Atta boy," Trace growled. "You dig those family jewels out of your pants and shake them at him. You outgrew taking his bullshit a couple thousand years ago."

"Maximilian!" Titus snapped, causing Mac to pivot to him. "This is no example to be setting for your son," he said, gesturing toward Fiona.

This time Trace was ready when Mac staggered backward. "Don't go all girly on me now, Mac, especially in front of Henry."

Mac couldn't stop staring at the young boy clinging to Fiona as if she were the only solid thing in the room.

"Henry?" Mac whispered. "He's my . . . the child's my *son*?" Mac looked at Titus. "But how? When?" He looked back at the boy, then at his father again. "Who's his mother?"

Apparently realizing that he'd gone about the introductions all wrong, Titus blew out a heavy sigh. "Cordelia Penhope," he said, darting a worried glance at the boy.

But Fiona had moved to the far corner of the room and was sitting on the floor, occupying the kid by playing with Misneach.

"Well," Trace whispered, letting go of his friend once he was certain that Mac's legs would hold him. "At least now you know why she suddenly sent you away."

Titus stepped closer to Mac. "It's Cordelia's brothers who have been trying to kill you," his father quietly told him, "in order to keep control of Henry." He reached out and set a hand on Mac's shoulder. "Cordelia became ill and died three months ago, Maximilian. It took her servant over two months to escape and make his way to Atlantis to tell us that Cordelia's dying wish was for you to claim your son."

"Delia's dead?" Mac whispered.

"You never knew she was having your child, son?"

Mac shook his head as he lifted his gaze to his father, but Trace suspected he was only seeing his dead lover's image. "I didn't know. I was going to ask Delia to marry me, but . . ." Mac shook his head as if trying to clear it. "She suddenly came to me one day and said that for as much as she'd enjoyed our time together, I was starting to bore her. And when I went back to my apartments, her brothers were there, and they told me that if I ever came near their sister again, they'd kill . . ."

He fell silent and turned away to face the doors.

"I find it hard to imagine you feared a threat on your life," Titus said. "Nor can I believe they'd make such a threat to begin with, especially to your face."

"Their threat wasn't against me," Mac said softly, still turned away. He canted his head back to stare up at the ceiling, his hands balling into fists. "That means it was all a pretense. Delia suspected I was going to ask for her hand in marriage." He spun toward his father. "I never lied to her about who I was. And being my lover was okay, obviously, whereas being my wife was . . ." He darted a glance toward Fiona, then to Trace, then back to his father. "Apparently, Delia felt that having a theurgist for a husband, as well as Titus Oceanus as her father-in-law, would be more trouble than it was worth."

"Or too dangerous," Trace said quietly. "If she realized she was pregnant and feared her brothers would use your child for their own gain."

"Where are they now?" Mac asked, his hands balling into fists again.

Titus gestured dismissively. "One of them has gone home with what's left of his manhood dangling between his bloody legs, and the other two are fertilizing a new sea grass I'm developing off the East African coast."

"So the storm's over?" Trace asked.

Titus nodded. "Except for the low-pressure system cloaking this ship. Come, Maximilian," he said, grasping his arm. "It's time you met your son."

Mac gently but firmly pulled away. "How did you get him?"

His father's eyes hardened. "The bastards actually brought Henry with them, either believing I would do nothing as long as they held my grandson or hoping he might have enough power to protect them. Come," he said, reaching out again.

Mac stepped away. "What did you mean about Fiona being my betrothed?"

Titus gave Trace a sidelong glance, then looked at Mac. "You have a son now, Maximilian; it's time you settled down. Miss Gregor obviously loves children," he said, gesturing toward the corner of the room. He smiled tightly. "And she seems to have not only the resilience it will take to be your wife but also the courage. So, I've decided it's in everyone's best interest for the two of you to wed."

"You've decided," Mac repeated deadpan. And damn if he didn't find the gonads to actually arch his brow. "Did you think to ask Fiona if *she* agreed with your decision?"

"Or me?" Trace added, deciding to get plan B moving. "Because I have first dibs on her." He waved toward Mac. "Hell, your boy here might love her like a sister, but I'm the one she stripped naked for."

Titus's complexion darkened. "Excuse me?"

Trace nodded, raising his voice enough to carry across the room. "The thing is, Fiona has totally embraced the twenty-first century, and being *anyone's* wife doesn't really hold any appeal for her," he said, casually reaching into his pocket when he saw Fiona stand up with Misneach tucked under one arm, her free hand firmly gripping Henry's as she slowly started toward them.

"But Mac knows nothing about raising a child," Titus growled, obviously getting hot under the collar—although he did try to soften his glare when he looked at his son. "Miss Gregor would make you a good match. There's no denying she's beautiful, and I'm certain she'll settle in nicely once you get her with child."

"Hell, do you know *anything* about her?" Trace asked as she quietly approached. "Fiona likes the idea of openly living with a guy as his *girlfriend,* and I know she's looking forward to having a kid out of wedlock just because she can." He shot Titus a grin. "She's really a bad girl at heart, and she's found a time and a place where she can finally be herself." Trace arched a brow himself at the old goat. "Isn't that what *free will* is all about, what you and your son are working your tails off to protect?"

"But he has no other prospects!" Titus snapped, an edge of desperation creeping into his voice. His face now a deep, dark red, he glared at his son. "You will marry Miss Gregor or lose your powers for an entire century!"

Damn; now they needed a plan C.

"Wait. What about all the magic stuff he's already done?" Trace asked before Mac could say anything, drawing the elder wizard's thunderous glare. "Like the lobsters fulfilling their destinies and my fancy television and nice leather recliners; would those tricks still be up and running?"

"Huntsman," Mac hissed tightly, "that's enough!"

Titus's eyes bulged with anger, and he raised his hand. Not knowing what the old goat had up his sleeve, Trace depressed the button in his pocket.

He hadn't expected to actually hear anything, but he did count to three before the floor shifted slightly beneath them, gently at first, and then in shuddering waves that increased enough to make things in the room rattle.

Titus stilled with his finger pointing at the ceiling, his gaze snapping to the door just as a deep-bellied moan came from below.

The floor they were standing on tilted ever so slightly.

Trace grabbed Mac's arm. "You take your son," he said, shoving him toward Fiona. "Oh, for chrissakes, just pick him up! We'll introduce you later," he growled as he plucked Misneach out of her arm, took hold of her hand, and started dragging her to the door. He had to stop long enough to shove Mac ahead of him, giving the wide-eyed Henry a wink as the kid bobbed on his daddy's shoulder when Mac flung open one of the doors and ran into the hall.

Trace was less than a step behind him. "Head to the airlock where we came in, only find a way that's not anywhere near that bathroom," he called ahead to Mac. He pulled Fiona up beside him and shoved Misneach back into her arms. "You follow Mac."

She grabbed his sleeve when he turned back. "We need to stay together."

"I'm right behind you, sweetheart, I promise." He gave her a quick kiss, then pushed her after Mac. "Just don't leave without me," he called out as he ran back into the room to find Titus still standing in the same spot—only instead of his hand being in the air, it was now holding what looked like an ancient cell phone up to his ear.

The elderly wizard, his face nearly purple with rage, suddenly stopped talking to whoever was on the line. "Is sinking my ship not enough for you, Huntsman," he growled, "such that you feel it necessary to return and finish me off?"

"One year," Trace said quietly. "You leave Mac alone for one full year, and I promise you'll finally get the son you've always wanted."

"What in the name of Zeus do you think one year will accomplish, when he's had thirty-five hundred of raising nothing but havoc?" He waved toward the hallway. "He just ran out of here with a son he didn't even know he'd fathered, as irresponsible as ever, creating yet another mess I'll have to clean up." He stepped closer. "Only this time, there is more than a petty war at stake. Mac doesn't know the first thing about children, and you expect me to leave my grandson in his hands for an entire year?"

"I know a lady who can help him with Henry."

"You've already made it quite clear that Fiona is spoken for."

"No, another lady. She's the widow of a friend of mine, and she lives right here in Maine, up in the mountains. She runs a program for parents and their kids. One year, Titus, and you have my word you won't regret it."

The ship gave a loud, shuddering groan and settled into a steeper list.

The mirror image of Mac's eyes, though far older and deeply wise, swirled with the emotions of a heart torn between its duty to mankind and the singular love of one soul for another. "Three hundred and sixty-four days," Titus said quietly, "and if you fail, Huntsman, I will own your soul."

"Deal," Trace said with a nod. He grinned. "And if you want to give me your e-mail address, I can keep you and your wife updated and even send pictures."

The old goat actually spun around and walked to a desk, and wrote something down on a piece of paper. He came back and handed it to Trace. "Toss a weighted jug with the photos overboard at those coordinates, and we will get them."

Well, hell, the king of the drùidhs was actually a big sap. Trace gave a wave with the paper and turned and headed out of the room.

"Huntsman," Titus said, causing him to stop at the door. "How did you know you could blow a hole in my ship and I couldn't retaliate?"

"The lifeboats."

"Excuse me?"

"I saw the first one in the boarding room, then a couple more stowed next to other airlocks on our way up here. I admit, I was baffled about why the most powerful wizard in the world needed lifeboats on his ship, but then, when you said the storm was over except for the low pressure cloaking you, it finally made sense. You might have a hell of a lot of power but it *is* limited, and I figure it's going to take most of your energy to save your ship—which Mac obviously knows, because he didn't feel the need to stay behind to cover our escape."

"But you planted your explosive charge before you had all of your information."

Trace shrugged. "I like keeping my options open."

Up went that brow again, into his hairline. "Including your options with women?"

"I'm still working on that one."

"You give me back my son and grandson in a year, strong and healthy and happy, and I will see that you succeed."

"No offense, but no thanks. I believe Fiona has a pretty good handle on matters of the heart, so I'll just wait and see what sort of magic *she* conjures up for me." He grinned. "Like you taught your son, life is meant to be embraced, and some challenges are more rewarding if we don't take shortcuts."

Trace started to turn away but hesitated. "He's a good man, Titus; he just needs you to trust him. You've given Mac the tools to fulfill his destiny, so maybe it's time you stepped out of the way and let him." He grinned again. "According to my uncle Marvin, your job description changes the moment your children have children, because that's when you stop being a parent and just become *grand* to a whole new generation of brats."

The ship gave another shudder, and the brick-sized cell phone on the desk started ringing. "Huntsman," Titus said, ignoring the phone when Trace started to leave, "your military was foolish to kick you out of their war."

"No, I believe they were very, very smart. Because the thing about a lethal weapon is, there's always the danger of it exploding in your face." He gave Mac's father a quick salute. "I'll see you in a year."

"You must come visit us in Atlantis and meet Mac's mother," the wizard said just as the ship gave a truly ominous groan, a series of loud explosions sounding over the shouts of men and a blaring alarm. Again ignoring the small disaster happening around him, Titus Oceanus smiled—rather tightly if not somewhat nastily. "I know Carolina would love to see you again, as she has yet to stop talking about you."

Trace ran as if the hounds of hell were after him, the old theurgist's booming laughter chasing him down the hall.

Chapter Twenty-one

✦

"*I* can't believe you had the nerve to blow up my father's ship," Mac said over the commercial coming out of the television's state-of-the-art surround-sound speakers.

Trace hit the mute button and looked across the granite-topped table sitting between them. "For the tenth time, I only blew a small hole in it, just big enough to keep everyone busy while we made our escape."

"But it forced him to release the storm in order to put his energy toward saving his ship—which is now limping home with only marginal camouflage."

Trace took a sip of his beer, remembering the sight of that massive submarine—which had been double the size of a goddamned aircraft carrier—listing precariously to starboard as it headed back to wherever the hell Atlantis was. He snorted. "Don't think I didn't see that smile on your face when you looked out the lifeboat window and saw him surface. Come on, Oceanus, admit it. Doesn't it feel good to stick it to the old man once in a while?"

"At the cost of my power." Mac sighed and looked down to rub his thumb over the label on his bottle of beer. "And without my powers, I'll be forced to live the next hundred years in real time." He glared across the table. "No more jumping centuries or popping in and out of countries, and no more impressive tricks to capture a woman's interest."

Trace stopped with his beer halfway to his mouth. "That's your pickup line? Magic? What, do you pull a bouquet of flowers out of your sleeve or something? No, wait, don't tell me," he said, straightening the back of his recliner. "I bet you walk up to a woman in a bar, pull a cute little rabbit out of your hat, and ask if she happens to have any lettuce back at her place."

Mac turned to look at the muted television.

"Are you completely powerless now?" Trace asked quietly.

The defunct wizard looked over at him again, and Trace caught the hint of a grin. "Do you honestly believe I've spent the last several thousand years thumbing my nose at my father without thinking to bank some of my powers for a day such as this? You're not the only one who likes to have a plan B."

Trace sat up even straighter. "You mean, you can still do stuff?"

Mac shook his head, even as his grin broadened. "I can't waste my reserves on trivial matters, but I have enough energy set aside for three, maybe four epic . . . tricks."

Trace relaxed back with a sigh. "Four tricks in a hundred years is sort of like the kid who's granted three wishes by the genie." He waved a finger in the air. "How will you know if something's important enough to make a withdrawal from your bank?"

Mac took a long swig of beer, then shrugged as he swallowed. "I'll decide when the time comes. What took you so long to catch up with us on the ship?"

"I was *humbly* asking your father for a one-year cease-fire between you two."

Mac stilled. "And?"

"And he said that in three hundred and sixty-four days, if you don't show up on his doorstep with Henry, the both of you healthy and happy, he's going to own my soul."

Trace had expected to get a good rise out of him, but Mac merely went back to rubbing his beer label. "You may have just foolishly bargained away your fate, my friend." He looked up, his eyes dark with . . . hell, the guy looked like he'd just swallowed a whale. "I'll be lucky if Henry is *alive* a year from now. My father wasn't criticizing when he said I know nothing about raising a child but stating a fact." He looked toward the bedroom hallway, then back at Trace, and leaned closer. "I'll admit to you, Huntsman, I've never been this scared in my life."

Trace snorted. "All this time you've been telling me not to be afraid of having a kid of my own, and here you are shaking in your shoes." He leaned on the table. "He's nothing more than a miniature you, Mac. Whatever worked for your dad will work on Henry." He frowned. "But the first thing you need to do is find out if he's got any magical powers and take them away from him ASAP." He sat back with a shudder. "Can you image a six-year-old with even a tenth of your powers?"

"He won't really have full use of them until he reaches puberty."

Trace shuddered again, deciding that a teenager with that kind of power was even scarier. "As for raising Henry, I happen to know a lady who might be able to help you."

Mac glanced toward the hallway again, his face awash with relief when he looked back at Trace. "You're right. Fiona can take care of him."

"No, she can't, because she's going to be too busy taking care of *me*. I'm talking about a woman who runs a year-round camp for parents and their kids. She's the widow of a buddy of mine who was killed in Iraq four years ago." He gestured at the bedrooms. "In fact, I think her daughter is just a little bit older than Henry."

"Where does she live?" Mac asked, eyeing him suspiciously. "If I'm stuck in this century, then I prefer to stay near people I . . . know."

"She lives right here in Maine, up in the mountains, in . . ." Trace chuckled, just now realizing that fate had one hell of a sense of humor. "Oh, you're going to love this, Oceanus. The town's called Spellbound Falls."

Mac didn't even crack a smile. "How far is it from here?"

"About a three-hour drive, but her camp, called Inglenook, is another ten miles outside of town."

Mac shook his head. "I don't wish to be that far from the ocean." He leaned back in his chair with a sigh. "I'll just find a place here in Midnight Bay, and Fiona and Eve and Madeline can help me with Henry."

"You got any marketable skills that will help you get a job?"

"Why would I need a job if I already have more money than I can possibly spend in a hundred years?"

Trace sat up again. "You're rich?"

Mac shot him a smug grin. "Energy's not the only thing I tucked away for a rainy day." He leaned on the table. "I could probably pay off your nation's debt and still have enough left over to buy you an entire fleet of boats."

"Where is all this money?"

Mac waved toward the window. "My big blue friend is keeping it safe for me."

"Are you saying there's a whale swimming around out there full of money?"

Mac chuckled. "No, he's merely guarding my luggage. What, do you think I travel with all of my belongings tied up in a hobo sack?" He looked toward the hallway again. "Maybe I should ask Fiona to show me how to organize everything so I can do away with a couple of the chests." He suddenly shook his head. "No, I'll need to keep them for Henry's belongings now."

Trace ran a hand over his face, trying to wipe away the image of several treasure chests full of loot sitting out on the ocean floor—being guarded by a *whale*. When that didn't work, he downed the rest of the beer in his bottle. But just as he was about to unmute the television, Fiona quietly walked into the living room from the hallway.

"He went to sleep, finally," she told Mac, smiling warmly, "once I agreed to let Misneach stay the night with him. You need to sneak in and see them, Mac. Henry insisted that Misneach get under the covers and share his pillow. He's a beautiful little boy, and rather smart and well-spoken, as well as quite brave. Even after all he's been through, from losing his mother only three months ago to meeting his fa-ther for the first time in the middle of a war, he's amazingly calm. You must be excited to discover that you have such a remarkable son."

Trace snorted when Mac remained as mute as the television. "Oh yeah, our boy here is trembling all over with excitement."

"Well, I believe I'll go upstairs now," she said, heading toward the kitchen.

"Wait!" Mac yelped, suddenly finding his voice. He closed the footrest on his chair and sprang to his feet. "You can't just *leave*."

"I've had a rather trying day, Mac, and I need to lie down before I fall down."

"But what about Henry?" he said, this time in a whisper, glancing toward the hall. "What if he wakes up and can't find you?"

"You'll be here, won't you?"

"Well, yes, but what if he wakes up and gets scared? It would be better if you slept down here so I won't have to come up and get you."

Trace saw Fiona smile at the panicked wizard. "If he wakes up, he only needs to see that his *father* is here."

"But I'm a stranger to him!" Mac cried in a whisper. "What if I do or say something wrong and he starts crying or something? What am I supposed to do then?"

"You do exactly what you'd want someone to do for you if you were in Henry's place," she told him calmly. She touched his arm. "You simply follow your heart, Mac, and lie down and gather Henry in your arms and tell him there's no need to be afraid because you're here for him. And if your heart tells you to hold him out here in the recliner while he has a glass of milk and a cookie, then you try that." She cupped Mac's pale cheek. "All Henry needs is to know you're here for him, and that you'll love him forever and ever, and never let him down."

"But I can't make promises I might be unable to keep," he whispered desperately, pulling her hand down to clutch it in his. "You heard my father's dictate today; I'm completely powerless now. I can't even make a glass of milk or cookies appear."

"Daddies are the most powerful entity in the world, Mac, in the eyes of their children. You need only to look at your own father to realize how Henry feels about you." She patted his hand still clutching hers. "And your son already knows a great deal about you, thanks to his mother having told him what a good, kind, strong man you are every day of his young life. So really, all your son needs is for you to be yourself."

She tried to pull away then, but when Mac refused to let her go, Trace quietly closed the footrest on his recliner and stood up.

"Anything you want," Mac growled. "Name your price, and it's yours. Just don't leave me alone with him."

"You will survive this, Mac," Trace said, freeing Fiona from his grip. "And in about ten years, I promise that instead of being afraid of him, you're going to want to strangle the belligerent little punk."

"Dammit, Huntsman, where are you going?" Mac hissed as Trace led Fiona away. "You can't leave me, too!"

"I'm just walking the lady home," he said over his shoulder. He helped Fiona into her coat and stepped onto the porch behind her, only then letting loose his laughter. "I think the poor bastard would rather face screaming demons than a six-year-old kid."

"I'm afraid Mac is far more traumatized than Henry is," she said, her voice laced with amusement as she slipped her hand into his. Only instead of heading along the side porch toward the front of the house, she pulled him down the steps and out into the dooryard. "He'll eventually get the hang of fatherhood." She sucked in a deep breath as she looked up at the sky, then blew it out slowly. "Such a beautiful night it's turned out to be, with the stars shining and the air so calm after such a turbulent day." Turning to face him, she shoved her hands into her pockets. "I want to thank you for stopping Mr. Oceanus from marrying me off to Mac today." She smiled up at him. "I might be able to tell my brothers to go to hell, but I didn't quite have the nerve to tell the king of the drùidhs that *he* isn't the boss of me, either."

"Don't you ever be afraid to tell anyone that you are the boss of yourself."

"Can I also tell them I'm your girlfriend, like Mac claimed today on the ship?"

He shoved his own hands in his pockets. "Do you want to be?"

"I don't know," she said, stepping closer to toy with a button on his shirt. "Do girlfriends have sex with their boyfriends in this century, or do they only hold hands and steal kisses when no one is watching?"

"Oh, they do way more than hold hands and make out. In fact, the boyfriend will usually drive his girlfriend to a secluded spot, sweet-talk her out of her clothes, and make love to her under the moonlight." He pulled a hand out of his pocket to tilt her chin up. "And sometimes, if the girl decides she likes him a lot, and she trusts that he'll always treat her as an equal, she might even move in with him."

She gasped softly, stepping away. "Without their being married?"

He nodded.

"But what would everyone think of her? Would the townspeople shun her?"

He nodded again. "Some would—usually the fuddy-duddy old women, and then only because they're just jealous." He closed the small gap between them. "But I happen to believe that thumbing noses at fuddy-duddies is the best part of two people openly living together. Women in this century—especially strong, resilient, independent women—like causing a bit of a scandal . . . just because they can."

She leaned into him and started toying with his button again. "So, at what point in their relationship do two people start living together?"

"Usually when the boyfriend realizes he'd be the luckiest guy in the world to wake up every morning with his arms wrapped around a beautiful, sexy woman he never dreamed he'd stand a chance of getting," he said, wrapping his arms around her.

She looked up. "So, the boyfriend simply asks his girlfriend to move in with him?"

"Sometimes. But if he's shy or scared or just downright dumb, sometimes the girlfriend has to drop a few hints that it's time for their relationship to move on to the next level."

She ducked her head to toy with his button again, but not quickly enough to hide her frown. "Have you ever lived with a woman before?"

"As in sharing a closet, deciding who does what chores, and having our mail delivered to the same address?"

She nodded, still not looking up.

"No, I can't say that I have. The nearest I've been to that sort of arrangement is when my mother moved in with Jack about a year before she married him."

That brought her head up. "Your mother lived with a man who wasn't her husband?"

Unable to resist, Trace gave her a quick kiss on her shocked lips, then smiled at her. "Mom finally discovered she's actually a bad girl at heart—much to her surprise and everyone else's."

"Including you?"

"Nope. I suspected it was there all along, only I didn't know how to get her to see it. It's easy to forget who you are if someone's been telling you for seventeen years that you're nobody."

She went back to toying with his button. "So your mother wouldn't think any less of a girlfriend who moved in with you?"

"Are you kidding? She'd be so happy I managed to find a woman willing to put up with me, she'd probably go out and buy monogrammed towels."

He gently tugged on her braid to tilt her head back, and was just leaning down to devour her sweet, beautiful lips when a set of headlights landed on them as a rattling pickup pulled into the driveway. Fiona scrambled out of his arms before he could stop her, the headlights revealing bright red cheeks in danger of bursting into flame.

He sighed, figuring they were a long way from living together if she got this embarrassed when someone caught them only kissing.

The truck pulled up right beside them, the engine shut

off, and the door opened. "I've been calling your cell phone all evening," Rick said as he climbed out. "What's the use of owning a phone if you never *answer* it?"

"Sorry. I guess it got wet. Rick, have you met Fiona Gregor?" Trace asked, having to grab her hand when he noticed her inching away.

Rick shot her a grin. "I've heard quite a lot about you from Gabriella," he said, extending his hand. "It's good to finally meet you. I'm Rick, Maddy's brother." He nodded toward Trace. "As well as this slacker's fishing partner."

Fiona wiggled free to shake Rick's hand, then tucked her hands behind her back. "Gabriella has told me a lot about you, too," she said, taking a step away. "Like how sweet you are to make her hot cocoa and sit up with her after she's had a bad dream."

Rick shrugged off her compliment and looked at Trace. "The Coast Guard called and told me they found our boat drifting about six miles out." He shook his head. "They said they had a hard time getting hold of it, though, because a bunch of whales kept getting in their way. It seems every time they tried to hook a line on the bow to tow it in, the whales would bump it out of reach." He grinned. "The mid-shipman said he'd swear those whales thought it was a new toy or something and were playing keep-away with them. Have you ever heard anything so ridiculous?"

"Not lately," Trace muttered, wondering if he was going to have to carry a harpoon when he went out fishing now.

"So, you coming to work tomorrow, or are you still *re-covering*?"

"I'll be there," Trace said, watching Fiona inching away.

She lifted a hand to cover a yawn even as she took

another step. "If you don't mind, I believe I'll turn in for the night. It was nice meeting you, Rick."

"Oh, I almost forgot," Rick said as she turned to leave. "Gabriella said to tell you she'll bring some boxes with her when she comes over tomorrow and help you pack."

Fiona darted a frantic glance at Trace, then back at Rick. "Thank you for giving me her message," she said as she continued walking backward, just before she spun around and ran for her stairs.

Trace beat her to the steps and blocked her way. "What's he talking about?"

"I've decided to give Mac my apartment so he and Henry can get acquainted with each other in a more intimate setting. If they continue living with you, Henry won't know which one of you is his father, because Mac will rely on you to do everything."

"And just where do you intend to live?"

She had to crane her neck to look up at him, and there was enough moonlight for him to see her mutinous glare. "I haven't decided yet." She suddenly sighed. "But I'll let you know as soon as I do, so you can forward my mail."

"Who in hell sends you mail?" he asked. Instead of asking her if she was out of her friggin' mind!

"Winter writes to me all the time." She stepped closer. "Would you happen to have any suggestions as to where I could live?"

Trace felt beads of perspiration break out on his forehead despite the freezing night air. "Not right this very minute, I don't."

She dropped her gaze, and he saw her shoulders slump.

She yawned again, quite loudly. "Well," she said brightly, smiling up at him, "I'd better get to bed."

Dammit to hell, he didn't want her moving out!

Then say something, you ass. Tell her she can move in with you.

But she wants to be independent, you idiot.

Promise you won't step on her toes. Not once. Never.

Are you forgetting she doesn't even like men? If she believes husbands are more trouble than they're worth, why would she think a boyfriend was any better?

Give her your word you won't ever complain about her messing with your stuff. Not once. Never. And tell her you won't leave your dirty clothes on the floor, you'll get a haircut and shave every damned day, and she can babysit twenty kids if she wants. Just beg her to give you a chance to prove you really are a nice guy.

Are you forgetting that I ran out on her that day down in the safe room?

Then you swear to God you'll never, ever run out on her again, no matter how scared you are.

I'm not scared; I'm just . . . I don't want to . . . goddamn it, I don't know what to do!

For chrissakes, you ass, just tell her you love her!

"Fiona, I—" Trace looked down and then spun one way and then the other. "Fiona? Goddamn it," he growled, glaring up at the light shining out her kitchen window. How in hell had she managed to sneak past him?

"So, you're talking to yourself now?" Rick asked, walking over to him.

"I thought I was talking to Fiona," he muttered, running a hand through his hair and then rubbing the back of his neck with a sigh.

"She went upstairs two minutes ago, cousin. So, you coming down to the harbor with me or what? The Coast Guard should be arriving with our boat just about now."

Trace gave one last glance up the stairs, then strode to Rick's truck. "Yeah, I'm coming. And I don't care if I have two broken legs; the next time I tell you I'm taking the day off work, you drive over here and drag me down to the docks at gunpoint if you have to."

"Don't get me wrong," Gabriella said, pulling some of Fiona's clothes out of her closet. "I think Mac is really nice and handsome and everything, but I don't know if I could ever marry someone like him." She tossed the clothes onto the bed. "I'd be afraid when the priest asked me to say 'I do' that I'd faint dead away. Weren't you scared? I mean, really, you came that close," she said, holding her thumb and finger apart, "to marrying a magic maker."

Fiona carefully folded a sweater, set it in the box, and picked up another one. "I was scared out of my mind." She smiled over at her friend. "Until Trace showed up and told Mac's father that it wasn't going to happen."

"Trace Huntsman, your hero," Gabriella said dramatically, placing the back of her hand on her forehead. She laughed and headed to the bureau. "Did he sweep you into his arms and vow his undying love, so Mac's father would believe your hearts belonged to each other?"

"No, he basically asked Mr. Oceanus if he wanted a daughter-in-law who slept with men she wasn't married to."

Gabriella bumped into the bureau and swung toward Fiona. "He told Mac's father that you're a fallen woman? The cad!" But then she suddenly smiled. "It was a good idea, though, as it obviously worked."

"No, I'm pretty sure Trace blowing a hole in the side of his ship is what worked."

Gabriella filled her arms with undergarments, carried them to the bed, and dropped them into one of the empty boxes. "I think it's very generous of you to give up your apartment to Mac and Henry, but do you really want to go live all by yourself in that big house Eve found for you to rent? I know her friend Susan Wakely lived there all alone, but it's more secluded than this place. And when Maddy drove me by it this morning, I noticed it's surrounded by woods. Won't you be scared?"

Fiona folded the box closed, then turned and sat down on the bed. Yes, Eve had called her friend Susan, who had run off with one of the MacKeage men last summer and now lived in Pine Creek, and asked Susan if she would be willing to rent her house. "I have Misneach, and Trace promised to show me how to shoot a gun."

Gabriella sat down beside her. "But won't you get lonely living all by yourself?" She nudged Fiona's shoulder with her own. "I could still be your roommate, and we could still open a child-care business together, couldn't we?"

"Not if you plan to be a nurse or a doctor, Gabriella," she said, taking the girl's hand. "I would love for us to be roommates, but it'll be easier for you to concentrate on your studies if you live with William and Maddy until you go away to college."

"But it's too hard," Gabriella said, standing up. "There are a whole bunch of difficult subjects I have to take to get accepted at a college. School's not just about learning how to read and write; I have to study things like biology and chemistry and mathematics, all of which have nothing to do with practical living. Why do I need to know what's inside a person's blood to stop them from bleeding to death? And why are there all sorts of chemicals to cure a disease when plants do a better job?"

Fiona walked over to her. "You must learn everything you can so people won't be able to take advantage of you. Knowledge is power, Gabriella, and ignorance is imprisonment. Think back to your old time, and remember how the learned ruled and the ignorant toiled." She took hold of the young girl's shoulders. "You must learn everything you can about this wondrous new world, so you can rule yourself."

"You're not going to school. Aren't you afraid people will take advantage of you?"

"If I were eighteen, I'd be going. But right now, I have to focus on my dream before I grow too old to bear children. In the meantime, I will be haunting the library and reading everything I can get my hands on, as well as watching all of those wonderful science and history channels on television. I might not become a doctor, but I'll never stop learning." She gave her friend's shoulders a squeeze. "Take your second chance and run with it, Gabriella, because the true gift of this century is that women can be *anything* we want." She grabbed a box and carried it into the kitchen. "Come on, let's take everything down to the porch so we can organize this place before Mac gets home."

Gabriella followed, also carrying a box. "Did you see the look on Henry's face when we drove in this morning? He got truly excited when you told him the truck had the power of several hundred horses."

Fiona opened the door and carried her box outside. "It was very sweet of Maddy to take Mac shopping to buy Henry some new clothes."

"I think Henry felt better about leaving you when he saw Sarah in the backseat," Gabriella said. "And when Mr. Getze brings the children on Monday, the boy will have someone closer to his age to play with." She dropped the box on the porch next to the house, beside the one Fiona had set down. "Oh, I forgot," she said as she straightened. "You'll be watching the children at your new place." She suddenly smiled. "Maybe Mac can bring Henry over there to play with them."

"I'm sure he will," Fiona drawled, heading back upstairs. "He's already offered to hire me to watch Henry while he goes to buy a truck and then learns to drive it."

"Omigod, I hope he doesn't let William teach him," Gabriella said with a laugh. "Is Mac truly powerless now?"

"It appears so. He told me Trace persuaded his father to give him a year to learn how to be a father himself, but apparently the deal didn't include getting his powers back." She headed into the second bedroom. "Personally, I think that's a good thing. Here, help me take the door off this cupboard."

"Why is it a good thing?" Gabriella asked, frowning at the cupboard.

"Because now Mac will be forced to deal with Henry like any normal father. Here, put this mattress over the porch rail to air it out."

"Why do you have a mattress in a cupboard?"

"Because bogeymen never think to look in cupboards."

Gabriella just blinked at her. "Then why are we taking off the door?"

"Until Mac can get Henry a proper bed, I thought the boy might like sleeping in here. It'll be cozy and make him feel protected, but I want to take the door off because I don't want him to think he's hiding from anything." She nudged her friend to get her moving. "I hope Maddy remembers to buy Henry some books and toys today."

They spent the rest of the morning preparing the apartment for Mac and a good deal of the afternoon preparing several simple meals Mac would only have to heat up on the stove. By three o'clock, Fiona and Gabriella were sitting on the porch, throwing a stick for Misneach to chase as they talked about all the different things Gabriella could be—including, but not exclusively, a mother.

Maddy finally pulled into the dooryard and shut off the truck, and Mac got out and opened the back passenger door. He leaned inside, and when he straightened, Fiona smiled at the sight of his sleeping son in his arms.

"Take him upstairs," she whispered, "and put him in the cupboard in the second bedroom. There's a bed all made up for him in there."

She saw Mac hesitate as he eyed Trace's kitchen door and gave him a gentle nudge toward her stairs.

No, they were *his* stairs now, she reminded herself.

"Everything's ready in your new home, Mac," she said, giving him another shove. "And you need to begin as you intend to go on."

He walked off carrying Henry, and Maddy and Sarah and Gabriella came over with their hands full of shopping bags.

"It was quite a day," Maddy said with a tired sigh. "I swear I don't know who was worse, Mac or Henry. Mac wouldn't even consider buying stone-washed jeans, insisting that his son wasn't wearing pants that looked used, and Henry kept wandering off to gawk at everything." She nudged her daughter with her hip. "If it wasn't for Sarah dragging him back every five minutes, we'd still be hunting for the kid."

"Mr. Oceanus sure can holler loud," Sarah said, grinning.

Maddy laughed. "Once, when we couldn't find either Henry or Sarah, Mac shouted Henry's name so loud everyone in the store stopped in their tracks. I'm surprised you didn't hear his roar in Midnight Bay." She stepped closer to Fiona and lowered her voice. "He was a ball of sweat the entire time, and I thought he was going to break down and cry when I said we could go home. He pulled me aside and offered to pay me a month's salary if I leave him behind the next time Henry needs something."

"We can't let him buy his way out of his responsibilities," Fiona whispered as they walked toward the stairs. "Surely he'll calm down once he realizes Henry's not going to break if he makes a mistake here and there."

"You know, I actually caught Henry patting Mac's arm a couple of times. I'm afraid the poor kid's going to end up parenting his father." She stopped and handed her bags to Gabriella. "You guys take everything upstairs and leave it in the kitchen. Sarah, you can show Gabriella what we bought."

Maddy turned back to Fiona when they left with Misneach racing up behind them.

"Mac said Trace told him about a woman in the mountains who runs a camp for single parents and their kids. And he said Trace suggested he and Henry should attend a few of the sessions. I really like the idea, but Mac said he doesn't want to leave Midnight Bay. What do you think?"

"Oh, I think it's a wonderful idea," Fiona said. "But probably not right away. Mac needs to learn to drive and get more comfortable with Henry. Maybe in a month or two."

"Yeah, I thought the same thing," Maddy said, nodding. "Come on, let's put your boxes in my truck, and I'll drive you over to your new house and help you get settled in. Gabriella and Sarah can stay here and babysit Mac."

"Thank you, but Kenzie plans to take me over later, so he can have a good look around and make sure everything is safe. You and Sarah and Gabriella can head on home." She chuckled. "Mac will probably have a nap after his trying day, and I think I'll sneak downstairs and watch my show on Trace's new television while I wait for Kenzie," she said, anxious to be alone so she could . . . think.

The dooryard was hauntingly quiet less than ten minutes later. But instead of going inside to watch her show, Fiona sat down on Trace's porch steps and buried her face in her hands on her knees with a sob.

Dammit, she didn't want to leave. She wanted to be the indecisive lout's girlfriend!

Chapter Twenty-two

Trace shut off his truck and stared through the windshield at the lights blazing out of every window of his upstairs apartment, and decided he wasn't an ass or an idiot or even a gullible chump.

No, he was an outright *coward*.

He dropped his head on the steering wheel with a groan, not wanting to walk into an empty house that didn't smell of delicious food cooking, or spend an evening in front of his brand-new television guzzling beer until he finally staggered down the hall and crawled into an empty bed.

He wasn't sure exactly when he'd fallen in love with Fiona, only that he had.

She'd certainly gotten his heart's attention when she'd crawled into that tunnel to save him, and then when he'd watched her firing the gun he'd given her back into the tunnel. And his heart had to have been soundly engaged when he'd run out on her that day in the safe room. What else would have sent him running to a bar three towns away to drown his sorrows if he hadn't been half in love with her then?

But if he had to come up with one defining moment, he'd have to say it had been when she'd told him how she'd walked halfway across Scotland, all alone and heavy with child, that his heart had started pounding with the realization that he was soundly and passionately in love with her.

So, how the hell hard would it have been to say four stupid little words last night, anyway? He'd been repeating them like a litany all day, for chrissakes, as he and Rick had hauled in trap after trap teeming with giant lobsters. He'd tried out *I love you* at first, but thinking that sounded a tad presumptuous—considering she might not feel the same way—he'd eventually settled on *Move in with me,* having decided that had a far less threatening ring to it.

Because he really didn't want to scare her off; he just really wanted her.

Any way he could get her. If Fiona wanted him to hold her hand and steal kisses when no one was looking, then he'd live like a monk the rest of his life—just as long as he was still holding her hand on his deathbed. And if she wanted babies, then, by God, he'd give her a dozen. But if she discovered she did need a ring on her finger, he'd marry her tomorrow, just as long as he could wake up every morning with his arms wrapped around her inviting body.

How in hell could he have let her go?

Trace straightened and got out of his truck, and quietly stood staring at the empty barn before sliding his gaze to his pitch-black windows.

Christ, he was a coward.

He finally went inside and walked through the house without bothering to turn on any lights, dropping his clothes where he shed them on the way to the bathroom. After flipping on the light, he turned on the shower, then stepped under the spray without even waiting for it to heat up—figuring it had to be warmer than the ice in his veins. He stood stiffly, letting the water beat his tired muscles as he tried to decide what to have for supper other than a six-pack of beer. He felt around for the shampoo and squirted some into his palm, but he stopped with it halfway to his head when he smelled roses.

"Goddamn it," he growled, washing it off under the spray.

There was no way in hell he was going to spend the night smelling her.

What was rose-scented shampoo doing in his shower, anyway? Had she picked up on his cue last night about girlfriends having to drop a few hints when it was time for a relationship to move to the next level, or had she sneaked in and deliberately left behind a little reminder of what his silence had cost him?

Opening one eye, he grabbed his shampoo with a snort, deciding that he hadn't needed to save her from Mac's father after all, since she obviously knew more about fighting dirty than all of them put together. He lathered up, washed his hair and rinsed off, and shut off the water; his blood nearly boiling now because he could *still* smell her.

But if he thought he was fired up with righteous indig-nation over shampoo, it was nothing compared to the feel of a knife plunging into his heart when he grabbed a towel so soft and fluffy he nearly dropped to his knees. Only half dried off before he couldn't stand the softness of the towel any longer, he noticed that his hand was trembling when he went to pick up his comb.

He stopped in mid-reach.

All of his toiletries had been pushed to the right side of the vanity, and on the left side, perfectly organized, was a bunch of . . . girly stuff—a wooden hairbrush, a tiny basket of barrettes and ribbons, a bottle of perfume, a jar of hand cream, and what appeared to be tubes of lip gloss lined up like little soldiers according to height.

He pulled open the medicine cabinet and found that it had also been reorganized, his stuff shoved to the right and more girly stuff neatly stacked on the left.

He shot out of the bathroom and into his bedroom, snapped on the light, and yanked open the closet door. Again, his stuff was shoved to the right—though mostly just piled on the floor as usual—and on the left were women's clothes hung on hangers according to length, sweaters folded on the top shelf by color, and four pairs of shoes and a pair of slippers lined up on the floor, toes pointing out.

He spun around to the bed and found it perfectly made, with half a dozen crisp pillows stacked in descending order by size, and on the right nightstand was his alarm clock, a lamp with a ratty old shade, a dog-eared paperback, and other small items haphazardly strewn as usual. On the left nightstand was only a box of tissues and three books neatly stacked—with the smallest on the bottom and the largest on top.

Trace stiffened and slowly turned around.

If he'd thought her beautiful golden eyes had been

scared and vulnerable the day she'd become his tenant, it was nothing compared to the stark fear in them now. He watched her gaze lower and then snap back to his as two tiny flags of pink appeared on her pale cheeks, and he realized he was standing there naked, staring at her.

And still he didn't move, afraid she might vanish.

"I can have all of my things gone in five minutes . . . if you want," she whispered, going completely pale again as she clutched her hands to her stomach.

"No."

"If I stay, my brothers are probably going to kill you."

"They're welcome to try."

"You have my word of honor, I won't mess with any of your stuff." Her gaze darted to the pants he'd shed on the hallway floor, then back to him. "But I could wash your clothes when I wash mine, if you want."

"I'd like that."

"And I'll tell Mr. Getze that I can't watch his children anymore. Or I could rent a place in town to watch them, if I get enough children to cover the expenses."

"This is the best place for kids, with a big yard that's far off the road."

A good deal of color returned to her cheeks, but he didn't miss that her hands, still clutching her stomach, had tightened. "I saw on television that there's a pill that prevents a woman from getting pregnant, and I intend to ask Maddy to help me find a doctor so we won't need to . . . worry."

That knife still piercing his heart twisted painfully. "The pill raises havoc with a woman's hormones sometimes, so don't bother asking Maddy anything."

"Can I buy condoms at the grocery store, then, when I go shopping for food?"

"I'll take care of the birth control. And I'll stop swearing," he offered, figuring he'd better cough up a few concessions of his own before she realized what a bum deal she was getting.

He saw her shoulders slump. "Does that mean I have to stop swearing, too?"

"For chrissakes, no."

And there it was, just a hint of a smile as she shoved her hands into her pockets.

"I have only two questions," he said quietly. "One, would you mind very much when you're organizing your things to straighten mine up, too?" he asked, knowing that if he didn't let her keep a perfect house, she would eventually explode. Or burn it down in sheer frustration.

"Oh yes, I'd love to do that for you. What else?" she asked eagerly.

"I want you to tell me why."

That sure as hell dampened her mood. "Why what?"

When he said nothing, her hands shot out of her pockets and started clutching each other again, and she dropped her gaze to his feet. "I found out that being strong and brave and independent is really quite lonely." Her eyes lifted to his. "And decided I would very much like to wake up every morning wrapped in the arms of a handsome, sexy man that I never dreamed I would fall in love with."

The knife in his chest withdrew so suddenly that his heart started pounding even more painfully, and he had her in his arms before she could finish gasping, putting everything he couldn't say into his kiss. Hell, who needed four stupid words, anyway, or even three, when two were all that really mattered? He reared up before he lost the nerve to say them.

"Marry me."

She went utterly, perfectly still, her golden eyes staring up at him for an eternity of heartbeats, and Trace realized that finding his courage had brought him right back to being an ass.

Fix it, you idiot. Say something!

No, kiss her again.

Oh, for chrissakes, just tell her you love her!

He opened his mouth, but not quickly enough.

"I'd rather not," she whispered, her eyes still locked on his. "Because I was really looking forward to being your girlfriend," she continued in a rush, her eyes taking on a sparkle. "So I can thumb my nose at all the jealous old fuddy-duddies. And I would also like to drive my brothers insane." She pressed a hand to his jaw. "Can we just take this one step at a time, Trace? Just so we can be sure I don't drive *you* insane?"

"I've been crazy since I met you."

"I'm sorry," she said—though she was smiling as she said it. She twined her arms around his neck. "There's an open condom under your pillow," she whispered, her cheeks turning a lovely pink again.

"No, I want to give you a baby."

She patted his shoulder, her beautiful eyes filling with amusement again. "One step at a time, okay? It's not like we can stuff the kid back inside if we change our minds." Her sparkle turned mischievous. "And I was quite looking forward to seeing how a condom works."

Was she serious?

Deciding that she wasn't going to vanish on him—at least, not until after she saw a condom in action—Trace tilted her head back and kissed her again. And just to prove that he could also multitask, he slipped the elastic off the end of her braid while continuing to feast on her mouth. He drew in the scent of roses mixed with his own soap, and discovered that the combination turned him on almost as much as the idea of her messing with *all* his stuff did.

Apparently not having anything to do since he was already undressed, she started driving him crazy by running her delicate fingers through his damp hair. He was never going to threaten to cut hers again, he decided, remembering how it had cascaded over her shoulders and tickled his chest that day down in the safe room. But when she tried lowering her arms, presumably to go after more interesting parts of his anatomy, he also remembered how she'd taken control of their lovemaking.

Which meant that he'd better get a handle on that particular problem before this turned into a repeat performance.

"Huntsman, your door is locked!" Mac shouted just before he knocked hard enough to rattle the window. "Did Fiona come down here?"

Trace cupped her head to him when she tried to pull away. "He'll leave."

"Fiona! Huntsman! Come on, hurry up. Henry's upstairs all alone."

She relaxed into him. "He probably just has a question about heating up dinner."

"Dammit, Huntsman, come open the door!"

Trace set her away but held on to her shoulders. "You don't

move from this spot, you understand? Not one inch. Promise me."

She smiled, nodding.

He started to let her go but stopped. "Don't even finish unbraiding your hair, okay? Promise," he growled, squeezing her shoulders when she frowned.

"Okay," she said, giving him a quizzical look.

"For the love of Zeus, open this friggin' door!"

He headed for the hall.

"Trace, your pants," she said, gesturing at him.

"Screw it," he muttered, figuring that answering the door in his birthday suit would send the bastard scurrying back upstairs quickly enough.

Trace yanked it open in mid-knock. "What?"

Mac took a step back, then finally regained his composure enough to glare at him. "Could you not have the decency to grab a towel? I didn't mean to get you out of the shower, but I thought Fiona was down here." He looked around the dooryard, then back at Trace, and frowned. "I didn't hear Kenzie drive in to pick her up. She was just upstairs a few minutes ago but left shortly after you got home, and I thought . . ." He shrugged, turning away. "I'll call her cell phone, then."

"Don't bother. She won't be answering it the rest of the evening or all night."

It took the idiot several seconds to catch on, and both of his brows shot into his hairline as he glanced down the porch. "All of her belongings were in boxes out here when I got home this afternoon. May I ask where they are now?"

"Unpacked in my bedroom and bathroom."

Another several seconds went by before the wizard slowly smiled, then suddenly reached out and patted Trace's upper arm. "You do know that if Kenzie doesn't kill you, de Gairn will make you wish you'd never been born."

"They'll have to go through their sister to get to me."

"Then I guess congrat—" There was a sudden crash on the kitchen ceiling, and Mac's eyes nearly bugged out of his head. "Sweet Neptune, I forgot about Henry!" he cried, bolting down the porch and disappearing around the front of the house.

Trace softly closed the door and locked it—like the smart woman waiting in his bedroom had done earlier— and silently walked down the hall, wondering if he'd find her right where he'd left her. He stopped just short of the door and peeked around the corner, and saw her standing in the exact same spot, staring at the bed, her hair still half braided and her hands balled into fists at her sides.

So, his new roommate was forming her plan of attack, was she?

He silently sighed, knowing that a repeat performance could kill any chance of this working out. He reached around the corner and turned off the light, and heard her spin around with a gasp of surprise.

"I've had some time to think about what really happened that day down in the safe room," he said from the doorway. "And you know what I finally realized?"

"N-no. What?"

"I realized that I'd gotten upset with you for all the wrong reasons." When she said nothing, he took a step toward her. "What I mistook as a submissive eagerness to please was really a rather aggressive attack."

She gasped again and took a step back. "I didn't . . . I wasn't attacking . . . You *asked* me to kiss you."

He stepped closer. "I also gave you the option to slap my face," he reminded her. "But you didn't quite dare, did you, uncertain if you could control my reaction, whereas kissing me kept you in the driver's seat instead of making you a passenger being taken for a ride."

"I—I don't understand."

"It's a twenty-first-century analogy for being the person in control."

Having good night vision, he saw her go perfectly still, her hands balling into fists again. "Are you implying that I was trying to control you?" She snorted, gesturing in his direction. "I'm not so foolish as to think I could control a man nearly twice my size."

"No, you're not foolish. In fact, you're far smarter than any of those bastards a thousand years ago." He closed the distance between them but still didn't touch her. "I'm not one of them, Fiona," he said quietly. "So I would appreciate it if you'd stop treating me as if I am."

She backed up against the bed. "But I'm not," she cried softly, lifting her hand as if to hold him at bay. He saw her take a shuddering breath, and her head dropped. "This isn't going to work, is it?" she whispered. She looked up, straining through the darkness, trying to read his expression. "You claim it doesn't matter, but you can't get past the fact that I've been with several men, can you?"

"Do you trust me, Fiona?"

"I thought I did."

He reached around and gently pulled her braid over her shoulder, holding on to the curls at the end. "Okay, let's go with your suggestion to take this one step at a time. Do you trust that I won't ever physically hurt you?"

"Yes."

He slowly started unraveling her hair. "And how about emotionally? Do you trust me enough to drop the defenses you've erected around yourself?"

"But I already have." She blindly reached out to clutch his arms. "Would I have moved in with you if I believed you would break my heart?"

He released a quiet breath, sensing that they were slowly making progress. "No, that was definitely a gutsy move." He brought her hands down to her sides, guided her away from the bed to the middle of the room, and let go. "Then I guess the next step would be to see if you trust me enough to give up control of our lovemaking."

"I thought that's what I was doing," she growled.

He chuckled. "Sweetheart, you're a bigger control freak than I am."

"I am not!"

He laughed outright at that, waving toward the bed and then the closet, not caring if she could see him or not. "God forbid anything should ever be out of place in your neat little world." He pulled her into his arms when he saw her stiffen, and cupped her head against his chest with a heavy sigh. "I'm betting it's a habit you formed a thousand years ago," he said gently, "right around the time you were abducted. When you lost control of your body, you took control of the only things you could, like cooking and cleaning and organizing everything around you." He tightened his embrace when she violently shuddered. "And eventually, you learned how to gain control over the very men who were using you."

He lowered his lips to her ear. "You discovered that even

though you didn't have any choice about having sex with them, you could refuse to be a victim by controlling the act itself—all while making the bastards think they were in the driver's seat." He squeezed her gently. "That's not lovemaking, Fiona, because nothing is being *shared*. So, I guess what I'm asking is, do you trust me enough to drop your emotional defenses, so I can show you how special it can be for two people who love each other?"

Three pounding heartbeats went by, then a dozen, and then an eternity, before he felt hot tears on his chest, and that knife plunged back into his heart.

"I love you more than life itself, Fiona," he whispered thickly against her hair. "Please let me show you what that means."

"But I don't know how," she quietly sobbed, clinging to him in a death grip.

"Then I guess it's a good thing that I do," he said with a chuckle, hugging her just as fiercely. "And I'm betting you catch on to lovemaking just as quickly as you learned to shoot a gun—which, now that I think about it, is really quite scary."

She wiped her eyes with a shuddering sigh, and he was pretty sure he felt her wipe her nose on his chest. And then he heard her take in a really deep breath as she straightened and stepped away.

"So, can I get undressed now?" she asked, obviously determined to try.

The only thing was, judging by her stance, the woman apparently thought lovemaking was going to kick just as much as a gun did!

Chapter Twenty-three

◆

Fiona stood stiffly to keep from trembling, suddenly glad that the room was too dark for Trace to see her fear. She wasn't exactly sure what to do, and she really didn't like that she didn't know what to expect—which is why she jerked when his fingers threaded into her curls and ran all the way to the ends before he let them fall over her shoulders.

"Easy now," he crooned, cupping her face and tilting her head up. "I know it goes against every instinct you have, but please try to relax. Try taking a deep breath and letting it out slowly," he whispered, his mouth only inches from hers.

Not knowing what else to do, she did as he suggested, but just as the last drop of air left her lungs, he touched her lips with his tongue, making her flinch again.

"Say you love me," he quietly commanded against her mouth.

"I—I love you."

"Again."

"I love—"

His tongue swept inside, curling around hers as if he could taste her words, his hands on her cheeks canting her head to deepen the kiss. But the moment she tried to kiss him back, he straightened away and started unbuttoning her blouse, her nipples pushing against his hands when she took another shuddering breath.

Okay, she could handle this, knowing that some men liked to undress a woman, sometimes slowly, as if they were opening a surprise package. It had always made her uncomfortable, though, because it usually meant she was in for a long night. But she'd learned how to speed things up once the man got enough of her exposed, just by rubbing her naked breasts against his arms or chest or especially his face. And if that didn't work, she could . . .

Fiona suddenly stiffened.

Trace stilled on the third button down. "Easy. Tell me what you're thinking."

"You're right," she whispered in shock, straining to read his expression. "I always did everything in my power to control them." She clutched his arms, digging her fingers into his muscles. "If they insisted on undressing me, I'd wait until they had . . . until I was naked, and then I . . . I'd do enticing things so they'd get it over with."

He pressed his hands to her face and brushed a thumb across her cheek, and she realized she was crying.

"And that's how you refused to be a victim," he said, "making you smarter than all of them put together." She heard Trace pull in a shaky breath of his own. "I swear I'm not wanting you to relive it, Fiona. But even though

I can't ever know how being with a man makes you feel, I can empathize with your being afraid of losing control, because I've been there myself." He pulled her to him again, gently holding her head against his beating heart. "What if we both just get naked and crawl into bed together, and spend tonight sleeping with our arms wrapped around each other?" He tilted her chin up. "How would that be for taking this one step at a time?"

She pulled her chin free so she could rest against his strongly beating heart again. "I'm not afraid, Trace, I'm just sort of . . . angry for some reason. How about if we just do it any way we can this first time, so I can get past those memories by making new ones with you?" She leaned back to smile up at him, not knowing if he could see her. "It's been a thousand years," she softly growled. "So I don't give a friggin' damn if we have to wrestle each other for control, as long as it just finally *happens*."

His laughter caught her off-guard as much as his arm coming under her knees did, as he swept her off her feet. "Christ, I love it when you talk dirty." He tossed her down onto the bed and quickly followed. "Please tell me you intend to fight dirty, too."

Her heart racing with the joy of being set free, Fiona took full advantage of the fact that she was fully dressed and he was fully naked, and wrapped both of her hands around his manhood just as he started after the buttons on her blouse again.

He reared up with a strangled shout of surprise and nearly fell off the bed, barely catching himself at the last moment. "Not fair! You're supposed to wait until you're naked, too."

She sent her mouth after her hands. "*Everything* is fair in love and war."

He grabbed her shoulders as he dodged her advance, flipping her onto her back and pinning her under him with the weight of his body, and then suddenly popped off the remaining buttons on her blouse with a sinister chuckle. He lifted her just enough to slide her blouse down over her shoulders, effectively trapping her arms against her sides. "So I guess that means using my superior strength is fair, too. What the . . . you're not wearing a bra!"

"I don't like them. Why in hell do women in this age stuff their bosoms into such confounding undergarments, making it impossible to breathe?"

"Damn, you do fight dirty," he muttered as he dropped his head to her left breast. He licked her nipple—once, twice, around in a maddening circle—and then closed his mouth and gently suckled.

She bucked at the wonderful sensation and started struggling to free her arms. But she went perfectly still when his lips made a fiery trail across her chest and he gave her other nipple a maddeningly slow, wet lick. She shuddered, moaning her pleasure when he blew on it, her fingers digging into the blanket as she lifted her hips into his groin. His manhood poked her intimately through her slacks, and she gave another keening moan when he slowly slid its length over her pelvis.

"I . . . my clothes . . . they're making me quite . . . hot," she said raggedly, hoping he could hear her over the soft slurping noises his mouth was making on her breasts.

"Hmmm? Did you say something, sweetheart?" he murmured, his lips burning another fiery trail over her skin to her neck. He used his head to nudge her chin out of the way, pulling another moan from her when his mouth found her racing pulse.

Having moved from unfair into the realm of sweet torture, Fiona decided that if he thought he was having his wicked way with her using brute strength alone, he was about to learn she really was stronger than she appeared.

And as he'd very kindly pointed out, also quite smart. She gave another moan—really loud so he could hear it—and lightly nipped his ear.

He reared up in surprise. "Did you just bite—"

She used his momentum to buck him off, and was out from under him and had her arms free before he landed on the floor.

"Goddamn it! There's no need to get physical!"

She silently slipped off the opposite side of the bed and then ducked under it—glad she'd sent the dust bunnies scurrying days ago—squirming out of her pants and panties as she quietly rolled to the other side.

"Where in hell did you go?" he growled as the creaky old bed dipped above her. "Fiona! Dammit," he muttered just as the bed shuddered violently when he flopped down onto it. "I am such a friggin' ass."

She silently rolled out and stood up. "Would that be a horse's ass or a skunk's?" she asked, throwing herself on top of him.

Only he must have seen her coming, dammit, because he caught her in mid-pounce with a grunt of laughter and spun them both around so she was right back beneath him—except now she was just as naked as he was.

He sobered, going still above her. "Say you love me again," he said thickly.

"Not until you say it again."

He sighed hard enough to move her hair. "How about we say it together?"

"How about we try that condom on for size, and then we'll say it together when you're inside me?" She touched his cheek, then slowly brushed the tip of her finger back and forth over his lips, stopping to dip it inside to make it wet before sliding it over his lips again. "I want to *feel* the words moving through me like a warm breath of air."

His arms on either side of her quivered with restraint as he lowered his face to hers. "God, I love you," he muttered against her mouth.

She wrapped her arms around him to toy with the fine hairs at the nape of his neck as she kissed him, pulling his tongue inside her with a soft sigh of contentment.

He leaned to one side, and she felt him fumbling around the pillows, even as he continued kissing her. Assuming that he was going after the condom, she reached up and found the packet and slid it into his searching hand.

She pulled her mouth away. "I want to see you put it on," she said raggedly, running her foot up his leg and shivering at the feel of his muscles growing tauter.

"Next time," he growled, rolling onto his hip beside her. "Don't you dare move," he ground out when she reached toward him. "I promise, next time, the light stays on, and I'll even let you put it on me."

"But I want to do it this time," she said in a pouting tone to torment him further.

"There won't be a *this* time if I let your hands anywhere near me," he finished in a strangled hiss, jackknifing away when she lightly brushed her finger over his scrotum. "Are you *trying* to kill me?"

Since she could no longer stifle her laughter, she ended it with a dramatically loud sigh. Oh yeah, she could fight dirty with the best of them. "No, I believe I'm trying to hurry you along. You really need to work on that, Trace." She tugged on his shoulder, urging him back on top of her. "Because I'm so hot. And wet. And *so* eager to feel you moving hard and fast inside me." When she realized he was still fumbling with the condom, she shrugged. "I guess I'll just have to start without you," she whispered, reaching down between her legs.

"Go ahead, keep talking like that," he growled, pulling her hands up to pin them over her head as he finally lifted himself over her, "and we really will be spending the night just holding each other."

She could feel the tension humming through him as he let her go to brace himself above her, his knees gently spreading her thighs as he slowly lowered his hips.

"Guide me into you," he thickly petitioned. "Rub me through that hot and eager wetness you were just talking about, and take me inside you, Fiona."

Lost in the cadence of his tender commands, her breaths now coming in short bursts, she reached down between them as he lifted just enough to give her room. She didn't know what she'd been expecting, but the condom felt exactly like it looked, like nothing more than a sheer second skin. "It's as if you're wearing nothing," she said, having to raise her voice over his moan when she folded her fingers around him.

"Not quite nothing," he said roughly, his entire body

trembling now. "Want me, Fiona. Show me how much. Open yourself and guide me inside."

His words fanned over her like the warm updrafts that used to slip under her wings, gently lifting her so high she had thought she could touch the sun. His wanting her to want him made her feel like a hawk again, soaring powerful and free on the fresh new wind of change welling up inside her.

She opened for him, urging him forward with soft mewling sounds and raising her hips to meet him halfway. "Omigod," she crooned as he slowly entered her, "whatever you do, don't stop. Omigod, yes!" She clutched his arms, throwing her head back to arch into him. "Promise me you won't stop."

"Not for a lifetime," he said through gritted teeth.

And when he pulled back and she cried out in protest, he thrust into her deeply, turning her cry to one of sweet, pure pleasure. He set his arms on either side of her head, his fingers splaying through her curls as he moved strongly against her.

She couldn't speak, couldn't think, could barely breathe, rocked by a host of unfamiliar sensations. She curved her arms under his and gripped the backs of his shoulders, digging her fingers into his warm, solid muscles to steady the drumbeat pounding through her.

"Easy, sweetheart," he whispered against her ear. He kissed her forehead, then trailed his lips down her cheek. "Fly away with me, Fiona," he whispered. He reached under her backside and lifted her into his thrusts, then slid his hand to press his thumb against her sensitive bud. "Soar into the sky with me, little hawk."

"I—I don't know what's happening!"

"Yes, you do. You've done it a thousand times. Open your wings and let the whirlwind lift you away. Soar, Fiona, and take me with you."

The urgency of his invitation enticed her to the edge, his powerful surges creating that whirlwind he spoke of. She felt her muscles gathering with tension begging for release, and she clung to him desperately. His thumb moved slickly against her with each of his thrusts, causing her instinctively to slide her legs up the length of his, spreading herself for him as she tossed her head back in response to his deepening thrusts.

And then she stopped breathing altogether as his relentless rhythm tugged her right up to the rim of the precipice and she grew afraid again.

"Jump, little hawk," he whispered, the warmth of his mouth sending her careening over the edge.

She cried out, tumbling through the whirlwind.

"Open your wings, Fiona," she heard as if from a distance. "Soar into the air!"

She touched the sun, its molten heat shooting through her in fiery waves of blinding ecstasy. She cried out in wonder, holding Trace to make sure he stayed with her as she rose and fell on the whirlwind he'd created, and convulsed around him.

Her cries suddenly turned to violent sobs. Burying her face in his neck, she wailed like a babe taking its first breath. She didn't know why she was crying, much less why she couldn't stop, the true wonder of it being that she really didn't care.

His strong and tender hands smoothed her hair off her

face, his lips sipping her tears as he murmured words of love, calling her his beautiful little hawk.

"H-how did you kn-know?" she rasped between sucking breaths.

He very thoughtfully, though a tad late, lifted some of his weight off her so she could breathe as he raggedly responded. "I guessed that you were happiest when you were a hawk soaring free, and thought that if you could remember what it felt like, you'd let yourself go to feel it again." He kissed her flushed cheek. "Only with me this time."

"And did you . . . . soar with me?"

"Oh yeah," he said thickly. "Higher than I ever have before."

She shuddered with a lingering sob and gently but firmly pushed him off her. He flopped onto his back with a heavy sigh and then muttered something under his breath.

"Excuse me?" she said, trying not to sound as shaky as she felt, wiping her cheeks with the palms of her hands. She couldn't believe she'd actually bawled like a baby during sex, much less in front of Trace. But really, she hadn't known sex could be so maddening and scary and exciting and so . . . wonderful.

And she sure as hell had never expected that she would ever ask if they could do it again.

"You were supposed to say 'I love you' when I was inside you," he said loudly.

She rolled toward him, resting her chin on her arm over his heaving chest. "I'm sorry, I guess I forgot." She gave him a pat. "Maybe I'll remember next time. Want me to get you another condom so we can try again? Or is one good for the entire night?"

His chest stopped heaving beneath her. "Are you *serious*?" He snorted and started breathing heavily again. "Hell, I don't even know where the damned thing is." He waved his free arm and then let it drop back to the bed. "It's either inside you or blown halfway across the Gulf of Maine."

She gasped, lifting her head to gape at him. "Are you serious?" He gave a startled grunt when she pushed off him to sit up. "I could be getting pregnant this very minute! What in hell good are condoms if they come off?"

"They're only ninety-something percent reliable as birth control."

"Then what's one hundred percent reliable?" she snapped.

He had her flat on her back before she could even gasp. "Abstinence," he growled, though she could hear the laughter in his voice. He settled between her thighs, spreading her open to him. "You going to let the possibility of making a baby clip your wings? Because I think I should remind you that neither one of us is getting any younger. And kids need parents who have enough energy to stay one step ahead of them, not some doddering old fools they can outrun as well as outfox."

She stopped breathing, wishing the light were on so she could see his expression. "You *truly* want to have children?"

"That would depend on how many we're talking about. Two? Four? A dozen?"

She did notice that the amusement had left his voice. "I was thinking . . . eight."

He was off her and standing in the middle of the room before she even heard the bed creak. "Goddamn it, you can't tell a man something like that *after* he's fallen in love with you!" She sensed him step toward the bed. "Why in hell are you always doing everything upside down and backward?"

She rolled onto her side and propped her head on her hand. "I do things properly; it's the rest of the world that does everything upside down and backward." Oh yeah, this fighting-dirty thing was really quite exciting. She loudly patted the bed. "Come back, Trace, and let's see if we can't make just one child first and worry about the other . . . seven later."

"Not unless you agree to marry me."

"My word of honor, if I get pregnant, I will marry you before the baby is born."

She heard him sigh loudly. "You are such a recalcitrant woman," he muttered. "I'm beginning to wonder if you were even born in the eleventh century." She sensed him moving closer and confirmed her guess when he spoke from the foot of the bed. "Will you at least agree to wear my engagement ring?"

She flopped onto her back, sighing even louder than he had as she folded her hands beneath her head. "I'm wondering if you were born in the twenty-first century," she muttered. "I will agree to *consider* wearing one."

"I was born in the twentieth century," he said just as she felt the bed dip. He lowered his weight down the length of her and ran his fingers through her hair to hold her facing him. "And a man feeling possessive about his woman is a timeless affliction. Especially if he loves her so much that he can't live without her. Besides," he said, giving her a quick kiss, although it was long enough for her to realize he was smiling, "I figure if we're at least engaged, Kenzie will only beat the hell out of me instead of outright kill me."

Fiona spread her legs until he was intimately nestled against her again and stretched her arms over her head to push her breasts into his chest. "Do you think I haven't noticed your little habit of getting what you want by letting others make the final decision?" she whispered, smiling when she felt him stiffen. She unfolded her hands and gently pressed them to his cheeks. "Thank you, Trace, for dropping your own defenses to let me into your heart. I will love and cherish you for the rest of our natural lives and beyond, and give you my heart to hold safe on our journey together."

He said nothing, not moving, barely breathing, although she felt his cheeks lift in a smile. "Yeah, me, too," he said thickly, slipping deeply inside her as he caught her gasp of surprise in his mouth.

Chapter Twenty-four

"Are you going to just lie there all morning staring at me," Trace asked without moving, probably because he couldn't, "or are you going to get up and cook me breakfast?" He opened one eye to see Fiona lying on her side, her head propped on her hand, smiling at him. "I don't know if you happened to notice, but I didn't get any supper last night. And with what calories I burned at work yesterday added to what I burned last night, it's a wonder I even have the energy to talk."

Though he did find the energy to roll onto his side, prop his head in his hand, and smile back at her. Lord, but if she had been beautiful before, this morning she was positively radiant, her wild mess of curls fanning over her like a waterfall of sunshine, her cheeks a warm dusty pink, and her sleep-laden eyes as intoxicating as whiskey.

"I haven't decided yet," she said huskily.

For the life of him, Trace couldn't figure out what she

was talking about—that is, until he heard a hollow rumbling sound coming from his stomach. He flopped onto his back. "I hope you know the only reason boyfriends ask their girlfriends to move in with them is so they'll get home-cooked meals."

"Aye, I suspected as much." She shrugged her shoulder, causing her hair to move just enough to expose one beautifully pink, well-loved nipple. "But since my boyfriend never actually *asked* me to move in with him, I can only assume he must not need someone to prepare him home-cooked meals." She flipped her hair over her shoulder, fully exposing both of her breasts as she leaned toward him. "In fact, it's been my understanding that boyfriends in this century often serve their girlfriends breakfast in bed. And they help do the dishes and take out the trash and actually place their dirty clothes in the hamper."

"On *soap operas*. But if you watch them long enough, you'll see that all that romantic stuff only lasts about a month. After that, the boyfriends revert to no-good lazy slackers, and the girlfriends start nagging and whining, and the relationship goes to hell in a handbasket." He rolled toward her and pulled her hair back over her breasts, because he honestly didn't think he had the strength to make love to her again—at least not until he got some food down to his rumbling belly. "But we can avoid all that ugly slacking and nagging if we divide up the chores into you doing the cooking and cleaning and me working really, really hard to earn our living."

It didn't help his libido any that she stuck out her well-loved lower lip in a cute little pout or that she went and flipped her hair back over her shoulder again just before she laid her delicate—and very talented—hand over his suddenly pounding heart. "So, you're never going to serve me breakfast in bed?" Her finger started drawing lazy circles through his chest hair. "I was so hoping to see what it's like to have a man hand-feed me strawberries that are dripping in chocolate and whipped cream, and feel what it's like to have him sip champagne off every inch of my skin."

He had her flat on her back and was looming over her before she got half a laugh out. "That does it. I'm locking out the Soap Opera, WE, Oxygen, and Lifetime channels, along with that Discovery and science junk. That leaves you only Martha Stewart and Animal Planet."

She clutched his arms, and he felt her thumb brush over his right bicep as she started to respond, but her eyes suddenly narrowed on her hand. "How come you have a hawk on your arm?" she asked in surprise.

"Sorry, sweetheart, but that's a good old-fashioned American bald eagle. I got it when I first went into the military."

"I'm sorry, sweetheart," she purred, this time poking his bicep, "but that's a good old-fashioned red-tailed hawk."

Trace rolled off her and sat up, twisting his arm to look down at his tattoo, only to blink in surprise. Damn, it sure as hell looked like a hawk.

She sat up beside him, running her finger over it. "How did you know?" she whispered, her gaze meeting his. "It's obvious you had this done long before we met. What made you choose a hawk?" She suddenly smiled, pressing her palm over his tattoo. "It was your destiny speaking to you, before you could even know your heart would belong to me."

No, it was Mac the Menace. Trace had thought it strange

last night when Mac had patted his arm, but now he realized why. Apparently, the wizard had enough spare magic kicking around to change an eagle to a hawk. Only when Trace saw Fiona's beautiful gold-rich eyes were filled with such certainty, he didn't have the heart to burst her bubble. "Yeah, I guess it was destiny."

"Ye have five seconds to open this door, Huntsman, before I kick it down!" Kenzie's voice suddenly boomed just as Trace was in mid-pounce.

Only he found himself pouncing on nothing, as Fiona was halfway across the room before he could untangle himself from the blanket she'd tossed over him.

"Your feet so much as hit that floor," she growled from the doorway as she slipped into her bathrobe, "and I swear, everything you eat for the next month will come from a goat." She pointed at him. "I don't need you fighting my battles for me."

Trace relaxed back on the bed, folding his hands behind his head. "Or we could tactically retreat down to our hidey-hole by using the secret door behind the bureau," he suggested as she tightened the belt on her robe.

"Huntsman!" Kenzie shouted, making every window in the house rattle.

"Stay put," she snapped, disappearing down the hall.

Trace was off the bed and hopping into a pair of jeans before she reached the kitchen. But he stopped and grabbed a shirt off the closet floor, figuring the less naked he was, the less angry Kenzie would be—assuming the highlander didn't outright explode when he saw his sister wearing nothing more than a bathrobe and a wild mess of love-tangled hair.

Trace silently crept down the hall but turned into the living room, being careful of where the floor creaked, and stood just out of sight in the kitchen doorway.

"Son of a bitch!" Kenzie shouted. "I will kill the bastard!"

Trace heard what sounded like someone being pushed up against the open door, and he stepped out into the kitchen, but when he saw *Kenzie* righting himself, he quickly stepped back into the living room with a grin.

"You may kill him," Fiona said calmly, "but only after you kill me."

"Dammit, ye lied to me yesterday afternoon. Ye told me not to come get you because you were staying the night to watch Henry."

"I had too much on my mind yesterday afternoon to also have to deal with your antiquated proprieties. But if you wish to discuss them now, I'm willing to hear what you have to say—that is, if *you* are willing to listen to *me*."

"You'll not live with a man who's not your husband," the highlander snapped, apparently in no mood to discuss anything. "Can ye not see yourself? Ye look as if ye . . . that you've been . . ."

"Well loved?" Fiona finished for him. "Aye, I have. And if you think I look the worse for wear, you should see my boyfriend."

Was she serious? Trace rubbed a shaky hand over his sweating face as he wondered if Kenzie had brought his sword.

Although come to think of it, the highlander's fists could be lethal weapons.

Assuming the soul warrior didn't decide to turn into a panther instead.

"Where is the cowardly bastard?" Kenzie snarled.

"I've got him tied up to the bedposts," she drawled.

Was she friggin' serious?

"And I would appreciate that you not refer to the father of my future children as a coward or a bastard," she continued. "And from now on, I prefer that you call ahead first, rather than come to our home unannounced. Sunday morning is the only time Trace and I will have to relax together, as he works daylight to dark six grueling days a week, and he drives to Bangor for supper with his mother on Sunday afternoons."

They would be driving to his mother's on Sunday afternoons, not *he*. What, did she honestly think he was going to let her out of that one?

"This isn't right," Kenzie ground out, although Trace heard more desperation than anger in his voice now. "Ye may have had no choice in the matter before, Fiona," the highlander said more gently, "but ye . . . you're still acting . . . dammit, sister, you dishonor yourself by willingly sleeping with a man you're not married to."

Trace silently stepped into the kitchen just far enough for Kenzie to see him.

"So, you're saying Eve was no better than a whore when she slept with you before she married you?" Fiona asked evenly.

"Nay!" Kenzie shouted, taking a step back. "She's my wife!"

"I don't remember seeing a ring on her finger that week the two of you camped out on the bluff while your home was being rebuilt, and you made love to her every night, all night long."

Trace leaned back against the wall, folding his arms over his chest, smiling at Kenzie's shock.

"How in hell do ye know about that?"

Trace saw Fiona shrug, and he'd bet his boat she was grinning like a kitten with a belly full of *cow's* milk. Man, did the lady fight dirty, or what?

"Contrary to belief, hawks have fairly good night vision, dear brother. And my favorite roost just happened to be an old oak tree out on that same bluff."

Kenzie was the one now wiping the sweat off his face. "Sweet Christ," he whispered. "Ye *watched* us?"

Trace straightened away from the wall at the sound of a truck speeding into the dooryard and skidding to a halt, its door slamming shut a second after its engine died.

Kenzie turned to look out, then suddenly stiffened and turned back and pointed at Fiona. "Ye don't say one word to her about seeing us," he growled. "She'd be horrified, and I don't want her getting upset this close to her birthing day."

Eve came running—or, rather, waddling—into the house, already looking upset. She stopped just inside the door, her eyes widening as she took in Fiona's disheveled appearance, and then turned to her husband. "You'd better be here congratulating your sister on her falling in love." She poked him when Kenzie opened his mouth to say something. "You say anything, it better be an apology to your sister and to Trace for disturbing their Sunday morning."

Apparently Kenzie wasn't apologizing quickly enough, so Eve spun around and did it for him. "I'm sorry we both stopped by unannounced this morning," she said. She shot Trace an apologetic smile, then looked back at her sister-in-law. "And I promise it won't happen again," she said, shooting a quick nonapologetic glare over her shoulder at her husband before looking at Fiona again. "Maybe one evening this week, we'll have you and Trace over to dinner."

Another vehicle drove into the dooryard and slid to a halt, although this one sounded more like a snowbank stopped it rather than its brakes. The three people standing by the door all looked out. "You called William for backup?" Eve cried.

But Trace heard another vehicle come barreling down the driveway just as the Irishman came barging through the door—holding his goddamned *sword*.

Both Maddy and Gabriella came charging in behind him, and Maddy grabbed her husband's arm and spun him around. "What in hell do you think you're doing?"

Ignoring his wife, William pointed at the door. "Ye get back in the truck, Gabriella. Ye have no business seeing what's going on here."

"Oh, get real!" Maddy said with a snort. "She sees people wearing a hell of a lot less doing a hell of a lot worse on television." She shot Fiona a sheepish grin. "I'm sorry for barging in unannounced and so early like this, but I did try to call and warn you, only your phone kept going to voice mail."

"I shut if off . . . yesterday afternoon," Fiona said softly.

And Trace would bet his boat her cheeks were bright pink.

God love her, the woman had orchestrated an attack on him yesterday that rivaled the D-day invasion, yet had somehow managed to make him feel as if *he* should be claiming victory.

Which, come to think of it, was a very scary thing.

His belly rumbled loudly enough that everyone stopped glaring at each other and all turned in unison to glare at him.

Well, except for Peeps, who was smiling way too smugly.

Fiona walked over, wrapped her arms around his waist, and melted into him with a sigh. "You don't listen very well, do you?" she said, though she was smiling up at him as she said it. "At least you put clothes on this time."

Holding her possessively against him, Trace had to brush her hair out of his way when some of it caught on his unshaven jaw so he could grin at all the people crowding his kitchen. "Not that I don't appreciate the impromptu housewarming party, but I think it's time you ladies took your husbands home and fed them breakfast, so my girlfriend can feed me mine."

"Or we could all go to the Port of Call for breakfast," Peeps suggested.

"Sorry," Trace said, shaking his head. He looked at the clock on the stove, then back at everyone. "Because in about three hours, my mom and Jack will be here. I invited them to come spend the afternoon and have Sunday supper with me and my new girlfriend in my nice clean house."

"You *what*?" Fiona cried—which was echoed by Maddy and Eve. Fiona stepped away, her eyes wide with horror. "Your mother's coming here? Today? For *dinner*? In three *hours*? With her *husband*?" She grabbed her hair, only instead of pulling it out like her expression suggested, she started trying to tame it into submission as she spun toward the women. "His mother's coming here! Today! For dinner! In three hours! And she's bringing Jack!" She suddenly spun back toward him, her eyes narrowed in suspicion. "When did you have time to call her?"

"Last night . . . um, after you fell asleep," he said, darting a worried glance at Kenzie and William, who, he noticed, both appeared as horrified as the women. He smiled down at Fiona. "Mom's been bugging me to let her and Jack make the drive down here at least every other Sunday since I bought the place. She even offered to bring dinner, but I kept refusing because . . ." He waved around the kitchen. "Well, because I didn't want her to see that I lived like . . . that I had all I could do to . . ." He took hold of her shoulders and gave her an encouraging smile. "That I lived like a pig," he finally admitted. "But you've got the place looking so beautiful, and you're so beautiful, and I wanted her to see how happy you've made me so she'll quit worrying that I'm going to turn into some old hermit, and so I . . . I thought that . . ."

Christ, this wasn't going at all well.

And for the life of him, he didn't know *why*.

"Goddamn it, what's the problem?" he finally just asked. "I thought you were looking forward to meeting my mother. You both have a lot in common, not the least of which is that you both *love me*," he thought to remind her.

"But not today!" she cried, stepping away to grab her hair again. "The house is a mess. I'm a mess. And I don't have anything prepared for dinner." She spun toward the women. "His mother is coming here in three hours!"

"You are such a stupid ass," Maddy hissed, walking over to wrap an arm around Fiona and leading her into the hallway, Eve and Gabriella following, both of them giving Trace a vicious glare. "Don't you worry about anything," Maddy continued to his now-sobbing girlfriend. "The three of us will help you get everything together in time. Not that you need to worry about trying to make a good first impression, anyway. The minute Auntie Pam finds out you love her son enough to actually live with him, she's going to be so over-joyed she'll probably cry."

Maddy's encouragement, every word seconded by the entourage following, ended with Trace's bedroom door shutting with deafening softness.

"Sweet Christ, Huntsman," William said, his sword hanging limply in his hand, "do ye truly not know what an idiot you are?"

"Apparently not." Trace shook his head. "Because I still don't see what all the fuss is about. It's my mother, for chris-sakes, not the queen of England."

"Ye don't tell a woman your mother's coming for dinner in three hours," Kenzie said, looking equally appalled. "Ye *ask* her if it wouldn't be nice to have your mum come visit and *when* would be a good time. You're going to pay dearly for this, my friend," the highlander said, although his smile was anything but friendly. "Which is the only reason I'm not sending you to rot in hell right now."

"For the record, I asked your sister to marry me, and she outright refused." Trace headed to the counter and started opening cupboard doors, trying to remember where the coffee filters were. "Hell, I only just barely got her to agree to consider wearing an engagement ring." He found the filters, grabbed a spoon, and headed into the living room. "And also for the record," he continued as Kenzie and William followed. He plunged the spoon into the Christmas cactus, just now noticing the damn thing was in full bloom.

"Your sister fights dirty, Gregor." He stopped spooning what he hoped was mostly coffee into the filter and pointed at Kenzie. "And I got to tell you, that woman's got an arsenal of weapons the Pentagon would envy. And she's sneaky and quick, and she doesn't like losing."

William snorted. "Have ye ever met a woman who did?"

"Yeah, well I think—" Trace stopped spooning again when he heard laughter coming through the wall from the bedroom, and the knot in his gut finally started to relax at the realization that the women had calmed Fiona down.

That is, until he heard Maddy shout out the word *condom*, which was quickly followed by more laughter. He sighed, heading back into the kitchen, wondering if he was going to find his bedroom decorated with condom balloons tonight.

No, they'd probably stuff them in the closet so his mother wouldn't see them, and he'd get ambushed by them when he went to bed. He set the filter in the coffeemaker, filled the machine with water, and hit the on button just as the kitchen door opened. Henry and Misneach came racing inside, Mac right behind them. The kid and his four-legged sidekick ran through the kitchen and straight into the living room, and Trace saw them both jump into one of the recliners, the pup settling beside Henry as the boy grabbed the remote control and turned on the television.

Children and technology, apparently, was a timeless combination.

Which reminded him: he'd better start learning how to block out channels.

"Is there a reason you're having a breakfast party and Henry and I weren't invited?" Mac asked, strolling over to the fridge and looking inside. When he didn't find anything to his liking, he turned and grinned at Trace. "What are we celebrating, the fact that Kenzie hasn't killed you yet?"

"He's decided my having to live with his sister is punishment enough," Trace drawled, taking four mugs out of the cupboard. "You know what I just realized, Oceanus? You're the only one of us who's still single."

"A state of being that, Providence willing, will remain so," Mac said, suspiciously eyeing the coffeemaker when Trace handed him a mug. "Did you buy new coffee?"

"Yeah, on my way home from work yesterday." Trace gave William and Kenzie a warning glare as he handed them each a mug. "So, Mac, have you given any more thought to you and Henry attending my friend's camp up in the mountains?"

"I told Madeline about it, and she thought it was a wonderful idea," Mac said, rolling his eyes. "But she also believes I should wait a few months before going, so I can get used to living in this century without my powers." He looked toward the living room, then back at Trace, and sighed. "I have a whole new appreciation for mothers," he said quietly. "I woke up in a cold sweat no fewer than six times last night, and had to sneak into Henry's room and make sure he hadn't suddenly . . . vanished." He looked at Kenzie and William and grinned. "I can see now why Mother Nature designed it so that we're given nine months to get used to the idea of being parents."

Trace grabbed the coffee carafe before it was fully done brewing and went around and filled everyone's mug, then quickly shoved it back onto the sizzling burner. "I thought you said you couldn't waste your reserves doing menial tricks," he said, turning his arm toward Mac and lifting his sleeve. "So, how come you changed my eagle to a hawk last night?"

The wizard gave Trace a small salute with his mug. "Because I believe all men should wear a token of their true love." He then used his mug to salute William. "Be it a medallion or a tattoo."

Trace recalled that Maddy had given William a medallion to wear, but Mac had changed the knight on a horse she'd originally picked out to a heart with the ancient symbol of a strong arm on it. "So what did you give Kenzie to wear as a token of Eve?" Trace asked.

Mac's face darkened. "I couldn't give him anything, because I can't get past de Gairn's magic." He suddenly grinned. "But it's obvious the highlander wears his heart on his sleeve for his wife."

"Drink up, Mac," Trace urged, lifting his own mug in salute. "If you're stuck in this century, then you need to get used to drinking a strong cup of coffee with your friends every morning if you want to get your day off to a good start."

Chapter Twenty-five

"See, that wasn't so bad, was it, sweetheart?" Trace said, resting his chin on her head so she couldn't look up and see his smile. "You went into a panic for nothing this morning. Mom fell in love the moment she laid her eyes on you, just like I did."

Trace was sitting in his recliner with Fiona on his lap, his belly stuffed so full it was a wonder he could breathe, watching his *fiancée* eyeing the delicate stone on her left ring finger and listening to her sigh every couple of minutes.

"I feel like a nobleman's hawk, wearing hunting traces," she muttered, fingering the ring. She leaned back against his arm to look at him. "That was a dirty trick, asking your mother to bring your grandmother's ring with her today and then proposing to me right in front of her. You set me up, knowing I wouldn't refuse with your mother being so excited she could barely contain herself."

"Uh-huh," he said, nodding. He took hold of her left hand so she'd stop fidgeting with the ring and brought it up to his mouth and kissed her palm. "Let's just call it payback for moving in with me and *then* asking if it was okay." He gave her a squeeze. "And an engagement ring isn't a means of restraint. It's merely a symbol telling the world that your heart is already spoken for."

She rested her head on his bicep—or, more specifically, on his tattoo—and smiled up at him. "A symbol I can always take off, whereas you will still be wearing your hawk into the afterlife."

"My grandmother never took off that ring for fifty-four years, and I expect you to still be wearing it in your afterlife," he growled. "And the second you know you're pregnant, the matching wedding band is going to be sitting right next to it."

"Ooh," she said, her eyes widening as she leaned away in mock terror. "So decisive you've become all of a sudden." She started toying with the buttons on his shirt, and he felt the first button open and her hand move to the next one. "But it will be a moot point if we don't make a baby," she whispered, her fingers moving to the next one.

He reached up and stilled her hand. "The door's not locked."

"Yes, it is. And Mac took enough leftovers upstairs to last until morning, the woodstove is set for the night, my cell phone is shut off—and hidden—and Misneach is with Henry." She reached over and shut off the lamp on the table beside them. "There, that's better. I learned on my first night here that the landlord doesn't like a lot of lights left on, because, he informed me, electricity doesn't grow on trees," she said huskily, shifting so that she was straddling him, her hands going to his belt buckle. "Come, my big, bold, mystical warrior. Take me soaring to new heights on *your* powerful wings of love."